ROBERTA
KRAY
CHEATED

SPHERE

SPHERE

First published in Great Britain in 2023 by Sphere

1 3 5 7 9 10 8 6 4 2

A CIP catalogue record for this book
is available from the British Library.

ISBN 978-07515-8138-6

Typeset in Garamond by M Rules
Printed and bound in Great Britain by Clays Ltd, Elcograf S.p.A.

Papers used by Sphere are from well-managed forests
and other responsible sources.

Sphere
An imprint of
Little, Brown Book Group
Carmelite House
50 Victoria Embankment
London EC4Y 0DZ

An Hachette UK Company
www.hachette.co.uk

www.littlebrown.co.uk

Through her marriage to Reggie Kray, Roberta Kray has a unique and authentic insight into London's East End. Roberta met Reggie in early 1996 and they married the following year; they were together until Reggie's death in 2000. Roberta is the author of many previous bestsellers including *No Mercy*, *Exposed*, *Survivor* and *Stolen*.

CHEATED

1

Rex Darby came from a long line of losers, feeble thin-faced miserable men who had achieved nothing in their lives beyond enough activity between the sheets to ensure yet another generation of failures. They had staggered through life, living hand to mouth while barely managing to keep above the poverty line. But he had broken the mould. He had built an empire that stretched across London and beyond, a vast portfolio of hotels, houses, clubs and restaurants. It was an achievement that would ensure a permanent change of fortune for his own offspring.

Along the way Rex had killed a man, wounded others, and imposed his will on anyone foolish enough to try and cross him. He had built his empire on guile and intimidation, on natural intelligence and his ability to take a well-judged risk. While his fellow villains had squandered their cash on tarts, gambling and booze, he had invested wisely and reaped the rewards.

Today, on his seventieth birthday, glasses were being raised and toasts given. He was, quite deservedly, the centre of attention. As he gazed around the table, he wallowed in self-satisfaction. His chest puffed up with pride. He had risen from the slums of the East End and knew that if he got to his feet, walked across the room and pulled back the heavy drapes, he would be able to look down on Upper Belgrave Street with its stylish terrace of white stucco houses. Not bad for a man who had gone hungry as a child, and who had always had holes in his shoes. Alfred, Lord Tennyson had once lived in this street.

Rex swigged his champagne and contemplated his journey from poverty to wealth. The war had brought opportunities and he had taken full advantage of them, breaking into warehouses and hijacking lorries to feed the black market with whisky, tobacco, nylons and furs. There had been forged ID cards for deserters and fake petrol coupons. Post-war, there had been new profits to be made in property and illegal gambling. He had lined his pockets and made it his mission to always be one step ahead of the law. Some villains saw jail as an occupational hazard, but not him. He had used his brains, greased the right palms and kept a clean sheet.

He looked at each of his girls in turn. Marian, Hazel and Carmen all had the same oval face as their late mother, the same long dark hair, olive skin and wide-mouthed smiles. But only Carmen, his youngest, had inherited her slate-grey eyes. No parent was supposed to have a favourite, but she was his. For the past ten years, after her sisters had married and flown the nest, the two of them had lived here alone. Soon, with Carmen's own wedding on the horizon, she'd be gone too, and he'd be left in this house like a dried pea rattling around in a jam jar.

Rex frowned as he thought about his future son-in-law, believing – as he had believed with his other daughters' choices – that he was not good enough for her. Clive Grainger was smart, ambitious and charming, but whether he was a suitable match was another matter altogether. If Rex could have sliced him open and examined his intentions, he would have. It annoyed him that Clive wasn't present tonight. A dose of flu had, allegedly, consigned him to bed.

Being a father wasn't an easy business. Rex lowered his gaze and sighed softly into his champagne. Had he been too strict with his girls? Too lenient? It had been tough raising them without a wife by his side, especially as they got older. He knew what boys were like and how easily they could take advantage. Sometimes he had not been as patient as he should have. Sometimes he had let his short temper get the better of him.

As he looked back, he wondered how it had all slipped by so quickly. The last ten years especially. The 1960s had come and gone, John F. Kennedy had been assassinated, man had walked on the moon, the Beatles had split up, and still Rex had clung on to his power. Now, four years into a new decade, he knew that it was time. There came a point in every man's life when he had to relinquish the reins. Tonight, he would make the grand announcement. Finally, he was going to step down, retire and split his assets equally between his girls. Better they had it now than when he was dead. Better he was here to witness their gratitude. He would keep enough to live off and the rest would be theirs.

When Rex looked in the mirror, he didn't see an old man, just the same man he had always been only with a few more lines on his face. His hair, slicked back and silver grey, was still abundant. He was tall and upright, not stooped or hunched like some of his peers. But he had felt himself slowing down in recent years, his brain not as agile as it once was, his instincts not as true.

Yes, it was time to take his place among the legion of the retired, to hang up his hat and slip quietly into the background. But still he didn't speak up. Soon, he thought, not quite prepared. What would he do when he was no longer commander, when people no longer hung on his every word, when his word was no longer law? How would he occupy his days? The prospective emptiness filled him with a creeping dread.

He nodded and smiled as the conversation flowed around him. There was travel, of course; he could go abroad, see something of the world, while away the time in foreign hotels and on pavement cafés. He could play golf. He could swim. He could pick up women and spend lazy afternoons between crisp white sheets. He could . . .

Pat Foster, who was sitting to his left, gave him a gentle slap on the shoulder. 'Are you ready, Rex?'

Of his eight guests, only Pat knew of his intentions. The two of them went way back. Pat was his right-hand man, his closest aide, a financial wizard who could turn the annual accounts into a believable work of fiction. But loyalty was what Rex valued above all else, and Pat had given him that in spades.

'A minute,' Rex murmured.

'Having second thoughts?'

Rex shook his head. His gaze roamed the table again as the coffee and brandy were served: Marian and Hugh, Hazel and Jonny, Carmen. Pat's wife, Annie, was wearing her usual sour expression, as if it pained her to be here – she could never be accused of being the life and soul of the party – although it didn't stop her shovelling up his food or knocking back his booze. The old cow had never liked him and never tried to hide it either. Her loyalty and affections had always lain with his late wife, Rosa. Next to her was her son, Eddie, a quiet, dull bloke who kept his own counsel. Pat's other son, the bastard one, was a livelier sort, but putting Milo and Annie together over a dinner table was asking for trouble.

'You sure?' Pat said softly.

'What are you two whispering about?' Marian said.

Rex tapped the side of his nose and smiled at her. 'Business. Private business.'

'You're not allowed to talk business on your birthday.'

'How are those two grandsons of mine?' Rex didn't see as much of the boys as he'd have liked. During term time they boarded at that fancy school, and during the holidays they always seemed to be busy. Summer had come and gone with him barely clapping eyes on them. Charlie and Gray were rapidly becoming strangers.

'Fast asleep, I should think. They'll be home for Christmas.'

Rex didn't approve of boarding schools, but Marian reckoned it was the best start they could have, that they'd make connections there, friends that would be useful to them for the rest of their lives. What *he* reckoned was that it was turning them into a pair of pansies with prissy accents and a sense of entitlement. He thought boys should be boys, rough around the edges and able to fight their way out of trouble should the need ever arise.

Pat was looking at him, waiting.

Rex drank some brandy, took a deep breath, clinked the side of his glass with a knife and rose to his feet. 'Now I'm not one for lengthy speeches, so I'll keep this short and sweet. Thank you all for sharing this birthday dinner with me. There's nothing better than having friends and family around.' He paused, knowing that what he was about to say couldn't be unsaid. Although he had spent the last few months thinking about it, poring over the books with Pat, now the moment was here he had to gird himself to carry on. 'I know you'll be surprised to hear this, but it had to come eventually. I've decided that it's time to retire, to step back and split the business between my three beautiful daughters.' He raised his glass to each of them in turn. 'I know you'll take good care of what I've built up over the years. I know I can rely on you.'

There was a shocked silence in the room.

Hazel's husband, Jonny Cornish, was the first to break it. 'Bloody hell, Rex. I never thought I'd see the day.'

Rex sat down, casually flapping a hand as if it was the most normal thing in the world to drop a fortune into the laps of his children. 'It's been fairly divided, a one-third share each.' He took three white envelopes from his inside jacket pocket and laid them on the table. 'All the details are in here. Don't open the envelopes now. Leave them until you get home. And no arguments, please. You've got what you've got and that's the end of it. All you have to do is sign the papers and it's done.'

Marian's gaze flicked between the envelopes and Rex. 'Thank you, Dad. Thank you so much.' She laid a hand on her heart and her voice trembled a little. 'This means ... well, *everything*. It's so appreciated. I can't tell you how much. I'm completely overwhelmed. You've been so kind and generous. You know how much I love you – more than anything or anyone – and that's never going to change. I couldn't have asked for a better father, not in any way, and I promise I won't let you down.'

Rex smiled and passed the envelope to her. Her response pleased and gratified him, and he looked towards Hazel, keen to hear more of the same.

Hazel cleared her throat and dabbed at her eyes as if she was fighting back tears. 'Lord, what can I say? This is such a surprise. I can hardly believe it. Thanks, Dad. I love you too, of course, and I'm so grateful for everything you've done for us. I know it can't have been easy. Every day I wake up and thank God I've got a father like you. You're the best, you really are. I realise how hard you've worked to bring us up and to build the business, and I hope one day you'll be as proud of me as I am of you.'

Rex passed the second envelope along the table. He was enjoying himself now, basking in the praise from his girls. A warm glow was spreading through him. And didn't he deserve this moment? He had worked his fingers to the bone to make sure they were always fed and clothed and happy. Now he was setting them up for life, passing on a legacy that few fathers could.

Eagerly, he turned to Carmen. It was her response he would value most of all. It was her tribute, her fulsome compliments, her expressions of love and gratitude that he was really looking forward to. He sat back, sipped his brandy, and prepared to be delighted.

'Thank you,' she said softly.

'Speak up,' Rex said. 'Don't mutter. We can barely hear you.'

'Thank you,' she repeated, raising her voice. 'It's very kind of you to do this.'

Rex smiled again, but the smile gradually faded when she didn't go on. An uneasy silence filled the room. A frown settled on his forehead. 'Is that it? Haven't you got anything else to say to your old dad?'

2

Carmen heard the sudden cold edge to his voice. She could feel his eyes boring into her and was aware that she was the focus of everyone else's scrutiny too. Her mouth was dry. She had listened to her sisters' fake flattery, to their empty compliments and hollow words, knowing that it was all lies. What they really felt about him was something quite different: what they said behind his back would make his toes curl. But this was all about money. Those two would fall on their knees and kiss his feet if that's what it took to prise the cash from his fingers.

'Carmen?' he prompted. And then demanded again, 'Speak up! What's the matter with you, girl? Cat got your tongue?'

Carmen inwardly flinched, reminded of all the other times he'd tried to bully or manipulate her. She remembered his harsh words when he came home drunk and angry, when someone had crossed him or slighted him, or a business deal had gone wrong. She recalled how often bitterness had risen to the surface, how he'd rant and rave about the world, the lack of respect shown by his offspring, his regret at not having had a son. Often, he would lash out, indifferent as to where his blows fell. She'd had the bruises to show for it. But for all that, she had never turned her back, never raised her voice or walked away, but instead had taken care of him, comforted and pacified him, and done her very best to be a dutiful daughter.

'You know what my feelings are, Dad. Don't I show them every day?'

Rex gave a snort. The colour had risen in his cheeks.

Even as she said it, Carmen knew it wasn't enough. He wanted more, much more. He wanted the obsequious praise that her sisters had given. He wanted a very public declaration of love and gratitude. And she did love him, even if it was despite his character rather than because of it. So why not just speak the words? Why not pander to him? Because she shouldn't have to, she thought. She shouldn't have to go through this embarrassing charade in front of everyone. Her actions proved her love seven days a week, fifty-two weeks a year. Anyway, anything she said now would just sound insincere or forced.

'It appears my daughter has nothing good to say about me.'

'That's not true, Dad.'

'So spit it out, why don't you? We're all waiting.'

'Why are you doing this?' she said, her discomfort growing by the second.

'My youngest daughter, everyone,' Rex said, gesturing towards her. 'Who apparently can't bring herself to express even a few loving words for the man who raised her.'

'You're not being—'

'Nothing, nothing at all.'

Carmen saw her sisters smirk. Eddie pressed his elbow against hers, although she couldn't tell if he was being supportive or prompting her to give in to her father's demands. She wished that Clive was here.

Rex's eyes flashed and his fingers curled around the final envelope, crushing the edges of it. 'What kind of daughter behaves so badly, shows such disrespect, when she's being handed a fortune on a plate? I thought better of you, Carmen. You've disappointed me. No, worse than that. You've shown me what you really are – a daughter who doesn't deserve what I'm giving her, a daughter who's beyond contempt.'

Carmen knew he was drunk – he'd been drinking all day – and that he had passed the point of rationality or of listening to anything he didn't want to hear. 'You're taking this all the wrong way.'

'The wrong way,' he repeated sneeringly. 'What other way is there to take it? You've made yourself perfectly clear.'

'Leave her alone,' Annie said. 'You're being ridiculous.'

Rex turned on her. 'And what bloody business is it of yours?'

'Someone needs to tell you what's what. You're acting like a fool. That girl's put up with you for years without a single complaint. You should be the one being grateful. *She* deserves a bleedin' medal.'

'You don't know what you're talking about.'

'Oh, I know all right. I've got eyes, haven't I? I've got ears.'

Carmen wished Annie would stop, even though she was defending her. It was only adding fuel to the fire. Her father couldn't stand Annie Foster. In fact, he couldn't stand anyone who stood up to him or had a different opinion from his. Even when he was sober, he hated criticism, and when he was drunk ... well, it was pretty much guaranteed to tip him over the edge.

'Control your wife, can't you?' Rex snarled to Pat. 'She's getting on my goddamn nerves.'

Annie peeled out an empty laugh. 'Control his wife? Jesus, Rex, what century are you living in? It's 1974, for heaven's sake.

You might be able to bully your employees, even your daughters, but you can't do the same to me.'

Carmen shifted in her seat, leaned forward, and made an attempt to bring hostilities to an end. 'Look, Dad, I'm sorry if . . .'

Rex's gaze shifted to her face, and his upper lip curled. 'Are you still here?'

Carmen recoiled, his response hitting her like a fist to the stomach. His voice was icy cold. Knowing that he wouldn't back down now, that it had all gone too far, she quickly pushed back her chair and rose to her feet. 'If that's what you want, then I'll go.'

'Don't let me keep you.'

Carmen moved swiftly out of the room without looking back. Silence accompanied her steps. She was angry now, as well as upset. Her face burned with indignation and shame. If he'd only been prepared to listen, to try and understand what she'd been attempting to say, things needn't have reached this stage. Now all she wanted was to get as far away from him as possible.

She grabbed her bag from the hall table, took a coat from the cupboard and fled through the door. The evening air smelled of dust and exhaust fumes. It wasn't cold, but she still shivered as she pulled on her coat. Then, walking as quickly as she could in her high heels, she made her way to the end of the road, glancing over her shoulder – no one was coming after her – and keeping her eyes peeled for a cab.

The row was going round and round in her head: what he had said and what she had said and how the whole evening had gone to hell in less time than it took to drain a glass of champagne. It wouldn't have been safe, she knew, to stay in the house. Her father would have come looking for her after everyone else had gone, drunk on brandy and rage and resentment. He would have made her pay for what she'd done – or rather for what she hadn't.

It was another few minutes before she saw the light of a black cab, hailed it and gratefully tumbled into the back seat. 'Poland Street, please,' she said. As the driver moved off, she sat back and took a few deep breaths. Her heart was beating wildly. She felt sick and clammy, dismayed by the confrontation. The only person she wanted to be with now was Clive. She gazed out of the window and willed the cab to shift faster through the dark London streets.

3

The party broke up shortly after Carmen's abrupt departure, the atmosphere having taken a turn from which it wasn't going to recover. They left in pairs, in quick succession, their good-byes hurried and awkward. Only Pat Foster remained, loyal as always, reluctant to leave his boss alone after the night had plunged from celebration into disaster.

Once outside, Hugh Loughton looked at his wife, rolling his eyes. 'Christ, that was even worse than usual.'

'Stupid cow,' Marian said. 'What's wrong with her?' She felt no sympathy for her younger sister, thinking that Carmen should have known better than to refuse their father the adulation he demanded. 'All she had to do was give him what he wanted. A few gushing words and he'd have been happy. How hard is that? Instead, she had to ruin the whole evening.'

'Your father's a bloody tyrant.'

'Tell me something I don't know. And *she* needs her head examined. Idiot.' Marian's comment about the evening being ruined was not entirely true, as nothing could have dampened the elation she felt at finally getting her hands on the inheritance she had been impatiently waiting for. If she experienced any guilt at all over what her sister had had to put up with over the years, it was smartly brushed aside. 'What's that saying about looking a gift horse in the mouth? She's got a screw loose if you ask me.'

'Rex didn't give her a chance.'

'All she had to do was tell him what he wanted to hear. It doesn't take a genius.'

'Yes, well, not everyone shares your ability to twist the truth, darling.'

Marian shot him a glance, a frown appearing on her forehead. 'It's a good thing I've just come into money, or I might take offence at that.'

'I wouldn't count your chickens.'

'What's that supposed to mean?'

'All I'm saying is that I'd check out the small print before you break open the champagne. Knowing Rex, there's probably a catch.'

Hugh saw a cab coming and stepped into the road, raising his arm. Marian tore open the envelope as soon as they were on their way back to the hotel. She quickly scoured the contents, checking out her share of the inheritance. Overall, she wasn't disappointed – a fast mental calculation put the value at over two million – but she hadn't got everything she'd wanted. She read out the list and said, 'There's no mention of Lola's.'

'He'll have given that to Carmen. Clive's been running the place for the past three years.'

'So what?' Lola's was her father's most profitable club, raking in thousands every week.

'So it makes sense to give it to her. Continuity and all that.'

'Lucky old Clive,' Marian said drily. 'There's nothing like marrying the boss's daughter.'

'You haven't done too badly.' Hugh stretched out his legs and lit a cigarette. 'Perhaps we can get the roof fixed now.'

Marian scowled into the gloom of the cab. There was nothing she wanted less than to waste her money on Hugh's old family pile. The Suffolk house was an endless drain on their resources, with something always in need of repair. If it had been up to her, she'd have put a match to the dump and replaced it with a building that wasn't perpetually cold and draughty. 'I might buy an apartment in town.'

'What for? Any time you come up, you can stay at the Gryphon for free.'

The Gryphon, a fashionable hotel in Bloomsbury, was where they were going now. It was also one of the businesses her father was passing over to her. There was nothing wrong with the place – it was smart and plush with spacious rooms and a decent restaurant – but it lacked the one thing she desired most: privacy. Everyone knew her there. She couldn't do what she wanted, with whom she wanted, without it rapidly becoming public knowledge. And Marian had plans. After twelve long years of tedious marriage, she intended to escape from the country as often as she could and use her newly acquired wealth to have a little fun.

'I might sell it,' she said. 'If you want that new roof, I'll have to liquidate some assets.'

'Rex won't be happy about that.'

'It won't be any of his business once the papers are signed.' Marian could still hardly believe her luck. She had spent the last few years convinced that all her father's talk of retirement was nothing but talk. Now that he'd finally done it, she would no longer be reliant on his grudging handouts or Hugh's meagre housekeeping.

'I hope Carmen's all right.'

'Huh?' Marian said, still revelling in the thought of the financial freedom coming her way.

'Carmen. Do you think she's all right?'

'She'll be fine. What are you worrying about her for?'

'She was upset, in case you didn't notice.'

'She'll get it over it. They both will. By this time tomorrow it'll be ancient history.'

Hugh smoked his cigarette and stared out of the window. 'I wouldn't be so sure.'

But Marian wasn't listening. She had no interest in her youngest sister's trials and tribulations. 'I'll ring Hazel as soon as we get back and find out what she got.'

'Your family never cease to amaze me.' Jonny raised his eyebrows as they walked the few steps from the house. 'Your old man was on top form tonight. One hell of a performance. Carmen put on quite a show too.'

'I'm glad we keep you entertained.'

'And here was me thinking that tonight was going to be duller than ditch water.'

Hazel stopped by a red MG parked under a streetlamp and held up the envelope. 'Still, we came away with more than happy memories.'

Jonny unlocked the passenger door of the car and opened it for her. 'So long as he doesn't change his mind.'

'Why would he do that?'

'Why does Rex do anything? He's a law unto himself.'

Hazel slipped into the MG and waited for Jonny to join her. She had to fight against the urge to rip into the envelope. For all she knew, her father could be watching from the window. Don't open it until you get home, he'd said, and she wasn't going to take the risk of being seen to disobey him – not after what had happened with Carmen.

Jonny walked around and climbed into the driver's seat.

'Are you sure you should be driving?'

'I'm not drunk. Well, not *that* drunk.'

'If you say so.'

Jonny shot her a glance. 'Get a cab if you'd rather.'

'All right. No need to get narky.' Hazel stared at his handsome square-jawed face, his dark eyes, and the mouth she had never stopped wanting to kiss. Even after ten years of marriage she still lusted after him, but that didn't mean she always liked him. He could be moody and deceitful. He lied, thieved, drank too much, gambled too much and was probably less faithful than he should have been.

'Let's get out of here.' Jonny made a slight adjustment to the rear-view mirror, taking the opportunity to check that his reflection was still as sublime as it had been when he'd looked at it three hours ago, shoved the key into the ignition, revved up the engine, released the handbrake and manoeuvred the car away from the kerb.

Only when they were out of sight of the house did Hazel tear open the envelope. Greedily she devoured its contents.

'So?' Jonny asked, trying to peer at the papers.

'Keep your eyes on the road. I'll read it to you.' She went through the list – the businesses, then the properties – only pausing when Jonny interrupted.

'We could move into that Mayfair flat. How big is it? Do you know?'

'Bigger than our place. Three bedrooms, I think.'

'It's about time we had somewhere decent to live.'

Hazel was as tempted as Jonny by the thought of a Mayfair address. It would be a step up from their modest Camden flat and something to boast about to her friends. She kept on reading out loud. 'And we've got the Capri in Brewer Street.'

'That's only a coffee bar.'

'It does all right, though. The kids spend their money there. We've got the Royal too. That's a decent club.'

'Not as good as Lola's. Nothing like.'

'It could be,' Hazel said. 'It just needs some cash spending on it.' For all Jonny's quibbles, she could tell that he was pleased. No more money worries. No more squabbling over debts. No more awkward conversations with the bank manager. As soon as the papers were signed, she'd be a rich woman – and he'd be a rich woman's husband.

Jonny beeped his horn at someone walking along the pavement, lifting his hand from the steering wheel to give a cheery wave.

Hazel looked up but was too late to identify the recipient of his greeting. She glanced over her shoulder but could only see the back of a tall man's head. 'Who was that?'

'That, my dear, was the filthy rich Lord Lucan.'

'And since when were you so chummy with the good Lord?'

Jonny grinned. 'I'm not. But he'll spend the rest of the evening wondering who I am.'

Hazel didn't bother asking why that mattered to him. Like her father, Jonny envied and despised the aristocracy in equal measure. He would have liked to move in their circle, to share in their privileges, but his working-class roots denied him entry. Although money could provide access to that world, it couldn't provide acceptance. He had a chip on his shoulder about it all, a simmering resentment, an inferiority complex that he couldn't shake off.

'He's a big-time gambler. Rarely away from the tables, allegedly.'

'Good for him,' she said.

'They call him Lucky.'

'And is he?'

'Not as often as he'd like. I've heard he loses more than he ever wins, thousands in an evening sometimes. He must be bloody rolling in it.'

'Perhaps we should open a casino.'

Jonny gave a snort.

'Why not? What's to stop us?'

'Because that Clermont lot don't gamble just anywhere. They don't like mixing with the riff-raff.'

Hazel knew the Clermont, an up-market gambling establishment in Berkeley Square. 'Well, they're not the only people who like a flutter.'

'Yeah, but Lucan and his sort have got deep pockets. And they don't kick off when they lose. There's always plenty more where that came from. You run a casino like that, and the cash keeps on rolling in. Big stakes, big profits.'

Hazel pulled a face. 'And big pay-outs too when the punters win.'

'The house always comes out on top in the end.' Jonny gave a shrug. 'They win it one day and give it back, and more, the next. That's how it rolls. What I'm trying to say is that they keep it between themselves. They only gamble where they feel comfortable, and where they feel comfortable is with each other.'

'So? That's never going to change. It's just the way it is.' Hazel reckoned Jonny was the only man who could find something to whine about after his wife had come into a fortune. 'Why does it bug you so much?'

'I've just explained why it bugs me. Weren't you listening?'

'Yes, I was listening. The rich boys like to play with the rich boys. So what? There's plenty more fish in the sea. Who needs that lot looking down their noses?' Hazel suspected that Jonny felt short-changed by his marriage to her, as if getting hitched to one of Rex Darby's daughters hadn't quite provided all the advantages he'd hoped for. Still, he could hardly complain now. Finally, they were free of her father's control, financially independent and answerable to no one.

No sooner had this thought entered her head than her gaze alighted on the final, convoluted paragraph of the papers concerning exceptions, exclusions, terms and conditions. The gist of it, so far as she could gather, was that for the next year nothing could be sold without Rex Darby's permission. She sucked in an audible breath.

'What is it?' Jonny asked.

Hazel folded over the papers and put them back in the envelope. 'Nothing,' she said, unwilling to provide him with any further reason to moan. 'I'll call Marian when we get back. I want to find out what she got.'

4

Carmen paid the cabbie, leapt out of the cab, walked quickly along Poland Street, and stopped outside Clive's flat. She pressed the bell of the green door and waited. A few yards further along people were going in and out of Lola's, a steady flow of Friday-night customers, groups of men and women, couples smiling and laughing. Their carefree expressions were in stark contrast to her own. The journey from Belgravia had done nothing to calm her down or ease the tension in her body. Her stomach was still churning, her throat tight, her mouth dry. Tears pricked her eyes, and she smartly wiped them away.

She glanced at her watch – almost eleven o'clock – and wondered if Clive was asleep. He had sounded sick when he'd called this afternoon, crying off from the birthday dinner. A dose of flu, he'd said, apologising for not being able to make it. Her father had been irked by the last-minute cancellation, believing that nothing short of imminent death should prevent a guest from fulfilling their promise to attend.

Carmen rang the bell again, three long rings while she shifted impatiently from one foot to the other. Perhaps Clive had taken a sleeping pill. Or a couple of stiff whiskies. What if she couldn't wake him? Find a phone box perhaps and see if the telephone would do what the doorbell couldn't. Or spend the night in a hotel. But the thought of being alone at a time like this filled her with dismay. She needed someone to talk to, a shoulder to cry on. She needed Clive.

Carmen stared with frustration at the door, willing it to open. It didn't. It was then, gradually, that a new anxiety began to seep into her. What if Clive was seriously ill? What if he had collapsed on the floor and was unconscious? He could have been lying there for hours. Panic gathered in her. Just because things had been bad tonight didn't mean they couldn't get a whole lot worse. She had to *do* something.

She looked along the street again towards Lola's. One of the regular doormen, Henry, was out on the pavement and she hurried towards him. 'Have you seen Mr Grainger?' she asked, her voice high and faltering.

'He's inside, miss.'

'I know.' She gestured back towards the flat. 'I've been ringing the bell but there's no reply.'

'No, I mean he's in Lola's.'

'What?'

'Come on in and I'll go and get him for you.'

Carmen's panic subsided, only to be replaced by surprise and a faint feeling of resentment. If Clive was so ill, what was he doing in the club? 'Oh, right. Thank you.' She forced a smile, gathered herself and followed Henry into the foyer. A few customers were milling about, depositing or collecting coats, waiting for taxis or for partners to emerge from the toilets. She could hear the soft jazzy beat of the music.

'I'll only be a minute, miss. Why don't you wait here?'

Carmen nodded but was too impatient to wait. The second Henry had passed through the heavy interior doors she was hot on his heels. Inside was dimly lit, noisy and crowded. A long bar, strung with fairy lights, ran along the back while the central dance floor was surrounded by tables. It would have taken her a while to locate Clive if she hadn't been able to follow Henry's movements: the doorman glided effortlessly through the busy room, knowing exactly where he was going.

Carmen saw him stop by a table of eight and bend down to whisper discreetly in Clive's ear. She hurried forward, desperate to be with him, but then stopped dead in her tracks as her brain belatedly translated what her eyes were seeing. A woman was sitting to the right of Clive, a woman who would strike fear into any fiancée: a stunning blonde with the face and body of a goddess. This Aphrodite had her elegant hand placed somewhat proprietorially on Clive's arm and was leaning in a little too closely. As Henry left, Clive said something to her, and she threw back her head and laughed.

Clive stood up, smiling, and began to walk towards the door. It was a few seconds before he noticed Carmen. He gave a slight start, a response that could have been down to surprise – Henry had probably told him she was waiting in the foyer – or guilt at being caught out doing something he shouldn't. Either way he quickly recovered himself, strode over, leaned down and kissed her cheek.

'Darling, what are you doing here?'

'I need to talk to you. There's been ... something awful has happened. A row. A big one.' And then, because she couldn't help herself, she glanced over at the table and said, 'Who's that woman?'

'Oh, that's just Paul Stanton's latest squeeze. Tara something.'

'She seems very ... friendly.'

23

Clive raised his eyebrows. 'Very drunk, more like. I was only keeping her company until Paul gets here. He's been held up and . . . Anyway, he spends a lot in the club, so I need to keep him sweet.'

Carmen could have said that there were six other people at the table to keep Tara company, but kept the retort to herself. She didn't want to come across as the clingy, jealous type. Men didn't like that. And after all, what had she seen? Nothing more than some over-familiarity. She knew, of course, that other women found Clive attractive. Why wouldn't they? He was smart and handsome and charming, and it was his job to keep people happy. She gazed at his fine-boned face, his fair hair and clear blue eyes. She wasn't so naïve as to think that girls wouldn't flirt with him – or he with them – and knew better than to make a big deal out of it. Despite that, she still murmured, 'She's very pretty.'

Clive took her elbow and gently led her towards the bar. 'Actually, she's a dreadful bore. A Yank who can't stop talking. Stanton owes me big time. Let's get a drink and you can tell me all about this row.'

Once the brandies had been collected, they went to sit at a table in a quieter if not quiet corner.

'I thought you were ill,' Carmen said, trying not to sound too accusatory. She had already fallen out with one person tonight and she didn't want to get into an argument with Clive too.

'I am. I feel like hell. I'm sure I've got a temperature. I'd be tucked up in bed right now if it wasn't for bloody Stanton. But I could hardly say no, could I? It all comes with the job, unfortunately. Now come on, tell me what happened tonight.'

Carmen began talking, trying to explain. In the cab she had gone over and over the exchange with her father, trying to get everything straight in her head, but now her account was disjointed and rambling. She stopped and started, corrected herself, carried on. Eventually she got the main points of the story out, but not in any coherent order. She sighed, looked at Clive and gave a light shrug of her shoulders. 'That's it.'

A frown had appeared on Clive's forehead. 'So you just threw a fortune back in his face?'

'I wasn't throwing anything. It wasn't like that.'

'All you had to do was play the game like your sisters did.'

Carmen didn't care for the way he was reacting or his look of disappointment. 'But it's not a game, for God's sake – or at least it shouldn't be.'

'You know what your father's like.'

'What are you saying? That it was all my fault?'

Clive raked his fingers through his fair hair. 'No, no I didn't mean that. I'm sorry. Of course it wasn't your fault. I just meant . . .' He placed his hand over hers and squeezed it. 'Poor you. What a night! Give the dust time to settle, huh? I'm sure he'll come round when he's had time to think about it.'

'He's not exactly the forgiving sort.' Carmen sipped her brandy. She had hoped for more support from him, some affirmation that she had not been in the wrong, but she suspected that he thought her as foolish as her sisters did. 'I didn't mean to insult him or sound ungrateful. I thanked him but that wasn't enough. And then he wouldn't let it rest. He kept going on and on . . .'

'It was just the booze talking, love. Don't worry. He'll realise what an idiot he's been in the morning. You can go home and talk to him, sort this out.'

'Not tonight, though,' she said. 'I can't go back there tonight. I can stay with you, can't I?'

Clive hesitated. 'Do you think that's a good idea? I don't want you catching whatever I've got.'

'I'll take the risk.'

'And Rex won't be happy if he finds out. It might just make everything worse.'

Despite it being 1974, Rex Darby persisted in the ludicrous belief that decent women should be virgins when they married. That boat had, of course, sailed long ago – she was twenty-one for God's sake – but the pretence was still upheld. So long as Carmen was back in her own bed at a respectable hour, her virtue remained theoretically intact. 'I'm not going home,' she said firmly.

'Perhaps a hotel would be better. You could go to the Gryphon. Why don't I drive you there?'

Carmen had no desire to go to the Gryphon where she would, undoubtably, run into Marian and have to endure a patronising lecture on how to deal with their father. She felt her eyes filling with tears again. 'Don't you want me to stay with you?'

'Of course I do,' Clive said, squeezing her hand again. 'There's nothing I'd like more. I'm just trying to be practical, to not rub salt into the wound. Your father's got old-fashioned ideas.'

'When it suits him,' she said. 'He's not so fussy when it comes to his own affairs. It's one rule for him and another for the rest of us. Maybe it's time he faced up to reality. We're engaged for God's sake. He can't tell us what we can and can't do.'

Clive pondered on this for a moment and eventually nodded. 'I suppose you're right. Come on, finish your drink and we'll get out of here.'

Carmen smiled, relieved that he'd come round to her way of thinking. But even so, something was niggling, a feeling that he was not entirely on her side. There had been an expression on his face while she'd been talking. Irritation? Disapproval? Perhaps she had not explained it properly. She thought of her father's glowering stare, the way he had dismissed her, and felt that churning in her stomach again.

As they were leaving Lola's, Carmen glanced across the room.

Tara was flirting with some other bloke now, twisting her silky blonde hair between her fingers. Feeling Carmen's gaze on her, the girl lifted her eyes and gave her a long assessing look. Then her mouth slid into a sly smile. What did that mean? Carmen linked her arm into Clive's, sending what she hoped was a clear message: he was taken, hands off. Unimpressed, Tara tossed her head and returned her attention to her latest admirer.

It felt chilly outside after the warmth of the club. They walked the few yards along the road to the flat, Clive unlocked the door and they went upstairs. Inside, with the lights on and the curtains closed, the place had a cosy feel. She looked around, taking in the pale green walls, the leather sofa and the lamps. Although she had been here many times before, and everything was familiar to her, she had never previously stayed the night.

Carmen slipped off her coat and slumped down on the sofa, feeling the stresses of the evening finally beginning to subside. She was safe now. If she could not forget about the night's events, then she could at least push them temporarily to the back of her mind.

'I'll run you a bath,' Clive said. 'You look all in.'

He went into the bathroom and shortly after she heard the sound of water running. She tipped back her head and closed her eyes. But her new-found state of calm didn't last for long. Clive returned to the living room and said, 'You relax and have your bath. I'll be back in ten minutes.'

Carmen's eyes blinked open. 'Where are you going?'

'I just need to sort out a few things at the club.'

'What things?'

'Someone is going to have to lock up later and put the takings in the safe. I'll get Prescott to do it. I won't be long.'

And then, before she could say another word, Carmen was alone again.

5

Other than his father, Eddie Foster and his mum were the last to leave the party. He took her arm as they walked along Upper Belgrave Street, aware that she was upset and angry and that nothing he could say was likely to change that. He wasn't surprised by how the evening had panned out; there was always drama in the Darby household. It had been the same for as long as he could remember. He had only accepted the invitation because he'd felt obliged; now, he wished that he had made an excuse to get out of it like Clive Grainger.

'Bloody Rex,' Annie muttered. 'That man . . .'

'Perhaps Dad can talk some sense into him.'

Annie gave a dry laugh. 'Fat chance. The blind leading the blind. That's all that is.'

'It's because he sprung it on her. Carmen, I mean. She got all flustered. She didn't know what to say.'

'She said thank you. What more did the old bugger want? He didn't need to show her up in front of everyone.'

'No,' Eddie agreed. He didn't know Carmen well, not like

he knew her sisters. He was of an age with Marian and Hazel, and they had played and holidayed together as children. By the time Carmen had come along her older siblings were nine and eight, and not best pleased to have an attention-seeking baby sharing the house.

'Rosa will be turning in her grave.'

Rex's wife had died before Carmen was six months old. Eddie remembered her as a beautiful but unhappy woman. But then who could be happy married to Rex? He was not the sort of man who valued the art of compromise and had ruled over his family, just like his business, with a rod of iron. No wonder Marian and Hazel had married young: it had been the easiest way to get away from him. 'You tried, Mum. What more could you do?'

Annie, whose eyes had been cast down towards the pavement, briefly raised them to look at her son. 'For all the good of it. What if he cuts off that poor girl without a penny?'

'It won't come to that. And even if it does, she might be better off. Money doesn't bring happiness. Isn't that what they say?'

'And a lack of it doesn't bring much happiness either. That money will give her independence, the freedom to do what she wants. It will set her free from Rex.'

But only as far as Clive Grainger, Eddie thought. There was every chance she would simply be exchanging one controlling man for another. But he kept this concern to himself. He suspected that his mum would have left his dad long ago – as soon as she'd found out about his affair, about his illegitimate son – if she'd had money of her own. With his father's ability to cook the books, she wouldn't have got much from a divorce. And there had been the Darby girls to think of back then too. She would have known that Rex would never let her see them if she was separated from Pat.

They had reached Buckingham Palace Road by the time

Eddie was able to hail a cab. He gave the driver the address in Victoria, and they climbed inside. As the cab moved off, Eddie sat back, reflecting on the evening.

'Did you know Rex was retiring? Did Dad mention it?'

'Not a word.'

'Will Dad do the same, do you think? He's still got a few years before he's sixty-five.'

'You'll have to ask him that – if he bothers to come home tonight.' Annie shifted in the seat and stared out at the night streets. 'Anyway, whatever Rex says, I can't see him retiring, not completely. He'll be watching those girls like a hawk, putting his oar in, making sure that precious business empire of his doesn't go down the drain. I don't imagine he'll be getting rid of your dad just yet.'

'Still, when he does stop working, you could move, couldn't you? Get out of London and buy a nice little bungalow in Eastbourne or Bournemouth. Or go abroad. How about the south of France? You always said you wanted to live in the sun.'

'He won't want to leave.'

Eddie did not state the obvious, that she could always go on her own. His father was well off and could easily afford to buy another place. And he owed her. No one could deny that. She had stuck by him through thick and thin, and there had been plenty of thin. 'You should think about it.'

'I've got more important things to think about tonight.'

'Well, you should think about yourself for once.'

'It's not just about me, though, is it? There's you and Rex and . . .'

Eddie knew who the 'and' was even if it wasn't spoken out loud: Milo. He hadn't been aware of his half-brother until he was thirteen when Marian had gleefully informed him that his dad had fathered another son, now nine years old, by a West

30

End stripper called Sylvie Grant. He had gone red in the face and called her a stupid stinking liar and she had said that he was the stupid one, that everyone knew but him, even his mother.

Eddie shuddered as he recalled that day. Suddenly so many things had made sense: the rows between his parents, the oblique references in his presence, the stony silences. It had been a long time, years, before he'd talked to his father about it. And even longer before he'd broached the subject with his mum.

For her sake Eddie always tried to avoid his half-brother. To have formed any kind of relationship with him would have been like adding insult to injury. And anyway, Milo was not pleasant to be around. Whenever their paths crossed, Eddie could feel the resentment emanating from him, a rancour that his fake affability did nothing to disguise.

Marian had taunted him mercilessly about Milo. Although, of course, she had taunted him over pretty much anything she could. He could remember her full lips drawn back into a mocking smile, her brown eyes flashing with pleasure. God, now that he had started thinking about her, he couldn't stop. She had always enjoyed tormenting him. She had known that he'd been infatuated with her, that he'd loved her beyond all sense or reason. The crueller she was, the more he'd adored her. It had been like a sickness eating away at his insides. When it had been announced that she was marrying Hugh Loughton he had thought that it would kill him.

Eddie barely recognised that teenage boy now. Over time his passion had shrivelled and died. Although he still preferred not to see Marian if he could avoid it, she no longer occupied his every waking hour. These days his world rarely collided with hers. His job at Egan's, a small bookshop on Charing Cross Road, didn't bring in much money but it brought him a certain kind of peace.

It was interesting, he thought, how you could love someone without liking them. This contradictory situation applied both to his relationship with his father and, once upon a time, to Marian too. It required a peculiar trick of ensuring one part of his brain didn't make contact with the other, of placing his emotions in neat little boxes with the lids fixed on tight.

'At least you stood up for Carmen,' he said. 'That's more than her sisters did.'

'Those two always had each other's backs. Thick as thieves they were, growing up. But it was different with Carmen. They were never close to her. She's had to cope with everything on her own.' Annie's hand moved restlessly, touching her face, her neck, before falling into her lap again. 'I should have kept my mouth shut. I just made it all worse.'

'Don't say that, Mum. None of this is your fault. They'll sort it out. I'm sure they will. That family are always at each other's throats, but it eventually blows over. You know what Rex is like.'

'I do know what he's like. That's the trouble. I know *exactly* what he's like. One way or another, he's going to make that poor girl pay.'

6

Milo Grant was perched on a bar stool in Lola's, drinking what must have been his third or fourth whisky, while he watched the pretty people at play. He didn't usually come here – it wasn't his sort of establishment – only the pubs had shut, and he wasn't ready for home yet. Resentment simmered inside him. It was something he was familiar with, an emotion never far from the surface. Earlier this evening he'd had a blazing row with his mother.

Milo snarled as he went over the exchange in his head. Her grand announcement that she was sodding off to live in Spain with her latest fancy man hadn't come as any great surprise. What had shocked him was that she was planning to sell the flat before she went – *his* home, the place he'd grown up in.

'So you're leaving me without even a bloody roof over my head?'

'You're twenty-five,' she'd said. 'Get your own flat. You're working, ain't you? You're old enough to take care of yourself.'

But Milo didn't see why he should have to fork out when he

didn't need to. He had as much right to that damn flat as she did. Come to that, she owed him big time for all the money she'd squeezed out of Pat Foster. If she hadn't got up the duff when she had, she'd still be taking off her clothes in some sleazy Soho joint, flashing her tits without a penny to her name.

He sipped his whisky and lit a cigarette. When he'd been a kid his mother had always been pressing Pat for cash – cash for school uniforms, for shoes, for haircuts – but little of it had ever come his way. She'd spent most of it on booze and fags and going out. Pat had paid her maintenance every month, but it had never been enough.

Yeah, she'd done pretty well, all things considered, out of what had been no more than a casual fling. Pat had even bought the flat for her. It was in a six-storey block, had two bedrooms and a decent-sized living room, and was in a handy location too, just off Tottenham Court Road. That was the price she'd demanded for keeping quiet about little Milo, and Pat had paid it. Course it hadn't stayed a secret for ever, but by the time Pat's missus found out, Sylvie had already taken him for a fortune.

Milo's feelings towards his father were hostile, although he was careful never to show it. There had been a series of blood tests after he was born, the results of which showed that Pat *could* be his dad but provided no definitive proof. That proof had come later as, fortunately for his mother, Milo had grown to look just like Pat, with the same stocky build, the same red-gold hair and pale blue eyes. The similarities were so striking that anyone could recognise them as father and son.

Although Pat hadn't shirked his financial responsibilities, Milo had always been aware of being second best, a dirty secret, the child who was kept in the background. Take tonight, for instance. It was Rex Darby's seventieth birthday, but he hadn't got an invite. No, Pat had taken his missus and Eddie with him.

34

And hadn't it always been like that? While Pat had swanned off on holidays abroad with his 'real' family – to Monte Carlo, the Dordogne, Florence – Milo had been lucky to get a day out in Southend.

Milo's resentment, towards both his father and his mother, ran deep. But in the former's case he was careful to keep it under wraps. For the past ten years, ever since he'd left school, he'd been cultivating their relationship, arranging it so they saw as much of each other as possible. His father, after much wheedling, had even been persuaded to get him a job working for Rex. Follow the money was Milo's mantra, and the real money lay with Rex Darby.

Milo had started off by running errands, criss-crossing London with letters in white envelopes, but he had never complained. On the contrary, he had always kept a smile on his face, showed willing and proved himself to be a thoroughly reliable employee. After a while he'd progressed to delivering small brown parcels full of money. He'd never nicked a penny either. Not that he hadn't been tempted. Knowing there was cash in his hands, bundles of notes wrapped in plain brown paper, would be enough to tempt even an honest man. And he certainly wasn't one of those. However, Rex's bribes were always safely delivered, proof that Milo could be trusted. It would have been easy to take the money and run, but he was playing the long game.

As he'd grown older and stronger, his duties had extended to rent collector. Although not especially lucrative, the job did have one redeeming feature: he got to spend more time with Rex Darby. The two of them would chat in the office and at least once a week go for a drink, along with Pat, to the Plumbers Arms down the road. Milo knew that Rex liked him, that he found his banter entertaining, and he went out of his way to ingratiate himself. He flattered the older man – not too obviously – nobody likes an arse licker – and made it clear that he looked up to him.

In his head, Milo was trying to put together some great scheme. A better position in the firm was part of it, more responsibility, more power, more opportunities. He was hoping that Rex would eventually recognise his potential and reward it accordingly. There wasn't much sign of this yet, but he wasn't giving up.

Marrying the boss's daughter had been part of his original plan, but this had long since gone by the wayside. With Marian and Hazel already spoken for, he'd turned his attention to Carmen. But when he'd tried to chat her up – always out of earshot of Rex – she had just stared back at him through those cool grey eyes of hers, as if he was speaking a foreign language she didn't understand. 'Stuck-up bitch,' he muttered under his breath.

Milo knew that when his old man kicked the bucket, there wouldn't be much in it for him: a few quid perhaps, but most of the inheritance would go to Eddie. His face twisted in anger. How was that fair? It bloody well wasn't. He was sick of always being at the back of the queue, of only ever getting the crumbs. Even thinking about Eddie enraged him. The boring fart worked in a bookshop, for God's sake. What kind of job was that for a man?

He looked around the club, his gaze resting briefly on one girl after another while he marked them out of ten and debated whether he would screw them or not. It was something to do, a way of passing the time. He might not be the best-looking bloke in the world, but he never went short when it came to a bit of skirt. Women – well, *most* women – couldn't resist a slice of Milo Grant.

The barman picked up Milo's ashtray, emptied its contents, gave it a wipe, and put it back in front of him.

'You want another?' he asked, gesturing towards the glass.

Milo nodded. 'Sure.'

While he was waiting for his whisky, Milo looked around again. This time his gaze fell on Clive Grainger. He wondered why Carmen's fiancé wasn't at Rex's bash, and why he appeared to be chatting up a very glamorous blonde. Trouble in paradise? He hoped so. He would find out when he next saw Marian. Carmen might think he was beneath her, but her sister didn't have any such scruples. In fact, being beneath her was exactly where she liked him to be.

7

It was nearer forty minutes rather than the promised ten before Clive came back to the flat. Carmen had finished her bath, dried herself and gone to bed. She had lain there for what had felt like an eternity, the lamp on, her eyes fixed on the alarm clock – what was he doing? Why was he taking so long? – trying not to think about the glamorous Tara, trying not to think about her father, until she finally heard the key in the lock.

Clive came into the bedroom, shrugging off his jacket and opening the wardrobe to hang it up. 'Sorry, I didn't mean to be so long.'

Carmen propped herself up on one elbow and watched him. 'Is everything all right?'

'Oh, only the usual. You can guarantee there's always someone who wants a "quick word" just when you're trying to make a hasty exit.' He loosened his tie, pulled it over his head and placed it over the back of the chair. He unbuttoned his shirt and took it off. 'Milo was there, propping up the bar.'

'Did you talk to him?'

'No.'

Carmen wondered if Milo had seen her in the club earlier, if he'd guessed something was wrong. She didn't like the guy, mainly because he was so sly and lecherous, but also because of Annie. Although it wasn't his fault that he was Pat's illegitimate son, she felt it would be disloyal to be on any more than nodding terms with him. Not that she wanted anything more. She wrinkled her nose. He had a habit, when he was hanging around her father's office, of looking her up and down like a piece of meat.

'He doesn't often come to Lola's, does he?' she said.

'Not often. He'd had a skinful, I reckon. Perhaps he had the hump at not being invited to your dad's.'

'Annie wouldn't have taken too kindly to that. Having her husband's love-child sitting across the table probably isn't her idea of a perfect evening.'

Clive grinned and went into the bathroom. She heard him splash water on his face, and then brush his teeth. He came back, sat on the edge of the bed, leaned down to undo his shoelaces and then eased his feet out of his shoes. Carmen studied the curve of his back. She wanted to reach out and touch him, to run her fingertips from the nape of his neck to the base of his spine.

'It's the first time I've ever spent the whole night here,' she said.

Clive removed his socks, stood up, took off his trousers and then slid into bed beside her. 'You should get some sleep. It's been a long day.'

This wasn't quite the romantic response she'd been hoping for. What she wanted was for him to hold her in his arms, to comfort her, to press his mouth against hers. What she wanted was love and passion. Instead, he had turned on his side with his back to her. A cold shoulder if ever she'd seen one. She could place an arm around him, curve her body around his, but she sensed that the physical contact wouldn't be welcome. Was it because he was feeling unwell, or something else? Fearing rejection, and not confident enough to make the first move, she kept to her own side of the bed.

Clive switched off the lamp, and there was quiet in the room. Carmen gazed into the darkness. She could hear his soft breathing, the ticking of the clock, the sound of footsteps on the street outside. It was odd, she thought, how lonely you could feel even when someone was lying right beside you.

8

Carmen had a night of interrupted sleep, repeatedly waking to a stone-cold feeling of dread. When she did fall back to sleep it was only to dream of terrible things, of being pursued, hunted, by an unknown predator. When she ascended from these nightmares the fear was still with her, and she could feel her heart's heavy thump and the dryness of her mouth. She would have tossed and turned had she not been afraid of waking Clive. Instead, she lay very still, dazed and panicky.

When morning finally came, she turned her head to look at the alarm clock, rubbed her eyes and saw that it was twenty past eight. She saw too that Clive was no longer in bed. A thin clattering broke through the silence. She got up, slipped on his discarded shirt, and padded through to the kitchen.

Clive was standing at the counter, fully dressed. The smell of coffee and toast wafted through the air. 'Good morning. Did you sleep well?' he asked.

'Yes, thanks,' she replied automatically, thinking that she had done enough complaining without adding to the quota. 'You?'

'Oh, so-so,' he said, as if he had been the one lying wide awake for half the night.

'Are you feeling any better?'

'Not too bad. I've taken some aspirin. Sit down, I'll have breakfast ready soon.'

Carmen perched on one of the two chrome stools and watched him while he whisked eggs in a glass bowl, added salt and pepper, and dropped them into a pan where a knob of melted butter was starting to sizzle. He put two plates on the counter. He stirred the eggs. All of his movements were clean, efficient and economical, his slender hands using the minimum of effort to maximum effect. Clive was one of those men who always knew exactly what he was doing, even if it was only making breakfast.

She could clearly remember the first time she'd laid eyes on him, a couple of years ago now. Her father had been on a mission to teach her about the business, taking her here, there and everywhere, showing her the ropes and introducing her to the staff. Eventually they had ended up at Lola's. Clive, with his easy manner, handsome sculpted face and air of sophistication, had made an instant impression on her. A man rather than a boy, she'd thought, as she'd sneaked interested glances. Over the following weeks she'd contrived ways to bump into him, found questions to ask, and made it clear that she enjoyed his company. Eventually he'd taken the hint and invited her to dinner.

Carmen had never been in love before, had never felt those butterflies in her stomach or experienced that dreadful and yet wonderful yearning. She had hung on his every word, beguiled. He had seemed the epitome of everything she desired in a man: intelligent, strong, protective. Over the past couple of years nothing had happened to change that, and although she knew he wasn't perfect – he could be cool, even distant – she was still convinced that she wanted to spend the rest of her life with him.

Clive placed the scrambled eggs in front of her, along with a mug of coffee. She wasn't hungry, but as he'd gone to the effort, she forced herself to eat, forking in tiny mouthfuls and making small noises of appreciation.

'Have you thought about what you're going to say to your father?' he said.

'I'll just apologise, I suppose, claim I was overwhelmed by the occasion or something.'

'That sounds vague.'

'Does it?'

Clive gave her one of his impatient looks. 'This is your future we're talking about, Carmen. It's important. You can't afford to get it wrong.'

'So what do you think I should say?'

He put down his knife and fork. 'Whatever it is, it needs to sound genuine. And contrite. None of this was your fault, but that's not how he's going to see it. Just bite your tongue and tell him what you think he wants to hear.'

'Should I go down on my knees while I'm at it?'

Clive threw her another look, as if her sarcasm was unbefitting to the situation. His mouth drooped a little at the corners. 'If that's what it takes.'

'But nothing's going to sound genuine, is it?' Carmen frowned. 'I can't repeat anything that Marian or Hazel said. And anything I do say, well, he's going to pick fault with it. Nothing will be good enough for him, *nothing*.'

'You sound like you've given up before you've even started.'

Carmen sighed into her scrambled eggs. 'He's a man who bears grudges.'

'You're his daughter, for God's sake. He isn't going to . . . Just say you're sorry, all right? Tell him you were taken by surprise, that you couldn't find the words to say how grateful you are. He'll have calmed down by now. I'm sure he'll hear you out.'

Carmen didn't think he knew her father very well if he thought he was the forgiving sort. Or that he'd have calmed down. She had known him sulk for weeks over far less. But she nodded, as if what Clive said made sense and she was reassured by it. 'Let's hope so.'

'Don't look so worried. Nothing's so bad that it can't be put right. Now finish your eggs, and I'll drive you over there.'

9

Carmen almost hoped for an accident – nothing serious, just a minor scrape that would delay their arrival at Upper Belgrave Street. She didn't feel prepared. She stared out through the windscreen, chewing on her lower lip while she battled with anxiety. Autumn sunshine, palely yellow, slanted down from a turquoise sky. She smoothed out the creases in her frock. With nothing else to wear she'd had to put her party attire back on, and she felt overdressed for a Saturday morning.

Clive drew the car up outside the house but kept the engine idling. 'Home sweet home,' he said, raising his eyebrows.

'Are you coming in?'

'Best not. This is between the two of you. I don't think he'd want me interfering. I'll give you a call later and you can tell me how it went.' He leaned across and kissed her on the cheek. 'Good luck. And don't forget what I said.'

'Be contrite.'

'Be *very* contrite.'

Carmen got out of the car, closed the door, and walked

towards the house. Clive beeped his horn and gave her a wave as he disappeared down the street. He could have offered to wait for her, she thought. But then this wasn't going to be a quick fix. It might take the best part of the morning to start getting back in her father's good books – and even that was being optimistic.

She paused on the threshold, took a deep breath, pulled out her key and unlocked the door. In the hall she stopped again. Mrs Cooper, the cleaner, was hard at work. She could hear the noisy rumble of the Hoover coming from the first floor. Then she heard another noise closer at hand – the chink of glass against glass – and her heart missed a beat. Her father. He was in the living room. She was tempted to bolt, to sprint upstairs, but knew that she would have to face him eventually.

Carmen swallowed hard, put on her penitent face, nudged open the door and went into the room. She was braced for confrontation, but it was only Marian. Her older sister was standing by the drinks cabinet and helping herself to a large brandy.

'Oh, hello.'

Marian held up the bottle. 'Want one?'

Carmen shook her head. 'It's a bit early for me. Is Dad here?'

'No, fortunately for you. He's at the office. I've just been to see him.' Marian picked up her glass and took a gulp of brandy. 'Hence the need for this.'

'How is he? Or shouldn't I ask?'

'Fuming. Furious. I've never seen him so mad.'

Carmen winced.

Marian sat down in the armchair by the fireplace and studied Carmen over the rim of her glass. 'What got into you last night?'

'Nothing got into me. I just . . . I just didn't know what to say.'

'You didn't need to storm out.'

'I didn't storm. He told me to go.'

'Out of his sight,' Marian said. 'Not out of the house.'

'It didn't sound like that to me.'

'You just made everything worse. Where did you go? Clive's?'

'Yes.'

Marian sighed. 'He won't be happy about that either. Look, if I was you, I'd stay out of his way for a few days.'

'And how am I supposed to do that? I live here, remember.'

'Go back to Clive's. Or a friend's place. Or the Gryphon. Give it a day or two, maybe three, and he might have calmed down. Now is not the time for whatever conversation you think you're going to have with him. He said if he saw your face today, he'd say something he'd regret.'

'And what's that supposed to mean?'

'Well, I wouldn't hang around to find out. You don't want to be on your own with him, not when he's in this sort of mood.'

Carmen, who was hovering just inside the room, listened for the sound of the front door opening. 'Do you know when he's coming back?'

'He didn't say.'

'Is anyone else at the office?'

'Only Pat. Although I think he was planning on going home. I'm not sure. He might have gone by now.'

Carmen shifted from one foot to the other, wrapped her arms around her chest and tried to work out what to do next. 'You could come with me,' she said tentatively. 'To the office, to see Dad.'

Marian pulled a face. 'Don't go dragging me into this. I've got enough problems of my own, thank you very much.'

'I just thought—'

'Have you not been listening to anything I said? He's in a rage, Carmen, thoroughly pissed off. Please don't ask me to take sides because I'm not going to. You created this situation, so you can deal with it. If you've got any sense, you'll pack a few things and get out of here.'

Carmen didn't need any further persuasion. She nodded and retreated into the hall, ran upstairs to her bedroom, took a small suitcase from the bottom of her wardrobe and flung it on the bed. She pulled fresh underwear from a drawer, and changed out of her dress into jeans, a white shirt and a navy-blue cashmere sweater. What to pack? Just the bare essentials, she decided, enough to get her through the weekend. Hopefully by Monday her father would be in a better frame of mind.

Quickly she stuffed clothes into the bag, and retrieved her toothbrush, toothpaste and make-up bag from the bathroom. She went over to the window and glanced up and down the street to make sure her father wasn't on his way back. Then she had a moment's hesitation – would it be better to stay and face the music, to get it over with? – before Marian's warnings came flooding into her head again.

Carmen ran into Mrs Cooper on the landing. Their cleaner, who had been with them for years, was a benign-looking woman in her sixties, small and plump with a round powdered face, dimples in her cheeks and a halo of soft grey curls. Appearances, however, could be deceptive. Her small, shrewd eyes saw everything, and she gathered gossip as efficiently as the Hoover gathered dust.

'Good party was it, last night?'

'Lovely, thank you,' Carmen said.

'It must have been nice for Mr Darby to have all his family round him like that. You're not seventy every day.' A sly smile crept on to her lips. 'I suppose the champagne was flowing. That would account for the mood on him this morning. A touch of the hangovers, I dare say. Almost bit my head off, he did.'

'Oh dear,' Carmen said. 'I am sorry.' Although she didn't see why she should apologise for her father's incivility, it was a habit she'd got into over the years. Good cleaners were hard to find, and Mrs Cooper was one of the best.

'Don't you worry about it, love. Water off a duck's back. I know what he's like, least I should do after all this time.' Mrs Cooper's gaze fell on the suitcase Carmen was holding. 'Going away, are you?'

'Just for the weekend,' Carmen said too quickly, seeing in the older woman's expression a curiosity that would need to be sated. 'To see a friend. I'll be back on Monday.' She glanced at her watch as if she was working to a strict timetable, as if somewhere across London, at Victoria or Waterloo or Euston, was a platform waiting for her to walk on to it. 'Well, I'd better get a move on, or I'll miss the train.'

'You all right, are you love?'

'Me? Yes, of course. Why wouldn't I be?'

'You're looking a bit peaky.'

Carmen's free hand rose to her face. 'No, I'm fine. Really. It was a late night, that's all.' She smiled thinly. 'And perhaps I had a drop too much champagne.' Then, before Mrs Cooper could interrogate her any further, she said her goodbyes, dashed across the landing and hurried down the stairs.

Carmen put the suitcase down in the hall and went into the living room. Marian was smoking a cigarette and still nursing her glass of brandy, or perhaps it was a fresh one. 'Do you want to share a cab to the Gryphon?'

'Not going back to Clive's then?'

Carmen had only made her mind up seconds ago. She had the feeling that Clive wouldn't be happy about this latest development, that he was expecting her to have sorted everything out and would want to know why she hadn't. It might be wise to wait a while before breaking the bad news. 'No, he's not well. He's got the flu.'

'Oh, I thought that was just an excuse to get out of Dad's birthday bash.'

'Why would you think that?'

Marian expelled a long thin stream of smoke. 'God, Carmen, you don't half ask some stupid questions. A night in the company of Rex Darby isn't everyone's idea of a good time. Surely even you must have wondered if Clive was telling the truth.'

'Well, he was,' Carmen insisted loyally. She was used to her sister's jibes – she'd lived with them for as long as she could remember – but, whatever the truth, she wasn't going to give her the satisfaction of thinking she was right on this occasion. 'He *is*.'

But Marian just grinned and said, 'He must have been kicking himself when he found out about Dad's big announcement. Fancy not being there when his fiancée is about to be made a rich woman.'

'I'm sure it doesn't bother him one way or the other.'

'If you think that you must need your head examining.'

Carmen stared at her. 'Do you want to share this cab or not?'

'Or not, I'm afraid.' Marian flicked some ash into the ashtray. 'I have to wait for Hugh. He's gone off to buy some new wellingtons. Can you believe it? Bloody wellingtons! We're about to come into money and that's his idea of a celebration.'

'I'll see you later then.'

'Probably. I'm not sure what our plans are yet.' Marian drained her glass and looked back at Carmen. 'I'd get a move on if I was you. You don't want to run into Dad.'

Carmen left the house, carrying her suitcase. Her heart was in her mouth as she stood on the pavement, glancing up and down the street. Her pulse raced. She dreaded seeing him, feared that awful temper of his. When no cab loomed into view, she began walking quickly in the opposite direction to the office. She had come here in the hope of achieving a reconciliation but was leaving with nothing.

10

Marian stubbed out her cigarette, stood up and went over to the window. A smirk appeared on her face as she watched her sister walk off down the street. She felt no regret, no remorse, for what she'd just done: if Carmen was stupid enough to believe the bullshit she was told, she deserved everything she got. Marian hadn't even seen their father this morning – she wasn't due at the office for another ten minutes – but she never let an inconvenient truth get in the way of stirring up trouble.

Getting one over on Carmen always brought her pleasure. And it hadn't been a complete lie. Odds on, Dad probably *was* still mad. Rex Darby liked to nurture his grievances, to feed and cultivate them. Carmen's failure to deliver a prompt and fulsome apology wouldn't sit well with him.

Marian turned away from the window, slipped into her coat, examined her reflection in the mirror above the fireplace, and made a few adjustments to her long glossy hair. She glanced towards the telephone, tempted to call Milo, but decided to take a rain check. Mrs Cooper was upstairs, and there was no knowing what those big flapping ears of hers might overhear.

Outside, she strolled down to Lower Belgrave Street and took a right into Ebury Street. While she walked her thoughts returned to Carmen. She could not remember a time when her little sister hadn't got on her nerves; she'd been a thorn in her side since the day she was born. And not just *her* side.

Her mother hadn't even wanted another child. She couldn't face, yet again, that post-natal darkness, the dreadful desperation, that always descended on her. Late at night, creeping out on to the landing, Marian had listened to the long bitter rows between her parents, the shouting (her father) and the crying (her mother), rows that only ever took them round in hopeless circles. Her father, of course, would not sanction an abortion, and not because of the risk to life or because it was illegal, but only because the child she was carrying inside her might just, this time, turn out to be a boy.

Marian recalled her mother in the months after Carmen's birth, lying very still in bed, silent and unresponsive, staring out of the window at the grey oblong of sky. And later, wandering barefoot around the house, zonked out on whatever pills the doctor had given her, seeing nothing and saying nothing and all curled in on herself like a wounded animal.

'She'll be all right,' Annie Foster had said. 'She'll get through this eventually.'

But Annie had been wrong. Having to deal with another baby had been too much for her: she had struggled, weakened and eventually given up. An accidental overdose was what their father said, but Marian couldn't see anything accidental about swilling down all those pills with half a bottle of vodka. Carmen had stolen her mother from her, and for that Marian would never forgive her. That such a judgement might be harsh did not enter her mind; in fact, the more she dwelled on it the more convinced she became that Carmen had, quite literally, got away with murder.

In later years, just to add insult to injury, their father had made it perfectly clear as to which child he favoured. It was Carmen this and Carmen that, and why couldn't she and Hazel be more like bloody Carmen. Always well behaved, always neat and tidy, never answering back. Even her school reports had been exceptional. Little Miss Perfect ... until now.

Marian could not deny that she was pleased by what had happened last night. The money had been the main event, but Carmen's failure to live up to expectations had been the icing on the cake. What a laugh to see her the subject of their father's wrath for once. And then her showing up this morning, all wide-eyed and fearful like a rabbit caught in headlights. The temptation to make more waves had proved impossible to resist. Well, what could she say? The girl was a credulous moron.

By the time she reached the office – the ground floor of a three-storey conversion on Ebury Street – Marian was in a thoroughly good mood. She rang the bell and got buzzed in by her father's secretary. Elizabeth Holmes, a smartly dressed fifty-something woman, had been around for decades: she was brisk and efficient and had once, when she was much younger, taken down more than dictation.

Marian's good humour faded at the thought of the two of them sneaking around behind her mother's back, probably even screwing right here in the office. The old bag disgusted her. He'd probably bought her the flat she lived in too; she could hardly afford it on the wages of a secretary. What had Elizabeth hoped for? To slip into the shoes of her mother, probably, to become wife number two. Marian felt a ripple of satisfaction. At least her father hadn't been stupid enough to go that far.

'Good morning, Mrs Loughton. Mr Foster is in his office.' Elizabeth gave Marian a nod. 'You can go straight through.'

'I need to see my father after. Will you tell him?'

Elizabeth hesitated, glancing down at the diary open on her desk. 'He's quite busy this morning.'

'I'm sure he can spare five minutes for his daughter.'

The secretary's lips pursed. The days of being his mistress were gone, but Elizabeth remained steadfastly loyal. She guarded reception like a hungry rottweiler, keeping out the uninvited and the undesirables. God forbid that anyone would give her beloved boss grief.

'I'll let him know.'

'That's very kind of you,' Marian said, making a mental note to get rid of Elizabeth at the first opportunity. Once her father had stepped down, she would employ another secretary, someone who showed her some respect, and someone whose loyalty would lie with her rather than the man she used to shag.

Pat Foster had the smaller of the two internal offices. He seemed less buoyant than usual, a result perhaps of having to endure her father's bad temper for most of the morning. Neither of them mentioned the previous night. For the next hour, Marian was subjected to a lengthy explanation of how the inheritance would work.

'The company has been split into three, each one with a new name,' Pat said. 'I'm in the process of opening bank accounts so I'll need your signature on the paperwork. Once the transition period is over, the three of you will have responsibility for your own businesses.'

'Transition period?' Marian echoed, alarm bells going off in her head. Hazel had been muttering something about terms and conditions on the phone last night, but she never took much notice of what her sister said.

'About a year, probably, just to make sure everything is running smoothly. I'll be staying on and so will Elizabeth, and I dare say your father will drop in from time to time. During this period, we'll be overseeing the changeover and you'll need a second signature, mine or his, on any cheques you write.'

Marian should have guessed that her father wasn't just going to hand everything over. No, he'd be standing over her for the next twelve months, watching her, making sure everything was done the way *he* liked it done. There wasn't going to be any windfall, at least not in the immediate future. 'What if I want to do something? Sell some of the rented properties, for instance?'

Pat frowned. 'Why would you want to do that? They bring in a good income, regular money every month. And they'll only appreciate in value. They're an excellent addition to any investment portfolio. No, I wouldn't advise it.'

Marian didn't much care what he advised, but she was careful to keep her tone respectful. 'I hear what you're saying, and perhaps you're right. I just mean, they're a lot of hassle, aren't they? Half the time the tenants don't pay, and the other half they're moaning about repairs that need doing.'

'You might want to employ a general manager at some point, someone to oversee the day-to-day running of the company. They can deal with all that. You've obviously got other responsibilities, a family, and you can't be in London seven days a week.'

'Yes, I'll think about that. I do intend to spend more time here, though.'

'Will Hugh be all right with that?'

Marian couldn't see what business it was of his what Hugh's opinion was, but she kept her thoughts to herself. 'He'll understand. It's important, isn't it? I don't want to leave it all to someone else.'

Pat went on to explain about the various assets, how they

fitted together, how they'd been chosen and how they would work together as a whole. Marian could have told him that she'd grown up with her father banging on about the business, that she knew all the ins and outs and didn't need them explaining to her, but she pretended to be interested while she switched off and started thinking about Milo instead. He looked like his father – same eyes and mouth, same solid build – but he hadn't got his brains. Still, it wasn't his brains she wanted him for.

It was the secrecy she liked, the sneaking around, the fast, frantic sex whenever they got the opportunity. Milo was rough around the edges, unpredictable, dangerous. He knew how to turn her on and they had a good time together, no strings attached. She would have a look through the properties later and see if there was an apartment she could use, somewhere in town, somewhere they could meet in private. Neither Pat nor her father could possibly object to her having a base in London.

Marian knew that she had married too young, and for all the wrong reasons. In a bid to escape the control of her father, she had walked blindly into another kind of prison. At the time Hugh had seemed glamorous, a minor member of the aristocracy, a man with the kind of social standing that would open doors for her and provide a superior lifestyle. What she had ended up with was a glorified farmer who bored her rigid.

The family pile, impressive at first sight, had turned out to be a wreck. She had hoped for dinner parties and balls and witty conversation but had found herself stuck instead in a village where all people talked about was pigs and sheep and whether the barley would thrive that year. Well, she'd had enough. She had done her duty, given Hugh an heir and a spare, and now it was time to enjoy herself.

At the end of the meeting, Marian politely thanked Pat, said she looked forward to working with him and left the office glad to have the obligatory talk over and done with. Her good mood had slipped into disappointment and resentment. She felt like a child who had been promised an expensive present, only to be told that she couldn't have it for another year. Her eyes flashed. She pushed back her shoulders and strode towards reception. Now for her father.

11

Marian, smugly informed by Elizabeth that her father was on the phone and that she would have to wait, sat down in one of the stylish leather chairs and drummed her fingertips on the arms. No offer of coffee was forthcoming. She watched Elizabeth shuffle papers, open and close drawers, and then begin clacking away on the typewriter. The noise got on her nerves. Five minutes passed, and then ten, before a buzzer finally sounded.

'He can see you now,' Elizabeth said, like a queen bestowing a gift on one of her minions.

Marian gave her a brusque nod, assumed her loving daughter face, and walked through into the short corridor that led to her father's office. She knocked lightly on the door and went in.

'Hello, Dad,' she said, pulling out a chair opposite him. 'How are you today?'

Rex, immaculately dressed in a grey silk suit, sat back, folded his arms, and threw her a scrutinising look. 'I presume you've seen Pat?'

'Yes, just now.'

'And you've come to try and persuade me to change my mind about something. What aren't you happy about?'

Marian knew better than to question his judgement, or his decisions. 'No, no, not at all. Why would I? I'm perfectly happy. And Pat was very informative, very helpful. No problems at all. I just wanted to say thank you again. And to check that you're all right. I know last night didn't turn out quite the way you expected.'

Rex's face twisted, his mouth turning down at the corners. 'I presume she'll show up with an apology at some point today.'

Marian made a point of shifting awkwardly in her chair, of looking away, of acting as if there was something she would rather not tell him.

'What is it?' Rex said. 'Come on, spit it out.'

'No, I don't want to upset you. I mean ... only, well, I suppose you'll hear it from Mrs Cooper anyway.'

'Hear what? For God's sake, Marian, what's going on?'

'Nothing. It's just ... Carmen was at the house earlier. She picked up some of her things, clothes and stuff. She won't be coming to see you. She doesn't seem to think she's done anything wrong. I tried to talk to her but ... You know what she's like. Once she's made her mind up, nothing's going to change it. She's as stubborn as a mule, that one.'

Rex's cheeks coloured. He unfolded his arms, leaned forward, and placed his hands on the desk, his fingers curling in two tight fists. 'Where has she gone?'

Marian shrugged. 'Clive's, probably. That's where she stayed last night.'

A low growl came from the back of Rex's throat. 'What's wrong with the Gryphon?'

When Marian had been winding up Carmen earlier, she

hadn't intended to take it any further. It had just been a spur-of-the-moment thing, a chance to score some easy points. But after hearing what Pat Foster had to say, having learned that her fortune was dependent on twelve months' probation, her frustration was getting the better of her and she wanted to lash out. 'Exactly. I said why not come back with me, we could share a cab, but she wasn't having any of it.'

'What else did she say?'

'Oh, nothing much. Just that she didn't want to see you right now. Honestly, from the way she was acting, you'd think *you* were the one who'd done something wrong. I'm surprised Clive didn't try and talk some sense into her; he must be as pig-headed as she is.'

'If he had any respect for me, he would have.'

'Yes,' Marian said. It had occurred to her while she was waiting in reception that Clive Grainger was going to receive one third of her father's money. As soon as he married Carmen – and that was only six months away – her inheritance would be his. And she was in no doubt at all that Carmen would let him do what he liked with it. The man had her wrapped around his little finger. 'If it wasn't for you, he wouldn't even have a job.'

Rex gave her a long hard stare.

Afraid that he might have seen right through her, might have seen the metaphorical knife that she was busily plunging into Clive's spine, Marian quickly added: 'Still, I suppose he's only heard her side of the story. I don't want to judge. He might just think he's being loyal.'

But she needn't have worried. Rex was too preoccupied by what he perceived as the unforgiveable conduct of his youngest daughter to guess her motives. 'Carmen needs to understand that she can't have everything her own way,' he said. 'She needs teaching a lesson. One she won't forget.'

12

Jonny was walking round the inside of the Royal with Hazel. The club looked even shabbier in daylight than at night, with its chipped paintwork and worn furnishings. There were fag burns on the tables and stains on the carpet. The decor was old-fashioned – it had probably been the same since the fifties – and desperately needed an update. The main room, although large, was stuffy and smelled of stale fag smoke.

'Some inheritance,' he muttered.

'It's not that bad. Nothing that a lick of paint and some new furniture won't put right. It just needs a bit of imagination.'

'If you say so.'

Jonny had been in a foul mood all morning, ever since he'd found out about the provisions in the inheritance. Hazel was trying to put a positive spin on it, to explain that it wasn't that disastrous, that there'd still be some money coming in, that twelve months wasn't that long to wait, but he wasn't in the mood for looking on the bright side.

'There's nothing to stop us making changes. Dad's not

going to object if he can see it will bring in money in the end. Speculate to accumulate and all that.'

'No one with money is going to want to come here.'

'Well, not as it is, obviously, but we can tart the place up, give it a more glamorous feel.'

'It'll cost a bloody fortune to bring this dump up to scratch. Is he going to give us a fortune? No, I don't think so.'

'Jesus,' Hazel said, 'stop being so damned negative.'

Roy Dempsey, the current manager, strolled over to join them. He was an overweight man in his late fifties, with a florid face and what appeared to be a wasteful amount of breakfast down the front of his jacket. He'd been around for a long time and knew how to run a club with the minimum of effort – and clearly, judging by the club's takings, he'd been putting the minimum of effort into it.

Handshakes were exchanged. Pat Foster had rung ahead to apprise Dempsey of the situation and ask him to give them a tour.

'Your old man's retiring then,' Dempsey said.

'Not straight away,' Hazel said. 'He'll be staying on for a while.'

Dempsey nodded, gazed around, and turned his head to look at her again. 'You planning on making some changes?'

'It could do with a facelift,' Hazel said.

'Mr Darby always says it ain't worth spending nothin' on it, not with what it brings in. Good money after bad is how he always put it.'

'You see?' Jonny said to Hazel.

Hazel ignored him. 'There's a basement here, isn't there? Could we take a look?'

Jonny perked up when they went downstairs. The basement was a decent space, and although at present it was being used as a storeroom and general dumping ground, it had potential. He poked around in the corners, tapped the concrete pillars with his fist and paced out the floor size. With some redecoration, a carpet and comfortable furniture, it could be turned into a reasonable gambling den.

'What do you reckon?' she said.

Jonny shrugged, not willing to share his plans. 'I still reckon it's a dump.'

Dempsey chuckled, unoffended. 'It ain't never been mistaken for Annabel's, that's for sure.'

Jonny thought that if Dempsey was worried about his job, he certainly wasn't showing it. Or perhaps he had the same cavalier attitude towards his employment as he had towards eating his breakfast. He would have to go. They needed a manager like Clive Grainger for the club, someone with a bit of panache, someone who looked the part. But all in good time. For now, until they made some decisions, Dempsey would do to keep things ticking over.

When they were back out on Beak Street, Hazel looked at him. 'You could run that place better than him. We could make it as good as Lola's.'

He didn't reply for a while but then he said, 'What's your father playing at? First, he's retiring, then he's not. It's a bloody joke.'

Hazel repeated what she'd been saying all morning. 'We only have to keep him sweet for a year.'

'You think? And what happens if he still isn't satisfied? Another year, another two? He could keep us dangling for a bloody decade.'

'It won't come to that.'

Jonny gave an irritated shake of his head. 'And how do you know?' She didn't, of course. It would be just like Rex to try and keep control, to pass on the business purely on his own terms, taking the credit for his own largesse while holding on tight to the purse strings. Jesus, he hated that man. Promise the world and then snatch it away. That was how he played the game. Frustration rose inside him. What was the point of being rich on paper if you couldn't spend it? 'Talk to Marian. See what she thinks.'

'Where are you going?'

'I need a drink,' Jonny said.

13

Milo Grant was propping up the bar at the Black Lion, indulging in that most effective of cures for a hangover – the hair of
the dog. He had drunk too much last night and now his head
felt like it was held in a vice. He knocked back a double whisky,
put the glass on the counter and gestured to the barman to pour
him another. While he waited for the top-up, he ran his gaze
over the other customers.

The Black Lion was a villains' pub, frequented by armed rob-
bers, thieves, pimps and pickpockets. Milo, who wasn't averse
to a spot of criminality when it suited him, scoured the faces,
searching for anyone who might have a job going. He was open
to most things, from violent intimidation to receiving stolen
goods. He could easily dispose of fags or booze to the tenants
he collected rent from. It was a nice little set-up where everyone
benefited, and although the profits weren't huge, it put some
extra cash in his pocket.

Thinking of tenants reminded him of his own precarious
position as regards accommodation. His bitch of a mother

wasn't going to change her mind about flogging his home from under him, so he'd have to find somewhere else to live. One of Rex Darby's properties might become available, but they were either dreary dumps, barely fit for human habitation, or completely out of his price range.

Despite the foul taste in his mouth, Milo lit a cigarette. Unfortunately, none of his regular contacts were around today. He recognised a few faces, but nobody who was likely to put any business his way. While he brooded on his mother's selfishness, he kept an eye on the door to the pub, hoping that someone useful would come in.

It was getting on for one when Jonny Cornish entered the Black Lion and walked over to the bar. He ordered a pint, nodded at Milo, and said, 'All right?'

Milo wasn't surprised to see him. Jonny often hung out here, as well as in some of the other dodgier pubs in Soho. He was a tall, good-looking geezer, a ladies' man, a gambler, pleasant enough but moody with it. Today his expression – his mouth turned down at the corners, his eyes cold and dark – suggested that all wasn't well in the world.

'Good do last night, was it?' said Milo, who was still nursing his resentment at being excluded from the party.

Jonny paid for his pint and took a long swig before replying. 'Fuckin' surprising,' he eventually said.

'Yeah? What happened?' Milo gave a thin laugh. 'The champagne run out?'

'Rex announced his retirement.'

This brought Milo up short. 'What?'

Jonny drank some more of his beer. 'He's stepping down and splitting the business between the three girls.'

'Christ, how come I haven't heard about it?'

'You just have,' Jonny said.

'Why didn't my old man say nothin'?' Milo didn't like surprises, especially the sort that could threaten his livelihood. 'Have I still got a job? Shit, this is all I need.'

'Sworn to secrecy, I should imagine. Your old man, I mean. And I wouldn't worry about your job: the work's still going to be there, isn't it? I can't see anything changing in a hurry, and they may as well use you as anyone else.'

Milo thought of all the hours he'd spent trying to ingratiate himself with Rex Darby, and silently cursed. What a waste of time! Still, there was always Marian. If she now owned one third of the business, she'd be rolling in it. And come to that, so would Jonny's missus. 'Why are you looking so naffed off?' he said. 'I'd have thought you'd be celebrating.'

'Turns out there are strings, mate, the main one being that Rex isn't going anywhere for at least a year. We can't do a damn thing without his say so.'

Milo could tell that Jonny had been drinking, that he'd been in a few other pubs before this one. The booze had loosened his tongue. Or maybe he just thought that Pat would eventually tell him all this anyway. 'Ah, keeping tight hold of the cash, is he?' Never one to pass over the opportunity of revelling in someone else's disappointment, he suppressed a smirk. 'Can't say I'm shocked. Rex Darby don't trust no one with his hard-earned dosh, not even his nearest and dearest.'

'Tell me about it,' Jonny said bitterly.

Milo knew that Jonny must have been anticipating good times: big stakes at the poker table, fancy holidays abroad, Savile Row suits and Rolex watches. Of course, in time, he would have all this, but Jonny wasn't the patient sort. 'Bit of a spanner in the works then.'

'He's a bloody wind-up merchant. He knows exactly what he's doing.'

'You'll just have to hope for the best.'

'And what would the best be?'

'Rex is getting on. He can't live for ever. Maybe he'll get sick, have a nasty accident or something.'

Jonny stared at him over the rim of his pint glass. 'And what are the odds of that happening?'

'Who knows? Whatever you want them to be, I suppose.'

A smile slowly crept on to Jonny's lips.

14

Carmen had booked into the Gryphon for a couple of nights, taking a room overlooking Bloomsbury Square. She had called Clive on her arrival but got no reply from his home phone. Since then, she'd been trying every half hour. She had phoned Lola's too but, like she'd suspected, it was too early for anyone to be there.

After unpacking she'd ordered coffee from room service and sat by the window with the cup and saucer balanced on her lap. Where was Clive? Had he gone back to bed and switched the phone off? Gone to see some friends? Gone to see ... no, she wasn't going to start stressing over that Tara woman again. Maybe he'd just gone for a drive. She considered going round to the flat again but dismissed the idea. Something about last night still sat uneasily with her, a sense of having disappointed him, of having been disappointed.

At two o'clock she went for a short walk around the square and sat down on a bench. The thin sunshine barely warmed her. Other people strolled across the grass, hardly noticed, drifting by like ghosts. She sighed. All this business with her father made her feel ill. She wanted it finished, over and done with, apologies made and accepted. But she was too nervous to approach him when he was this furious.

When half an hour had passed, she returned to the hotel and asked the receptionist if Mrs Loughton was back yet.

'Oh, I think . . . Hold on a moment,' the girl said, pulling the signing-in book on the counter towards her. 'Yes, Mr and Mrs Loughton checked out a couple of hours ago.'

'They've gone?' Carmen had been hoping to talk to Marian again, to see if there was any more news about her father. 'Did she leave a message?'

The girl checked the cubby holes behind her. 'No, sorry, no messages.'

Carmen was disappointed, but unsurprised. Marian had made it clear that she didn't want to get 'involved'. All the same, she could have let her know she was leaving. It didn't take much to pick up a phone. 'Thank you,' she said to the receptionist, and headed back to her room. Now she was stuck on her own with no one to even have dinner with.

It had always been the same with her older sisters, she thought, as she climbed the stairs to the first floor: neither of them had ever shown the slightest bit of interest in her, unless it was to tease or torment. Being so much younger, Carmen had never felt a part of their lives. And by the time she was a teenager, they were both married and living away from home.

And soon she'd be married too. Only six months to go and she'd be Mrs Grainger. This cheered her up. She'd be starting a new life, creating a new family, and she couldn't wait. Clive was her soulmate, the only man who made her pulse race, who made her feel loved and desirable. Well, not so desirable last night, but that had only been down to the circumstances.

71

Carmen went into her room, closed the door and walked over to the window. She stood, unsure as to what to do next. The rest of the afternoon stretched ahead of her, long and dreary. Should she call Clive again, try and catch him before he went to work? She could go to Lola's as soon as it opened but she knew he'd be busy tonight; on Saturdays the place was always heaving. No, she would convey the news by phone.

Carmen was just about to reach for the receiver when the phone suddenly started ringing. She jumped, her hand briefly rising to her chest, before snatching it up. 'Hello?'

'There's a Mr Grainger here to see you,' the receptionist said.

'Tell him I'll be right down.'

Carmen quickly ran a comb through her hair, checked her reflection in the mirror, and rushed downstairs. He was stand-ing in the lobby, and she would have flung her arms around his neck, but something in his stance, in the expression on his face, held her back. Instead, glad that he had tracked her down, she smiled broadly and said, 'How did you know where I was?'

'An educated guess. I called you at home and your father said you weren't living there any more.'

Carmen's smile faded away. She frowned, confused. 'What? No, I just . . . Why would he say that?'

'Rex told me you'd packed a suitcase and gone. He thought you were with me, but I put him straight on that.' Clive glanced across at the receptionist – it was quiet in the lobby – and then took Carmen's arm and led her towards the lounge area. 'Come on, let's go somewhere we can talk in private.'

The lounge was empty apart from a middle-aged couple taking afternoon tea. Clive chose a pair of armchairs on the other side of the room. No sooner had they sat down than a waiter approached them.

'No,' Clive said brusquely, waving the man away. He turned

his attention back to Carmen. 'What's going on? Did you have another row?'

'I didn't even see him. Marian was there. She said he was in a rage, that he didn't want to talk to me, so I thought I'd keep out of his way for a while.'

Clive leaned forward, his face tight and serious. 'He's expecting an apology, and instead you're holed up here. How is that going to solve anything?'

Carmen had never told him about her father's temper, at least not the extent of it. But she thought he must have some idea. He'd worked for him long enough. And you didn't rise from the gutters of the East End by spreading sweetness and light wherever you went. There was a hard, cruel side to her father, and even his own daughters weren't exempt from it. 'Sometimes it's better to avoid him. Believe me, you can't have a rational conversation when he's in this frame of mind.'

'He's in this frame of mind because you *haven't* been to see him.'

Carmen shook her head. 'I don't understand why he's saying I've moved out. I only took a few things, just enough to see me through the weekend.'

'So there's been a misunderstanding. This is getting out of hand. Look, I've got the car. We can go there now, get it over and done with.'

'Did he sound like he'd been drinking?'

'He sounded angry.'

Carmen shrank back into the chair. 'I don't want to see him when he's angry.'

'The longer this goes on, the worse it's going to get.'

'I thought you were on my side.'

Clive heaved out a sigh, his voice exasperated. 'Don't be childish, Carmen.'

Carmen stared at him. 'There's nothing childish about it.' She must have said it louder than she'd intended because the middle-aged couple stopped eating their scones and gazed across the room at her. She lowered her voice. 'He was unreasonable last night, and he's being unreasonable now. I won't go and see him when he's like this.'

'You're as stubborn as he is. Do you want me to lose my job?'

'It won't come to that. His argument's with me, not you.'

'We're engaged. As far as your father's concerned, I'm as guilty as you in all this. Aiding and abetting and all that. I had to tell him I slept on the sofa last night, not that he believed me. He thinks because I let you stay at the flat that I'm supporting what you're doing.'

'He's not going to fire you; you're the best manager he's got.'

'Are you really willing to take that risk?'

'Are you really willing to let him manipulate you?'

Clive gave another of his sighs. 'So he likes to have things his own way. We both know that.'

'He's a bully.'

'For God's sake, Carmen. Why are you doing this? It's your future at stake, *our* future. Can't you just swallow your stupid pride and apologise?'

'I didn't say I wouldn't apologise. I'm just not going to do it when he's in one of his rages.'

'You need to grow up, stop sulking and get a grip.'

Carmen had never heard Clive speak like this before – well, perhaps a hint last night – and she didn't appreciate it. She had always respected him, looked up to him as someone older and wiser, but she didn't like what she was hearing. There was a hardness in his voice, a scathing anger. She'd had enough of that from her father. 'When I'm ready,' she said, determined not to be browbeaten.

'Yeah, well, when you're ready could be too late.'

'Why are you being so horrible?'

'Jesus, I'm just being realistic, trying to get you to see sense. What's the matter with you? It's like you *want* to throw it all away: us, your future, everything.'

'This isn't about us,' she said. 'Nothing's changed between us.'

Clive rose to his feet. 'I've had enough of this. Are you coming or not?'

'I've already told you I don't want to see him when he's in this mood.'

'You won't be on your own. I'll be with you.'

But how did she explain that she feared what would happen after he'd gone, when there wasn't a witness? It was something she couldn't talk to him about. And anyway, she wasn't going to crawl to her father in front of Clive. It would be too humiliating. When she did it, when she finally plucked up the courage, it would be on her own terms.

Carmen shook her head. 'Not today.'

Clive scowled down at her. 'You're being foolish.'

As she looked up, as she met his gaze, she felt like she was seeing a stranger. Where was the supportive partner she'd always believed him to be, the loving fiancé, the man who would stand by her whether she was right or wrong? She gave a shrug. 'If you say so.'

'Don't blame me when you find yourself cut off without a penny.'

'Why would I blame you?'

'Call me if you change your mind.' And with that he strode out of the lounge without a backward glance.

Carmen's jaw dropped for a moment, before she hurriedly closed her mouth. She fought against the urge to stand up and run after him. It was what he expected. They had never fallen out before, at least not like this. She suspected that, with the right persuasion, some gentle cajoling, she might have given in, but he had made the mistake of presuming she'd do exactly what he wanted. He had pushed all the wrong buttons and made her even more determined.

Carmen gripped the arms of the chair, feeling that everything was spiralling out of control. It would pass, she told herself. She would make up with Clive, make up with her father. Nothing was irrevocable. So why did she feel so strange, so adrift, as if the ropes that had been mooring her had suddenly been severed?

15

Jonny was drunk, but not so drunk that he could forget all his problems. When you owed Joe Quinn over a grand, no amount of booze could chase away the knowledge that unless you came up with the cash you were going to get a beating – or worse. Quinn was a vicious bastard who enjoyed inflicting pain on others. The gangster ran most of the East End these days, ruled it with an iron fist, and no mercy was shown to anyone who didn't pay their debts.

Jonny's love of poker, of any kind of gambling, had got him into trouble on more than one occasion. He didn't usually stray out of his West End territory, but when he'd heard about the game in Kellston – high stakes, big rewards – he'd been unable to resist. A massive mistake. Now he was having to constantly look over his shoulder in case one of Quinn's henchmen had come to collect.

Last night, when Rex Darby had announced his retirement, he'd thought he'd finally caught a break. Pennies from heaven. But that hope had soon been extinguished. Of course Rex wasn't going to let his daughters play fast and loose with his hard-earned cash; he would keep tight hold of the business for as long as he could. A snarl curled his lip. Christ, he loathed that man.

Milo, he thought, had a point. Who would grieve for Rex Darby if he was to meet with an unfortunate accident? Certainly not his immediate family. Well, Carmen perhaps, but after last night's ordeal even her affections must be at breaking point. Not that he cared one way or the other about Carmen's feelings. He had more important things on his mind.

There were various means by which a man could 'accidentally' meet his end: a hit-and-run, a violent mugging, drowning, a burglary gone wrong. Once Rex had been disposed of, there would be nothing to stop Hazel getting her hands on the money. Pat Foster wasn't going to stand in her way when his boss was six feet under. How could he? She could sell whatever she wanted. All that would take a few months but, in the meantime, there would be plenty of undeclared cash to share out. Men like Rex always had a hefty stash in the safe, a fallback in case of emergencies.

Jonny played out this fantasy in his head as he walked unsteadily down Brewer Street. He was too distracted to take much notice of what was going on around him. The faces in the Soho crowd were a blurred mass, a merging of anonymous features. It was Saturday night and all the joy-seekers, the hustlers, the tarts and the pimps were out in force. A good time could be had – if you had the money to pay for it.

He stopped at the opening to an alley and took a packet of fags out of his pocket. As he struck a match and put the flame to the cigarette, he sensed rather than heard the movement behind him. Too late he remembered about always looking over his shoulder. An arm snaked around his neck, and he was shoved forward into the shadows. The blows came fast and hard. He was too slow, too drunk, to even try and protect himself.

Quickly his legs gave way and he crumpled to the ground. A few final kicks and it was over almost as soon as it had begun. As he lay among the rubbish, the dirt and the vomit, he could taste blood in his mouth.

Milo was considering his future. Following his conversation with Jonny, he decided, in the early evening, to head over to Belgravia and ambush his father in the Plumbers Arms. Even on a Saturday the two old cronies, his father and his boss, were usually to be found in the pub after a hard day's work exploiting the poor and filling up the coffers. But Rex, on this occasion, was absent. Only Pat Foster was there, brooding over the last inch of a pint of best while he gazed surreptitiously at the curvy barmaid.

Milo bought him a fresh drink and settled down to interrogate him. 'I bumped into Jonny earlier and heard about Rex's retirement. Bit of a bolt from the blue, that. So do I still have a job or what?'

'Course you have a job. Nothing's changed. Everything carries on as normal for the next twelve months.'

'And then?'

Pat gave a shrug. 'The girls are still going to need people to work for them. I'll put in a word. I'm sure you'll be fine.'

Milo didn't fancy working for a woman, and especially not Marian. It upset the balance of things, collecting a salary from the woman you were shagging, but neither of the other two were going to keep him on. By the time Jonny had finished there wouldn't be a business to run, and Carmen couldn't stand his guts. He drank his Guinness and considered his options. Could Marian be persuaded to leave Hugh? It was worth thinking about. Screwing a wealthy woman was all very well, but marrying her was an entirely more profitable option.

'And what about you?' Milo said. 'What are you going to do?'

'Stay on for as long as they need me. Annie says I should retire too, but I'm not sure if I'm ready for that yet.'

Just the mention of Pat's wife caused Milo's guts to twist. It reminded him of that other family his father had, the one that was more important to him, the one that always came first. He was careful not to betray his feelings, though. Instead, he nodded and shrugged and said, 'Well, perhaps you should. It won't be the same without Rex around.'

'I'll see how it goes. I'm not one for sitting back and doing nothing.'

Milo reckoned he'd been born to the wrong woman. If Annie Foster had been his mum his whole life would have been different: there would have been food on the table, holidays, respect and standing and, most importantly of all, Rex Darby as his godfather. He would have grown up with opportunities, the chance to be someone. Instead, it was his half-brother who'd got all these things, and he didn't even appreciate them.

'How's Eddie doing these days?' Milo said, smiling as if he cared. 'Still at the bookshop, is he?'

Pat gave an exasperated shake of his head. 'Yeah, still there. I don't know what's wrong with him. Why would you throw up a damn good job in the City to go and work in a place like that? It doesn't make any sense.'

Milo had only met Eddie half a dozen times, but that had been enough for him to form an opinion. The bloke was cold and stand-offish. It had been clear from the start that Eddie didn't want anything to do with him. It was like Milo was someone he'd prefer to forget about, someone who caused him embarrassment. Not so much a half-brother as a dirty secret that he preferred to keep swept under the carpet. Any time they bumped into each other, Eddie couldn't wait to get away.

It pleased Milo that Pat didn't have a great relationship with his other son. And what pleased him even more was that he was part of the cause of the rift between them. Sides had been taken after the affair had come to light and Eddie had taken his mother's. That was the thing about secrets; when they came out, there was always hell to pay.

'What else did Jonny say?'

From the way Pat posed the question, Milo instantly knew that something else had happened last night. He could have asked straight out, but Pat tended to keep schtum when it came to Rex's private affairs. 'He'd had a few bevvies,' he said, as if to imply that Jonny had been less than discreet. 'You know what he's like when he's been on the bottle.'

'It'll blow over. These things always do.'

'Do you think? Jonny didn't seem so sure.'

'What does Jonny know? He hasn't got a clue. He hasn't got kids of his own.'

'Yeah, that's true. Still . . .'

Milo waited, let the silence settle between them, until eventually Pat told him all about the events of the evening. If anyone had been going to ruffle Rex's feathers, Milo would have put his money on Marian, with Hazel running a close second. But it was Carmen, apparently, who'd refused to play ball in the game of Happy Families. 'Why would she even do that?' he asked, bemused. If he'd been offered a bloody fortune, he'd have said anything, done anything, to get his hands on it.

'It wasn't all the girl's fault.'

'Just the same, you'd think she'd know better. Well, let's hope it all works out.' He said this, but what he was thinking was something quite different. Advantage could always be taken in times of trouble – and there was never more trouble than when a family was at war.

*

Marian glanced at the clock on the mantelpiece – it was after eight – and felt simultaneous waves of relief and satisfaction flow over her. She tucked the phone under her chin while she lit a cigarette. 'If she's not there by now, I shouldn't think she's going.'

'Not this late,' Hazel said. 'Not if she's got any sense.'

Marian knew what she meant. Their father's black tempers increased in proportion to the amount he drank, and at this time on a Saturday night Carmen would guess that he'd be in the mood from hell. When she'd found out that Clive was under orders to deliver Carmen to the house, she'd been sure that her sister would be summarily delivered. Clive was nothing if not efficient. That they hadn't shown up was a blessing – for her at least. Although she could talk her way out of most things, she'd still been worried that Carmen would land her in it and blab to their father about the advice she'd passed on this morning. 'What's going on, do you think?'

'God knows. It's not like Carmen to do something like this. She's usually so ... docile.'

'How did Dad sound when you called?'

'Furious.'

Marian smiled into the receiver. 'Maybe she'll go and see him tomorrow.' She paused and then added, 'What does Jonny think about it all?'

'About Carmen?'

'No, the other stuff: about the inheritance, the business and everything.'

'He's got the hump, of course. He thought we'd be able to do what we liked – spend, spend, spend – and now he's realised that it all comes with strings. Jonny doesn't care for strings.'

Marian rolled her eyes. 'Is he there?'

'No, he's out drowning his sorrows someplace. Probably getting plastered. We went to see the Royal today, but he just

82

kept saying that it was a dump. I reckon we could do something with it, if we had the cash, but we don't so … We'll just have to wait, I suppose.'

'You might not.'

'What do you mean?'

'There are ways round everything. I'm sure if we put our heads together, we can come up with a plan.'

Hazel didn't sound convinced. 'But Dad's going to be keeping a close eye on everything. I don't reckon he'll let Pat Foster countersign a single cheque without asking permission from him first.'

'Don't be so defeatist.' Marian wasn't going to let a few terms and conditions get in the way of her ambitions. 'Since when did Dad ever stop us doing exactly what we wanted?'

16

Terry Street was doing as he was told – for now. If Joe Quinn said jump, he'd ask how high. If Joe Quinn told him to kiss his arse, he'd get down on his knees. If Joe required him to find Jonny Cornish and give him a beating, he'd do exactly that. Nothing bothered him because he knew it was only a matter of time before he'd never have to dance to Quinn's tune again.

Terry was young, strong, smart, and he was going places. As he strode through Soho, he rubbed his knuckles, only lightly bruised from the recent encounter. Cornish hadn't put up much of a fight. Well, if the truth be told, no fight at all. The bloke had been too pissed to even try and defend himself. Terry had delivered the message with his fists and left his victim lying in the alley. He didn't feel bad about it. It was the way things were, the price you paid when you crossed the likes of Quinn. Everyone knew the risk and there was no point whining about it.

There was bad blood between the Quinns and the Darbys. That much Terry knew, but he didn't know all the ins and outs. Some ancient history, something to do with Darby's wife, he'd heard, although you couldn't always believe what people told you. The East End was rife with rumour and gossip, and half of it wasn't worth repeating. Anyway, with Cornish being Rex Darby's son-in-law, Joe Quinn had taken extra pleasure in ordering the beating.

Terry took in the sights while he drifted through Soho. He was feeling good, feeling chilled. He had big plans for the future. The East End was all well and good, but it was here up West where the real money lay. Quinn was too stupid and too lazy to grab the opportunities that were lying here: he had no vision, no ambition. The Soho streets were paved with gold, with gamblers, with addicts, with punters wanting girls. The very air smelled of possibilities. Terry breathed it in, filling his lungs.

He had been involved with the Quinn firm for a few years now, using his guile to gradually worm his way into the inner circle. Quinn, who preferred to be a big fish in a little pond, worked out of Kellston, running the manor with all the tact and diplomacy of a ruthless dictator. Terry never openly questioned him. No, he was playing the long game, pretending to be respectful, pretending to admire his boss. It wasn't hard to win a man's trust if you really put your mind to it.

It was this trust Terry was relying on, along with Quinn's inflated sense of self-importance. Such was the ageing gangster's ego he could never imagine one of his subordinates betraying him. Terry smiled. His walk had a jaunty swagger to it. He was already imagining what it would be like to be in control, to give orders rather than take them. What he was going to do was both dangerous and daring, but he had the nerve to go through with it. He knew that killing a man was different from giving him a beating, that it came with a different set of consequences, and he was prepared to take the risk. Quinn was past his sell-by date, a relic of the past. He needed taking out before it was too late.

Terry felt no guilt over his plan to eliminate Quinn. The world would be a better place without him. The old gangster was living off past glories and using brute force to keep himself in power. He was vicious and greedy and stupid. Everyone was sick of him, and eventually someone would act. That someone might as well be him.

He had spent months going over the plan in his head, making sure there were no loose ends, nothing that could bring the law to his door. The beauty of the murder would be that he'd get shot of Connor too, Quinn's older son who had the same nasty streak as his father. Two for the price of one. And then the firm would be up for grabs, its leadership open to the man who had the guts to step forward and take Quinn's place.

Not everyone would accept him. There would be members of the firm who wouldn't follow someone so young, who'd sneer at his aspirations, or try and stab him in the back. But he didn't care about those losers. Over the past few years, he'd used his charm to form alliances with the men who mattered, the ones who would stand by him. The rest could go to hell.

Terry strolled past the sex shops, the peep shows, the strip joints and the bars. Yes, there was money here, opportunities for those who had the nerve to grab them. And he had the nerve, the guts and the will. One day his name would be on everybody's lips. He was about to rise from obscurity and take his place in London's underworld.

17

It was the early hours of Sunday morning and Jonny was sitting at the kitchen table with a wad of cotton wool pressed against his nose. Hazel was giving him the third degree, asking the same questions in a different way over and over again as if she didn't entirely believe his story and was torn between suspicion and sympathy. A mugging, he'd claimed, a couple of blokes who'd dragged him into an alley, given him a beating and stolen his wallet. She wasn't disputing the beating – that was clear to see – but she had her doubts over the motive.

'Why pick on you?' she said. 'You're hardly the smallest bloke in the world.'

'Because I'd had a few. They probably followed me out of the pub.' Before coming home, Jonny had taken the precaution of emptying his wallet and dumping it in a bin, caching the few notes he had left down the side of his sock. He hadn't wanted to take the risk of Hazel finding it and catching him out in a lie. The less she knew about his debt to Quinn, the better.

'I still don't get why you didn't report it. You should have gone to the police.'

'What for? I couldn't give a description. I wouldn't know them if I passed them in the street. What's the point of spending an hour down the nick when it's not going to make a blind bit of difference?'

'Even so. They shouldn't be allowed to get away with it.'

Jonny ached all over, but his ribs hurt the most. Maybe one of them was cracked. He gently probed his right-hand side, wincing as his fingers pressed against the bruised skin. He'd be sure to keep his eyes peeled from now on and keep his wits about him. This was just a warning. Next time he'd end up in hospital – or worse.

'You didn't even get a glimpse?' Hazel persisted.

'How many times have I told you? They came up behind me. It was quick. They pushed me into the alley and . . . Christ, I don't know. It was dark in there. I struggled and so they slapped me around a bit.'

'More than a bit. Is your nose broken, do you think?'

Jonny shook his head, a gesture he instantly regretted. A sharp pain ran through his nostrils. He put the bloodied cotton wool on the kitchen table and gingerly touched the bridge of his nose. 'I reckon it's just swollen. Give it a few days and it'll be all right.'

'Have you upset anyone recently?'

'Like who?'

'You tell me.'

'Give it a rest, love. I was robbed, pure and simple. Don't go making it something it isn't.'

'I can't believe no one saw it happen. I mean, there's always a crowd in Soho. Someone must have—'

'Change the subject, can't you?' Jonny dabbed at his nose

with the cotton wool. 'I've had enough bleedin' grief for one night.'

'You should be careful where you drink then, shouldn't you?'

'Yeah, well, I'll know better in future.' Then, in an attempt to distract her, he said: 'So what have you been up to? Did you talk to Marian?'

'Yes, and then I went to see Dad. I thought I might be able to persuade him to let us have the Mayfair flat.'

'And did you?'

'No.'

'There's a surprise.'

'It didn't help that he's still got the hump over Carmen. He was just going on and on about her. Anyway, do you know what he said in the end?' Hazel didn't wait for a reply. 'He said that if we wanted more space we should move into the house with him. I mean, can you imagine it? I knew you wouldn't be interested so . . .'

But Jonny, far from agreeing with her, was instead thinking back to the conversation he'd had with Milo Grant. 'Maybe we shouldn't be too hasty.'

'What? Are you kidding?'

'It's a big house,' he said. 'And a good address. I reckon we should think about it. Carmen's going to be moving out after she's married, so there'll only be the three of us.' What he didn't mention, but what was foremost in his mind, was what Milo had said about accidents. If most of them happened at home – hadn't he read that somewhere? – then maybe Rex's home was exactly where they ought to be.

18

When Monday finally arrived, Carmen felt both relieved and anxious. It had been the longest Sunday she could remember, one of those days that dragged on and on, as if time itself was conspiring in some scheme to prolong her agony. She had hoped Clive would call her, but he hadn't. And staring at the phone apparently didn't make it ring. She had picked it up, intending to call *him*, at least a dozen times, but then placed the receiver back in its cradle. Something had held her back, perhaps simply the instinctive knowledge that giving in would be the wrong thing to do.

Pleasing Clive had been Carmen's *raison d'être* since they'd become a couple. She had laughed at his jokes, sympathised with his troubles, and done her best to be the perfect girlfriend. All she was asking for in return was a little moral support. But they seemed to have reached an impasse on that front. He wasn't giving any ground, and she wasn't shifting either.

This trouble would pass, she thought, as she re-packed her suitcase and prepared to leave the Gryphon. It was just a glitch, a bump in the road, and once she was reconciled with her father, she and Clive would get back on track again. Although she wasn't looking forward to what she had to do this morning, there was no shirking it. She would be glad, however, when it was over and done with.

It was still early, only half past seven, but she wanted to get home before her father left for work. At least he would be sober at this time of day. Not in a good mood, she was sure of that, but less inclined to completely lose the plot. She would be suitably sorry, he would give her a lecture on how a daughter should respect her father, and everyone would be happy.

Carmen went down to the lobby with her case, told the man at the desk she'd like to check out and asked for the bill to be put on the Darby account. The receptionist, a man she'd never met before, was middle-aged and dressed in the smart silver-grey livery of the Gryphon. He exuded an air of slick efficiency, but his professional smile suddenly faltered.

'I'm afraid we're unable to do that,' he said, his face taking on an apologetic expression.

'I don't understand.'

He glanced around the lobby, even though it was empty, and lowered his voice. 'We've received instructions from Mr Darby that your bill ... that it shouldn't go on the company account.'

Carmen stared at him, mortified. 'Are you sure?' she asked, although she already knew the answer to the question. That her father was being this petty, this mean spirited, shouldn't have come as any great surprise, but she was still taken aback.

He gave an awkward nod and pushed a slip of paper across the counter with the cost of her two-night stay neatly written out on it.

'Fine,' she said, fumbling in her bag for her chequebook. She could feel her cheeks burning at the sheer embarrassment of it all. Quickly she wrote out the cheque, eager to get out of the place. The man must be wondering what this was all about, but she wasn't going to enlighten him. She took her receipt, thanked him, picked up her case and left with as much dignity as she could muster.

Out on the street she quietly cursed her father. This was what he was like, always trying to control her, to make her dance to whatever tune he was playing that day. He was impossible. And unkind. And vengeful. By refusing to pay for the hotel he was sending her a message: do as I say or there'll be consequences. It almost made her want to run in the opposite direction. But Carmen knew that she wouldn't. This wasn't the time for resistance or rebellion.

Instead, she hailed a cab, gave the Upper Belgrave Street address, and climbed inside. While she travelled through the streets of London, she dwelled on her father's constant need to exert his authority. It was like a compulsion. He always had to call the shots, always had to have the last word. It was like living with one of those tyrannical Roman emperors.

Carmen was still quietly seething when she stepped out of the cab in Belgravia. She took a moment to get her thoughts in order, to take a few deep breaths before advancing on the front door. *Just stay calm*. Anger was the last thing needed right now. She had to bite her tongue and just get on with it.

She put down her case, took out her key and put it in the lock. But the key wouldn't turn. She tried twisting it, to the left, to the right, but nothing happened. What was wrong with the damn thing? She jiggled it again, but the result was the same. Eventually, with no other choice, she had to ring the doorbell.

It was Mrs Cooper who answered the door with a dustpan and brush in her hand. 'Oh, hello, dear.'

Carmen smiled apologetically. 'Sorry, but there's something wrong with the lock. I can't get my key to work.'

'He had it changed, love. Yesterday, so he said. Must have cost him double on a Sunday.' Mrs Cooper gave a long sigh and added: 'He also said that if you showed up, on no account was I to let you in.'

Carmen stared at her in disbelief. 'What? That's ridiculous! Is he here?'

'No, he gave me my instructions and stormed off. Gone to the office, I expect. I take it you two have had a falling out? I won't ask. It's none of my business.' Mrs Cooper paused, inclining her head to one side, as if Carmen might volunteer the information despite her declared disinterest in the subject. When this didn't happen, she said: 'I can't let you in, love. I'm sorry. It's more than my job's worth.'

Carmen stood on the doorstep, trying to process this latest development, shocked that her father had gone this far. To be denied access to her own home. It was beyond the pale, crazy! She stood there, open-mouthed, tearful, at a loss as to what to do next.

Mrs Cooper was holding tight to the side of the door, but pity came into her eyes. 'Well, I won't pretend to know what's going on, but it's a rum do when a father throws his own daughter out.' Mrs Cooper's gaze slid down to Carmen's belly. 'I'm guessing you're in some kind of trouble.'

Carmen's eyes widened and she quickly shook her head, anxious to prevent that particular rumour from doing the rounds. 'Oh, no, I'm not . . . I'm not. Honestly. I swear. It's nothing like that. We just had a row and then . . .' She gave a helpless shrug.

Mrs Cooper looked up to Carmen's face, as if trying to work out how truthful Carmen was being – and what sort of row, if it wasn't over an unplanned pregnancy, could have possibly ended in a drama of this magnitude. 'That must have been some argument.'

'I'm sure we'll work it out eventually.'

'Sooner rather than later, I hope. You take care of yourself, love. You've got somewhere to stay, I take it?'

Carmen nodded and picked up the case. 'Yes, I'll be fine.' It occurred to her that she could just push past Mrs Cooper – she was younger and stronger – force her way in and refuse to leave. But what would that achieve? Only more wrath from her father. And maybe even a very public ejection. It wasn't worth the grief. 'Goodbye, then.'

Carmen began walking back along the road, head held up and shoulders back, drawing on those rapidly dwindling reserves of dignity that had been so much in demand this morning. Where now? She would go to Clive's, of course. There was nowhere else she could go – or wanted to go. They might have had words, might have disagreed, but when he heard what her father had done, he'd be as astounded as she was.

19

Clive's smile was wide, even faintly triumphant, when he opened the door, but the smile quickly faded when he saw Carmen's suitcase. 'What's going on?'

'Dad won't let me in the house.'

'He won't what?'

'He's lost the plot,' she said. 'I can't believe it. He's thrown me out.'

Clive's face fell. He hesitated for a moment before taking the case from her. 'Jesus. You'd better come on up.'

When they were in the flat, he put the case down beside the sofa and turned to her.

'What did you say to him?'

Carmen heard that accusatory edge to his voice again, and immediately became defensive. 'I didn't say anything. I haven't even seen him. I went to the house this morning and my key wouldn't work. Mrs Cooper – she's the cleaner – answered the door and said that Dad had changed the locks and she was under strict instruction not to allow me in.'

'So you haven't even talked to him? That's insane, Carmen.'

'How could I?'

'You've had all weekend. I even drove you over there on Saturday.'

'He was in a rage. I've already told you. It wasn't a good time.'

'It was as good a time as any. Now you've just made him even angrier.' Clive reached for the telephone and said: 'I'm going to call him right now and get this sorted.'

Carmen put her hand firmly over the receiver. 'No, you can't. I don't want you to. I'm not going to grovel to him. Why should I? He's the one who's being unreasonable. What kind of a man changes the locks over a stupid argument? It's not normal. If he doesn't want me there, then fine. I'll go somewhere else.'

'There's no need for any of this.'

'Try telling him that.'

'For God's sake, Carmen, one of you has to be the bigger person. This has to stop. I understand how you feel, I really do, but your father isn't going to give in. He never does. So just do it for *our* sake, why don't you? Let's put this to bed and get on with our lives. We've got a wedding to think of, a future.'

'We don't need him for that,' Carmen said.

'And how are we going to get married if I don't even have a job?'

'He won't get rid of you, and even if he does, you can get another job, a better one. You're good at what you do. And we don't need a fancy wedding. We can go down the register office and get married there.'

Clive didn't seem overly impressed by this idea. 'We can't live off air. Even this flat goes with the job. Where exactly are we going to live?'

'We'll find somewhere.'

'You're not being realistic.'

'You can't expect me to beg. He's changed the locks, Clive. That's not a man who's going to be satisfied with a simple apology.'

'So make it a sincere one.'

'It's too late for that.'

'It's never too late.'

Carmen stared at him. She understood his concerns, but he didn't seem to understand hers. Her father had crossed a line, barred her from her own home, and a few obsequious words weren't going to change anything. Rex Darby wasn't the sort of man who backed down. He'd want his pound of flesh, and she wasn't prepared to give it to him. 'I'm not going back there. I can't.'

'So where are you going to go? I don't think it's a good idea for you to stay here.'

Carmen's heart missed a beat. She hadn't expected this, although maybe she should have done. 'Why not?'

'Because it's like throwing petrol on the fire. No, if you won't go home, you should go back to the Gryphon, or stay with one of your sisters. Let's not make everything worse.'

Carmen didn't see how it could get any worse. Even Clive was turning his back on her now. 'If that's what you want.'

'It's not to do with what I *want*,' he said. 'It's what's for the best.'

The best. Carmen shook her head, dismayed to find herself at loggerheads with him again. She had come here looking for understanding, love and tenderness, but all she was getting was cool disapproval. 'We don't need him,' she repeated, hoping that if she said it often enough, he might eventually agree with her.

Clive released an exasperated breath. 'You're not being realistic. How exactly are you proposing to live? If your father cuts you off, you'll have nothing. And I'll be in the same situation if he fires me.'

'I wouldn't expect you to keep me,' she said quickly, concerned that this was what he was anxious about. 'I'll pay my way. I can get a job. I've got qualifications and I can type.'

Clive's eyebrows arched. 'Typists don't earn much. You're used to having everything you want, Carmen. You've only ever had to ask, and it was yours.'

'Not everything,' she retorted, offended by the remark. It made her sound like a spoiled child. Was that really how he saw her? It was true that she didn't work a nine-to-five job or have to pay the bills, but she had never been idle. She had studied hard for her History of Art degree, taken care of her father, and spent much of the holidays working in his office. 'Money isn't the only thing that matters.'

'The only people who say that are the ones who don't have to worry about it.'

Carmen felt a tightening in her chest. They were fighting again, not with raised voices or physical contact, but fighting all the same. She knew it shouldn't be like this. She knew that they should be standing together, united, and the fact that they weren't didn't say much for them as a couple.

Clive suddenly smiled, reached out and gently stroked her cheek. 'You're a sweet girl, Carmen, but you have no idea how the real world works. Please let me take you to see your father. For me. For *us*. This feud has gone on long enough.'

For a moment Carmen had softened at his touch, but she immediately bristled at his 'real world' comment. There he was, treating her like a child again. Patronising her. She might be inexperienced, but she wasn't completely naïve. She instinctively withdrew, taking a step back. 'He won't change his mind.'

Clive's hand dropped to his side and his face hardened. 'I don't feel like I know who you are any more.'

The feeling was mutual. There was a coldness about him,

Carmen thought. Had it always been there? Perhaps she had been too besotted, too blind, to recognise it before. 'I'm the same person I always was.'

'Are you? Only the Carmen I knew wouldn't have hesitated, wouldn't have thought twice about doing the one thing that would guarantee our future.'

Carmen knew in that moment that without her father's money, without the prospects that came with marrying Rex Darby's daughter, he would never be prepared to commit to her. It struck her with a dreadful force, a breath-removing blow to the heart. Panic gathered inside her. She was tempted to agree to his request, to agree to anything in order to keep him, but she knew it would be pointless. The Clive Grainger she had fallen in love with wasn't this man; he was someone quite different, a figment only of her imagination perhaps.

Before she could embarrass herself, Carmen quickly picked up her suitcase. 'I'd better go.'

'Where to? Where are you going?'

'To the Gryphon,' she lied. 'Call me if you want to.'

Clive didn't try and stop her going. He didn't even say good-bye. It was over.

20

Carmen walked quickly, trying to put as much distance as she could between herself and Clive. What was she thinking about? Nothing of importance. Her mind couldn't absorb it all yet and so she pushed it away, hiding it from the daylight, squashing it down into a dark corner. She concentrated on the simple things: one step in front of another, the clip of her heels on the pavement, the sound of the traffic swooshing past.

By the time she reached Oxford Street, the suitcase, even though it wasn't large, was beginning to feel like a lead weight. She found a café and went inside, grateful to be able to sit down for a while. The room, half empty, smelled of breakfast, of fried eggs and bacon. Carmen took a table by the window, and when the waitress came she ordered a small pot of tea.

It was only then, as she gazed out at the busy street, that everything began to tumble in on her. What was she going to do now? Where was she going to go? Why didn't Clive love her like she loved him? This last was too painful to dwell on and so she concentrated instead on the practicalities. First on the list was somewhere to stay. The Gryphon was out of the question – she couldn't afford to go there again even if she wanted to. Marian wasn't going to take her in, and Hazel's flat was too small for three. Anyway, Hazel always followed Marian's lead. If Marian said no, Hazel would say it too.

There was her best friend Lucy of course. Except Lucy was in Paris, supposedly studying at the Sorbonne, but spending most of her time, from what Carmen had gathered from the pale blue airmail letters, with a distracting French student called Benard. Anyway, she didn't have her passport with her and even if she had, would she really want to play gooseberry?

Carmen had other friends, but they were not the sort who could be called upon in a crisis like this. They were girls she met for casual drinks or the occasional lunch, and she could not imagine ringing them up and begging for a bed for the night. She would have to explain why, and it would be too embarrassing, too shameful.

The waitress arrived with her tea, placing the bill beside the pot. The little slip of paper reminded Carmen of the state of her finances. How much did she have in the bank? About fifteen pounds, she thought. Every month her allowance came in, and every month she spent it. Now she was wishing she had been more frugal. If only she'd put a little aside for a rainy day.

Carmen poured the tea and went back to contemplating where she would sleep tonight. Annie Foster was the next option that sprang into her head. Annie would never turn her away, but it would be bound to cause problems between Pat and Carmen's father. And between Pat and Annie, probably. No, that wouldn't do at all.

Having run through her short list of possibilities, and rejected them all, the only option left was a small hotel or B&B. But not round here. She would have to head for somewhere cheaper, somewhere she could eke out her money until she got a job. But to even get a job she would need appropriate clothes. Jeans and a jumper were hardly suitable for an interview. And nor was a little black cocktail dress. Suddenly she wished that she *had* pushed past Mrs Cooper, not so she could stay and face the music, but so she could have filled the suitcase with more useful attire.

Carmen took her time drinking the tea. She was making plans and yet they didn't seem quite real, as if it was someone else's life she was thinking about, someone else's future. She could barely comprehend the enormity of it all and so she didn't try. One step at a time. It was easier that way.

Eventually, when the teapot was empty, Carmen stood, picked up her case, paid at the counter and went back out on to the street. She was nearing a bus stop when she saw a red double-decker approaching with the destination 'Kellston' displayed on the front. She knew where Kellston was, had even been there once – a long time ago – and decided on impulse that this was as good a place to go as any. It was in the East End and so it would be cheap. She could get a room there, maybe even find a job.

Before she could have second thoughts she joined the back of a short queue, took a few deep breaths, and prepared herself for the tricky business of starting all over again.

21

Rex had been drinking steadily since Friday: never enough to become incapable, but just enough to keep the bad thoughts festering. He sat in his office in a fug of smoke with a cigar in one hand and a glass of Glenfiddich in the other. All weekend he had been waiting for Carmen to come to him. That she had failed to show up was both painful and infuriating. Nothing. Not a word. Not even a phone call. Such utter disrespect could not be forgiven.

Something had snapped in him on Friday. Carmen had spoiled his night, just like her mother used to spoil everything. She had looked at him through those slate-grey eyes and he had seen the same expression Rosa used to wear. Contemptuous? Insolent? Accusing? He had never quite been able to put his finger on it, but it had always made him angry. It had made him want to shake his wife, to slap her, to wipe that look off her face. Perhaps he even had, once or twice – a man could only be provoked so far – but she had never learned her lesson. Soon that look would be back, and he would be forced to deal with it all over again.

Michael Quinn jumped uninvited into his head. The two of them had been close once, like brothers. They had gone to school together and later drifted into a life of crime. They had been solid, tight, loyal, unwavering in their friendship. For years nothing could come between them. Until Rosa. Yes, as always, Rosa had ruined it all.

Rex could not remember the first time he'd set eyes on her. Michael had been the oldest of eight siblings and his home had always been full of snotty-nosed kids. But he remembered, of course, the first time he'd *noticed* her. She'd just turned nineteen then and had become an extraordinary beauty, one of those girls who took your breath away and transformed you into a tongue-tied teenager again.

If he had expected Michael to give his blessing to the pursuit of his little sister he'd been quickly disabused of the idea. 'Forget it,' Michael had said. 'Leave her alone. You're too old for her, and I know what you're like with women.'

There was an age difference, that was true. He had been in his thirties by then. And Michael knew all about his womanising, and the careless way he acquired and as quickly disposed of the women in his life. None of this had bothered Michael before, but the rules weren't the same when it came to sisters. However, the problem with forbidden fruit was that it instantly became more desirable. Rex was used to getting what he wanted, and he wanted Rosa.

Whenever Rex thought of her, a thin shiver ran through him. It was not his fault that she'd done what she had done. No one could blame him. She was weak, that was the problem, weak and not right in the head. How had he been supposed to deal with the black moods or the volatility or the sheer bloody craziness? By the time he'd discovered all that it was already too late: they were married, parents, and there was no way out. It wasn't like today when divorces were two a penny, when wives could be easily discarded and a superior one acquired. No, he'd just had to make the best of it.

There had always been a wildness about Rosa, something almost feral. That was what had fascinated him so much at the beginning. She'd been unlike any other girl he'd met before. He'd pursued her with single-minded determination, with yearning and lust, until he'd finally got that ring on her finger. Marry in haste, repent at leisure, is how the saying went and it was true: he'd had years to regret ever having fallen for her. He should have listened to Michael. What a fool he'd been!

Rex sucked on his cigar and breathed out the smoke. He gazed around his office, taking in the deep-pile carpet, the rosewood desk and the paintings on the walls. Everything expensive, everything befitting a man of his status. Despite his disappointments, he had still achieved most of what he'd wanted from life: success, money and respect. Only a son had been denied to him. Rosa, although unable to prevent herself from falling pregnant, had in some way contrived to never let those babies be boys. It had been her revenge on him, he thought, her final victory.

Rex lifted the glass to his lips and drank. When they were growing up, he had seen traces of Rosa in Marian and Hazel, in their strong personalities and headstrong ways. But Carmen had been different. At least that's what he'd always believed. Now he was starting to realise that she was more her mother's daughter than either of her sisters. Stubborn and coldly indifferent to his feelings. Ingratitude ran in her blood. Like a venomous snake, she had lain coiled in his affections, ready to strike when he least expected it.

She would get a wake-up call soon. All weekend he had waited for her to come, pacing the office, pacing the house, watching from the windows. Even after Marian had told him that Carmen had been back, that she'd packed a bag and left again, he'd still refused to believe that she wouldn't return. Now he'd put a stop to any free rides at the Gryphon, now he'd made it clear to her sisters that her staying with them would not be appreciated, now he'd marked Clive's card too, where else could she go? It was only a matter of time before she came crawling home.

Well, she'd be in for a shock. No one could humiliate Rex Darby in front of everyone and expect to get away with it. Such behaviour could not be tolerated. Changing the locks had been the right thing to do, the only thing. Once she realised that she wasn't free to come and go as she wished, Carmen might finally face up to her mistakes.

Rex drained his glass, reached for the bottle and poured another drink. His attention shifted to Clive Grainger, a spineless bastard who should, if he had any backbone at all, be standing by his fiancée instead of trying to pander to his future father-in-law. It was yet another example of Carmen's poor choices. She hadn't the sense to spot a gold-digger when she saw one. Clive might be suave and charming, even the best club manager Rex had ever had, but he was a man with an eye to the main chance. It had been ambition rather than love that lay at the heart of his marriage proposal.

Rex suspected, not without glee, that all wasn't rosy on the romantic front. Clive had failed to fulfil his promise of delivering Carmen and had sounded less than happy about it on the phone. There had been something abrupt in his manner, something that smelled worse than simple disappointment. He was not the sort of man, apparently, who dealt well with contrary women.

Rex gazed into the middle distance for a while, his hand still tight round his glass. Time passed: a minute, maybe longer. When the office came back into focus, he was not entirely sure where he was up to in his musings. These days he was prone to losing his train of thought. Yes, of course: Clive Grainger. He pulled a face before swatting the image out of his mind.

From outside in the street came the sound of a woman laughing. Rex stiffened. There was something about the sound, too high-pitched, too artificial, that reminded him of the noise that used to come out of Rosa's mouth. He lifted his chin, and a thin hiss escaped from between his lips. Even now, twenty years after her death, she wouldn't leave him in peace.

22

When Carmen alighted from the bus at Kellston train station she couldn't say for sure whether any of her surroundings were familiar. It was ten years, maybe eleven, since she'd last been here, and then she'd been in the car with her father. He had driven the dark red Bentley slowly around the streets, pointing out places of interest like a London tour guide, only instead of the Houses of Parliament and Westminster Abbey, it had been the old Roxy cinema, a run-down pool hall and the primary school he had once attended. The house he'd grown up in, if she remembered rightly, was somewhere behind the station, a small, cramped terrace bordering the railway line. He had parked the car outside and stared at it for a long while.

'Seven of us lived there,' he'd said, 'crammed together like sardines in a tin. A right dump with damp on the walls, and an outside lav and all. You girls don't know you're born.'

Carmen hadn't known what to say, and so she'd said nothing. But now, looking back, she thought she might have seen a hint of nostalgia in his face. He may have left behind the squalor of the place, the unforgiving hopelessness, but for all his wealth and success, he had not been able to buy himself happiness.

She was aware that her mother had hailed from Kellston too, but he hadn't mentioned her, and although she'd been curious, she hadn't asked. He never talked about her, but she had no idea if this was because the memories were too painful or for other reasons altogether. In fact, she knew very little about her mother, other than the bare brutal horror of her suicide. And what was she supposed to do with that information? It was too big a burden, too painful a truth, to examine too closely. For the most part she simply tried to forget about it, to push it deep down inside her into that dark corner where all her other fears and insecurities lay buried.

For a moment, as she stood wondering where to go next, Carmen's feelings towards her father softened. She wondered if she wasn't being ridiculous running away from home like some angry kid with a knapsack over her shoulder. But then she recalled the changed locks, his blazing eyes at the birthday dinner, and Mrs Cooper's declaration that on no account was she to be allowed in; she knew there was no going back.

Across the street Carmen could see a row of B&Bs, most of them shabby with their windows covered in dust and their paintwork peeling. They looked less than desirable, but they also looked cheap. Her eyes scanned the row. Which to choose? She shifted the case to her other hand. Then, aware that she was blocking the pavement, she moved back and went to stand by a place called the Station Café. Immediately she was tempted by the thought of getting something to eat – she'd had no break-fast and her stomach was rumbling – but knew she had to start being careful with her money.

As she was weighing up her hunger against the price of

relieving it, her attention was drawn to a handwritten notice in the café window:

Waitress wanted. Apply within.

Perhaps the fates were smiling on her. Before anything as mundane as a lack of experience or the absence of any references could blunt her enthusiasm, she pushed open the door and went inside.

The woman behind the counter was in her fifties, tall and skinny with short brown hair framing a red-cheeked face. She was busy buttering a sliced loaf, the knife skimming quickly across the bread.

'Yes, love, what would you like?'

'I saw the notice in the window,' Carmen said. 'Are you still looking for someone?'

The woman stopped buttering and stared at her. Her gaze was appraising, taking in everything about Carmen from her face to her expensive clothes and the case in her hand. The verdict didn't seem entirely favourable. 'Got any experience, have you?'

'Not exactly. But I'm a hard worker, and reliable.' Carmen, sensing that this wasn't enough to satisfy her would-be employer, rapidly added: 'And I'm a quick learner. If you give me a chance, I won't let you down. I promise.'

'What's your name, love?'

'Carmen.'

The coffee machine chose this exact moment to emit a loud belching sound, followed by a long hiss, and her name was partly lost in the noise.

'Carly?' asked the woman.

Carmen suddenly had second thoughts about using her real name. It was unusual and could make it easier for her father to track her down, perhaps even to come and cause a scene. She nodded. 'Carly Baxter,' she said, appropriating Lucy's surname as it was the first that came to mind in the moment.

'And where are you from, Carly?'

Again, Carmen felt the need for caution. 'Over Notting Hill way.' She thought about trying to provide a plausible reason as to why she had left, but decided it was probably best not to start embroidering unless she had to.

The woman wiped her hands on her apron. 'I'm Mrs Devlin, Joan Devlin.' She folded her arms across her chest and gave Carmen another of those long assessing looks. 'Well, I suppose I could give you a trial run. Shall we say to the end of the week and see how it goes? It's an eight-hour shift, six till two with a half-hour break at eleven thirty. I need someone Monday to Friday. Do you think you could manage that?'

Carmen smiled widely. 'Absolutely. No problem at all. Thank you. Thanks. That would be great.'

'Twenty pounds a week, and you get to keep any tips that you make. Not that they're over generous round here so I wouldn't get your hopes up.'

Carmen was shocked by how little it was but took care not to show it. She would manage somehow, cut her cloth to . . . whatever the saying was. She could manage. She'd have to. 'When would you like me to start?'

'As soon as you can. Would tomorrow suit?'

'Yes, I'll be here on the dot.'

Mrs Devlin's gaze slid down to Carmen's expensive high heels. 'You'll need a pair of comfy shoes. You'll be on your feet all day.'

'Of course. And is there a uniform?'

'There's an apron out back you can use.'

'Right,' Carmen said. 'I'll see you tomorrow, then. And thanks again.'

'No need to thank me, love. I've had that notice in the window for over a week now and you're the first girl who's come in to ask about it.'

Carmen, who'd been quietly congratulating herself on the good impression she must have made, faced a quick reality check. Not so much the best candidate as the only one. Still, she'd managed to secure the job and that was all that mattered. 'I don't suppose you know of any decent B&Bs round here, do you?' And then in case Mrs Devlin suspected she might only be passing through, she rapidly added: 'Just until I get sorted with a permanent place.'

Mrs Devlin gestured towards Station Road. 'You could try Mrs Jordan's. She's up there, opposite the laundrette. I can't rightly remember what the number is, but it's got a door with one of those stained-glass thingies above it. A window type thing. You know what I mean? She might not be the cheapest, but it's clean . . . and respectable.'

From this Carmen could only surmise that some of the establishments were *not* respectable. 'Thanks. I'll give it a go.'

'Can't guarantee she'll have any vacancies, mind.'

'I'll go and find out. Thanks again, Mrs Devlin. I'll see you tomorrow.'

'Call me Joan. There's no need to stand on ceremony here.'

Carmen said her goodbyes and left, pleased to have secured a position even if it had been by default. That was one problem solved. Now all she had to do was find somewhere to live.

23

Carmen walked along Station Road until she came to the laundrette. Directly opposite, just as Joan Devlin had said, was a Victorian terrace with a stained-glass fanlight over the door. She crossed over, dodging between the cars and buses, and stood in front of the house. Compared to its neighbours, the building was in good condition, the exterior paintwork pristine and the windows sparkling. In one of the front windows was a sign saying Vacancies.

A tiny, frail-looking woman answered the door, her face wrinkled, her hair sparse and grey. Her eyes, however, were two bright beads and her voice was strong and firm. 'Hello, dear.'

'Mrs Jordan? I'm looking for a room. Mrs Devlin recommended that I try here.'

The old lady gave Carmen one of those up-and-down assessing looks that appeared to be the norm in Kellston. 'For the week, is it?'

Carmen wasn't sure if she wanted to make a seven-day commitment – what if she didn't like the room? – but decided she couldn't afford to be fussy. She was starting work tomorrow and needed to be settled somewhere. 'Yes, please, for the week.'

Mrs Jordan continued to examine her, searching perhaps for any outward signs of lack of decency or virtue.

Carmen stood up straight and tried to look respectable.

Eventually, as if she had passed muster, Mrs Jordan said: 'It's £3 a week, dear. In advance. Would that be agreeable to you?'

Carmen, who only had the rates of the Gryphon and her father's other hotels to go by – it was cheap in comparison – nodded. 'That would be fine, thank you.'

Finally, Mrs Jordan stood back and allowed her over the threshold. Carmen followed her up the stairs and into the room that was going to be hers. She quickly took in the surroundings. It was a decent-sized space, not too small, and contained a single iron bedstead, a wardrobe, a chest of drawers, a bedside table, a chair, a sink and a gas fire.

'The bathroom's just along the landing,' Mrs Jordan said.

'Thank you. I'm sure I'll be very comfortable here.'

Mrs Jordan took a bunch of keys from her cardigan pocket, slipped one from the ring and passed it to Carmen. 'This is for the room. I lock the front door at nine o'clock sharp, so if you're in any later you'll have to ring the bell.'

'I won't be keeping late hours.'

Then, as the landlady continued to hover by her elbow, Carmen remembered about the rent in advance and quickly took out her purse. She counted three one-pound notes into Mrs Jordan's palm.

'Breakfast is between seven and eight weekdays, seven and nine at the weekends.'

'I won't be needing breakfast during the week,' Carmen said. 'I start work at six.'

Mrs Jordan didn't offer a discount on the breakfasts that

would remain uneaten but instead said: 'I prefer my guests not to bring strangers into the house. You have to be careful these days.'

'Of course.'

'I don't think I caught your name, dear.'

'Carly Baxter,' Carmen replied, the name still sounding foreign to her.

'Well, Miss Baxter, I'll leave you to get settled in. I'll be downstairs if you need anything.'

Once the door had closed, Carmen stood and had another good look round. The room was light, with a large window overlooking Station Road, but noisy too from all the traffic going past. The decor was old-fashioned: a faded flowery wallpaper of roses and ivy, a worn, brown-patterned carpet and brown curtains. But it was clean at least, without a speck of dust. She made a determined effort not to compare it to her own lovely room in Upper Belgrave Street. This was perfectly adequate, she told herself, knowing that comparisons would only evoke regrets, and regrets would lead to the kind of thoughts she preferred not to deal with. The room would do until she could find something more permanent.

Carmen unpacked the few things she had in her case, making a mental list of everything she would need to buy before she started work tomorrow. She hung up the little black cocktail dress she had grabbed before going back to Clive's on Saturday (she'd been hoping to spend the evening with him at Lola's) and it swayed softly on the hanger in the wardrobe, looking lost and out of place. She placed some other items – a pale blue T-shirt, a change of underwear – in a drawer, and put her make-up, comb and perfume on the top of the chest of drawers.

When all this was done, and before she could start feeling sorry for herself, she shoved the empty suitcase under the bed, picked up her handbag, left the room and locked it behind her. Downstairs, the hall was empty. Apart from Mrs Jordan, everyone was probably at work. The door to a lounge area was open, and she saw a collection of mismatched armchairs and a TV set. She wondered what her fellow residents were like but decided to try and avoid them as much as she could. She didn't want to lie to people, but she didn't want to tell them the truth either.

The sun was shining as Carmen walked down to the junction and turned right on to the high street. She had an afternoon of shopping ahead of her: soap, shampoo, deodorant, towels, work clothes, sensible shoes and an alarm clock. Aware of her dwindling reserves of cash, she would have to choose carefully. Her days of spending without thinking were over.

The sun's rays, she noticed, didn't do much to brighten the area. The street was shabby and run-down, many of the shops boarded up and the pavements covered in litter. She faltered, wondering not for the first time what she was doing. Could she really live here? It felt strange and alien, daunting. In the distance she could see the three tall towers of a council estate. They loomed on the horizon, grey and gloomy, their tiny square windows like a thousand watching eyes.

Carmen was aware of the people around her, of the unfamiliar faces and unfamiliar smells. She knew she had entered a different world: a place where, for the moment at least, she didn't belong. A brief flurry of panic rose in her chest, and her fingers closed tightly around her bag, afraid that someone might try and snatch it. Suddenly it all felt too much. But what was the alternative? Running home with her tail between her legs, admitting she couldn't cope, and begging for forgiveness? No, that was completely out of the question.

24

There were twelve tables in the Station Café, arranged in three rows of four. By seven o'clock on Tuesday morning most of them were occupied, and Carmen was flying up and down the aisles with full English breakfasts and mugs of tea. There was a never-ending stream of orders and by the time one set of customers had left another quickly replaced it. It was mainly men, early starters, construction and factory workers, who all had huge appetites and a ready supply of banter. Discovering a new waitress on duty, some of them weren't slow to try and see how far they could push the boundaries. Carmen fixed a smile on her face as she swatted away the suggestive comments and the occasional roaming hand.

'Don't let that lot take advantage,' Joan said, as she shovelled sausages, bacon and eggs on to plates. 'Give 'em an inch and they'll take a mile.'

Carmen nodded, knowing she was on probation and intent on making a good impression. 'Don't worry, I can deal with it.'

It was all much more frenetic than Carmen had expected.

She had to take the orders – written neatly enough for Joan to be able to read them – and then deliver the right breakfasts to the right customers, make out the bills, take the money and give the correct change, and then clear and wipe down the tables at double-quick speed as soon as they were vacated. Turnover was everything. She was caught up in a whirlwind of activity, and so focused on the here and now that she didn't have time to think about anything else.

While Joan sweated over the stove, a girl washed up the pots out back. Lottie was Joan's granddaughter, about fifteen or sixteen, and wore the resigned expression of someone who had only a bowl of hot soapy water to look forward to. When they'd first been introduced, Lottie had stared intently at Carmen, frowning, as if examining an odd, alien creature who had inadvertently wandered into the Station Café but then almost immediately lost interest and gone to find her rubber gloves.

By eight o'clock there was a new set of customers, office workers smartly dressed in City attire, getting their breakfasts before boarding the train. Carmen noticed immediately that some of these people, although far less familiar and superficially more polite than their predecessors, actually complained a lot more: the bacon wasn't cooked enough or was cooked too much, the toast was too toasted or not toasted to the right shade of brown, the tea was too strong or too weak. Carmen tentatively relayed these criticisms back to Joan, not sure what else to do, but worried about upsetting or insulting her. She didn't want to be the messenger who got shot on her first day.

But Joan only raised her eyes to the heavens and said: 'Ignore them, love. They'd complain about the quality of the water if they were on fire, and you hosed them down. I'd like to see them get a better breakfast round here for the price.'

And so Carmen quickly learned to keep the complaints to

herself, apologising to the whiners while nodding sincerely and assuring them that she'd be sure to pass on their comments to the cook. She noticed that despite their grumbles, they always managed to clear their plates.

The rush was over by nine, and she was able to relax a little. How was she doing? Well, her feet, even in the so-called comfortable shoes, were hurting already, her jaw ached from smiling so much, and she felt thoroughly frazzled, but otherwise it wasn't going too badly. Although that, of course, was down to Joan to decide. A few errors had been made, some orders mixed up, but she was learning from her mistakes.

Carmen got a break at eleven thirty and was able to sit down and have something to eat. She devoured the food like a starving woman, wondering how many calories she'd burned this morning hurrying up and down the café aisles. She drank a strong coffee and suppressed a yawn. She hadn't slept well last night, being frequently woken up by the sound of creaking floorboards, the flush of the toilet, and cars going by outside.

Lottie came and sat down opposite her, stared at her left hand, at the ring on her finger, and said: 'You getting married, then?'

Carmen thought about Clive and inwardly flinched. 'One day, I suppose. No time soon.'

'What's his name?'

'Don,' Carmen said, plucking a name out of the air.

'What does he do?'

Carmen, unprepared for all these questions, picked a random occupation, but one that would account for frequent absences. 'He's in the Army.'

'Is that a real diamond?' Lottie said, staring at Carmen's left hand.

'No,' Carmen lied, thinking that a real diamond, and

especially one of this size, might provoke even more interest. 'It looks real, though, doesn't it?'

Lottie played with her lank brown hair, twisting strands around her finger. She had an oddly vacant air about her. Her eyes darted around the café before coming back to rest on Carmen again. 'I don't have a boyfriend.'

'I dare say you're better off without one.'

Lottie giggled. 'Gran says men are nothing but trouble.'

'She could have a point.'

'Is Don trouble?'

Carmen was saved from answering this by a couple of blokes coming through the door, one in his mid-twenties, the other about ten years older. They sat down by the window and looked around for a waitress. Joan was out in the back and Lottie showed no intention of getting up, so Carmen rose to take their order. Her break was almost over anyway.

'Two teas, please, love,' the younger one said. He was a handsome guy with short dark hair, chestnut-coloured eyes and sharp cheekbones. His suit was expensive, and he wore a flashy gold watch on his wrist. 'I've not seen you here before.'

'Just started,' Carmen said. 'This is my first day.'

'How's it going?'

'Good, thanks.'

'I'm Terry, Terry Street.' He flapped a hand towards his companion. 'And this ugly sod is Gordie. We're both in here from time to time.'

'Okay,' she said, edging away. 'Two teas coming up.'

'And what's *your* name?'

'Carly,' she said.

'Nice to meet you, Carly. What brings you to Kellston?'

Carmen shrugged while she thought about it. 'The job, that's all.'

'Not to mention the lovely scenery.' Terry smiled and glanced out of the window at the dismal London street with its run-down houses and relentless traffic. 'You can't beat a view like that. Do you ever drink in the Fox? It's the pub just along the way. I'm there most Friday nights.'

'Ignore him,' Gordie said. 'He can't help himself.'

'I'm only asking,' Terry said. 'Just being friendly. You don't mind, do you, Carly?'

Carmen shrugged again. 'If you don't mind waiting for your tea.'

Terry grinned. 'I'd better give it a rest, then. Old Gordie's spitting feathers here.'

Carmen went back to the counter and poured two mugs of tea. She could hear Joan in the back, chopping and slicing, sorting out food for the lunchtime service. She wasn't bothered by Terry's interest; in fact, she was faintly flattered that a man so good looking would even give her a second glance. After the break-up with Clive – was he really gone for ever? – her confidence was at an all-time low.

Carmen delivered the teas along with a saucer with the bill on it.

'What's this?' Gordie said, taking the slip of paper and holding it up.

'The bill,' Carmen said, bemused. 'I'm sorry, did you want something else?'

Gordie, who looked as though he'd been in more than a couple of scraps – two cauliflower ears and a nose that had clearly been broken in the past – gave her a long hard stare. 'We don't pay, love.'

Carmen glanced from one to the other, wondering if this was some kind of childish prank. Were they pulling her leg? Testing her because she was new? Trying to get a free cuppa?

121

Gordie's expression had turned a little belligerent, but Terry was sitting back as if he didn't have a care in the world. 'And why's that, then?'

'Because that's the way it is,' Gordie said bluntly.

'Don't mind him,' Terry said. 'He left his manners at home. If you ask Joan, she'll put you in the picture.'

Carmen retreated to the counter and went through to the kitchen. She still wasn't sure if this was just a bad joke and worried that Joan would think badly of her for not being able to deal with the situation on her own.

'There are two guys out there,' Carmen said. 'They're saying they don't need to pay.'

Joan wiped her hands on a cloth, put her head round the door and nodded. 'Yeah, don't worry about a bill for them. They work for Joe Quinn.'

Carmen gave a start. Quinn was her mother's maiden name. 'Joe Quinn?'

Joan kept her voice low. 'Quinn runs things round here.'

'He owns the café?'

'No, love, what I mean is that he runs things in Kellston. He's the boss. He don't pay for nothin' if he can help it. It's more the other way round if you get my drift.'

'You pay *him*?'

'Everyone pays him, at least everyone who knows what's good for them. All the local businesses. You won't survive long if you don't put your hand in your pocket every Friday.'

Carmen was now desperately hoping that she wasn't related to this man. What were the odds? Quinn wasn't *that* unusual a name, but the Kellston connection was hard to ignore. 'So he's . . . what, some sort of gangster? You should go to the police.'

Joan gave a hollow laugh and shook her head. 'And what are they going to do about it? They're just as bleedin' bad, taking

122

backhanders to look the other away. They all expect to get somethin' for nothin'. You'll never catch a copper paying if he don't have to. That lot down Cowan Road – that's the local nick, love – they all think they can have a free ride.'

Carmen glanced over her shoulder at the two men sitting drinking their tea. She wasn't completely naïve – she'd heard about intimidation, about protection – but had never expected to find herself so close to it. She looked back at Joan. 'It's not right, though, is it?'

'It's the way it is, love. No point moaning. At least I know where I stand with Quinn. This way I don't get no trouble.'

Trouble, thought Carmen, had been dogging her recently. Still, this wasn't any of her business. All she had to do was keep her head down and get on with her job. Teas and coffees, delivering plates of food and wiping down tables were the only things she had to concern herself with. She would stay well away from the rest – and especially from Joe Quinn. Whether he was family or not, she didn't want anything to do with him.

25

A pretty face always brightened up Terry Street's day. It was in his nature to flirt, to chat, to try his luck with any pretty girl who crossed his path. He liked the look of Carly even if she hadn't said much to encourage him. She had nice eyes and a good figure. He could tell from the way she talked that she wasn't from round here, that she was a class above. Well, he was a sucker for a challenge. Given time, he reckoned he could wear her down, exert the old Terry charm and persuade her to go for a drink with him.

Gordie was droning on about Connor Quinn, Joe's eldest, about how he was a liability, and someone should do something about it.

'It's Joe's problem,' Terry said, not wanting to be drawn, not ready yet to put his cards on the table. Little mistakes could come back to haunt you. 'Leave it to him.'

'He won't do nothin',' Gordie grumbled.

'Let the two of them sort it out themselves.'

'Someone's gonna end up dead.'

'Best to stay out of it.'

In truth, Terry had been dripping poison into Connor Quinn's ear ever since the man had come out of the slammer: hints here and there about how Joe didn't rate him, didn't trust him, and was cutting him out of the better deals. It hadn't taken much to push him to the edge, and then gently nudge him over it. Drunks, especially the paranoid ones, were always willing to believe the worst.

Connor had finally exploded a few days ago, charging into the Fox wielding a baseball bat and threatening to kill his father in full view of over fifty witnesses. It had been a stellar performance, guaranteed to stay in every customer's mind. He had been aiming for Joe's head but instead brought the bat down on the table with a shattering bang, showering everyone with glass and lager. Abuse had spewed from his mouth in a garbled tirade.

After disarming him, Terry had kicked the bat under a bench and retrieved it later, taking care not to spoil a perfect set of fingerprints. Now he had it safely stashed away. When the right time came – it wouldn't be long now – he'd be able to get rid of them both, father and son, in one simple move. Connor was an evil bastard, a chip off the old block, a sadist who found his entertainment in inflicting pain on others. The sooner he was out of the picture, the better.

'Are you listening to a bloody word I'm saying?'

Terry put down his tea and stared at Gordie. 'Yeah, I'm listening. You've got the hump with Connor. Join the queue: it's a long one.'

'I'm trying to have a conversation here and all you keep doing is gawping at that bird.'

'No harm in looking,' Terry said, glancing back over to where Carly was standing behind the counter. He tried to catch her eye, but she wasn't having any of it. She was staring out of the window, pretending to be absorbed and deliberately avoiding his gaze. He wasn't fooled, not for a second. Some girls were harder work than others but that didn't mean they weren't worth the effort.

'You ain't got a chance, mate.'

But Terry knew there was always a chance. So long as there was breath in his body and desire in his heart. Women were his weakness. Everyone had one. Gordie's was having no imagination. He was a bloke without vision, who didn't like change, who needed to know where his place was – even if that place was near the bottom of the pile. Would Gordie support him when he made his move to take over the firm? He didn't think so. No, Gordie wouldn't risk it. He'd be too afraid of backing the wrong horse, of ending up on the losing side, to take the gamble.

Terry picked up his mug again and drank some more tea. In his head he began going through his plans, making sure he hadn't overlooked anything. The baseball bat was ready to go. Connor's key to the cellar of the Fox – Quinn's other son, Tommy, ran the place – had been 'borrowed' when he was too pissed to notice, copied and returned, along with the keys to Joe's Jag. He would hide the bat in the cellar after killing Joe, somewhere it wouldn't be too hard for the law to find.

It would have to be done on a Friday. Nothing kept Connor away from the Fox on a Friday evening: it was the day of the milk run when money was collected from all the local businesses. He'd be there, like he always was, with his greedy hand stretched out for his share.

'There's been nothin' but aggro since he got out,' Gordie said. 'I'm sick to bleedin' death of it.'

'Tell me something I don't know.' When Terry thought about Connor Quinn, only bad stuff came into his head. Connor's last stretch inside had been for rearranging the features and numerous other body parts of a shopkeeper who'd refused to pay his dues. The man, who'd run a local hardware store, had gone to both the police and the press, the latter ensuring that the former couldn't sweep the violent assault under the carpet. Justice had been done, but at a price. He might have had his day in court and got his pound of flesh, but with the threat of further retribution hanging over him, the hardware man had been forced to accept police protection and move away.

Terry could see the useful side to all this. Others, who might have been tempted to revolt against the weekly payments, were now deterred not just by the threat of a beating but by the knowledge that if they informed there would be no going back. And who wanted to change their identity, move halfway across the country, never see their mates again and spend the rest of their life looking over their shoulder? It was easier to just pay up.

Grassing was a cardinal sin in the circles Terry moved in, something only the lowest of the low did. He frequently made his own opinions on the subject clear – grasses were dirt, disgusting, filth – while simultaneously exploiting what he saw as a perfectly legitimate loophole. Slowly, he was building up his own small group of narks: reliable contacts who, like double agents, would pass on information to the law. If another villain crossed him, or screwed him over, a whisper would soon find its way to Cowan Road station about a job going down or where some stolen property was stashed. Nothing could be traced back to him, and that was the way he intended to keep it.

You had to be smart in this game, Terry thought, one step ahead of the competition. Brutality could only take you so far. After a while, people got sick of it, started fighting back, and then what you had was all-round dissatisfaction and the soft murmurings of revolution. If he waited until Joe was overthrown, either by one of his own men or, more likely, by a neighbouring firm, his chances of slipping into the breach were greatly reduced. *Now* was the time to act, to grab the crown while it was still within his grasp.

'You know, I reckon I've seen that girl somewhere.'

'Huh?' Terry said, his mind still on other things.

'The waitress, the girl you've been eyeing up.'

'In your dreams,' Terry said.

'Nah, I'm serious. I've seen her somewhere before. I don't forget faces. It'll come back to me.'

They both looked across the café towards where Carly was standing.

26

Marian stood on the back doorstep of her home in Suffolk, gazing out across the garden to the fields beyond. It was approaching dusk, and the sky had assumed a thin greyish look, as though a blanket was slowly gathering around the day. In the distance she could see Hugh striding through the pasture, looking as small as the lead toy farmer she'd once owned as a child. Her husband wasn't small, of course, but quite tall really, with straw-coloured hair – receding slightly now – and a pink-cheeked, almost babyish type of face.

Hugh was what people would call a solid man, staunchly conservative and disinclined towards change. His habits were regular, his conversation mundane. She couldn't remember the last time he'd surprised her. Maybe never. Even his proposal had been predictable: a West End restaurant, flowers, an engagement ring that had once belonged to his grandmother.

Marian folded her arms across her chest and sighed into the silence. The truth was that he bored her, always had and always would. He bored her during the day, and he bored her in bed. Even after twelve years, twelve long and tedious years, he still had no idea of how to arouse her. She avoided sex with him as much as possible, faintly revolted by his body, turned off by his clumsy fumblings and grunting breath.

While she yearned for thrills and excitement, for the colour of her youth, for bright lights and cocktails, he was content to bury himself in the countryside. And as his wife she was obliged to live in this godforsaken place too. Still, that was all about to change. Now she had her inheritance – on paper at least – she had the perfect excuse to spend a lot more time in London.

After one last look out across the fields, she closed the door, went through to the drawing room and picked up the phone. She dialled Milo's number and listened to it ring. There was no answer. Disappointment furrowed her brow. He was probably down the pub or . . . no, she didn't want to imagine what else he might be doing. Although she felt no emotional attachment to him, it irked her to think of him with another woman. He was like a favourite dress or a special piece of jewellery: only worn occasionally but still her property and not to be borrowed by anyone else.

She put the phone down, picked up the receiver again and rang Hazel. This time she had more luck.

'Hello?'

'It's me,' Marian said. 'How's the packing going?'

'Slowly. Jonny's cleared off, of course, and left it all to you know who. Typical, isn't it? *He's* the one who wants to move but you don't see him for dust when the actual work needs doing.'

Marian was in two minds about the couple's unexpected decision to move to Upper Belgrave Street. On the one hand it could be helpful to have her sister there, keeping an eye on what the old man was up to, but on the other she didn't entirely trust Jonny. Was he hoping to be able to exert some influence, to cajole and wheedle, to try and persuade their father to loosen the purse strings? Not that there was anything wrong with that, so long as she got the benefit too. 'I still don't get it, why he's so keen. Who wants to live with their father-in-law? I thought it would be the last thing he'd suggest.'

'Don't ask me. I think he just fancies the idea of a good address. You know what he's like. He gets an idea in his head and there's no shaking it.'

'But what about you, what you want?'

There was a brief silence on the other end of the line, as though Hazel was considering the novel concept of her own feelings being considered for once. But Marian knew that she'd put up with anything if it kept Jonny happy. Her sister had married for love – more fool her – and had been reaping the consequences ever since: always stressing over what Jonny was doing behind her back, always anxious about him seeing other women, always trying too hard to please.

'Oh, it might not be that bad,' Hazel said finally. 'We'll see how it goes. If it doesn't work out, we can always come back to Camden.'

'Aren't you selling the flat?'

'No, we're going to hang on to it for a while and rent it out. You know, just in case. It's good to have a fallback position.'

Marian saw an opportunity and immediately grabbed it. 'I'll rent it off you. What do you say? I've been looking for a base in London.'

'What's wrong with the Gryphon?'

'Nothing, but it seems stupid taking up a room that someone could be paying good money for. Anyway, I'm sick of packing and unpacking. I want a base, somewhere more permanent, somewhere I can keep clothes and a few bits and pieces. And before you suggest using a room at Dad's, I've got no intention of living under the same roof as him ever again.'

'I wasn't going to,' Hazel said. 'I'll have a word with Jonny. I'm sure it'll be fine.'

'Thanks. Is everything all right with you two?'

'As it ever is. He's still in a huff about the whole inheritance thing.'

'Aren't we all.' Marian thought how crazy it was that they were both, theoretically, rich women and yet they remained cash poor.

Frustration suddenly burst from Hazel's lips. 'Dad's being such a shit about it. These terms and conditions are just bloody ridiculous. I mean, we're old enough to make our own decisions about what we do with our share. Why is he treating us like kids? A year, Pat said, but what if nothing changes after that? This could go on for ever.'

Marian gazed around the drawing room, at the lumpy old furniture and the wallpaper that hadn't been changed for over a hundred years. The whole house was like this, decorated in the dreadful taste and style of one of Hugh's ancestors. It was like living in a mausoleum. That anyone had got around to installing electricity was a miracle. If she had some money, some *real* money, she could at least put her own stamp on the place, brighten it up and take it into the twentieth century.

'You said you had a plan,' Hazel continued when Marian didn't say anything.

'I didn't say I *had* a plan, only that we needed one.'

'Fat lot of use that is.'

'For God's sake, Hazel, have some patience. The ink's barely dry on the papers. Has Dad heard from Carmen yet?'

'Not as far as I know.'

'Do you think she's with Clive?'

'He says not. Clive, I mean. Dad reckons there's been a falling out, that Clive's none too happy about the situation she's put him in.'

Marian smirked, happy to hear that all wasn't well with Carmen and her gold-digging fiancé. The path of true love – or whatever it was – clearly wasn't running smoothly. 'She'll be with that friend of hers, then. Lucy, is it?'

'Lucy's in Paris, I think. And Carmen's passport is still at the house. I went into her room and checked.'

'Well, wherever she is, she won't be gone long. Once the money runs out, she'll soon come running back. And I daresay Dad will forgive her for everything. She always was his favourite. If we behaved like she did, we'd never be forgiven.'

'He still seems pretty mad about it.'

Marian's smirk reappeared. Over the past few days, whenever she'd got the opportunity, she'd been encouraging her father in his bitterness towards Carmen, expressing astonishment at the behaviour of her youngest sister and shoring up his anger. 'If it had been you or me, he wouldn't have cared so much. It just goes to show, doesn't it?'

'Well, I wish she'd just come back and put an end to all this. It's all he ever talks about. It's getting on my nerves.'

Marian was of a different opinion. She'd started to hope that Carmen would never come back. What if she just disappeared for ever? Instead of a one-third share of the inheritance, she and Hazel would have half each. This seemed a much more satisfactory situation.

The thought lingered with her after they had said their goodbyes. She put down the phone, lit a cigarette, poured herself a drink and sat by the window. People disappeared all the time, walked out of their homes and were never seen again. Or met with accidents: stepped out in front of speeding cars, sustained fatal injuries from falling trees, or slipped and tumbled into the murky waters of the Thames. None of these scenarios seemed especially probable, but she still took pleasure in imagining them.

27

Jonny Cornish stood back, viewed the space they had cleared in the basement of the Royal, and wiped the heel of his hand across his brow. He was sweating from the exertion of shifting all the rubbish that had been dumped over the years. His ribs still ached from the beating he had taken on Saturday, and it hurt when he bent to lift stuff. But the pain and the effort had been worth it: now they could see the wood for the trees, the space was beginning to look more promising.

He sniffed the air, breathing in a smell of must and mould, like the stink of something that had died a long time ago. With his toe he scuffed at a brown stain on the concrete floor that could have been dried blood or old spilled beer. He gave Milo a nod. 'All we need is a lick of paint and some carpet and we're ready to go. We can hold two or three poker games a week here, maybe more. Minimal set-up cost. It's easy money.'

Milo shook his head. 'Didn't you just get the fuck beaten out of you for losing at poker?'

Jonny frowned, wishing he'd never shared that particular

piece of information and hoping that Milo would keep his mouth shut about it. 'Thanks for reminding me. I won't be playing, will I? Just taking a cut. The house always wins, yeah?'

'If you say so. What about whatshisname, the manager?'

'Dempsey,' Jonny said, 'Roy Dempsey. He won't give us any bother. I've told him we're going to be doing it up and that we don't want to be disturbed. It's no skin off his nose. We don't even need to go through the club; we can use the other entrance round the corner on Warwick Street. But we keep this between ourselves, yeah? Just you and me. Not a word to Rex or Hazel – or your old man, come to that.'

'I get you,' Milo said. 'I mean, I ain't going to go shooting my mouth off, am I? I'm supposed to be working full-time for Rex. He ain't going to be happy if he finds out I'm spending more time here than sorting out his tenants.'

Jonny still wasn't convinced that working with Milo was a good idea, but he needed the help – and later he would need some muscle in case there was trouble. Losers didn't always take defeat well. Did he trust the bloke? Not as far as he could throw him. But if he wanted to get his little gambling den off the ground, he couldn't afford to be fussy. Better the devil you know, as they said.

Milo leaned back against the wall. 'What if Dempsey talks to Rex?'

'What if he does? He won't know what we're doing down here. I'm going to get the locks changed on the two doors – the one that goes from here into the club and the one from Warwick Street – so he can't come snooping when we're not around.' Jonny smoothed back his dark hair and thought about it some more. 'Yeah, I'll tell Rex I'm poncing up the place, doing some painting and decorating so we can rent the space out for private parties.'

'This was Rex's first club,' Milo said, glancing up towards the ceiling. 'Years ago. I heard it used to be packed on a Saturday night.'

'He's let it go. It doesn't bring in much these days.'

'You'll be seeing a lot of him soon,' Milo said. 'Looking forward to living with the father-in-law?'

Jonny, maintaining the pretence that he was only moving in with Rex because it was what Hazel wanted, said: 'So long as the missus is happy. Happy wife, happy life. That's the trick, mate, in case you ever find yourself hitched someday.'

'I've never met a bloke who recommends it.'

Jonny grinned. 'It has its ups and downs.'

'What are you doing with your place, then? Camden, ain't it?'

'Selling it,' Jonny replied quickly, in case Milo got any ideas about moving in there. In fact, he'd persuaded Hazel to let the flat for a while, using the argument that if it didn't work out with Rex, they'd have somewhere else to go. The real reason, of course, was that he needed some fast cash to fund this latest venture, and a deposit plus a month's rent in advance would be more than useful at present. Selling the flat could take months. However, Milo wasn't the sort of tenant he wanted: he would always be late with the rent – if he paid at all – and probably didn't even know how to use a Hoover.

'I don't reckon Rex will be an easy man to live with.'

Jonny shrugged. 'There are compensations.'

'Oh sure, there are always compensations.'

There was something about the way Milo said it, with a sly smile, with a hint of cunning, that set Jonny's teeth on edge. He wondered how drunk Milo had been when they'd bumped into each other at the Black Lion, and decided not drunk enough. No, he'd remember what he'd said about Rex not living for ever, about getting sick, about accidents happening. His words had been stuck in Jonny's head ever since.

*

Milo knew that Jonny didn't trust him, but that was okay because he didn't trust Jonny either. He didn't mind doing business with him, though. Jonny had a certain reckless charm, and they were almost family. Pat was virtually a brother to Rex. Sadly, his own position in the Darby hierarchy didn't come with the same privileges that Jonny had, but there was still a connection there.

A For Sale sign had gone up outside his own home yesterday, his slut of a mother refusing to backtrack on her determination to flog the flat. He looked around the basement, at the large empty space, and considered the possibilities it contained. If the worst came to the worst, he could always doss down here. There was electricity, a water supply and even a bog. It would do, short term, if he couldn't find anything better.

Despite his current problems, Milo had ambitious long-term plans. He needed to inveigle himself deeper into the Darby family, and Marian was his way in. She was a rich woman now, even if she couldn't immediately lay her hands on the money. What had begun as a no-strings relationship, a casual fucking, suddenly had prospects.

He glanced over at Jonny, thinking that they both wanted the same thing: to be rich, to be respected, to be able to do what they wanted when they wanted. It was how they were going to achieve it that still needed to be properly worked out. Jonny, he was sure, was already scheming, his mind set on the big prize. But Milo had no intention of being left behind. Wherever Jonny was going, he was going too.

28

By the time Friday afternoon came around, Carmen was exhausted – her legs ached, her feet hurt – but she was also faintly proud of herself. She had arrived promptly every morning and could now negotiate the hectic breakfast and lunch service with the minimum of mistakes and a decent level of efficiency. She had mastered the art of doing several things at once and learned that a ready smile and a bit of banter could earn her the occasional tip – nothing life-changing, but every little helped.

During quieter moments, Carmen had also gleaned a fair amount about her boss. Joan Devlin had bought the café with her husband fifteen years ago, been promptly widowed, and had run the place on her own ever since. She had almost boundless energy, working from six till six Monday to Friday, and nine to five on Saturdays. Only on Sunday was the café closed.

Joan was the fount of all knowledge when it came to the female customers and knew everything about them. The café was a hotbed of gossip: whose husband was sleeping around, who was pregnant, who was up in court for shoplifting. From around eleven the local women came in, lugging their groceries, and settled, like a flock of starlings, in chattering groups around the room.

Carmen was already growing fond of Lottie. She was fifteen but young for her age, and she struggled with all but the most basic of tasks. Because of this she was rarely called upon to serve tables, even when the café was busy. By the time Joan had explained where table number six or table number ten was, Lottie had already forgotten. The girl was good-natured, though, and always tried her best. Like a curious child, she was forever asking personal questions, and Carmen, who didn't want the truth coming out, had to be careful how she answered.

She was starting to recognise the regulars now, even to learn a few names. She knew which blokes had straying hands and which were all bark but no bite. Terry Street hadn't shown his face again, but the other bloke, Gordie, had just come in and ordered a brew.

'Here,' Joan said, passing an envelope across the counter to Carmen along with a mug of tea. 'Give him this.'

Carmen could tell from the feel of the envelope that there was money inside. She went over to Gordie and placed both items on the table, trying to keep her expression neutral. Although it irked her that Joan had to hand over part of her hard-earned profit to a local thug – a thug whose boss she might even be related to – she wasn't stupid enough to let it show.

Gordie deftly palmed the envelope into his pocket and said, 'Cheers.' Then, before she had the chance to walk away, he asked: 'Where you from, love?'

'Notting Hill,' she said, sticking to the original story she'd told Joan.

Gordie pondered on this for a few seconds with his eyes firmly fixed on her. 'What's your surname, then?'

None of your damn business, is how she wanted to respond, but she knew that would only provoke even more curiosity. 'Baxter.'

Gordie's brow furrowed and she could sense the cogs revolving in his tiny brain. 'Baxter,' he repeated. 'You got a brother?'

'No. No brothers, no sisters. It's just me. Why?'

'You look familiar, that's all.'

There was nothing friendly about the way Gordie was looking at her, nothing to suggest that the reason he was asking these questions was down to a misguided chat-up technique or a clumsy attempt at small talk. She smiled, laughing lightly. 'Oh, people are always saying that. I must have one of those faces.'

'It'll come back to me,' he said ominously.

Praying that it wouldn't, Carmen returned to the counter. She wondered how their paths could have crossed, unable to imagine him at Lola's or any of the other places she and Clive had frequented. Perhaps it was just a case of mistaken identity. If it wasn't and he eventually put the right name to her face, she would have a lot of explaining to do.

Carmen glanced at Joan, debating whether to come clean or not. People didn't like being deceived. Perhaps she should tell her, reveal who she really was and why she'd left home. But then again, Gordie might have made a genuine mistake – or, if he hadn't, might never find the name he was grappling for.

'You all right, love?' Joan asked. 'Did that ugly sod say something to you?'

Carmen quickly shook her head. 'No, nothing. It's not that. I was just . . .' She searched her mind for a reasonable explanation as to why her face had assumed such an anxious expression, shrugged, and said, 'It just annoys me, that's all, the way they expect you to pay them like that.'

'Well, it's probably best to keep that opinion to yourself. For your own sake, I mean.' She paused and then added, 'And for mine too, come to that. Joe Quinn ain't the forgiving sort.'

Carmen hadn't had the pleasure of meeting Quinn yet, but already she'd formed an association in her head between him and her father: two bullies, two men who expected everyone to dance to their tune. 'Course not. I wouldn't ever say anything, not to their faces at least. Doesn't stop me thinking it, though.'

'You and me both, love.' Joan reached down under the counter and pulled out another envelope. 'Anyway, you get off now. It's after two. Here's your pay for the four days you've done.'

Carmen took her wages, already thinking of how she could spend them. 'Thanks.' She hesitated, wanting to ask if she'd passed her trial and now had a permanent position, and feeling on edge in case the answer might be no. 'I'll ... er, see you on Monday then?'

'Unless you've got something better to do,' Joan said.

Relieved, Carmen went through to the back, took off her apron, retrieved her handbag, said goodbye to Lottie and Joan, and left. Gordie was still sitting at the table, hunched over his mug of tea, his eyes squinting in concentration as if he was thinking hard about something. She could only hope that something wasn't her.

29

The weather had turned blustery with a chill wind blowing. The clouds were low, and the sky was as grey and gloomy as Station Road. Carmen shivered a little as she walked back towards the B&B, desperate to slip off her shoes, collapse on to the bed and take the weight off her feet. The one advantage to her exhaustion was that she now slept soundly at night, not rousing until the shrill ringing of the alarm clock jerked her awake at five thirty every morning.

Carmen already had her Saturday planned. There was a market, so Joan said, and she intended to go there tomorrow. She needed a dressing gown, something to slip on when she went to the bathroom. Although she was usually up before anyone else, there was always the danger of running into an early morning pee-er. The other guests – there were only three of them at present – were all middle-aged men, and although they were now on nodding acquaintance, she had no desire to meet them in her nightclothes.

Of course, if she was going to stay in Kellston she would

need to find a more permanent place to live. She had bought a local paper this morning, hoping there would be a bedsit or a flat share offered in the small ads at the back. She had ringed a few during her break, but none looked especially promising.

Carmen had been putting off this big step, partly because she hadn't been sure about the job, and partly because there was still a tiny hope lurking in the back of her mind that all the upheavals of the past week, all the angst and recriminations, might somehow be miraculously reversed and she would find herself reinstated as beloved youngest daughter and fiancée.

Beloved? She rolled her eyes. What was she thinking? There hadn't been much evidence of that, not from her father when he was changing the locks or from Clive when he had made it clear that his love was entirely dependent on a hefty inheritance from Rex Darby. Even though she knew all this, she couldn't quite let go of the hope.

Carmen felt her mouth go dry, her stomach shift. It was alarming to be out in the world on her own, with no one to fall back on, no one to talk to. She thought of her bedroom back home with its comfortable bed, deep-pile carpet and wardrobes full of clothes. She wished she could close her eyes and open them again to find herself in Belgravia. Was anyone missing her? Her father was trying to prove a point by barring her from the house, and she was doing the same by coming here to Kellston and getting herself a job. She didn't want to be the one to give in first, but the idea of it being for ever, of her *never* going home, filled her with a dull enveloping dread.

'Stop it,' she muttered, afraid that she was losing her nerve. 'Don't be such a baby. You can do this.'

'That's a bad sign, talking to yourself.'

Carmen jumped, whirling around to find Terry Street

144

standing right behind her. Her hand rose to her chest in surprise. 'Oh, it's you! You shouldn't sneak up on people like that.'

Terry put his hands in his pockets and grinned. 'I'm not sneaking. I was just walking behind you. Were you having a private conversation, or can anyone join in?'

Carmen felt her face colour, wondering how much he'd heard. 'Private,' she said firmly.

'Okay, only I'm a good listener if you've got something on your mind. You seem kind of—'

'Kind of what?'

'Like something's bothering you.'

'Or *someone*,' she said, arching her eyebrows and giving him a withering look.

Terry laughed, showing a row of straight white teeth. 'All right, I can take a hint.' He took a step back as if he was about to go, but then stopped and said, 'Have you thought any more about that drink?'

'No.'

'No, you haven't thought about it or no, you don't fancy it?'

'Both,' she said, holding up her left hand so he could see her engagement ring. It was surplus to requirement now, of course, but he didn't know that. 'Sorry, but I'm attached.'

'Not married yet, though. All is not lost.'

Carmen smiled, despite herself. Terry Street certainly couldn't be described as shy. He had the confidence that most attractive men had, and the cheek too. But she wasn't in the market for another charmer, and especially not one from the criminal classes. 'I have to go.'

'See you around, then.'

'Sure,' she said, hoping that she wouldn't, although that wasn't very realistic with him knowing where she worked. Terry Street was, she suspected, a man who wasn't used to women saying no to him. Still, at least he wasn't getting all miffed about it. Some blokes took offence when things didn't go their way.

'If you change your mind about that drink, I'll be in the Fox later.'

Carmen gave him a nod, but he had already turned away. She studied the back of his head before her gaze gradually slid down to the slope of his shoulders, the line of his spine and the movement of his hips. He walked with a confident swagger, as if he owned the world and everything in it. Then, aware that if he looked back over his shoulder he would see her gawping at him, she quickly averted her eyes and set off for the B&B.

30

Milo lay on his back gazing up at the ceiling. Sweat glistened on his skin. His heart was still pumping hard, his chest rising and falling as if he'd just completed a 100 yard sprint. Sated but peevish, he turned his face to look at Marian. Already she was propped up on one elbow, lighting a cigarette.

'Jonny told me he was selling this place.'

'Not this again,' she said, sounding bored. 'Why do you keep going on about it? I'm sure he will sell it – eventually.'

'I could move in here. Why not? You're hardly going to use it. Wouldn't you like me here waiting for you whenever you come to town?'

Marian inhaled and released the smoke with a thin sound like a sigh. 'That would be lovely, darling. But how am I going to explain your unfortunate presence when Hugh stays here? Three's a crowd, so they say.'

'You could book into the Gryphon like you usually do.'

'Well, that's going to seem a little odd when I'm renting this place. I thought you'd be pleased. Now I've got this flat we'll always have somewhere to meet up.'

'I'd be more pleased if I had a roof over my own head.'

Marian put the cigarette between his lips, waited for him to take a drag and removed it again. 'You're hardly living on the streets, darling. It'll be months before your mother finds a buyer. Something will turn up in the meantime. Have another word with Pat; he's got lots of flats on the books.'

Milo couldn't help feeling riled. It was all right for her with her big house in the country, and now another pad in town, but what did he have? Sod all was what he had. And the only thing Pat had to offer was one of Rex's run-down dumps that wasn't fit for a dog to live in. He placed his hands behind his head and frowned. Marian, like his mother, was a self-centred bitch who only ever thought about herself.

'Oh, don't sulk, darling. It's not a good look.'

'I ain't sulking.'

'So tell your face that. And how come you and Jonny are so pally all of a sudden?'

'What do you mean?'

Marian ran a finger down the length of his arm. 'You said he told you he was selling the flat.'

'I was in the office when Elizabeth gave him the keys to your dad's place.' And then, because Milo was in the mood for some stirring, he added: 'Doesn't it bother you, the two of them moving in with him?'

'Why should it?'

'I dunno. Call me suspicious but it seems kind of strange, this sudden interest in his welfare.'

Marian shrugged her lovely shoulders. 'I shouldn't imagine it's anything to do with his welfare. It was Jonny's idea. He just fancied a more desirable postcode – and a free ride, probably. You know what he's like, always broke, always looking for something better without having to pay for it.'

'Possession is nine-tenths of the law, ain't that what they say?'

Marian's eyes narrowed and she stared at him. 'What have you heard?'

'Nothin'. Nothin' much. Just got the impression from Jonny that *she* was the one pushing for it as much as him. You should watch out. That house is worth a fuckin' fortune. And now they've got their feet under the table . . .'

'It isn't like that,' she said.

'You sure of that?'

'She's my sister,' Marian said. 'She's not going to screw me over.'

Milo knew it wasn't wise to rock the boat too much while he was working with Jonny, but he couldn't resist the opportunity to wipe that smug expression off her face. 'I'm just looking out for you, babe. When it comes to money you can't trust no one.'

Marian got out of bed, slipped into her dressing gown, and made a point of looking at her watch. 'You'd better get dressed. I'm running late.'

'You trying to get rid of me?'

'Yes, I've got things to do.'

Milo reached out and took hold of her wrist. 'So cancel them. We can spend the afternoon here.'

'Another time. I'll give you a call next week.' And then, in case he hadn't got the message, she freed her hand from his, grabbed a towel and said, 'I'm going to take a shower. You can let yourself out, can't you?'

'What do you think Hugh would do if he found out about us?'

Marian stopped in her tracks and stared at him. There was something in his voice, something almost threatening. 'And why should Hugh find out?'

'I dunno. I'm just curious.'

'I should think he'd divorce me and kill you.'

Milo laughed. 'What, old Hugh? He's never struck me as the murderous type.'

'Oh, he wouldn't do it himself. He'd sell a few sheep and get someone else to do it.' Then, without waiting for a response, she went into the bathroom and locked the door. As she stood under the hot water, she decided that the anticipation of meeting up with Milo was often better than the reality. The sex was great, but once it was over, she had no desire to remain in his company. Especially when he was being sulky and resentful. She hadn't liked the question about Hugh. And what was he thinking, suggesting that he move in here? The very idea was ludicrous. What they had was casual, a fling, a relationship without strings. She didn't want a full-time lover living in her flat, cramping her style and making demands on her time.

She spent longer than usual in the shower, hoping that Milo would be gone by the time she got out. What he had said was preying on her mind. The stuff about Hugh finding out about them, and Jonny's plans as regards the house. She would need to keep an eye on her brother-in-law, make sure that she protected her interests. Although she'd been intending to go shopping this afternoon, she decided to head over to Belgravia instead; it wouldn't do any harm to spend some time with her father, perhaps even take him out to dinner this evening.

It was fifteen minutes before Marian emerged from the bathroom and thankfully the flat was now Milo-free. She got dressed, combed her hair, and did her make-up. She ripped off the sheets and threw them in the washing machine, took clean bedding from the cupboard in the hall and remade the bed. She removed the ashtray from the bedside table. In the living room she cleared away the two glasses and the half-empty bottle of wine, carried them through to the kitchen, put the bottle in the fridge, rinsed the glasses out in the sink, dried them and put them back on the shelf.

Only then, when everything was back to how it should be, did Marian stop and relax. She stood by the kitchen door and gazed at her living room. She liked her new bolthole in Camden. It had everything she needed, even if the furnishings weren't exactly to her taste. Still, she could soon sort that out. The first thing she had done on taking possession was to change the locks in case Hazel or Jonny dropped by uninvited. Yes, she thought, looking round, this was the beginning of a whole new life. Whether it would include Milo, however, was debatable. She was starting to wonder whether he was more trouble than he was worth.

31

It was only twenty-four hours since Jonny had moved into Upper Belgrave Street and already Rex was getting on his nerves. Lording it over them like they were the poor relations and should be bloody grateful to be allowed to live in his house. He felt the tension in his body, the anger bubbling up inside him. Hazel hadn't wanted to come here, *really* hadn't wanted to come, but he'd talked her round. And he didn't regret it, even if Rex was causing him grief. It was a means to an end, nothing else.

Jonny went from room to room, picking things up – a silver cigarette box, a bronze art deco statuette, a Chinese-looking vase – assessing their value and putting them down. It was the first time he'd ever been here on his own. Rex and Hazel had gone out for lunch, but he'd declined the invitation, saying that he'd wanted to finish the unpacking. Not that there was much to unpack. They had left all the furniture in Camden, so it was just clothes and other miscellaneous junk.

He opened and closed drawers, discovering a ten-pound

note in the drawing-room cabinet. His first instinct was to snaffle it, but then he wondered if it was a trap, whether Rex had deliberately left it there to be found. Some kind of test, perhaps, to see how honest his son-in-law was. Reluctantly he left it where it was.

The hallway had a marble floor and a high ceiling, giving the space an airy feel. He stood and looked up at the grand, blue-carpeted staircase. One shove in the back was all it would take to send Rex tumbling down those stairs. But it was risky. What if the fall didn't kill him? What if he remembered that he'd been pushed? No, when the time came, the 'accident' would have to be failsafe, beyond doubt, one hundred per cent certain, with no room for error.

Jonny continued to travel up the house. He investigated the fancy bathrooms and poked his nose into the bedrooms, most of them unused now, and eventually found his way to the master. It was, of course, the largest and grandest of all the bedrooms, with an ostentatious four-poster dominating the room. There were plush rose-coloured drapes and an expensive-looking pink and grey bird wallpaper, both of which he suspected had been chosen by Rosa rather than Rex. Apart from this there was no trace of her: no photographs, no reminders, nothing at all. It was the same downstairs: as if not content with her passing, Rex had gone on to try and obliterate every trace.

Jonny took a step inside, feeling his feet sink into the deep-pile carpet. On the wall opposite the bed was a striking portrait of a young woman in a blue silk dressing gown reclining on a chaise longue. Dark hair tumbled over her shoulders. Long legs with creamy thighs were revealed along with one shapely bare breast and a large brown nipple. A pair of wide dark eyes gazed out provocatively from the canvas.

He studied it for a while. It was erotic and sexy, the kind of picture you wouldn't mind staring at when you were in bed. Typical of Rex, he thought, to put porn on his wall and call it art. The woman looked a little like Rosa but not enough for it to actually be her. Hazel said her father had killed her mother, not in the literal sense – although he wouldn't have put it past the old bastard – but in the way he had treated her. Or maybe it was Marian who'd said it, and Hazel had just agreed. He couldn't remember. It had been a long time ago, in a West End restaurant, although he couldn't remember which restaurant either. Anyway, Hazel usually agreed with whatever her sister said: she was like the trusted sidekick, always playing second fiddle, always trying too hard to please.

Jonny turned away from the painting, skirted the bed and looked out of the window down on to Upper Belgrave Street, taking care to stand to one side in case Rex and Hazel suddenly appeared. Not that they would. They'd only been gone half an hour and Rex liked to enjoy a leisurely lunch. However, he would still have moved swiftly away if he hadn't seen Lord Lucan approaching.

Jonny studied the top of the man's head as he passed beneath him and noted his tailored suit and how he walked with that stiff Army gait. Richard John Bingham was the Seventh Earl of Lucan, an Anglo-Irish aristocrat with all the advantages that brings. Still, he didn't have everything. The gossip columns had been full of how he'd separated from his wife and was fighting for custody of the three kids. His wife still lived in the family home – a stone's throw away in Lower Belgrave Street – and Lucan had moved into a nearby flat in Elizabeth Street.

Jonny's upper lip curled a little. All it took was an accident of birth to determine whether you were top of the pile or the bottom. He felt envy and resentment and a simmering anger. Lucan wouldn't have sleepless nights when he lost at the games table, wouldn't have to worry about how to pay his debts or have bloody thugs queuing up to kick the shit out of him. No, all *he* had to do was get out his chequebook and sign on the dotted line.

But for all that, Jonny still wanted to make his acquaintance. He would contrive a meeting, a series of meetings, he thought. Two local residents passing on the street: what could be more natural than to stop and chat? Or maybe just a nod the first couple of times, a polite acknowledgement of the other's existence, before moving on to a comment about the weather or the state of the economy. Maybe a disparaging remark about Harold Wilson's return to power would go down well too.

Jonny watched until Lucan disappeared from view before stepping away from the window and continuing his tour of the house. He didn't probe too deeply into this desire to be on speaking terms with the lord, only telling himself that such contacts could be useful in a world that was run by the rich and powerful.

On the third floor he glanced into unused bedrooms, established there was nothing of interest in them, and moved on. The attic was the only place left to explore, but when he tried the door to the staircase it was locked. He rattled the handle, wondering where the key was kept. Down in Rex's bedroom, perhaps, or he might have it on him. Jonny was curious as to why it was locked. There was only ever one reason why people denied access to an area and that was because they had something to hide.

He kneeled and peered through the keyhole but all he could see were a few bare wood stairs. What could be up there? Or perhaps he should be asking who? Maybe Rosa wasn't dead at all but secured in the attic like that mad woman in that old black-and-white film, Jane something or other, that Hazel had once made him watch. Jonny grinned, knowing it couldn't be true, but still enjoying the idea of it. Rex was the type to have dark secrets.

He got to his feet again, wondering whether he should risk doing a search of Rex's bedroom for the key. There could be valuable stuff up there, items that could be pawned without anyone noticing, and then redeemed and put back before they were missed. A whole treasure trove, perhaps.

Unable to resist the temptation, Jonny quickly descended the stairs, hurried back into Rex's room, made a surreptitious survey of the street, and then set about carefully rifling through all the drawers and wardrobes. There was an almost full bottle of sleeping pills on the bedside table, and Jonny stopped his search for a moment. He unscrewed the lid, shook a few pills out into the palm of his hand and stared at them for a while before slipping them into his jacket pocket. Although he had no firm plan, he thought they might come in useful at some time in the future. Then, because he was a cautious man, he wiped his prints off the bottle.

Jonny made sure that he left everything exactly as he'd found it, moving nothing out of place, leaving no evidence that he'd ever been there, but after twenty minutes there was still no sign of the key.

Disappointed, he went downstairs and made a further search of the drawing room, the living room and even the kitchen. He found a few stray keys, but none that would fit the old attic lock. He hissed through his teeth, frustrated. Still, it wasn't the end of the world. The attic wasn't going anywhere; he just had to figure out how to get in.

32

It was six thirty and already the Fox was busy. Friday was payday for most of the locals and they came straight from work to meet up with their mates and start spending. There was a queue at the bar and most of the tables were occupied. Later the girls would arrive in their glad rags, coiffed and perfumed and looking for love. Friday night was party night. It was a little goldmine, Terry thought, as he sat with his back against the wall, surveying the room. One day he'd like to own a pub like this.

The point about the Fox was that it didn't cater to any one type of person: everybody, from villains to the law, from students to businessmen, frequented the place. It was a curious mingling that shouldn't have worked but somehow did. People came from out of the area, from all over the place, because the beer was good and the atmosphere convivial. There was rarely any trouble, which was why the incident with Connor and the baseball bat would stay in people's minds.

A few more of the firm had drifted in and the table was starting to fill up. Joe Quinn was sitting to Terry's right, and

Gordie was sitting opposite. Connor was complaining about something not worth listening to. Vinnie Keane – Terry's closest ally – was at the bar getting a round in. Most of them were in a good mood, the money having been collected and divided according to status and position. Terry had a thick wad of notes in his inside jacket pocket, his reward for keeping things running smoothly.

He glanced towards the door whenever it opened, mainly just to check on who was coming in, partly in case the lovely Carly changed her mind and decided to show up after all. What were the odds? Long, he decided, but it didn't stop him hoping. Vinnie came back with a tray full of drinks and distributed the glasses, Joe's first and then the rest.

Gordie sniggered into his pint. 'She ain't coming, mate. She's got better things to do on a Friday night.'

'Huh?' Terry said, pretending that he didn't understand. 'What are you going on about?'

'He's got the hots for that new bird at the caff,' Gordie gleefully explained to everyone. 'Couldn't keep his bleedin' eyes off her. Love at first sight. Shame the feeling weren't mutual.'

'Yeah, yeah,' Terry said. 'Like you weren't looking or nothin'.'

'She's out of your league, mate. You haven't got a chance. She's . . .' Gordie stopped, his mouth still open. 'Shit, God, yeah, I've just realised who she is. I knew I'd seen her somewhere before.' He rubbed his hands together and grinned. 'You might be interested in this, boss,' he said to Joe Quinn.

'What, some bloody bird?' Joe said sneeringly.

'Not just any bird. She's Rex Darby's daughter.'

At the mention of Darby's name, Quinn's face grew dark. His whole expression changed, his eyes narrowing to slits. 'What the hell would Darby's girl be doing working in a local caff?'

'I dunno, but it's her.'

'Or just looks like her.'

'Nah, it's her,' Gordie said insistently. 'I swear it, boss. I was on the door at Lola's over the summer. She's engaged to the manager – Grainger's his name, Clive Grainger – and she was there with him more than once. One of the other lads told me she was Darby's youngest daughter. I don't remember her name. It weren't Carly, though.'

'Carmen,' Quinn said. 'That's her name.' He looked at Terry. 'What do *you* think?'

'I've never seen her before. She's got a ring on her finger, though. A big flashy diamond. Claims she comes from Notting Hill but . . .' Terry gave a shrug. 'If she is Darby's kid, what's she doing in Kellston?'

Quinn's hands lay on the table, curled into two loose fists. His voice shifted down an octave, becoming a low growl. 'Find out for me, Terry. Find out what the fuck she's up to.'

And Terry, who had no objection to spending more time with the lovely Carly or Carmen or whatever her name was, gave a nod and said, 'Leave it to me.'

'You know where she's living?'

'I'll find out. Just give me a day or two.'

'Darby's daughter,' Quinn said, as if he still couldn't quite believe it. 'Rosa's girl.' Then he turned his attention back to Gordie and snarled, 'You'd better not be wasting my bloody time.'

But Gordie was sticking to his guns. 'I'm not, boss. I knew I'd seen her someplace else soon as I clapped eyes on her. Didn't I say, Terry? Didn't I say I knew her?'

Terry didn't get a chance to reply, because Connor, who was already on the wrong side of sober, decided to stick his oar in.

'She ain't got no right being in Kellston. That Darby lot ain't welcome round 'ere. She's taking bloody liberties.'

'Stay out of it,' Quinn said to his son. 'It's nothin' to do with you. It ain't any of your business.'

Connor's face twisted. 'This is *family* business. Don't go saying it ain't got nothin' to do with me. We all know what that Rex Darby done.'

'Yeah, and he'll pay for it. But you stay away from her, right? I'll sort this in my own way.'

Terry, who was still in the dark as to the details of the Quinn/Darby feud, kept quiet. He was one of the youngest in the firm and this must be ancient history, hostilities dating back to way before his time. If Carly was Darby's daughter, then Terry had given her brother-in-law a beating last Saturday night, something that would hardly recommend him to her. But she had given no sign of recognising his name, which suggested that Jonny had either kept his mouth shut or didn't know who'd attacked him.

It was another hour before the group drifted apart and Terry was able to pull Vinnie Keane aside and ask him about the feud. Vinnie lifted his eyebrows and said, 'You got any sense you'll stay well clear.'

'Yeah, but it's always useful to know exactly what you're staying clear of.'

Vinnie was about fifteen years older than Terry, a great bear of a man, well over six foot and with the kind of physique that deterred all but the most insanely stupid from ever picking a fight with him. They'd formed a bond over the past few years, a friendship based on mutual respect and a shared distrust of Joe Quinn. Now Vinnie leaned back against the bar, pulled on his fag, and had a quick look round to make sure nobody was listening.

'Rex Darby comes from round here, although you wouldn't think it to see him now. Fancy house in Belgravia, millions in the bank, the kind of lifestyle you and me can only dream about. But he was a right villain in his day. Anyway, he and Michael Quinn – that's Joe's cousin – were best mates growing up, in and out of each other's houses, always had each other's backs, you know the type of thing. They went on to work together and pulled off some decent jobs.' Vinnie paused to take a swig of his pint. 'So, everything's peachy, everything's coming up roses, until Darby sets his sights on Michael's little sister. Michael's none too pleased about this and it all kicks off, a major falling out, World War Three.'

'All over a bird,' Terry said.

'Not just any bird: a *sister*. It's different, ain't it? Darby was years older than Rosa and he had a reputation. Michael didn't want him screwing her over. Or screwing her at all, come to that.' Vinnie's eyes made another quick survey of the surrounding area. 'So the two of them, Darby and Rosa, want to get hitched, but Michael's putting his foot down, saying over his dead body and the rest of it. Anyway, they went ahead with the wedding, but it was never the same between Rex and Michael again. Then – and this is about six or seven years later – Michael disappears, walks out of his house and never comes back, and even though Darby swears it had nothing to do with him, there were rumours flying round.'

'Does Joe think he topped him?'

'When it suits him. Because Michael never came back, did he? And it gets worse. About twenty years ago, Rosa killed herself, and Joe blames Rex Darby for that too. Reckons he drove her to it. Whether he did or not . . .' Vinnie shrugged his enormous shoulders. 'Who's to say? From what I've heard about Rex Darby, he ain't the easiest bloke to get along with.'

'Were they close then, Joe and Rosa?'

Vinnie gave a snort. 'Nah, Joe ain't close to no one, is he?

Only person he cares about is himself. But it gave him another reason to hate Darby. And if this girl is Carmen, he'll be looking to see what use he can make of it, where the advantage might be.'

'But she's Rosa's daughter as well as Darby's.'

'Family only means something to Joe when it suits him. I don't reckon he'll be putting out the bunting any time soon. Nah, leverage is all he'll be interested in. He'll be thinking of the benefits, of the gain, of what he can do with this to manipulate Darby.'

'Not good news for Carmen, then.'

'I wouldn't hang around if I was her.'

33

On Saturday morning Carmen spent two hours at Kellston market perusing the stalls and making a few careful purchases. With her wages from the café, she bought a pair of black trousers to replace the skirt she'd been wearing for work – a safer option, she decided, when there were wandering hands to deal with – a dark red sweater, and some notepaper and envelopes so she could write to Lucy. She returned to the B&B at around midday, emptied her carrier bag and wondered what to do next.

After the noise and bustle of the market, her room felt oddly still. The traffic still roared past outside, but it had slipped into the background, a noise that was so constant she barely noticed it any more. It occurred to her, with a sinking heart, that she had proved nothing by her four days' hard work. Anyone could manage that. It was doing it long term that was the real challenge, the constant juggling of money, the struggle to make ends meet. When she looked ahead, she could only see all the difficulties and the loneliness.

Quickly she gave herself a mental shake. What about the

positives? She was answerable to no one. She could do what she liked (within certain financial parameters). She didn't have to put up with her father's rages or his constant manipulations. She would not just be somebody's daughter or somebody's wife, but a person in her own right. And yes, it was scary to be without a safety net, to know that the only person she could rely on was herself, but she could do it.

Carmen was considering this new version of herself – a self-sufficient, confident woman – when the doorbell went. She didn't take much notice – it was probably someone looking for a room – and so was surprised to hear a knock on her door a minute or two later. She opened it to find Mrs Jordan standing there.

The landlady's mouth was pursed and disapproving. 'There's a gentleman here to see you, Miss Baxter.'

'For me?' Carmen said. 'Who is it?'

'I've asked him to wait outside.' And with that, Mrs Jordan gave her a censorious look, turned, and walked away.

Carmen ran over to the window and peered down into the street but whoever it was must be standing in the porch. Anyway, she didn't need to see to know who it was. A thrill ran through her. It had to be Clive. He had found her, tracked her down and had come to beg her to give him a second chance. And suddenly all her thoughts of independence, of making it on her own, evaporated. So he *did* love her! He had realised what she meant to him and come to put everything right.

She quickly examined her face in the mirror, put on some lipstick, and ran a comb through her hair. She'd looked better, but it would have to do. Grabbing her jacket and bag, she headed out of the door and down the stairs. Slow down, she told herself. Don't look *too* keen.

She halted in the hall, took a deep breath, and opened the

164

front door, unable to keep the smile off her face. Instead of Clive standing on the doorstep, it was Terry Street.

'Oh,' she said, as her smile faded, and her dreams shattered into crushing disappointment. 'It's you.'

'No need to sound so pleased about it. How are you doing? Have you got a minute? We need to talk.'

'Talk?' Carmen repeated. She was aware of how snappy she sounded but didn't care. She felt foolish for ever imagining it could have been Clive. Humiliated too, as if Terry could see right through her and knew that she'd been hoping it was some-one else. 'Talk about what?'

Terry peered around her, suspecting perhaps that Mrs Jordan was still in the vicinity. 'Let's go somewhere else. I don't want to do this on the doorstep.'

'Do what?' she asked, still trying to work out what she and Terry could possibly have to talk about. Or was this just some dreadful follow-up to his chat-up attempt? 'Look, if it's about that drink . . .'

'It's not. It's nothin' to do with that. Come on, I'll buy you a coffee.'

'I'm busy,' she said stubbornly.

Terry gave her a long stare, shrugged, and reversed a few steps back. 'Okay, but it's about Rex Darby. I think you might want to hear it.'

Carmen jumped at the name, knowing in that moment that her secret was out. 'Who?' she asked weakly, and it sounded pathetic even to her own ears. Then, aware of some movement behind her, and worried that the landlady might be earwigging, she decided that Terry was right: the doorstep wasn't the place for this conversation. 'All right,' she said, moving forwards into the porch and closing the door behind her.

'Shall we go to the caff?'

Carmen quickly shook her head, not wanting Joan to see her with Terry. It would be like fraternising with the enemy. 'Somewhere else.'

'The Fox? Or there's another caff, Connolly's, up the road.'

'Let's go there,' she said. 'Connolly's.'

'Connolly's it is.'

'So what's this all about?' Carmen said while they walked side by side along Station Road. She could have persisted with her denial of ever having heard the name Rex Darby before, but knew it was pointless. 'Has he been here, looking for me?'

'Not that I know of. So what should I call you, Carmen or Carly?'

Carmen gave him a sidelong glance. 'Whatever you like.'

'I'll stick with Carly, then, seeing as that's the name you're using round here.'

They turned right on to the high street. Carmen was feeling anxious now, and somewhat defeated. 'How did you find out?'

'I'll explain at the caff.'

34

The street was crammed with Saturday shoppers, people emerging from the train station, mums with prams, and loitering teenagers. Carmen and Terry had to weave a path through the throng, their elbows occasionally touching. Knowing she was going to have to wait to get the major question answered, she tried a minor one instead. 'How did you find out where I'm living?'

'Lottie told me, but don't be mad at her. She didn't want to. I wheedled it out of her.'

'It's no big secret,' Carmen said. 'I was just curious.'

'Good. No damage done, then.'

Even in her nervy state of mind, Carmen noticed how women looked at Terry, the way some of them just sneaked glances and others blatantly stared. She didn't know why this annoyed her. Perhaps it reminded her of Clive's popularity with the opposite sex. Or maybe, because she *could* have been Terry's girlfriend – how were they to know? – she found it unpleasantly rude and predatory.

Terry, who'd been quiet for a minute or so, broke the silence. 'Who were you expecting to see when you came to the door?'

'No one,' Carmen said.

'The sort of no one who makes you look miserable as sin when you realise it's only me.'

'If you say so.'

'None of my business, right?' Terry said, and grinned. 'Sorry, I'll keep my nose out of it.'

Connolly's, up at the far end of the high street, was doing a brisk trade. They got one of the few remaining tables, sat down, ordered coffee from the waitress, and lapsed back into silence. All around them, voices rose and fell, mingling with the insistent hiss of the coffee machine and the sound of the radio. 'So?' Carmen said eventually, when Terry showed no sign of restarting the conversation.

'Yeah,' he said, frowning, as if he hadn't quite decided how to begin. Then he leaned forward, put his palms on the table and said, 'Look, I'm going to be straight with you: it was Joe Quinn who asked me to do this, to talk to you. He wants to know what you're doing in Kellston.'

Now it was Carmen's turn to frown. 'I don't understand. What's it got to do with him?'

'An old feud, apparently. Between him and your old man. He thinks you're up to something. He doesn't understand why you're here, slumming it in Kellston, instead of in your nice big house in Belgravia. Joe's got a very suspicious mind.'

'What on earth could I be up to?'

Terry lifted and dropped his shoulders. 'Hard to say what goes on in Joe's head.'

'How does he even know who I am?'

'Ah, that was down to Gordie. He recognised you from

when he was working on the door at Lola's. In the summer, I think it was. Couldn't wait to pass on the good news to Joe.'

Carmen nodded. Now all the questions Gordie had been asking her made sense.

'So why are you here?' Terry asked. 'What's the deal? Have you run away from home?'

'I'm not ten. I just fancied a change.'

Terry's expression was sceptical. 'In Kellston?'

'Why not? If it's good enough for you, why isn't it good enough for me?'

The waitress saved him from having to answer immediately. She put the two cups of coffee on the table and flashed Terry a smile before hurrying off to deal with another customer.

'Well?' Carmen prompted.

'I'm just making the best of a bad job. I wouldn't choose to live here if I didn't have to. You, on the other hand, have a perfectly good home but you're choosing to live in a crummy bed and breakfast with a landlady who disapproves of gentleman visitors.'

Carmen doubted if Terry could be classified as a gentleman but kept the thought to herself. 'It's not crummy. It's actually very clean and nice.'

'Yeah,' Terry said as if he didn't believe a word. 'But in comparison . . .'

'I still don't see why it's any of Joe's business. I don't even know him. I'm presuming he's related to my mother in some way?'

'Her cousin,' Terry said. 'I'm not sure what that makes the two of you, second cousins or something?'

'And I don't know anything about a feud. I only came to Kellston by chance. It wasn't planned. My dad brought me here once when I was a kid to show me where he'd grown up. So you can tell Joe that. My coming here has nothing to do with him.'

'You two had a falling out, you and your dad?'

Carmen lifted her mug, blew across the surface of the hot coffee, and took a sip. 'Something like that.'

'Must have been serious.'

'Serious enough.'

'If I were you, I'd go home. Or at least somewhere away from here.'

Both these options filled Carmen with dismay. She'd only just got settled in, found herself a job and somewhere to live, and now she was supposed to move on again. But then the full import of what he was saying struck her. Ice slid down her spine. She swallowed hard and said, 'What do you mean?'

'Just that Joe isn't the nicest guy in the world. He's got a problem with your old man and might try and use you to get to him in some way.'

'What sort of way?'

'All I'm saying is that you don't want to get in the middle of this feud.'

'I don't even know what this feud is about.'

'You've never heard anything about it?'

'If I had I wouldn't be asking.'

'Fair enough,' Terry said. 'That's families for you.'

'Are you going to tell me, then?'

Terry drank some coffee and looked round the café before returning his gaze to her. 'I can only tell you what I've heard, second-hand, you know? It was all years ago, before my time – and yours, come to that.'

'Okay, but anything would help.'

So Terry told her about her late uncle, Michael Quinn, and the hostility there had been towards her father marrying her mother. And then the disappearance of Michael and how suspicion had fallen on Rex Darby. And finally, her mother's suicide, of which Rex was not judged to be entirely innocent either. She listened carefully, filing the information away in her head, wondering how it was that she'd been completely ignorant of all this while she was growing up.

When Terry had told her as much as he knew, Carmen scowled and said rather more loudly than she'd intended: 'My father might be a lot of things, but he's not a murderer.'

Two middle-aged women at the next table stopped talking and stared at Carmen. Carmen stared straight back until they got the message and resumed their own conversation.

'He's not,' she said again.

'Hey, no need to shoot the messenger,' Terry said softly. 'I'm not saying that he is. I'm only telling you what Joe *thinks*. Well, if he thinks at all. He's not that big in that department.'

'Doesn't sound as if you like him very much.'

'Have you liked all the bosses you've worked for?'

As Carmen had a somewhat limited experience of being an employee – a fact she had no wish to share with Terry – she chose to ignore the question. 'So what are you going to tell him?'

'What you've told me,' Terry said. 'That you're not here to cause any bother, that Rex didn't send you, that you're just minding your own business and maybe he should do the same.'

'Not that last bit,' she said, horrified, until she realised that he was only joking. 'That's not funny.'

Terry didn't apologise. 'Just thought I'd lighten the mood.'

Carmen, her mood in no way buoyed, asked, 'Do you think he'll be happy with that?'

'I'll let you know.'

Not reassured by his answer, Carmen played with her coffee mug. 'If I'd even guessed this might happen, I'd never have come here.'

'It's not too late to leave. Why not go home?'

Carmen, who had no intention of going into detail about the row with her father, said instead, 'Why should I? And I can't just walk out on Joan. It isn't fair.'

'I reckon that's the least of your worries.' Terry took out a pack of cigarettes, offered her one and, when she refused, lit one for himself.' He inhaled, blew out the smoke, smiled and said, 'Bit of a family trait, is it? Feuding?'

'All families fall out from time to time.'

'So what's the deal with you and Clive Grainger?'

Carmen's gaze automatically flew to the ring on her finger. 'I don't want to talk about it.'

'Oh, like that, is it?'

Suddenly Carmen wanted to get away. She needed time alone to think. 'What happens next? With Joe, I mean.'

'He might want to talk to you.'

'And what if I don't want to talk to him?'

'Well, nobody *wants* to talk to Joe but . . .'

'But?'

'Sometimes we all have to do things we don't want to do.'

35

After Terry had walked Carmen as close as she'd allow to the front door of the B&B, he crossed the road and went into the Fox. She was worried, understandably, and he'd wanted to re-assure her, to tell her not to stress over it too much, that before long Joe wouldn't be a problem. Except, of course, he hadn't been able to say that. That was the sort of thing that might stick in a person's head and might just pop to the surface when they heard that Joe Quinn had been murdered.

The Fox had the usual Saturday afternoon crowd in it. Terry pushed through to the bar, ordered himself a pint and, while he was waiting for his beer, took to thinking some more about Carmen. She was a desirable combination of aloofness and vulnerability. Attractive, too. There were lots of pretty girls out there, but she had something more about her. While he was pondering on what exactly it was that got his pulse racing so fast, someone tapped him on the shoulder. He turned to find Gordie standing behind him.

'Oi, Joe wants a word.'

Terry didn't like that 'Oi', or the way it was delivered, as if he was some flunkey who could be talked down to. But he didn't react other than to give Gordie a dirty look. 'Two minutes. I'm just waiting for my pint.'

Gordie trotted back to his master like the obedient dog he was, while Terry turned his attention back to the bar and collected his drink. Eventually, when he was good and ready, he sauntered over to the table.

Joe was sitting in state, surrounded by his usual entourage. Terry grabbed a stool from a neighbouring table and squeezed in between him and Connor. Joe stank of sweat and the sort of pungent aftershave that made you not want to breathe too deeply.

'Where's the girl?' Quinn snarled. 'I told you to bring her here.'

'She wouldn't come, Joe. I reckon she's not the pub sort. We went up to Connolly's for a coffee instead.' Terry took a long pull on his pint and put his glass down. 'Anyway, we had a chat, and she don't know nothin' about you and her old man or what you fell out about or anythin' about Michael.'

'You believe her?'

'Yeah, I believe her. She's just a rich kid who's had a barney with her dad and wants to prove she can make her own way in the world – well, at least for a week or two.'

'What did they fall out about?'

'She wouldn't say.'

'You should have made her fuckin' say.'

Terry wondered how he'd been supposed to do that in the middle of a crowded café, and almost said as much, but bit his tongue. Joe didn't understand patience. Carmen would tell in her own good time.

'I'd have made her,' Connor said. He looked at his father. 'You should have let me speak to the tart.'

174

'Mind your language,' Joe said. 'That's Rosa's girl you're talking about.'

'Rosa gave up being a Quinn when she married Rex bloody Darby. It ain't no coincidence that her daughter's rocked up here. She and her old man are up to somethin'.'

Terry shook his head. 'She only came here 'cause Darby brought her here once when she was a kid. She remembered the place. It's nothin' more than that. No need to get stressed about it.'

'Who's fuckin' stressed?' Connor said. 'Did anyone say they were stressed?'

Connor always got belligerent after a few drinks. He was like his father, naturally bad-tempered, but the booze added an extra layer of aggression into the mix. Terry decided not to engage with him. Instead, addressing himself only to Joe, he said, 'I'll keep tabs on her if you like, double-check that she's kosher.'

Gordie chose that moment to stick his oar in. 'Terry's idea of keeping an eye out is to try and get her in the sack.'

Connor gave a snort. 'Yeah, and just 'cause she told you all that shit about why she's here, don't mean it's true. She saw you coming, mate.'

'She's not that smart,' Terry said calmly. 'She ain't got the brains to have an agenda.' He didn't feel bad about casting aspersions on Carmen's intelligence – so long as she wasn't around to hear them. His gut told him that her story was true, that she hadn't been stringing him a line, but it appeared no one was going to take his word for it.

'I want to see her,' Joe said. 'Sort it out, Terry. Arrange a meet.'

'She might not want to do that.'

'What, too good for us, is she?'

'Nah, I didn't mean that. But with you and her old man being, you know, not so friendly, she mightn't ...'

But Joe was already talking over him. 'Next week. Monday or Tuesday. Reckon you can manage that?'

36

All of Carmen's worst fears were confirmed when Terry Street showed up at the café on Monday morning. She knew even as she was walking down the aisle to take his order that it wasn't good news. She felt it in her stomach, in her throat, in every nerve end of her body. Clutching her notepad and pen, she approached the table with a forced smile on her face.

'Good morning. What can I get you?'

Terry grinned, as if her formality amused him. 'Just a brew, ta, Carly.'

She waited, knowing there was more and not wanting to hear it, but knowing too that unless she put her fingers in her ears she was going to have to.

'I saw Joe,' he said, his gaze briefly swerving away before coming back to rest on her face again. 'He'd like a word if that's okay. Nothing to worry about. This afternoon all right?'

She wondered why it was that when people said there was nothing to worry about, there nearly always was. 'What does he want? I mean, you told him, didn't you, that I'm not here to cause any trouble?'

'Sure, sure, I told him. He knows that. He just wants to meet you, you being Rosa's daughter and all that. Family, yeah? A chance for a catch-up. That's all it is.'

Although Carmen had been expecting it, her mouth still went dry. Family or not, she couldn't see any good coming from this get-together, but couldn't see any way of wriggling out of it, either. She had left Belgravia to escape from trouble, but trouble, apparently, was right here too. Maybe Quinn was just curious to meet her, but she doubted it.

'Connolly's,' Terry continued. 'Say, two thirty?'

I'd rather not, she wanted to protest, but what she wanted didn't seem to have much relevance. Quinn, she suspected, was not the sort of man you said no to. 'If I have to,' she said grudgingly.

Terry laughed. 'I'll tell him you're looking forward to it.'

On the basis of forewarned being forearmed, she asked, 'What does he really want to see me for?'

'What do you mean?'

Terry had put on an innocent expression, but she wasn't fooled. He knew exactly what she meant. 'I just . . . I don't really understand why he wants to meet up. What's the point of it?'

Terry was about to answer when the café door opened. A couple of women came in and settled themselves at a table. With reluctance, Carmen was forced to abandon her questioning. She went to the counter, put in his order for tea and went to serve the new customers. She would have gone back and pressed him further if there hadn't been a flurry of activity right then: more customers, more orders to take, and no opportunity to stop and chat.

By the time there was a brief hiatus, Terry had finished his tea and was about to leave. 'Two thirty then,' he said as he passed her in the aisle. 'Would you like me to walk up with you?'

Carmen shook her head. 'No, thanks. I know the way.'

When she went to his table to retrieve the empty cup, she found a one-pound note sitting under it. Enough to pay the bill, and a decent tip besides. What was all that about? The last time Terry had been in here he hadn't even paid for his tea. She dropped the note into the tip jar at the counter to share with Lottie. Strictly speaking, all the tips she made were hers, but she was happy to split them. She reckoned Lottie had a tough deal being stuck with her hands in the sink all day – not a job she'd like to be doing – and that she deserved a little extra.

The next few hours seemed to speed by in that way they always do when you're dreading the arrival of a particular time. Carmen kept glancing at the clock, her stress levels rising by the minute. When it came to knock off, she went through to the back, removed her apron, grabbed her bag, went to the bathroom, had a pee, washed her hands, undid her ponytail, ran a comb through her hair and put on some lipstick. She gazed at her reflection, wondering if she smelled of bacon and eggs. Just in case, she dug into her bag, took out a phial of Chanel, and dabbed a few drops behind her ears.

Even as she was doing all this, she wasn't sure why. It wasn't as if she wanted to impress Joe Quinn or make him like her or even spare his sensitive nostrils from the odour of breakfasts past. What did it matter what she looked or smelled like? It was for her own sake, she insisted, to bolster her confidence, to try and create the impression that she wasn't a woman who could be pushed around.

Carmen smiled thinly at this thought, knowing that she'd been pushed around by one man or another for most of her life. It was time to start standing up for herself. Whether this was the perfect moment, however, when she was about to come face to face with a ruthless gangster, was debatable.

Naturally she had no way of knowing that Joe Quinn was ruthless, but she figured that it followed. He wouldn't be running Kellston unless he was a man of a certain nature, and capable of engendering fear if not respect. The big question was whether he viewed her as Rosa's daughter or Rex's. If it was the former the meeting might be amicable. But if it was the latter . . . well, that might not go so well.

Carmen's anxiety levels rose another notch. She would have liked to stay in the bathroom, to hunker down and hide from her obligations, but that was impossible. She took one last look in the mirror, said a short prayer, and prepared to meet her father's enemy.

37

By the time she got to Connolly's, Carmen's entire body was tense, her pulse racing, her heart hammering in her chest. Even her hands were clammy. She pushed them into her pockets and immediately took them out again. Terry had given her a brief description of Joe and told her he'd be sitting at the back. She took a deep breath, pushed open the door and stepped inside. Abba's 'Waterloo' was playing on a tinny radio behind the counter. She made her way briskly towards the rear, trying not to look like the type of woman who was easily intimidated.

He wasn't hard to find. Joe Quinn had a presence, there was no denying that, and it was a disturbing one. Even at a distance, a sense of menace emanated from him. Although the café was busy, she noticed that the tables surrounding his were all empty. By coincidence or design? She had the feeling that no right-minded person would infringe on his space unless it was by invitation.

She was there, standing in front of him, before she

wanted to be. She cleared her throat. 'Mr Quinn? Hello, I'm Carmen Darby.'

Joe gave her a long hard look, produced the semblance of a smile, and then flapped his hand in a gesture for her to sit down. 'Rosa's daughter, eh?' he said.

Carmen nodded as she pulled out a chair. 'It's nice to meet you.'

If the feeling was mutual, Joe didn't express it. Instead, he kept staring at her, a slight frown on his forehead as if he was attempting to work out if she really was who she said she was. 'Yeah,' he said eventually. 'You've got her eyes.'

Carmen's lips widened. 'Have I? Do you think so?'

Joe didn't answer her directly. Instead, he said, 'Do you want a brew?'

Carmen didn't – she was reluctant to stay here any longer than she had to – but it seemed churlish to refuse. 'Thank you.'

Joe raised his hand, and a waitress came scuttling over. 'Get us another brew, will you, love.'

During this brief interaction, Carmen grabbed the opportunity to take a closer look at her mother's cousin. He was a big man, square, running to fat, with a large protuberant belly that pressed against the edge of the table. His face was round but drooping, with baggy eyes like a bloodhound, heavy jowls, sparse grey hair combed over a pink scalp, and a fleshy mouth. His teeth were crooked and stained brown as if he hadn't been near a toothbrush in years.

'Yeah,' Joe said, turning his attention back to Carmen. 'You got sisters, ain't you?'

'Two. Marian and Hazel. They're both married now.'

Joe's thick shoulders moved a little, an impatient shift of indifference, as if her sisters' marital status was neither here nor there to him. 'All the boys used to chase after your mum when she was young. Most popular girl in Kellston, Rosa was. A real stunner.'

Carmen could see his gaze roaming over her face, taking in her features one by one, judging her, perhaps, against the beauty of her mother. 'I never really knew her. She died when I was a baby.'

'Rosa always went her own way, did what she wanted. She wasn't one for toeing the line. We never saw much of her after she married your old man. Do you know why that was, Carmen?'

Carmen shook her head, although she had a pretty good idea.

'He ever talk to you about Rosa's brother, Michael?'

'Not much. Was he the one who disappeared?'

'Dead, not disappeared,' Joe said roughly. 'There's a difference. Michael didn't go nowhere. Someone made sure of that. It might be a long time ago but I ain't forgotten.'

The waitress came with the tea. Carmen thanked her, glad of the interruption. It gave her a few seconds to try and think of a reply. 'How awful,' she said, when she couldn't come up with anything better. She knew what he suspected – that her father had killed Michael – but had the sense not to react in the way she had with Terry. 'No, it's not the sort of thing you'd ever forget.'

Joe glared at her as if doubting her sincerity. 'I reckon your old man knew more about it than he ever let on.'

'What do you mean?' she said, deliberately frowning, trying to look like she didn't have a clue what he was going on about.

But Joe, instead of sharing his suspicions, abruptly changed tack. 'So what brings you to Kellston, love?'

'Oh, well, as I told Terry, I just—'

'I don't care what you told Terry. You're talking to me now.'

Carmen had never come across anyone quite as ill-mannered and aggressive as Joe before. Compared to him, even her father's arrogance seemed to fade into insignificance. But she kept a polite expression on her face, gave a small nod and said, 'I wanted to live somewhere else for a while. I came here when I was a child and remembered it, so ...'

'You had a bust-up with the old man, then?'

'A disagreement,' she said. 'These things happen in families, don't they?'

'A disagreement over what?'

Carmen could feel her jaw clenching, resentment rising in her throat like bile. What damn business was it of his? He might be top dog round here, might even be her mother's cousin, but that didn't give him the right to know all the ins and outs of her personal life. 'It was nothing important.'

'Important enough for you to pack your bags and scarper.' He raised his cup to his mouth and took a large slurping gulp of tea. 'Still, your old man always was a difficult sod. Likes things his own way, don't he? I told Rosa that before she married him. He'll always want to have the last bloody word, I said. She didn't listen, though. She always reckoned she knew best.'

'I'm not here to cause any trouble. I had no idea my mum still had family here.'

'Never mentioned me, then, your old man?'

'No, but then he doesn't like talking about the past. You know, with everything that happened.'

Joe gave a snort. 'What's he up to these days?'

'Semi-retired,' she said. 'But he likes to keep busy.'

'Yeah, Rex always liked to keep busy.'

From the way he said it, Carmen knew it wasn't a compliment. If Joe had been of a more amenable personality, she might have asked him about her mother, tried to learn some more about her, but she wasn't convinced that the questions would be welcome. Also, she didn't want to admit to her ignorance. It seemed vaguely shameful somehow to know so little about her own mum. The subject had always been taboo in the Darby household, the mere mention causing her father's face to darken and an icy chill to fall over the room.

'He still living in that fancy house in Belgravia?'

'Yes, still there,' Carmen said.

'You must be missing your home comforts,' he said sneeringly. 'You don't look like the kind of girl who belongs in Kellston.'

'I like it here,' she lied.

'You'd be the bloody first. Your mother couldn't wait to get out of the place.'

Carmen lifted the cup to her lips and took a small sip of hot tea. She held the cup firmly, afraid that her hands might shake. It was odd to think of her mother living here, walking these streets, maybe even drinking in this very same café. She still wasn't sure what Joe Quinn wanted, why he'd summoned her today, what he was *really* after. Terry's warnings about him remained at the forefront of her mind.

Joe still had his beady eyes on her. 'Does your old man know you're here in Kellston?'

She hesitated for too long, afraid of telling a lie in case she got caught out, but not wanting to admit the truth, either. The delay told Joe all he wanted to know.

'Nah, course he don't. And I doubt he'd be too pleased about it.' Joe looked smug when he said this. 'He reckons he's a cut above these days. He wouldn't want his daughter slumming it.' Then, as if another thought had just occurred to him, he said, 'Ain't one of your sisters married to Jonny Cornish?'

'Hazel,' she said.

'Yeah, I thought so.'

'Do you know Jonny?'

'As well as I want to,' Joe said. 'I see him around from time to time.'

'In Kellston?' Carmen said too quickly, alarmed by the thought of bumping into him. He'd be bound to go straight home and tell Hazel. And Hazel would tell Dad and . . .

Joe must have read her expression. 'Oh, you don't need to worry, love. He won't be showing his face round here anytime soon. He's keeping his head down, staying out of my way.'

This came as something of a surprise to Carmen, who'd had no idea Jonny knew Joe Quinn, or that he had good reason to stay away from him. She'd have liked to have known why but suspected Joe wouldn't tell her even if she asked. Or would he? While she toyed with the idea of posing the question, Joe followed up with something even more startling.

'I hear that him and his missus have moved in with your old man.'

'What? No, that can't be right.' Carmen saw Joe's mouth clamp shut and annoyance flash into his eyes at her contradiction. 'Sorry, I didn't mean . . . are you sure? It just seems odd, that's all. They've got their own place in Camden.'

'And now they've got an even bigger one in Belgravia.'

'But Hazel always said . . .' Carmen came to a halt, realising that what Hazel always said – something along the lines of rather being dead than living under the same roof as their father again – was best kept to herself. 'She said she liked living in Camden.'

'Seems she likes living in Belgravia even more.'

'It might just be temporary.'

'Not if Jonny Cornish has anything to do with it. He's a man with eyes bigger than his stomach if you get my meaning.'

Carmen felt an odd jolt inside her at the realisation she'd been so rapidly replaced. It was only ten days since the dreadful birthday dinner and already her father had filled the vacancy in his house.

'Well, it's been nice to meet you, Carmen,' Joe said, looking at his watch. 'Don't be a stranger, will you?'

It took Carmen a moment to realise she was being dismissed. Relieved, she jumped to her feet. 'Thanks for the tea,' she said, although she'd barely touched it. As she left the café, she had the disturbing feeling that she had inadvertently given Joe Quinn something that he wanted; she just wasn't quite sure what that something was.

38

Jonny got back to the house shortly after five. He'd been hoping to run into Lucan, had even walked around the block a couple of times, but there was no sign of him. He wondered what the man did all day. Maybe he just stayed home and counted his money. Gambling was usually a night-time occupation, although, for the hard core, some places were open in the afternoon.

He could hear Hazel moving about in the kitchen, the soft tread of her feet on the wooden floor, and he went through to join her. 'Is Rex home yet?'

'Lovely to see you, too.'

'Huh?'

Hazel glanced up from the percolator, her expression exasperated. 'Jesus, don't I even get a hello, a how are you, have you had a good day? You just walk in here and ask about Dad and that's it.'

'Yeah, yeah, I get it. So, sweetheart, you had a good day?'

'If you call Dad droning on about Carmen good, then yes, it's been beyond brilliant. Someone needs to find out where she is and drag her home before I go stark raving mad. And where have you been? You said you'd drop by the office.'

'Sorry, I got caught up.'

'Got caught up where? In the pub?'

Jonny wondered why wives always felt obliged to nag, as if it was some part of the marriage job description. 'Sorting out the basement in the Royal, actually. So is Rex here or not?'

Hazel made a show of looking round the kitchen. 'Does it look like he's here?'

'In the house, then. Is he in the house?'

'He's still at the office.'

'Good, 'cause I wanted to ask you something.'

Hazel slopped milk into mugs. 'What?'

'I noticed the other day that the door to the attic is locked. Do you know where the key's kept?'

'What do you want to go in the attic for?'

Jonny had already prepared an answer to this. 'I just wanted to take a gander. It could be good storage space, couldn't it? For all the stuff in our flat, the furniture and the like. You know Marian. She won't be happy with our taste. Give her a week or two and she'll want a new sofa, a new bed, a new kitchen table. We'll need somewhere to put all our things.'

'I don't think she'll bother. It's not as though she'll be living there permanently. She might only be there a few days a month.'

'Maybe. Maybe not. I still don't get why the attic's locked.'

'No one goes up there.'

'Why not?'

'What does it matter?'

'I'm just curious, that's all. Seems weird to lock it up.'

Hazel poured coffee into two mugs. She gave a long sigh, her eyes avoiding his. 'Because it's where she ... where Mum ... God, do I have to spell it out?'

'Shit, you're kidding. She killed herself in the attic?'

'Yes.'

'Jesus, sorry, I didn't know that. Christ, why didn't Rex flog this place, take you all to a house that wasn't full of bad memories?'

'You'll have to ask him that.' Hazel shoved a mug towards him. 'We never got a say in it. The door was locked and that was the end of it.'

'And you've never been up there since?'

'For God's sake, Jonny! Why would I want to do that?'

Jonny leaned against the counter, his gaze roving up towards the ceiling as if he could see straight through the floors to those sorrowful rooms at the top of the house. 'Yeah, sorry. Out of bounds, then. I get it.'

'Completely out of bounds.'

Which was like a red rag to Jonny. Tell him he couldn't do something and that was all he wanted to do. He recalled his search of the house and how there was nothing of Rosa Darby in it. Had it all been consigned to the attic? If that was the case, there could be a little gold mine up there. Although Rex wasn't a fool – he'd have put all the really valuable stuff in the safe – there might be enough in the leftovers to make his trespass worthwhile.

39

It was the end of the day, and apart from Rex the office was empty. He was studying the details of a block of run-down flats in Battersea, trying to decide if they were worth the investment or not. It was purely a distraction from the long list of things he didn't want to think about. Marian had been in earlier, trying to persuade him to let her move a desk into his office, but he'd refused. He applauded her enthusiasm, but he was used to working alone. Sharing Pat's office had been ruled out too. In the end he'd offered her a space in the corner of reception. She wasn't happy about it and Elizabeth, when she found out, wouldn't be either, but he wasn't ready yet to relinquish the sanctity of his four walls.

Then there was Jonny and the Royal basement. Of all the places he could have chosen to do up, why that one? Private parties, he'd said, but Rex couldn't see much of a future in the idea. He wished that he had sold the club years ago, got shot of it, but that wasn't his decision now. The place held bad memories for him. When was the last time he'd been down in the basement? He felt a tightening in his chest. No, he didn't want to think about that. What was done was done, and regrets were pointless.

Before he could move on to his next subject of concern, the phone started ringing. With no Elizabeth to filter his calls, he picked it up himself, put the receiver to his ear and barked out his name.

'Rex Darby.'

There was a long pause on the other end of the line. For a while he was sure it was Carmen – a smug smile tugged at the corners of his mouth – but he was soon disabused of the notion.

'How are you doing, Rex? Well, I hope. It's been a while.'

Rex felt his shoulders stiffen, his entire body tense. He'd have known that East End voice anywhere, even though it was years since he'd last heard it. 'What the hell do you want, Joe?'

'That's not very friendly, pal.'

'Since when were we ever pals? Don't waste my time. Like I said, what do you want?'

A hollow laugh floated into Rex's ear. 'I want my dough, of course. I can't wait around for ever.'

'What dough? What are you talking about?'

Another cackle of laughter. 'Oh, ain't Jonny told you? He must be getting forgetful in his old age. He owes me a grand and I want it pronto.'

'Since when have Jonny's debts had anything to do with me?'

'He's family, Rex. Thought you might want to help him out before I take matters further. I mean, that daughter of yours – Hazel, ain't it? – she's kind of young to be a widow.'

Rex's left hand formed a fist on the table. He'd be having words with Jonny when he got home. What was the stupid arsehole thinking mixing with the likes of Quinn? Poker, no doubt; it was bound to be. The fool didn't have the brains he was born with. 'Don't threaten me. You should know better. Whatever Jonny owes he can pay himself. I'm not his fuckin' banker.'

'Have it your own way, pal. Just don't say I didn't warn you.'

'Is that it?'

'Not quite.'

'Well, make it speedy, Joe, 'cause I'm a busy man.'

'Too busy to talk about Carmen?'

That caught Rex's attention. He stiffened again, his fingers gripping the receiver. 'What fuckin' business is Carmen of yours?'

'She's my business when she's on my patch. I don't remember inviting no Darbys into Kellston. Nah, I don't remember that at all. Still, seeing as she's Rosa's girl, I ain't going to cause a fuss. I mean, she's family, ain't she, of a sort.'

'You're talking crap.'

'You calling me a liar? That ain't very polite. Now your girl, she's got much better manners. Come to see me, didn't she? She ain't happy with you, Rex, not happy at all. Yeah, couldn't wait to look me up, tell me what a shit you are, and check out what she's been missing on her mum's side of the family.'

'She wouldn't go near you if you paid her.'

'That's where you're wrong, pal. Her and me, we got on like a house on fire. Yeah, we met up this afternoon, and had a good old chinwag. I reckon now that the two of you have fallen out, she's looking to acquire some less tiresome relatives. Can't say I blame her, neither.'

Rex spoke through gritted teeth. 'Fuck off. Carmen isn't in Kellston.'

'Yeah, sure, have it your own way. We weren't together this afternoon, either. And she ain't working at the Station Café, serving up brews to every Tom, Dick and Harry. 'Bloody waste of an expensive education if you ask me, but that's up to her.

You need to face up to it, pal. Your girl's not coming back. She ain't even using your name any more.' Quinn sniggered down the phone. 'You don't have much luck with your nearest and dearest, do you, pal? First Rosa and then—'

Rex hung up before Joe Quinn could say anything else. Rage was bubbling up inside him, an emotional volcano ready to explode. Of all the people Carmen might have turned to, Quinn was the worst. But that, of course, was why she'd done it. She had chosen Quinn to spite him, to stick the knife in, to cause as much hurt as she could.

He leaned down, opened the bottom drawer, took out the bottle of whisky, slammed it down on his desk and unscrewed the lid. Without bothering with a glass, he drank straight from the bottle, two big slugs that slid easily down his throat. Could Quinn be lying? No, he knew too much, and that gloating voice had been too full of triumph. The bastard had seen Carmen just like he'd said. Rex was sure of it. His youngest daughter, the one he had always loved the most, had betrayed him in the worst way possible.

40

Marian leaned forward in the chair, her eyes wide, her mind rapidly processing the possible consequences of the news her father had brought back from the office. If she could have compiled a list of things guaranteed to enrage him, one of his daughters having a cosy chat with Joe Quinn would have been right there at the top. Her mouth twitched and she had to fight against the desire to laugh.

'Do you believe him?' she said. 'What if it's just a pack of lies?'

Rex shook his head. He was pacing the room from side to side, his face florid, his arms held rigid by his sides. 'Quinn hasn't got the brains to come up with something like that. He's an evil sod, but he hasn't got any imagination.'

'Joe Quinn, though,' she said, rubbing extra salt into the wound. 'That awful man. How could she? *Why* would she? I don't understand what she's playing at.'

'What she's playing at is humiliating me, my dear. *Me*, her own father. I've done everything for the bloody girl, and this is how she repays me. It makes me sick to my stomach.'

Marian released a long sympathetic sigh. 'Sit down, Dad. You'll give yourself a heart attack.'

Rex didn't sit down. He marched over to the window, looked out for a second, gave a low growl, and then went to the drinks cabinet and poured himself a stiff Scotch.

'And a waitress,' Marian said with a slight shudder. 'I can't see Carmen waiting on tables.'

'Well she'd better get used to it because she's not getting another penny out of me.'

'You don't mean that,' she said, hoping that he did. 'Are you going to go and see her?'

'Why would I want to do that? If she imagines I'm going to waste my time running around after her, she's got another think coming. She's made her bed; she can damn well lie in it.'

'I don't know what's got into her. It's like she's just being deliberately hurtful. Do you think this is the first time she's seen Quinn or have the two of them been . . .?' Marian didn't finish the question, but let it hang in the air. Her father was always susceptible to conspiracy theories, especially when he'd had a drink or two.

Rex knocked back his Scotch and poured another. 'What are you asking me for? How would I know?'

'Something must have possessed her to behave like this.'

'Bloody ingratitude. That's what possessed her. But she's not getting away with it. So far as I'm concerned, she's no longer a member of this family. This is it, finished, done with. I'll be seeing my solicitor.'

Marian tried not to look too pleased. If that meant what she thought it meant, then half of Carmen's share of the inheritance was about to come her way. Well, unless he did something totally insane, like leave it to Pat or Elizabeth or the local dog's home.

Rex glared at her. 'And did you know about Jonny and the money he owes Quinn?'

Sensing that her father was looking for someone to take out his frustration on, she was quick to refute the suggestion. 'No, of course not. Why on earth would I? I shouldn't think Hazel knows, either. She'll have a fit when she finds out.'

'I'm not paying his debts for him.'

'There's no reason why you should. It's his problem, not yours. Do you think the mugging had something to do with Quinn? That was quite a beating Jonny took.'

Rex snarled, baring his teeth. 'Not half as bad as he deserved. I won't have him gambling away everything I've left Hazel.'

Marian, who had spent the afternoon on a tour of her properties, was glad now that she'd decided to call in at the house before returning to Camden. 'She won't ever dump him, if that's what you're hoping.'

'Do you know where he is? I need to talk to the stupid bastard.'

'No idea. He might not be back for hours.'

In frustration, Rex slammed his glass down on the top of the cabinet, making it shake. 'That man's never done a decent day's work in his life. He's a waster, a loser, a bloody parasite!'

'Have you eaten anything today, Dad? We could go to that new Italian down the road.'

'I'm not hungry.'

'You should have some dinner.'

Rex turned his blazing face on her. 'Did you not hear what I just said?'

'Yes, I heard.'

'So why don't you bloody listen?'

Marian, not wanting to be the third target of his rage, decided to quit while she was ahead. It was only a matter of time before he got on to her bad parenting skills and her inadequacies as a

197

wife and daughter. She had got what she'd come for – the latest on Carmen – and everything was rosy on that front.

'I'll leave you to it, then,' she said mildly, rising to her feet and shrugging into her coat. She didn't like being alone with him in the house when he was in this mood. Experience had taught her how quickly his rants could turn violent – and woe betide anyone who was in the vicinity when that happened. She was older now, less vulnerable, but she still knew what he was capable of.

Out on the street, Marian had a spring to her step. As she headed for her car, she was already making plans for tomorrow. Carmen shouldn't be too difficult to find. The Station Café had to be either in the station itself or close to it. She had to make sure that her little sister stayed exactly where she was, both literally and metaphorically. So long as Carmen remained in their father's bad books, there was money up for grabs – and Marian intended to have it.

41

Tuesday morning hadn't started well for Carmen. As she was leaving for work, she'd been waylaid by Mrs Jordan and informed that this would have to be her last week at the B&B as one of her regulars was due back and the room was needed. She suspected her forthcoming eviction might have more to do with Terry Street turning up on the doorstep, but there was nothing she could do about that now. Her landlady had a reputation to uphold, and Carmen was clearly lowering the tone.

Her second surprise came at around ten past ten. The door to the café opened and Marian swanned in. Carmen felt a rush of air enter her lungs. Her sister, wearing a tailored linen suit and gold accessories, looked as out of place as a peacock in a car park. She glanced at Carmen, gave a thin smile, and sat down at a table away from the windows. Carmen hurried over.

'Marian! What are you doing here?'

'Oh, that's a nice welcome when I've just slogged all the way across town to come and see you.'

'No, what I meant is how did you know where I was?'

'Is it supposed to be a secret?'

'No, but—'

Marian, either uninterested in the original question or unwilling to give a straight answer, swiftly interrupted her. 'Do you serve coffee here?'

'Of course we serve coffee.'

'Well, be a dear and get me one, will you? I'm dying of thirst. And then we can have a little chat.'

'I'm working, Marian.'

Marian looked around the café, which was virtually empty. 'I'm sure they can spare you for ten minutes.'

Carmen would have preferred to talk away from work, or even better not to talk at all. She couldn't imagine that Marian had anything to say that she wanted to hear. But she went over to the counter and asked Joan if she could take a short break. 'I'll make up the time later.'

'That's fine, love. We're hardly rushed off our feet.'

Carmen took two coffees back to the table and sat down opposite Marian. 'Did Dad send you? Is that why you're here?'

'God, no. He'd have a fit if he knew.' Marian sipped her coffee, pulled a face as if it didn't come up to her exacting standards, and placed the cup back on the saucer. 'Especially after all this Joe Quinn business. What were you thinking of, Carmen? Dad can't stand that man. And now Quinn's ringing up and saying the two of you are . . . well, I don't know what you are, but it's nothing Dad likes the sound of.'

Carmen felt her heart sink. Hadn't she known that no good would come from the meeting with Quinn? 'It's not like that. Joe came looking for me. I could hardly refuse to see him, could I?'

'I don't see why not. You've got a tongue in your head. You could have just said no.'

200

'Believe me, he's not the type of man you want to offend. And he's still Mum's cousin, no matter how gross he is.'

Marian rolled her eyes. 'Have it your own way. But you should know that this has been the final straw. Dad's had it with you, Carmen. I presume you're intending to go home at some point, so I ought to warn you that you won't get a warm reception. He says you've gone too far this time, and there's no turning back. So far as he's concerned, you're not his daughter any more – and you're certainly not welcome in his house.'

Carmen felt her chest constrict. She had known things with her father were bad, worse than bad, but hearing it spoken out loud made it all so final. She had been holding on to a tiny glimmer of hope and now even that was extinguished. There was a certain smug pleasure in Marian's relaying of the news that set her teeth on edge. So much for sisterly love: she had only come to gloat. 'And you came all the way across town to tell me this?'

'I didn't want you to embarrass yourself. I suppose you could go home and beg and make a scene, but I wouldn't recommend it. You know what he's like. He's not going to change his mind. He says you and Joe Quinn are welcome to each other.'

'Since when were you bothered about whether I embarrassed myself or not?'

Marian gave an elegant shrug of her shoulders. 'Don't be like that. None of this is my fault. If you hadn't been so bloody stupid this would never have happened.'

Carmen's hackles rose. 'I wasn't the one who got in a raging temper. I wasn't the one who changed the locks. Why are you putting it all on to me?'

'All right, calm down. There's no point having a go. You're talking to the wrong person. I only came to tell you what's what. I'm only the messenger.'

A messenger who enjoyed delivering misery, Carmen

thought. She glared across the table, her fierce expression hiding the tumult that was going on inside her.

'And I hate to tell you this,' Marian continued, without a hint of hating it, 'but he's seeing his solicitor this morning. I think you're about to be disinherited.'

Carmen's glare intensified. 'All the more for you, then.'

'I've told him he's being ridiculous, but he just won't listen.'

Carmen doubted whether Marian had said any such thing. A list had probably already been made of what to spend the extra money on. While she was still absorbing this latest bitter act of her father's, she watched Marian take out a cigarette, light it, inhale, and then exhale the smoke in a long, languid stream.

'Why are you even working in this place?' Marian wrinkled her nose as she looked around. 'You've got a degree, for God's sake. Surely you can find something better.'

Carmen wasn't about to waste her breath explaining how hard it was to get a job in the art world, especially without any experience. She'd applied for numerous vacancies since she'd graduated, but the London galleries and auction houses seemed to favour upper-class men and women, which left meagre pickings for the rest of the hopefuls. 'I like it here,' she said defensively. 'What's wrong with it?'

'What's right with it? Are you really going to wait on tables for the rest of your life?'

Carmen ignored the dig. 'I've still got things at the house. Do you think he'll let me in to pick them up?'

'I wouldn't count on it.' Marian took another drag on her cigarette. 'I suppose I could pack up some stuff for you when he's not around. What are you after, just clothes and the like?'

This sudden helpfulness was out of character, but Carmen wasn't about to look a gift horse in the mouth. 'Could you? Yes, my clothes, and everything in the top dressing-table drawers: my passport and letters. Oh, and the photo of Mum: it's on the bedside table.'

Marian's eyebrows arched. 'I don't know why you'd want a picture of Mum. It's not as though she even ...' She stopped suddenly and put her hand over her mouth as if she'd said something that she shouldn't.

'Even what?'

'It doesn't matter.'

'No, what were you going to say?'

Marian shook her head. She smoked some more of her cigarette, her gaze avoiding Carmen's. 'Just that ... well, you never really knew her, did you? She died when you were so young.'

'That's not what you meant.' Carmen had a sick feeling in the pit of her stomach. Prickles ran up and down her arms. 'Tell me.'

'There are some things you're better off not knowing.'

'I want to know.'

Marian hesitated, but then shook her head again. 'I shouldn't have said anything.'

'But you have. You did. If you don't tell me, I'll ask someone else. I'll ask Hazel. I'll ask Annie Foster. I'll keep on asking until I find out what you meant.'

Marian gave a long sigh, as if Carmen was being an exasperating child pestering her for sweets. 'In that case, I suppose you might as well hear it from me. But don't say I didn't warn you. You're not going to like it.'

Carmen waited on tenterhooks, but her sister took her time, clearly savouring the moment. Marian enjoyed having the upper hand, being in possession of sensitive information that she could choose to pass on or not. A silence settled over the table. Carmen's nerves were stretched tight. 'Oh, for God's sake, just get on with it.'

Marian's expression was artful, her smile small and without warmth. 'Look, what you have to understand is that Mum wasn't well. It's not any reflection on you.'

Those sentences alone were enough to strike fear into Carmen. 'What are you trying to say?'

'Well, there's no easy way of . . .' Marian stubbed out her cigarette and sighed again. 'Basically, because of the post-natal depression and everything, she didn't want another child after me and Hazel. You were something of an accident.'

'I'd kind of guessed that with the age difference between us.'

'But what I mean is that she *really* didn't want another baby. She knew what would happen after you were born and couldn't cope with another round of despair. It was just beyond her. All those months of misery stretching ahead. Giving birth triggered something in her, you see, an awful, awful depression. She knew it would finish her off.'

Carmen's cheeks were burning, and a lump was growing in her throat. 'So she didn't want me. I get it.'

'There were the most God-awful rows between her and Dad,' Marian continued mercilessly. 'They went on for weeks. She didn't want to go through with it, but he wouldn't let her . . . you know.'

Carmen did know. 'Get rid of me,' she said bluntly.

'I said you wouldn't like it. But you shouldn't take it personally. I mean, you weren't even a *person* then, not a proper baby, not someone with fingers and toes and the rest. Of course, abortion wasn't legal back in those days, but there were still places you could go if you had the money.'

Carmen was aware of Joan and Lottie watching them from the counter, Joan pretending that she wasn't, and Lottie quite blatantly staring. She kept her eyes on Marian, wishing that she'd never made her tell. Finding out that her mother had been desperate to abort her was too much to take. She felt winded, as if she'd been punched in the stomach. For a second, she thought her heart had stopped beating. In a small voice she eventually said, 'At least Dad wanted me.'

'Only because he thought you might be a boy,' Marian scoffed. 'He couldn't take the chance, could he? You know how much he always wanted a son. He didn't care about Mum, what he was going to put her through, so long as he finally got his son and heir. But he lost out on both counts, didn't he? He ended up with another daughter and no wife – and we've all been paying the price ever since.'

Carmen could almost smell the malice leaking out of Marian. And now, for the first time, she understood the resentment of her sisters, why they'd always treated her like they had, why nothing even approaching love had ever come in her direction. *She was the child who'd killed their mother.*

'I think we must be cursed, the whole Darby family,' Marian said. 'You're better off out of it, darling. You've had a lucky escape.'

Carmen's lower lip was clamped hard between her teeth while she tried to control her emotions. Why was Marian telling her all this? Yes, she'd asked, of course she'd asked, but there was no need for the whole appalling truth. She could have been spared that.

'Anyway,' Marian said, casually placing her cigarettes back in her bag, 'I'd better make a move. I'm meeting Hazel for lunch.' She paused, inclined her head, looked at Carmen and said, 'Now you're not going to dwell on all this, darling, are you? No one blames you for what Mum did.'

'*You* blame me.'

'Heavens, whatever gave you that idea?'

'Well, don't you?'

Marian, who could play the martyr to perfection, grew huffy. 'You should be grateful to me, not having a go. I don't see the others queuing up to check out how you are. No Dad, no Hazel, no Clive. I'm the only one who's made the effort to come to this godforsaken place and this is all the thanks I get.'

Carmen, gazing at her, wondered at her sister's amazing ability to turn everything around and make herself the victim.

'So what do you want me to do about your things?' Marian asked sharply.

Suspecting she would never see her belongings again if she didn't go some way towards placating her, Carmen forced herself to say softly, 'I am grateful. Of course I am. Thank you. I haven't got anywhere permanent to live yet, but it shouldn't be too long. I'll let you know when I've sorted something out.'

Marian rose to her feet looking partly – if not entirely – mollified. 'You'd better call me on Hazel's number. If I'm not there, leave a message on the machine.'

'Why Hazel's?'

'She and Jonny have moved in with Dad, so I'm using the flat as a base for when I'm in London.'

Carmen already knew, courtesy of Joe Quinn, about Hazel's new living arrangements, but she'd been unaware of Marian's. It seemed that everything was changing quickly, a kind of musical chairs on the accommodation front. 'Okay, I'll call you there.'

Marian gave a stiff nod and then, without another word, not even a goodbye, turned and walked out of the café.

Carmen stayed at the table for a while, too shocked to move, absorbing everything she'd been told. The past made more sense to her now, but the pain was hard to take. To know she'd been unwanted, unloved, and even worse, that she had been some terrible propellant for her mother's suicide, made her feel cold to the bone. Guilt wrapped around her. Her place in the Darby family may have felt fragile sometimes, but now it had been smashed into a thousand pieces.

42

It was almost midday before Jonny rose from his dreams and eased himself out of bed. He had a slight hangover but nothing too brutal. He thought about Mimi and the sex they'd had last night, and grinned. He'd been seeing the girl for a couple of months now although it was nothing serious. A casual fling, that was all. He enjoyed her company because she was fun and provocative and bloody good in the sack, but most of all because she never nagged or complained. She was easy-going and that was what he liked best in a woman. He just needed a little distraction in his life, an escape from the day-to-day routine.

Hazel, thankfully, was gone. She had said something, he remembered, about meeting Marian for lunch in the West End where, undoubtedly, she would take the opportunity to list his latest catalogue of failures.

She had woken when he'd come home in the early hours and instantly embarked on an interrogation: Where had he been? What had he been doing? And who the hell had he been doing it with? She'd had so much to ask she had barely drawn breath, barely known where to begin. And before he'd had the chance to answer any of the original questions, she'd launched into a tirade about his gambling, and more specifically his debt to Joe Quinn, which her father had spent the whole evening venting over.

'And that's what I've been doing,' he'd explained, alarmed to hear that Rex knew about the debt but quickly grabbing at this excuse for his absence. 'Staying out of your old man's way until he's cooled down.' Fortunately, Hazel was too wound up to wonder how he'd found out.

'He isn't going to bloody cool down.'

'I don't see that it's any of his business who I owe money to.'

'A thousand pounds. For Christ's sake, Jonny! What's the matter with you?'

And so it had gone on, to and fro, for a good half hour, with Hazel hissing at him like an angry cobra, and he, like an ine-briated snake charmer, trying to calm her down.

Jonny stretched and instantly regretted the movement. His ribs were still sore from the beating he'd taken. Hazel should have a bit more sympathy for him. Hadn't he suffered enough from his mistake? And yeah, okay, a grand was a lot of dough, but it wasn't as if they were paupers – or at least they wouldn't be if Rex would relax his tight-fisted grip on Hazel's inheritance. Rex was the problem, not him.

Jonny took a long shower, taking care to go easy on his multitudinous bruises. His skin was mottled with ochre, dun brown and violet, and his face still looked like he'd been in a car crash. Battle scars from Soho. Not that there had been much of a battle, but he preferred not to think about that. Damn Quinn! All he'd needed was a bit more time.

After fifteen minutes he switched off the water, stepped out of the shower, ran his palm over the steamed-up mirror, combed his hair, brushed his teeth, and had a leisurely shave. Then he went back into the bedroom and got dressed. Once he was ready to face the world, he cautiously opened the door and stood for a moment, listening to the sounds of the house. Or rather to the lack of them. Once he was certain that Rex wasn't lurking, he went downstairs to the kitchen and made himself coffee..

He was on his second cup and his second cigarette when he started thinking about the attic again. Last night when he'd come home to a dark house, he'd taken a moment to open the hall cupboard and go through Rex's overcoat pockets. Two sets of keys – one for the office, one for home – but neither set containing anything that looked like it would fit the attic lock.

Jonny wondered if he kept it at the office. That didn't seem likely, not if it meant traipsing round to Ebury Street every time he wanted access. Except he probably never did want access. There was always the safe, but if that was where it was, he was buggered. Not even Hazel knew the combination.

He was mulling over this dilemma when something struck him. Perhaps he'd been overthinking it all. He pushed back his chair, stubbed out his cigarette, flew out into the hall and took the stairs at a jog to the top floor. Here, a few feet away from the attic entrance, he hesitated, not wanting his hunch to be a letdown. He could hear his own slightly wheezy breath, his lungs pumping from the sudden exertion, the sound unnaturally loud in the silence.

His gaze lifted to the lintel, to the narrow ledge above the door. What better place to put a key if you simply wanted to keep it out of reach of your children's curious hands? It would have been years, more than twenty, since Rex had cleared the house of everything Rosa, stashed it all in the attic, and locked the door behind him. What would be more natural than to leave the key where it wouldn't be lost?

210

Jonny stepped forward, raised his right arm, and carefully felt with his fingertips. Dust came away and drifted down. He was prepared for disappointment, expected it, but suddenly his fingers dislodged something metal, and a heavy key fell clattering on to the wood floor. The noise made him jump, made his heart skip a beat, and he stood rigid, as if the sound might send someone running. But the house was empty apart from him. There was no one else to hear.

Hurriedly he crouched down, retrieved the offending object and straightened up again. The lock was stiff, and Jonny had to twist and turn the key a few times before it finally engaged and he heard the welcome click. He pushed the door open and found himself at the foot of a short flight of carpetless stairs. Almost immediately, a sour smell assailed him, like stale air rushing out of an opened tomb.

He instinctively drew back, and for a moment questioned the wisdom of what he was doing. He looked up into the dimness, a rare anxiety leaking into his veins. He shouldn't be doing this, he knew he shouldn't, but it could be weeks before he got another opportunity. Who could say when Rex and Hazel would both be absent from the house again? Not to mention the cleaner, whose hours he wasn't yet familiar with. He couldn't afford to hang about: time was money.

He noticed the light switch just inside the door, moved forward again and flicked it on. Instantly, the brown wood stairs with all their scuffs and scrapes were illuminated, and the room at the top was flooded with light. The sudden brightness chased away his reservations. Jonny took one quick glance over his shoulder, ascended to the attic, and looked around.

Stacked against the far wall was all the debris of family life: unwanted furniture, outmoded appliances, suitcases, blankets, cots and a lot of boxes. The room was dusty, full of cobwebs.

He could feel the dryness of the atmosphere in the back of his throat. Over to his right were eight large crates, set apart. There was a clothes rail too, the garments protected by opaque plastic covers.

Jonny was a man of limited imagination but even he couldn't fail to be affected by what he knew had happened here. The ghost of Rosa Darby seemed to hover, to watch him through accusing eyes. He couldn't help wondering where exactly she'd done it, at which precise spot in this dreary desolate space she had chosen to take her own life. Like one of those rubberneckers on the motorway, slowing down to view an accident, his gaze raked the four corners of the room.

But he mustn't get mired in the past. There were no such things as ghosts and ghouls, only real flesh-and-blood people. And if he wasn't careful, one of those people might come home to catch him poking around where he wasn't supposed to. He was here for a purpose, a practical one, and couldn't afford to indulge in fanciful notions.

Jonny went over to the crates and began going through them. The first contained sets of china, each piece of porcelain individually wrapped. Too heavy, he decided, and too fragile to be lugging around. He quickly moved on. The next had small paintings, all wrapped in brown paper and tied with string. He could feel the frames through the paper. He undid one and held it up: a seascape with a couple of young children playing on a beach. Was it worth anything? It looked like an original water-colour, not a print, but the signature didn't mean anything to him. Not that it would. He was hardly an expert when it came to art. He put it to one side and pulled out the next. Another wishy-washy watercolour, this time of a country village with winding lanes and a row of thatched cottages.

Neither of the pictures were his cup of tea – he preferred the nude in Rex's bedroom – but they might have some value. Jonny put them to one side. He was beginning to realise now that it would take hours to properly go through the crates, unwrap everything, and find the items that could be pawned for easy cash. But it also occurred to him that anything he took probably wouldn't be missed. It was clear that no one had been up here for years. And once Rex was gone – and he meant *permanently* gone – who would even know that items had been removed? It seemed unlikely that the girls would even be aware of what had been kept after their mother's death and what had been thrown away.

Jonny abandoned the crates and walked over to the clothes rail where hopefully the best items in Rosa's wardrobe were hanging. He moved from garment to garment, unzipping each cover far enough down to establish what was inside – dresses, jackets, silk blouses – before zipping it up again. He was almost at the end of the rail when he hit the jackpot with a long sable coat. He sucked in a breath and grinned. Now *that* was worth a few bob!

Jonny took it off the rail, draped it over his arm, picked up the two paintings and made a hasty exit. As he hurried down the stairs, he thought he heard a noise, a faint whispering from behind him. The hairs on the back of his neck stood on end. He briefly came to a halt, paralysed, convinced that he wasn't alone.

There are no such things as ghosts, the rational part of his brain pronounced again, but he still couldn't quite bring himself to glance over his shoulder. Chills were running through his body. A sudden rush of adrenaline propelled him into action. He took the last four steps in a couple of bounds, switched off the light and firmly shut and locked the door. After placing the key back where he had found it, he hurried downstairs to the safety of the bedroom.

43

Carmen was in a state and trying not to show it. Marian's revelations lay like a dead weight in her mind, cruel and crushing, squeezing out every other thought she had. She could have coped with being an accident – she would hardly have been the first in the world – but being unwanted, being the *cause* of her mother's death, was almost too much to bear.

Joan, seeing her upset, had made some gentle enquiries. 'Not bad news, I hope?' Carmen, forcing a smile, had brushed her solicitude aside. She was fine. There wasn't a problem. It was something and nothing. Bland words slipping from her lips while she tried to hold back the tears and stop her hands from shaking.

Lottie had been less discreet. 'Who was that woman you were talking to? She's very pretty. Is she a friend of yours? What's her name?'

'Don't go badgering Carly with all your questions. She's got work to do.'

And Carmen had been grateful for the intervention. She

knew Lottie meant no harm, but she couldn't cope with her curiosity today. She felt dazed, as if she'd been coshed over the head, and yet everything about the café was the opposite of blurred: the blue-flecked Formica tabletops, the scuffed lino, the windows that framed the constant traffic going past. All of it seemed so vivid, so perfectly in focus, like it was somewhere she had never properly seen before.

It was ten to twelve, shortly before the lunchtime rush was due to begin, when Terry Street came into the café. Carmen reluctantly went over to take his order. It seemed to her that wherever Terry was, trouble wasn't far behind.

'How did it go with Joe?' he enquired after asking for a brew.

'Hasn't he told you?'

'I wouldn't be asking if he had.'

'It was ... memorable,' she said, having left a short pause while she ran through a possible list of adjectives. 'And then he rang my dad to tell him all about it. I don't know exactly what he said, but it was enough to convince him that I've gone over to the dark side.'

'Yeah, sounds like the sort of thing Joe would do.'

'I don't see why he had to drag me into their feud.'

'It'll blow over,' Terry said with infuriating casualness. 'These things always do.'

Carmen could have told him, in no uncertain terms, that there wasn't going to be any blowing over, that this time her bridges were burned for good. But she didn't want to get into it with him. The less he knew about her business, the better. 'Just a tea then, is it?'

'Don't take it to heart, love,' he said, ignoring the question. 'What are you doing after work?'

'Why?'

'I thought you might like a chat about this Joe business,

somewhere more private.' Terry glanced briefly towards the counter where Joan, although she was chatting to an elderly customer, also had one eye on Carmen.

'I don't see what else there is to discuss. It's done, isn't it? I'd rather just forget about it.' And before he could reply, she walked off.

Fortunately, the café began to fill up, and once she had delivered the tea, she had an excuse for keeping her distance. What good could come of churning over the meeting with Joe? It wasn't going to change anything. It wasn't going to make things right with her father. And anyway, she wasn't convinced that this was Terry's real reason for wanting to be alone with her. She saw the way he looked at her, as if he was eyeing her up for another notch on his bedpost. She hurried up and down the aisles, smiling, taking orders and delivering lunches, while all the time her thoughts buzzed around her head like bees chasing pollen.

Carmen left the café at twenty past two with the local newspaper in her hand. Despite her best attempts, Terry had not been deterred but was waiting a few yards down the road. He was wearing his familiar grin as he strolled over to her.

'What are you doing here?'

He glanced at the paper she was holding, folded open to the small ads page. 'You looking for somewhere else to live?'

'Sort of,' she said stupidly, not wanting Terry to know too much but immediately realising that all those rings around the ads were something of a giveaway.

'Could be your lucky day, then. I've got a pal called Deana who's got a room going. She lives on the Mansfield.'

'Where?'

'The estate down the road. The three towers, yeah? You can see 'em from the high street.'

'Yes, right, I know where you mean.'

'You want to go round and check it out?'

Carmen quickly shook her head. She didn't want to go any-where with Terry Street. 'Thanks, but I've got things to do.'

'What's the matter? The Mansfield too downmarket for you?'

'No, I didn't mean ...' she began defensively, but then she saw his face and realised he was just winding her up. 'I'm sure it's very nice.'

'Oh, it ain't nice, just cheap and ... well, I was going to say cheerful, but it ain't really that either. Bit of a dump to be honest. The flats aren't bad on the inside, though, and it isn't too far from the caff.'

Carmen racked her brains trying to think of a good excuse as to why she wouldn't even go to look at it. 'I don't think—'

'She's a sweet girl, Deana, if that's what you're worried about. She's your age too, or thereabouts. I reckon you'd get on. So what do you say? I can give you a lift. It'll only take five minutes.'

Carmen hesitated, not wanting to come across as the kind of girl who was too stuck-up to live on the Mansfield or the kind who was unwilling to get into a car with him. At the same time, she couldn't see why it mattered a jot what Terry Street thought of her. She was under no obligation to go to the damn flat, so why didn't she just say she wasn't interested? Instead, the words that came out of her mouth were something quite different. 'Shouldn't you call first? She might not be in.'

Terry glanced at his watch. 'She's usually around in the after-noons. Come on, the car's parked at the Fox.' And then, as if it had all been decided, he started walking towards the pub.

Carmen held back, exasperated by her inability to say no and to make it sound like she meant it. Why did men – and by men she meant her father, Clive and now Terry – always pre-sume that she would do exactly as they wished? On principle, she considered taking a stand and refusing to budge, but then wondered if she'd just be cutting off her nose to spite her face. Finding somewhere decent to live could be a time-consuming business, so it was foolish to turn down this flat without even having viewed it.

Carmen had to hurry to catch up with him. 'So what does Deana do?' she said, when they were side by side, hoping to gather some useful information on her prospective flatmate.

'She works in a club.'

'Local or . . .?'

'Up West,' he said. 'You had enough of the B&B then?'

'It's had enough of me. Anyway, it was never going to be permanent.'

'Planning on sticking around?'

'For now,' she said cautiously.

Terry's car was a dirty white Ford with several dents in its rear. Inside it smelled of stale cigarette smoke overlain by a sharp lemony scent emanating from a cardboard air freshener dangling from the rear-view mirror. As they pulled out of the Fox, he wound down the window and placed his elbow on the ledge.

Terry drove with a careless disregard for other vehicles, even buses, as if he, and he alone, had right of way in Kellston. At the junction he took a right and sped up the high street. She could see the three towers looming up ahead, taller than anything else around them, solid chunks of concrete blotting a landscape that had hardly been picturesque to start with.

Carmen was overly aware of Terry's closeness to her, of his left hand on the gear stick, of his gaze which frequently slid between the road and herself. She couldn't help but be reminded of that warning drummed into her as a child: *Never get in a car with a stranger*. And here she was, having done exactly that. Except Terry couldn't really be classed as a stranger. But she didn't know him that well either.

'What's wrong?' he asked.

'Why should anything be wrong?'

'You look on edge, like you're waiting for something bad to happen.'

Carmen faked a snort and shifted in her seat. 'Something bad already has,' she said, not wanting him to know what she was really thinking. 'Slow down, can't you? Have you even passed your driving test? You shouldn't be looking at me. Keep your eyes on the road.'

'I'm a good driver,' he said.

'The back of your car begs to differ.'

'That's other people's bad driving, not mine. Trust me. I'll get you there in one piece.'

Carmen kept her gaze fixed straight ahead, trying to mentally rearrange her features into an expression of someone who had confidence. Of course, Terry wasn't completely unknown to her and there was nothing fundamentally frightening about him – well, if you didn't count what he did for a living – but she was still struggling to relax.

Her body tensed again as the car passed through the gates to the Mansfield. Everything was so grey and dreary and depressing. There was a sense of desolation about the estate. Graffiti adorned the walls and litter was scattered across the pathways. People scuttled by with their shoulders hunched and their heads down. Shifty-looking boys lurked in entrances to dark passageways. Her heart sank. Could she really live here? No, it was too awful. With luck Deana wouldn't be in, but even if she was, Carmen had already decided that this wasn't for her.

44

Carlton House was pretty much identical to the two other towers, one of which, Haslow House, stood beside it, and the second, Temple Tower, on the other side of the estate. Carmen walked with Terry to the main door and into a dank-smelling foyer with lifts and cracked tiled walls and yet more litter – cans, bottles, fag ends – scattered across the floor. On the ceiling a long fluorescent tube light flickered on and off, as if unable to decide whether it was day or night.

Following him into the nearest lift, Carmen was immediately hit by the pungent odour of urine. As the doors closed, she was tempted to interrupt the process and make a bid for freedom. The smell was diabolical. 'God,' she murmured, 'don't people have toilets here?'

'Yeah, stinks, don't it? They clean 'em out every now and again, but it makes no difference. Might be smart to hold your breath for the next fifteen seconds. She's on the ninth floor.'

The lift jerked its way slowly upwards, groaning like some ancient beast of burden. Carmen prayed that it wouldn't break down. The prospect of being stuck in this little metal box for hours was bad enough, but being stuck in it with Terry, she thought drily, would just be the icing on the cake.

'What club does Deana work at?' she said, trying to take her mind off breakdowns and confined spaces, and hoping that the club wasn't Lola's.

'Scandal. Do you know it?'

Carmen had heard of it, had even walked past it, but had never been inside. It was a private members' club for the well-heeled. There were rumours that it was called Scandal for a reason, that men went there for more than the burlesque cabaret and over-priced drinks. 'Dean Street, yeah?'

'That's the one.' Terry glanced at her and said, 'What?'

'What do you mean, *What*?'

'It ain't a knocking shop, you know.'

'I didn't say it was.'

Terry laughed. 'Try telling that to your face.'

The lift came to a halt and after a worrying pause the doors slid open. They turned left and walked along a shabby corridor with magnolia-coloured walls and stained lino on the floor. The smell of cannabis wafted through the air. There were flats on both sides, all the doors painted a uniform shade of industrial green, and Terry stopped at one that was about halfway down. He pressed the bell and they waited.

The girl who answered was tall and slender, a blonde with waist-length hair, a wide mouth and a warm smile. She was wearing blue tracksuit bottoms and a white vest that showed off her smooth honey-coloured skin.

'Terry, hon. What are you doing here?'

'You still got a room going, babe?'

Deana stood aside and waved them in. 'Yeah, still looking for someone.'

'This could be your lucky day, then. Meet Carly. She's after a place to live. I told her you're a nightmare, but she still wanted to come and see the place.'

Deana laughed. 'Don't listen to him, Carly. I'm an absolute angel. If anyone's a nightmare, it's him.'

The living room was a pleasant surprise: light and spacious with panoramic views over east London and beyond. There were long dark grey curtains and a paler carpet. The white walls were hung with framed monochrome prints and there were copies of *Cosmopolitan* and *Vogue* on the coffee table. It was all a far cry from the clean but thoroughly old-fashioned surroundings of Mrs Jordan's B&B.

'Come on,' Deana said, 'I'll show you the room. Terry, there's beer in the fridge if you want it. Help yourself.'

Carmen followed Deana's swinging hips along the hallway until they reached the very end. Deana told her the rent, much cheaper than the B&B, and said, 'It's smaller than the other two bedrooms so you pay a bit less. We thought that was only fair. You've got full use of the living room, of course, and the kitchen and bathroom. Beth's my flatmate, but she's not around during the day. She works at a women's refuge in Hackney.'

Deana pushed open the door and Carmen looked inside. The room had a single bed, a wardrobe and a dressing table squeezed in under the window. But it was still bright and comfortable. The carpet was the same grey as the living room and the curtains were a pale pink.

'It's nice,' Carmen said.

'We split the gas and leccy three ways and write down all the calls we make on the pad by the phone. We've only got a couple of house rules: clean up after yourself and no men staying overnight. I'm not bothered about the last one, but

222

Beth says she can't be doing with bumping into half-naked men first thing in the morning. Do you have a boyfriend? Are you and Terry—'

'No,' Carmen said quickly. 'He's just ...' What exactly was Terry? Hardly a friend, but slightly more than a passing acquaintance. 'I know him from the café where I work. We got talking and he mentioned that you might have a room.'

'Well, it's yours if you want it. You can move in whenever you like.'

'Really?' Carmen said, surprised by the speed of it all. 'Don't you want to discuss it with Beth first?'

'Oh, Beth won't care. She just wants someone to share the rent. Is there anything else you need to know?'

Although the inside of the flat was far nicer than expected, Carmen still had reservations about the Mansfield. 'You don't er ... get any trouble on the estate? I've never been here before and it looks a bit ...'

Deana laughed. 'Yeah, it looks rough, but it's not that bad. You'll soon get to know people. And if you're mates with Terry, no one will give you any bother. So what do you think? Do you fancy it?'

And in that moment Carmen knew that she was taking the final step, accepting that the past was past, and she wouldn't be returning to Belgravia. She took a deep breath, nodded, and said, 'Thanks, I will. I'll take it.'

45

Jonny was in a good mood. He had two hundred smackers in his pocket, which was two hundred more than he'd woken up with this morning. He'd managed to pawn the fur coat for ninety quid and had sold the two paintings for a hundred and ten to a gallery in Bond Street. Original Victorian watercolours, the man had said. Left to him by an aunt, Jonny had said, looking suitably doleful at her loss. He had gone up West wearing one of his best suits, shirt crisp and ironed, shoes gleaming. It always paid to look the part.

He'd been pleasantly surprised by the price he'd got for the paintings and already he was thinking of that crate in the attic where other similar pictures, wrapped in brown paper, lay ready to be liberated. There was only one niggling worry in the back of his mind: that the pictures would go in the gallery window and that Rex or even Marian or Hazel would walk past and recognise them. It was a risk worth taking, but next time he'd go further afield to sell his wares: some wealthy Home Counties town like Esher or Weybridge, where the well-heeled residents might be tempted by the opportunity to hang something old and pallid on their expensively decorated walls.

Jonny's afternoon was a productive one. After flogging the paintings, he went on to the Royal to oversee the laying of the carpet in the basement. The walls had been painted racing green and already it was starting to look more like a habitable space and less like a storeroom. What it still lacked, however, was style. It needed more character, more glamour. He would have to work on that. In his head he had a picture of a small, exclusive, and comfortable club where even the likes of Lord Lucan would feel at home.

After he was finished at the Royal, he went for a late lunch, followed it with a few neat whiskies in a backroom bar that didn't adhere to the usual licensing rules, and then walked through to Charing Cross Road where he hailed a cab and gave the Ebury Street address. He was going to have to face Rex eventually, and now was as good a time as any.

Autumn sunshine streamed down from a powder-blue sky, casting a golden glow across the London streets. Jonny sat back in the cab and gazed out of the window. He was feeling pleased with himself, devoid of any guilt as regards the property he had taken from the attic. What was the point of it just lying there? Nobody wanted it, so it may as well be disposed of. In a way he was doing them all a favour. It was just plain weird to hang on to all of Rosa's things like that, to stash them away where they couldn't be seen.

By the time the cab dropped him off at Belgravia it was ten past four. He prepared himself for what was to come – it wasn't going to be pleasant – and made a mental note to stay calm and take it on the chin. Remorse, guilt and shame were the order of the day. Then, when he was sure that this was firmly embedded in his skull, he strode into the office. Elizabeth looked up and frowned, as if he'd brought a bad smell through the door with him.

'Is Rex around?'

'Is he expecting you?'

Jonny shrugged, familiar with that barrier she always managed to erect when it came to anyone disturbing the boss. Or perhaps that tightness around her mouth was simply down to disapproval. Had Rex told her about his gambling debt to Quinn? Probably. He had the feeling that Rex told his secretary most things. Hazel and Marian couldn't stand Elizabeth – and made no secret of it – but he'd always tried to keep on the right side of her. A few compliments and a little fake flattery could go a long way with a woman, and there was no knowing when this one might be useful.

'Am I in the doghouse?' he said, leaning against the desk and bestowing his most charming smile.

'I believe so. Rex is very upset about it all.'

'Well, I've come to apologise. I've been a fool, haven't I?' Jonny ran his fingers through his hair and sighed. 'What an idiot! I should know better at my age. If I could turn back time, I would. Perhaps you could put a word in for me, tell him I'm not *all* bad. It would mean something coming from you.'

Elizabeth seemed to soften a little at this show of regret, shaking her head sadly as if someone upsetting Rex in any shape or form was beyond her comprehension. It was then, as her hand reached for the phone, that there was a muffled shout and the sound of an inner door slamming. Suddenly Rex came barrelling into reception, muttering wildly, his face white and his eyes wide.

For a moment Jonny thought that he was the subject of this outburst and braced himself accordingly. But Rex pushed straight past and ran outside. Startled, Elizabeth immediately stood up. Pat, hearing the commotion, left his office and hurried in to join them.

'What's going on?' Pat said.

Jonny shook his head. 'I've no idea.'

The three of them went over to the window and stared out at the street. Rex was rushing up and down, looking in both directions. He had one hand raised to his forehead, shielding his eyes from the sun, as he frantically scanned the surrounding area. There was a wild expression on his face, a jerkiness to his movements.

'What's he doing?' Elizabeth murmured.

'He appears to be looking for someone,' Pat said.

'Yes, but who?'

As none of them had the answer to that, they continued to stand and stare, bemused by the scene playing out in front of them, until Rex finally disappeared from view. Elizabeth nudged Pat and said, 'You'd better go after him, make sure he's all right.'

Pat nodded and hurried out of the office, following in Rex's footsteps until he too was out of sight. Jonny and Elizabeth stood side by side in silence. He could hear her slightly ragged breathing and see the tension in her shoulders.

'He's not been himself recently,' she said.

Jonny, who hadn't noticed any difference from Rex's normal malevolent self, made an incoherent noise that meant nothing but might possibly be taken for agreement. The minutes passed by and there was still no sign of either Rex or Pat. Elizabeth shifted impatiently from one foot to another. She had her nose pressed up against the glass, her gaze fixed on the street and the passers-by.

Then, eventually, the two men appeared again, walking slowly down the street. Rex was frowning and waving his arms as if trying to explain something. Pat was shaking his head. Elizabeth quickly returned to her desk and Jonny moved across the room to join her. They waited without speaking, both on tenterhooks, but probably for different reasons.

Rex strode back into reception, saw Jonny as if for the first time, glared at him and barked, 'My office! Five minutes.'

Elizabeth waited until she heard his door close before turning to Pat. 'What was all that about?'

Pat might have been more guarded in Jonny's presence had he not been so flustered. Instead, he blurted out, 'He thought he saw Michael Quinn walk past the office.'

Elizabeth looked astonished. 'What?'

'He swore it was him, said he'd know him anywhere.'

'But it can't have been.'

'You try telling him that.'

Jonny didn't know that much about Michael Quinn, other than that he'd been Rosa's older brother and had disappeared several years after she'd married Rex. Although, now he came to think about it, Hazel may have mentioned something about Rex and Michael being best mates once, a friendship that had fallen apart due to Rex's determination to marry Rosa.

'Isn't Michael Quinn dead?' he said bluntly.

Elizabeth looked briefly at Pat but was clearly too agitated by the whole situation to hold her tongue. 'Everyone presumed he was. I mean, it's been years since he went missing and he didn't take anything with him, never used his bank account again, didn't say goodbye to anyone. And Joe Quinn was convinced he'd been murdered. He even accused Rex of . . . well, the less said about that the better.'

'That was all nonsense,' Pat insisted. 'Rex would never have hurt Michael, not in a hundred years.'

'Of course not,' Elizabeth said. 'I wasn't . . . I didn't . . . I was only saying what Joe Quinn thought.'

Pat shot a pointed glance in Jonny's direction as if to imply that such talk was not advisable in front of Rex's son-in-law. 'Some things are best left unrepeated.'

'I'm sure it's nothing Jonny hasn't heard before,' she huffed.

Jonny was enjoying the exchange, sensing as he did the undercurrent of hostility between them. It didn't surprise him. Rex and conflict went together like two sides of the same coin, as if one could not exist without the other. 'My lips are sealed,' he said.

The colour had risen in Elizabeth's cheeks. 'You'd better go in,' she said sharply. 'You don't want to keep him waiting.'

46

Jonny could smell the whisky as soon as he walked through the door. The glass, half full, was sitting on Rex's desk, his right hand curled around it. There was a bad atmosphere in the room, something heavy and ominous. It didn't bode well. Jonny wouldn't have minded a drink himself, but he knew better than to ask.

'Wondered when you'd show your face,' Rex said aggressively.

Jonny smiled thinly, pulled out a chair and sat down opposite him. He was prepared to take a bollocking, expected it, and wanted to get it over and done with. 'I hear Joe Quinn called you.'

'Yeah, he fuckin' called me. A grand, Jonny. What the hell were you thinking?'

'Well, I wasn't thinking, was I? I screwed up big time. But I'll sort it out.'

'I'm not paying your fuckin' gambling debts for you. If you think that, you can think again.'

'No one's asking you to,' Jonny said, keeping his voice calm. 'It's my problem, not yours. I'll deal with it.'

'But you haven't dealt with it, have you? It was weeks ago. And now I've got Quinn giving me grief. You think I need that, Jonny? You think I need that scumbag on my back?' Rex took a generous swig of whisky and slammed the glass back on the desk. 'I'm not having it! And I'm not having Hazel giving you money, either. This is your debt, not hers.'

'And I'll sort it. I've already told you that.'

'Yeah, but what you say and what you do are two different things. How are you going to sort it? Where are you going to get a grand from? You can forget about Hazel. She's not seeing another penny from my estate until you've paid back Quinn in full. In fact, I'm starting to wonder if I've made a big mistake in handing anything over to her at all.'

Jonny could have retorted that Rex hadn't exactly passed over anything yet, at least nothing that translated into cold hard cash, but he had no desire to provoke him. All the same, this wasn't going quite how he had expected. He'd been anticipating a lecture, that's for sure, but hadn't reckoned on Rex's pique taking such a worrying direction.

'You shouldn't take this out on Hazel. None of this is her fault.'

'She bloody married you, didn't she?' Rex's eyes narrowed into slits. 'You think I'm going to sit back and let you squander the money I've slaved for? No chance! You're a bloody waster, Jonny. You're no good. Have you ever done a day's work in your life? If you have, I've never noticed. It seems to me that you live off my daughter, and no father wants a son-in-law like that.'

'That's a bit harsh, Rex. I've made a mistake, I admit that, but I've learned my lesson. I won't be going anywhere near Quinn or a poker table for the rest of my life.'

'And you expect me to believe that?'

'It's the truth. I swear.'

The glass made its way to Rex's mouth again. He mumbled something into the whisky, a few incoherent words. Jonny wondered if he was drunk. Perhaps this wasn't his first drink of the day. Or maybe Rex was losing his marbles. First the sighting of Michael Quinn and now all this nonsense. It was a complete overreaction. He stared at him closely. The man looked unwell, his face drawn, the hollows under his cheeks more pronounced than usual. It could just have been the shock of thinking he'd seen a dead man walking, but hopefully it was something more serious than that, more physical than psychological, like heart disease or cancer.

'Get out and leave me alone,' Rex said.

'But what about—'

'Are you deaf as well as stupid?' Rex roared. 'Get out of here! I can't stand the bloody sight of you!'

47

'He didn't mean it, though, did he?' Hazel said, staring at her husband. 'He can't take back what's done. I've already signed the papers.'

'How would I know whether he meant it or not? He's behaving like a crazy man, running after ghosts and getting hysterical over a stupid debt that no one expects *him* to pay. If you ask me, he's losing the plot.'

Jonny, who had got back to the house to find Marian and Hazel ensconced in the drawing room, helped himself to a large brandy from the cabinet. He drank half of it down in one and topped up his glass.

'What did he say *exactly*?' Marian asked, crossing one elegant leg over the other.

'Oh, I don't know, some rambling rubbish about how Hazel wouldn't see another penny until the debt was paid, that he wasn't going to let me squander his hard-earned cash, that he'd made a mistake in even thinking of handing over the inheritance.'

'You have to pay Quinn,' Hazel said.

'Thank you for stating the obvious, darling.'

Hazel flushed red. 'Don't have a go at me! I'm not the one who's got us into this mess. If you hadn't—'

'Spare me, Hazel. I'm really not in the mood. Quinn will get his money, okay? I'm working on it. I'll have it by the end of the week.' Already Jonny was thinking about the treasures in the attic, about what else he could take from the crates and turn into cash.

'Where are you going to get a thousand pounds from?'

'Let me worry about that.'

'But will Dad change his mind?' Marian said, looking almost smug.

'Of course he'll change his mind,' Hazel said. 'Once Quinn has been paid. Don't you think? Won't he?'

'You know what he's like once he digs his heels in. He gets an idea in his head, and nothing will shift it. What if he decides to cancel the legacy, to hang on to your share until he drops off his perch? Do you have a copy of the contract you signed?'

'Not yet,' Hazel said. 'Dad said Pat was sorting it out.'

'So theoretically there's nothing to prove that anything was ever signed. He can tear it up and throw it in the bin and there's nothing you can do about it.'

Jonny, irritated by Marian's self-congratulatory expression, decided to wipe the smile off her face. 'If that is the case, you should watch out too. You could be next.'

'Why would I be?'

'Why not? First Carmen, then Hazel. Bit of a theme going on if I'm not mistaken. How long do you think it's going to be before he adds you to the list? I reckon Rex has had second thoughts about handing everything over and now he's just looking for excuses to not go through with it.'

'Rubbish,' Marian said. 'He can't backtrack now.'

Jonny drank his brandy and shrugged. 'If you say so.'

'Well, *I* haven't done anything wrong. I mean, Jesus, I've been running around like a blue-arsed fly doing everything he wants me to do.'

'Nothing to worry about then.'

Marian glared at Jonny, and he had the feeling that she wasn't quite as sure of herself as she had been a minute ago. Everyone knew that Rex could turn with the least provocation, that what he said one day might not be true the next, and that when it came to money he was beyond ruthless.

'I'm not worried,' Marian said. 'You need to have a word with him, Hazel. Find out what his plans are.'

'And since when has Dad ever shared his plans with me? What if he chucks us out of the house?'

'He won't,' Marian said.

'If he chucks us out, we'll need the Camden flat back,' Jonny said to Marian. 'Maybe *you* should talk to him. You're the only one in his good books.'

'I'll think about it.' Marian held out her glass. 'Pour me another, Jonny, while you're on your feet. And tell me about this Michael Quinn business.'

'There's nothing more to tell. Rex was convinced he saw him walking past the office, went rushing out like a madman, but he wasn't there. Well, he wouldn't be, would he, not if he's dead. It was weird, though. Rex seemed pretty shaken up, like he'd seen a bloody ghost. Fortunately, he had me to take all his frustrations out on.'

Marian frowned. 'I dare say it's all this Joe Quinn business that's got him thinking about Michael again. Some kind of association thing.'

'My fault, in other words,' Jonny said.

'Oh, stop being so sensitive. And where's that drink? Come on, I'm gasping here.'

Jonny handed her a large gin and tonic. 'Maybe your old man's losing his mind. He is getting on a bit. There's no knowing what he might do next. He could disinherit the whole lot of you and leave all his money to Pat or Elizabeth.'

Marian snorted. 'Elizabeth!'

'Why not? Services rendered and all that. Perhaps he intends to repay all those years of loyalty, all those hot sweaty nights, with a generous bonus.' Jonny was starting to enjoy himself. Marian was always so supercilious, so full of herself, that it was fun to place a few doubts in her head. 'And Pat's been with him for years. They're tight, those two.'

Hazel frowned at him. 'I don't know why you're saying all this. Why should he disinherit us?'

Marian sighed into her glass. 'He isn't going to disinherit us, for God's sake. Jonny's just winding us up. Or trying to.'

Jonny grinned. 'Or what about Eddie? Perhaps he'll get the family fortune. Have you ever noticed how little he looks like Pat? More like Rex, now I come to think of it. Makes you wonder whether Annie and Rex didn't share a special moment together some time in the past. What do you reckon? Could Eddie be the secret son and heir?'

'Don't be ridiculous,' Hazel said. 'Dad can't stand Annie, and vice versa. They're always at each other's throats.'

'How easily love turns to hate,' Jonny said softly.

Hazel, her face tight, shot him a look. 'What's the matter with you? Why are you always so—'

'The only problem with that theory,' Marian interrupted, intervening before full-blown hostilities broke out, 'is that Dad can't stand Eddie, either. He finds him a crashing bore.'

'Or claims to,' Jonny said. 'Could just be a ploy to put us off the scent.'

Marian sipped her gin and raised her eyebrows. 'What a wonderful imagination you have.'

There was a short silence, then Hazel said, 'What if it *was* Michael Quinn he saw? I mean, they never found a body, did they?'

Jonny thought about the expression on Rex's face when he'd come hurtling out of the office this afternoon. It was hard to say exactly what had been written on his features: shock, fear, horror? Maybe all of them. But definitely not excitement, definitely not unmitigated joy at the possibility of his old mate showing up out of the blue. He thought of that dark stain on the basement floor of the Royal, the stain that looked like blood, and wondered if Rex had good reason to dread the sight of someone who was supposed to be dead.

'I need a slash,' he said. 'If you two ladies can spare me for a minute.'

'Take your time,' Hazel said.

As Jonny was walking along the hallway, he could hear Marian pronouncing in her cool, arrogant voice, 'You could always divorce him. That would bring some joy into Dad's life.'

48

Eddie leaned back against the sink and folded his arms. He had been about to go – he'd only dropped by to spend an hour with his mum – but now that his father had come home earlier than expected, it felt churlish to leave; it would be as if he didn't want to spend time with him, as if he couldn't wait to get away. All of which was true, but out of politeness he agreed to stay for another cuppa.

While his mother made the tea, his father took off his jacket, rolled up his shirtsleeves and sat down at the table. He was starting to look old, Eddie thought, his hair greying, the lines on his face becoming more pronounced.

'Something odd happened today,' Pat said.

'What was that?' Eddie said, although he wasn't much interested.

'Rex thought he saw Michael Quinn walk by the office.'

Annie seemed to freeze, her head caught in the process of turning, the teapot held aloft. 'What? Michael?'

'It wasn't him, of course. Or if it was, he must have scarpered pretty pronto. Rex ran out into the street and looked. He was convinced, sure of it. I had a job getting him back into the office.'

'I thought he was dead,' Eddie said.

Pat nodded. 'That's what everyone thought. Christ, he must be. No one's heard from him in years.'

Annie slowly put the teapot down. 'You think Rex made a mistake?'

'He can't have caught more than a glimpse. Just some bloke who had the look of him, probably. But Rex isn't having it. He went out to search again, up and down those streets for over an hour.' Pat gave a long sigh. 'He'd been drinking by then, had a skinful, so I had to stay with him. I was worried he'd get run over. When we finally got back to the office, he told me to go . . . well, not exactly in those words . . . so I did. There's no reasoning with him when he's in that kind of mood. Elizabeth will make sure he gets home safely.'

Eddie pushed away from the sink and rocked gently on his heels. 'It's only round the corner. I'm sure he'll manage to find it.'

'What if it *was* Michael?' Annie said.

Pat rubbed his face and sighed again. 'It couldn't have been. Why would he suddenly turn up after all this time? It doesn't make sense. If he was going to come back, wouldn't he have done it after Rosa died? Wouldn't he have come to the funeral?'

'He might not have known she was dead.'

'So why would he walk straight past the office and not come in? I know he and Rex weren't on the greatest terms but . . . well, all that was a long time ago. No, it couldn't have been him.'

Eddie thought his father was more shaken up than he was letting on. The skin around his eyes was tight, his hands clenched on the tabletop. 'You think Rex is seeing things?'

'I didn't say that,' Pat snapped. 'A mistake, that's all. We all make them. He's been under a lot of stress recently with the

239

Carmen business, and now Jonny. He had a real go at him this afternoon. Bad bloody timing that was, Jonny showing up at the same time as Rex thought he'd seen Michael.'

Annie poured hot water into the teapot and put the lid on. 'Over that Joe Quinn thing? Is that why Jonny was there?'

'Why else?'

Eddie's mother had told him about Jonny and his debt to Quinn. 'Jonny's an idiot. How's he going to pay that off? Or is Hazel going to pay it for him?'

'Not if Rex has his way,' Pat said. 'He's putting a stop on her money until Jonny sorts it out.'

'Could have a long wait.'

'I think he's having second thoughts about the whole inheritance situation. He's asked me to keep hold of the contracts until he's had another chance to look at them.'

Eddie laughed. 'Why doesn't that surprise me? Those girls aren't going to see a penny until Rex is six feet under.'

Annie poured the tea, passed the mugs round and sat down opposite Pat. Her mind, clearly, was on something other than the trials of the Darby girls. 'It never made any sense to me why Michael would just take off like that. It wasn't like him. God, it broke Rosa's heart when he disappeared. But who'd want to kill him? And they never found a body, did they? Perhaps he is still alive.'

Eddie didn't remember Rosa's older brother. He had seen photographs of him, though: a tall, swarthy-looking man with dark hair. 'Why would he have left without saying goodbye to Rosa?'

'He wouldn't,' Annie said.

'He might,' Pat said. 'If he had to leave in a hurry. Who knows what kind of trouble he was in? And he and Rosa ... they hadn't really got on since she married Rex.'

'Even so. It would be cruel to go and not even send a letter, a note, to let her know he was all right.'

Pat shrugged and drank his tea. 'True enough.'

'Why does Joe Quinn think that Rex killed Michael?' Eddie asked. 'He must have some reason for it.'

'Joe never could stand Rex. He can't stand anyone who's smarter or richer than himself. I'm sure it suited him to point the finger, to spread a few rumours.'

'Unless Rex *did* kill him and now he's got a guilty conscience,' Eddie said, playing devil's advocate. 'Maybe his mind is playing tricks, his sins coming back to haunt him.'

Annie shook her head. 'Don't say things like that, Eddie.'

But Eddie felt she'd said it just to keep the peace, to keep his father happy. He knew she disliked Rex as much as he did. And Rex had a temper on him; everyone knew that. He was more than capable of murder.

49

It was a long few days for Terry before Friday came around. He'd been trying to act normally, to behave the way he always behaved, to not arouse any suspicion. Even with Vinnie Keane, the man he trusted most, he hadn't dropped his guard. What people didn't know about they couldn't blab about. Not that Vinnie was any kind of risk on that score, but better to be safe than sorry.

Only one other person knew what was going to happen tonight, and that was a bent cop called Lazenby who hated Joe Quinn almost as much as Terry did: Lazenby would stop the Jag when Connor was driving home, find Joe's body in the boot and get himself an easy collar. Once Terry had taken over the firm, Lazenby would profit from it too, especially with a move into the West End. There'd be plenty of money rolling in and the cop would be taking a generous share. At some point, Terry knew, he might have to get shot of Lazenby too, but for now he was content to drink with the devil.

Terry put on his gloves, took the suitcase from the top of

the wardrobe, laid it on the bed and flipped open the locks. Carefully, he removed the baseball bat, the handle still covered with polythene film. He weighed it in his hand for a moment, imagining the sound it would make as it arced through the air towards its target.

He placed the bat in a navy-blue sports bag on top of a clean pair of trousers and a shirt. Although he was hoping to avoid getting blood on his clothes, it was best to be prepared for all contingencies. His heart was starting to pump now, the reality of what he was about to do sinking in. But he had no intention of backing out. This was his big chance to take what he wanted, and chances didn't come around every day.

Terry poured himself a stiff Scotch to steady his nerves. The foundations of his plan had already been laid with the call he'd made this afternoon from a phone box on the Caledonian Road.

'Joe, I need a word alone before you go to the Fox tonight.'

'Yeah, what's the deal?'

'It's good, but I'll tell you later. How about I pick you up around half eight? We can talk on the way.'

Joe, who was always paranoid about the law listening in to his phone, didn't press him. 'Half eight, then. And don't be bloody late.'

'I won't. Oh, and could you do us a favour? Don't tell Connor about this, will you? If he knows something's in the pipeline, he'll be on my back all night trying to find out what's going down. Let's just keep it between the two of us for now.'

'I don't tell him nothin',' Joe had grunted before replacing the receiver.

Terry emptied his glass, put it down on the table and checked his pocket for the keys. One set for the Jaguar, another for the cellar door at the side of the Fox. All present and correct. He looked at his watch, saw that it was time, grabbed the bag and went out of the door. It was dark now with a chill in the air. Ignoring his own car, he walked around the corner to where a white van was parked. He'd picked it up for a song – cash, no questions asked – and would dump it later this evening.

He climbed into the van, took the bat out of the bag, and slid it under his seat. Later, he'd remove the film from the handle and leave the weapon in the cellar for the cops to find. It wasn't far to St George's Court, a fancy block of flats with a marble-tiled foyer and balconies on every floor, and even driving at a steady pace he was pulling on to the forecourt in less than five minutes. There was no sign of the Jaguar, which was good news: it meant that Connor had gone on ahead to the Fox.

Once he'd pressed the buzzer and let Joe know he was here, Terry returned to the van and lit a fag. His hands weren't shaking but a thin trickle of sweat was running down the back of his neck. He knew that he would always remember this night, either as his biggest step on the ladder to success or the time he got himself banged up for life. Either way, nothing would ever be the same again.

As soon as Joe got in the van, he started griping about the state of it, the smell of it, as if his finer feelings were offended by travelling in a rusty heap of junk. Terry told him that his car was in the garage, that he'd had a bump over Hackney way. It was when Joe called it 'a fuckin' death trap' that Terry jumped a little, afraid that Joe, subconsciously, had guessed what he was planning.

To cover up his discomfort, Terry pulled the van back out on to the street and started talking about a dealer he'd met last night when he was up West with Liverpool Larry. 'A Colombian by the name of Mendez. I reckon we could do business with him.'

'We've already got a supplier.'

'Not a reliable one, though. How many times have we

been let down in the last year or so? And every time there's some wannabe ready to slide in and fill the gap. Supply and demand, boss. There's a fuckin' big demand and we ain't got a regular supply.'

Joe didn't look convinced.

Terry said the guy was kosher, that Larry could vouch for him. He kept on talking until he wondered if he was talking too much. Would Joe pick up on his nerves? Would he know something was wrong? Terry was just trying to fill the minutes until they reached the Fox. Had he covered every angle? What if there were customers in the car park? What if Connor, for the first time ever, had gone somewhere else tonight? Shit, the more he thought about everything, the more the doubts set in and the harder his heart thumped. Adrenaline streamed through his body.

The traffic lights on the junction of Station Road and the high street were on red. Terry inwardly cursed as he pulled the van to a halt. He tapped his fingers impatiently against the steering wheel. Fear was leaking from his palms. He tried to relax, to steady his breathing. Christ, what if he bottled it? No, he couldn't think like that. He was Terry Street, not some two-bit loser. There was still time for him to change his mind, but he knew where that would leave him: attached to a firm that was rotting at its roots. Joe wouldn't relinquish power until he was in his grave.

'Is Connor at the Fox?' Terry asked.

'Where else would he be?'

Terry nodded, relieved, one more thing ticked off the list. The lights changed and he shifted forward, switching on the indicator to show that he was turning right. And now they were at the Fox, sweeping gently into the car park, and his eyes quickly raked the space, alert to any customers arriving or leaving by car, searching for any stray drunks or crack-happy toms who might be doing business in the gloom.

Everything was quiet. Terry sent up a silent prayer of thanks. And there was the silver Jag parked in its usual place by the cellar door. He pulled the van up beside it, creating a visual barrier between the car and the street. This way no one passing on Station Road would be able to bear witness to what was going to happen next.

'Christ, Joe, what was that?'

'Huh?'

'I think someone's smashed into the back of the Jag.'

Joe was out of the van faster than a greyhound from a trap. 'Stupid fuckin' bastard!' he muttered, presuming that Connor had been practising his usual careless driving.

Terry, after one final look around, bent down and grabbed the bat from under the seat. He jumped out of the van and strode around to where Joe was hunched over, peering at the rear end of the Jag.

'I can't see nothin',' Joe said.

And those were the last words he ever spoke. In one swift, easy motion, Terry lifted the bat above his head and brought it down with all his force on the older man's skull. There was the cruel sound of wood on bone, a dull, dense fracturing, before Joe slumped forward, fell against the boot and slid slowly to the ground.

50

Carmen was woken in the early hours of Saturday morning by the piercing sound of sirens. From what she had gathered during her short stay, this was not an unusual occurrence in Kellston, but what was different this time was that the noise suddenly cut off almost as soon as the vehicles passed by. Too curious not to investigate, she got out of bed, went over to the window, pushed aside the curtain, and looked along the street.

To her right she could see the Fox lit up like a Christmas tree, the lights blazing upstairs and down. The car park was swarming with police. Her first thought was that there had been trouble at closing time but then she realised it was too late for that. The pub would have been cleared by eleven thirty or thereabouts. Maybe a break-in, then, although the police presence seemed a little over the top for that. So, something more serious.

Carmen pressed her face against the glass, trying to get a better look. She had never been inside the Fox, although Terry had invited her. Thinking about Terry reminded her that she hadn't seen him since he'd taken her to Deana's flat. He hadn't even been in the caff to collect the weekly dues; Gordie had come on his own. After the favour Terry had done her, she had half expected him to show up with that cheeky grin on his face saying that the least she could do was buy him a drink.

She thought about this. Perhaps he'd lost interest. And that was a good thing, wasn't it? Although it was hard not to like him, she guessed that he was the type who played around, who had girls running after him left, right and centre. And anyway, she had no intention of getting involved with a gangster. It had been nice, though, to have a man show some interest, to know that even if Clive didn't want her, somebody did. She felt a touch miffed that he appeared to have abandoned his pursuit, even though she'd made it clear that his pursuit was pointless.

Spotlights had been turned on at the Fox now, illuminating the car park and the side of the pub. Officers were going in and out of the building. The fuss had caused a stir among the neighbours and some of them had emerged from their houses to gather in groups and gawp at the spectacle. She was gawping too, of course, but in what she liked to think of as a more discreet way.

Carmen wondered if there had been a bomb alert – the IRA at it again – and instinctively drew back from the window, wary of shattering glass. But if that was the case, she reasoned, the police wouldn't be stomping all over the place, and they certainly wouldn't allow what could almost be classified as a crowd to be standing so close to the pub. No, this was something else entirely.

She moved forward, resuming her position. There was no ambulance, which presumably meant no injuries or fatalities. A drugs raid? That didn't seem impossible. By now Carmen was wide awake. Not including this one, she only had a single sleep left at the B&B. On Sunday she was moving to the flat on the

248

Mansfield and already her few possessions were packed. She felt relieved to have somewhere more permanent to go, but was anxious too about how she would cope on the estate.

Carmen watched for a while longer, but when nothing further happened, she closed the curtains and returned to her bed. She would find out from Joan what it was all about on Monday. Gazing up at the ceiling, her thoughts wandered from the Fox to Marian – she had called her twice to pass on her new address but got no reply – and on to Clive. Lola's would be closing round about now, the last guests leaving, another busy Friday night done and dusted.

What was Clive doing? Sorting the takings, perhaps, or seeing the last customers off the premises. Was he alone? And by alone, she meant was there a woman waiting for him? She squeezed her eyes shut, not wanting to believe that he might have moved on already. Surely there must be some small part of him that regretted what had happened, that wished she was still with him. But she knew deep down that Clive's emotions were inextricably linked to money and ambition, and that love alone would never be enough for him.

With these tormenting thoughts running through her mind, she eventually fell into a restless sleep and didn't wake up again until five past eight. The distant clatter of crockery and the sound of her fellow residents moving around reminded her that breakfast was being served. Starting work so early, she normally missed this meal – and last weekend she had been too shy to go downstairs – but decided that today she would gather her courage and get her money's worth in the time that was left to her here.

The first thing she did on getting up was to go over to the window and look along the street at the Fox. Everything was quiet now, all the police gone, although some bright tape, flapping in the breeze, sectioned off an area of the car park. A clue as to what had taken place, but not one that meant anything to her.

She went to the bathroom, washed, dressed, and then followed the smell of bacon and eggs to the dining room. Two men, one of whom shared her landing, were already tucking in. There was just one big table and so she had no choice but to join them. They both said, 'Good morning,' and she said the same back. A slight awkwardness hovered in the air, as it so often did when strangers were forced to eat together.

Fortunately, her fellow residents had more on their minds than social niceties. Almost immediately the older of the two, a thin man with a horsey face and prominent teeth, addressed her. 'So, quite a furore last night. Did all the commotion wake you?'

'It did,' she replied, pulling out a chair and sitting down. 'I saw the police at the pub. Do you know what it was about?'

Carmen could tell that her response was a welcome one, that he was pleased to have a new audience for his revelations. He sat forward, his fork poised mid-air and said, 'I do, but you might prefer to hear about it *after* breakfast rather than before.'

'Oh dear, that sounds ominous.'

'It's not very pleasant, that's for sure.'

Carmen waited, but he was clearly savouring his dramatic moment, not wanting to rush, intending to keep her in suspense for a few seconds longer.

'Murder!' the younger man suddenly blurted out, as if he couldn't hold it in any longer. 'Right on our doorstep!'

The thin man shot him a look, annoyed to have his thunder stolen. 'Murder indeed,' he said. 'It's a rum do. Very rum.'

Carmen looked suitably shocked. 'How terrible. Do we know who was murdered? Was it someone at the pub?'

'A man called Joe Quinn,' he said. 'Have you heard of him?'

Carmen started. She felt the blood drain out of her face. 'Yes, of course. Isn't he . . .?' Her mouth had suddenly gone dry, and her pulse was starting to race. A terrifying idea had just leapt into her head. Just how angry had her father been when he'd heard she'd met up with Joe? And she remembered sitting in Connolly's with Terry, saying, *My father is not a murderer.* When she spoke, her voice had a hoarse sound to it. 'I mean, was it some kind of gangland thing?'

'Murdered in the car park and bundled into the boot of his own car,' the thin man said almost gleefully. 'That fancy Jag of his.' He quickly wiped the smile off his face. 'Awful, naturally, but I dare say there'll be some round here who won't be grieving too much.'

Carmen swallowed hard. 'But do they know who did it?'

'Now this is where it gets truly gruesome,' the thin man said. He shot his companion another fast look, as if warning him not to interrupt again. 'Guess who they've arrested?'

'I've no idea.'

'His own *son*! Connor Quinn.'

Relief flooded through Carmen. Of course, she had never really suspected her father. Even *he* wouldn't go that far. But she was still hugely thankful that her unwanted meeting with Joe Quinn hadn't been the catalyst for his killing. 'How dreadful.'

'And Tommy Quinn too – that's Joe's other son. Although no one's saying that he had any part in the actual murder.'

'An accessory,' the other man said, feeling it was safe to make a contribution now that the juiciest information had been delivered. 'Helping Connor to dispose of the body. Not that they got that far. The police stopped the car and found Joe Quinn in the boot. It was a baseball bat he used apparently. He hit him over the head with—'

'I'm sure poor Miss Baxter doesn't want to hear all the gory

251

details,' the thin man said, suddenly solicitous now that he wasn't relaying the unpalatable details.

Mrs Jordan came into the dining room, gave a slight eyebrow rise as if surprised to see Carmen there, and nodded. 'Cooked breakfast, is it, dear?'

But Carmen had lost her appetite. Her gaze fell on the men's greasy plates, on the thin rinds of bacon and the eggy smears. Her stomach turned over. She wondered what they'd think if they knew she was related to Joe, that on Monday she had been sitting across the table from him in Connolly's. If she could have stood up and left, she would have, but she didn't trust her legs to carry her. 'Just toast, please.'

51

It was shortly after midday when Jonny heard the news. Milo called from a pay phone in the Black Lion and told him that Joe Quinn was dead. Even as he was speaking, Jonny could feel the tension draining out of his body. One less thing to worry about.

'So you're off the hook, mate. You can't owe money to a dead man. Time to celebrate.'

Jonny was pleased, but he'd have been even more pleased if Rex hadn't taken Hazel aside this morning and told her that he wasn't currently prepared to proceed with the share-out. It wasn't unexpected – hadn't Rex threatened as much in his office? – but he'd been hoping he might not go through with it.

'You're not responsible enough. That husband of yours can wrap you round his little finger. He'll fritter away every penny I give you.'

Or words to that effect. Jonny had been listening outside the drawing-room door, his hands clenched in two tight fists, his upper lip curled. Hazel had argued, of course, but to no avail. Rex had dug his heels in and that was that. So what now? It was a good question. They were back in limbo, without even Rex's limited largesse to keep them ticking over.

He still had the gambling club at the Royal, but that wasn't going to be up and running any time soon. A business like that couldn't be set up overnight. And even when it did open it would take a while for word to get around, to start getting the right customers through the door. He didn't want any old riff-raff in there. He wanted the big rollers, men with money to spend.

Jonny put a hand in his pocket and pulled out the sleeping pills he'd snaffled from Rex's bedroom. He held them in his palm and wondered how many a man would have to take to kill him. Too many to disguise in a glass of whisky. And they probably had a taste. Even drunk, Rex would know that something was wrong. An accidental overdose would be ideal, but he could see no means of achieving this outcome.

He had to find another way. A hit-and-run? A violent mugging? A robbery when Rex was alone in the house or the office? But someone would have to be paid to carry out the killing while the rest of them were covered by cast-iron alibis. It was always risky, though, bringing a third party into the mix. You could never trust a stranger.

He thought about Milo. He didn't trust Milo either, but he might still be the perfect candidate. After all, what did he have to gain by the murder? Nothing. On paper he wouldn't profit at all from Rex's death. He didn't stand to inherit and therefore had no motive. Well, no financial motive. And Milo needed money. Perhaps an arrangement could be made where everyone won. Once Rex was dead there would be plenty of cash to go around.

52

October arrived and brought with it a gold and red tinge to the trees. Rex had not set eyes on Michael Quinn again, or at least not as clearly as he had that first time when his old friend had walked past the window. Sometimes, though, he thought he caught a glimpse of him in a crowded place or when a bus went by or when he stepped out of his office of an evening and a figure was just disappearing round the corner. Occasionally, after he got home from work, he would hear a knock on the door, but when he opened it no one was there. Was his mind playing tricks? Or was Michael? There was only one way to find out, but Pat wasn't having any of it. When he'd made the suggestion, Pat had gone white as a sheet.

'Don't even think about it, Rex. Do you want to spend your last days in jail?'

'It was him,' Rex insisted. 'I saw him.'

But Pat just stared at him strangely, as if he was crazy, as if he was deranged. 'It can't have been. You know it can't.'

Rex knew he was drinking too much, but he had been driven

to it. How else was he supposed to cope? Just as Joe Quinn's son had turned on him, his own family was busy plotting against him too. He could see it in every look they gave, hear it in every word they spoke.

That waster Jonny thought he was off the hook because Joe Quinn was dead, but he wasn't getting away with it that easily. He'd got lucky, that's all, but it didn't mean Rex was going to trust him anywhere near the family fortune. Hazel rolled her eyes, said he'd learned his lesson, said she didn't understand why she was being punished for what *he'd* done. But she was as bad as him. If she couldn't control her own husband, how was she going to control the fortune that was coming to her?

And Marian. He knew what she was up to. Making a show of coming into the office, pretending that she was willing to work for her money when all the time he knew she was just waiting for the moment she could liquidise her assets and go on a spending spree. He could see straight through her. The high life was all she wanted, and freedom from a husband who bored her.

Then there was Carmen, who would rather slave as a waitress than apologise, who had gone behind his back and courted Joe Quinn, who had been the biggest disappointment of his life. Well, the second biggest. No one could ever nudge Rosa off that top spot.

When push came to shove, none of his daughters deserved what he had done for them, none were ready for the responsibility. He had been too hasty in handing over his fortune. The truth was that he had raised a family of parasites, girls with Rosa's blood and Rosa's ingratitude. They knew the price of everything and the value of nothing. It gave him palpitations to think of his empire reduced to ashes, of everything he'd built up being razed to the ground.

Once he was dead and gone, he would have no control over

that, but in the meantime he still had the power to keep them in their place. He would not let them take it for granted that they'd inherit. A few hints dropped here and there should be enough to remind them of their obligations. They needed to learn some respect, to learn that you didn't get something for nothing.

All of this was bad enough, but now the spectre of Michael hung over him, too. Sometimes, in the middle of the night, when Jonny and Hazel were asleep, he sensed a strange shifting in the air, thought he heard the sound of footsteps, the creaking of boards, but when he got up to investigate, no one was there. It creeped him out, this sense of another presence in the house, an invisible guest, as if the ghosts of his past would never leave him alone.

Marian looked across at Hugh, scowled and said, 'All this is Jonny's fault – and Carmen's. If it wasn't for them, Dad wouldn't be doing this. He won't even let me have any proper office space. I've got to share the reception area and stare at Elizabeth's ugly mug all day.' She stood up, crossed her arms and pouted. 'And please don't say *I told you so*. I'm not in the mood.'

'He's got cold feet,' Hugh said. 'Give him a few months and he'll calm down. He's just realised the immensity of what he's doing, and it terrifies him.'

'Well, he should have realised the bloody "immensity" before he made his grand announcement.'

'He hasn't said that he's not going to hand it over, has he?'

'As good as,' Marian replied. 'He's not interested in anything I suggest. Everything has to stay just as he arranged it. I can't sell any of the houses or flats. And Pat won't even give me a copy of the contract. It needs to be countersigned and Dad's dragging his feet. So basically, all the money is still going into the original company account, and I can't touch a penny of it.'

'Perhaps you should move out of the Camden flat. It's just

257

more expense, isn't it, when you can stay at the Gryphon for free?'

'I've only just moved into the damn place.'

Marian's frustration was palpable, a throbbing agony at how the prize had been dangled in front of her and then snatched away. She was thirty, for God's sake, and when she looked in the mirror, she could almost see her beauty slipping away. Before she knew it, she'd be past her prime, one of those women who were over the hill and a shadow of their former selves. None of this, of course, she could share with Hugh. Instead, she sighed and said, 'I wanted to take the boys on a decent holiday. We haven't been away in ages.'

'We were in Cornwall in the summer.'

'Oh, you know what I mean. *Abroad*. France, Italy, somewhere you can rely on the weather, somewhere the boys can run around in the sun. I want them to have the kind of holidays I had when I was young.'

'You always said you hated those holidays.'

'Only because *he* was there, spoiling it for everyone.' Marian exhaled an exasperated breath. She would have stamped her foot if she hadn't feared looking childish. 'He can't stand the thought of anyone enjoying themselves. He always has to ruin everything.'

'Oh, Carmen rang again,' Hugh said. 'She left her new address and number. I've written it down on the pad.'

'I told her to call me at Camden.'

'She said she's been trying but you never pick up.'

'Well, I've been busy, haven't I? I haven't got time to be running around after Carmen. If she wants her things, she can go and get them herself.'

Hugh sat back in the armchair, put a match to his pipe and gazed at her through puffs of smoke. 'If you told her that, she wouldn't have to keep on ringing here.'

'She doesn't need to keep ringing here full stop. You'd have thought she'd have got the message by now. And do you have to smoke that thing? It stinks.'

Hugh smiled mildly back at her. 'You'll get the money eventually. What's the point in stressing about it?'

Marian despaired of her husband's stupidity. It could be ten years, twenty, before her father died. In fact, he would probably live to a hundred just to spite them all. She looked around the drawing room and felt the walls closing in on her. Was this it? She could feel her life slowly dripping away, hour by hour, day by day. But she refused to be stuck here, mouldering in this dump. Tomorrow she would go back to London. She wasn't giving up yet. There had to be a way. She wasn't her father's daughter for nothing.

Milo knew what Jonny was getting at, what he was angling for, but he wasn't going to make it easy for him. If he wanted to ask, he could do it straight out. Instead, he'd been going round the houses for the last half hour, talking casually about the perfect murder and if it was ever possible to get away with it.

'The filth ain't stupid,' Milo said. He sniggered into his pint. 'Well, some of 'em, but not all. Family's the first place they always look. They're the ones who usually have the motive.'

'Yeah, but what if the family's in the clear? What if they all have alibis?'

'That don't mean nothin'. They could have paid someone else to do it.'

'And how would the law prove that?'

'Don't suppose they could unless they nabbed the hitman and he squealed. Although that's your next problem, ain't it? You gonna trust a stranger to keep his gob shut if he's caught? I mean, there ain't nothin' in it for him at that point. May as well sing like a canary and try and get a few years off his sentence.'

Jonny nodded, still pretending that this was all hypothetical, still just a casual conversation in a quiet Soho pub. 'It would have to be someone you trusted, I guess.'

'Trust! You can't trust no one in this game. No, you'd need to make it worth their while to do a proper job and keep schtum about it. Big risks, big rewards. And the filth are gonna check all the family bank accounts, make sure no suspiciously large sums have gone out recently. How do you get round that little problem? I mean, a job like that ain't gonna come cheap.'

'What if they were paid after, when all the fuss had died down?'

Milo laughed. 'Any self-respecting hitman's gonna want at least half up front. I mean, what if he does the job and don't get the cash? He can hardly go whining to the filth about it. Hey, officer, I wasted this geezer and now the bastard won't pay me what I'm due! He's up the creek without a paddle, ain't he?'

Jonny shrugged, smiled and drank his pint, like these were other people's problems, not his own.

Milo knew then that he wasn't going to ask him, not tonight. Jonny was being cautious. But when he got around to it, what would his answer be? On the one hand he didn't want to spend the next twenty years in the slammer, but on the other he didn't have a pot to piss in. If Darby money was going begging, it might as well be his as anyone else's.

53

Carmen had not seen much of Terry Street since the murder, but she had heard the rumours – or rather Joan had heard them and passed them on to her. Now that Quinn's rule had come to an end, there was a battle raging for who would take his place. Terry was trying to step into his shoes, to take control, but he was facing opposition from the older members of the firm, men who thought him too young, too inexperienced and perhaps too cocky to rule the manor with any effectiveness. While this internal war raged, neighbouring firms looking to extend their territory were also trying to move in on Kellston and pick up the spoils. Fights were breaking out, knives were being wielded, and the local hospital was doing a brisk trade cleaning up the injured and stitching them back together.

The only advantage to all this, so far as the Station Café was concerned, was that no one was coming to pick up the Friday afternoon pay-outs. Carmen had expected Joan to be pleased about this, but instead she was anxious that someone even worse than Quinn would take over, someone who would up her weekly payment to a level she couldn't afford.

'At least I knew where I was with him,' Joan said. 'He might have been a vicious old sod, but I didn't have sleepless nights wondering what was coming next.'

'Terry wouldn't charge you more, would he?'

Joan buttered the bread with fast, easy strokes, exactly the same amount across every slice. 'Terry's barely out of short pants. How's he going to take over that mob?'

But Carmen wasn't so sure. There was something about him, she thought, and it wasn't just his cheeky charm. 'He's not that young. I mean, he's older than me.'

'Well, that's not saying much.'

'I don't think he liked Joe Quinn,' Carmen said.

'Nobody liked Joe Quinn, love. That doesn't qualify him to take his place. If Terry isn't careful, he'll end up six foot under and that's the truth of it.'

'Who'll end up six foot under?' Lottie asked, coming out from the back and wiping her wet hands on her apron.

'No one you need worry about,' Joan said firmly.

Lottie, who knew when she was being fobbed off, looked to Carmen instead. 'Who were you talking about? Terry Street?'

'Those big ears of yours have been flapping again,' Joan said. 'You shouldn't listen in to other people's private conversations.'

'You should talk more quietly then. I can hear every word you say.' Lottie grinned, leaned against the counter and said, 'Terry likes Carly.'

'No, he doesn't,' Carmen said.

'Then why did he want to know where you live?'

Joan gave Carmen a curious look. 'Did he now?'

'I wasn't supposed to tell,' Lottie said, briefly clamping a hand to her mouth. 'I forgot.'

'It was ages ago,' Carmen explained quickly, not wanting Joan to get the wrong idea. 'And it was only because he'd heard about the room going on the Mansfield. He was just being . . . helpful.'

'You should watch that Terry,' Joan said. 'In my experience men are never "helpful" for nothing.'

'I've hardly seen him since then. Anyway, I should think he's got other things on his mind right now.'

'What sort of things?' Lottie piped up.

'Nothing you need to concern yourself with,' Joan said. 'Now sit down while it's quiet and I'll get you a brew.'

Carmen glanced at the clock. It was quarter past two and her working day was over. 'Okay, I'm off. I'll see you tomorrow.'

'Going anywhere nice?' Joan said, fishing for information, and perhaps with Terry Street still idling in her thoughts. She had noticed, no doubt, that Carmen was dressed more smartly than usual, had brushed her hair, and put on fresh lipstick.

Carmen put her straight before any scurrilous ideas could take root. 'Nowhere exciting. Only Victoria, I'm afraid. I'm going to meet an old friend of my mum's.'

'You have a good time.'

'Thanks.'

As Carmen left the café, she realised she was feeling faintly nervous. She had only called Annie Foster yesterday to let her know, somewhat belatedly, that she was all right, but Annie had insisted on them meeting up. It would be the first time Carmen had seen any of her family – well, almost family – since Marian had come by over a month ago. She hoped Annie wouldn't try and persuade her to go home. It seemed unlikely, bearing in mind the older woman's loathing of Rex Darby, but these days nothing was predictable.

Carmen felt guilty at having left it so long to get in touch – she remembered Annie standing up for her at the party, and all the other kindnesses through the years – and wished she had contacted her sooner. Why hadn't she? If she was being generous to herself, she would say it was because she had wanted to protect her from this feud, but she suspected it had had more to do with how her father, from her early childhood, had always made it clear that he did not approve of Annie Foster and wanted his daughters to keep their distance. Now, when she thought back on it, Carmen was ashamed of how she'd so blindly obeyed him.

Growing up, her carers had comprised an endless troop of housekeepers, nannies and au pairs, all of them pretty and none of them staying longer than it took her father to get them into bed and then grow bored of them. Annie's offers of help had fallen on deaf ears unless he was desperate. Only then, and grudgingly, had he allowed her a few precious hours with the children of her best friend.

When the bus arrived, Carmen went upstairs and chose an empty window seat halfway along the aisle. The bus wasn't busy – it would be a couple of hours before the rush began – and she settled down to enjoy the journey without someone else being squashed up beside her.

While the bus travelled through the streets, stopping and starting, she reflected on how much her life had changed in such a short period of time. It wasn't that long since her future had been mapped out, a future she had been perfectly happy with, in which she would never have to worry where the money was coming from to pay the bills or grab a cab or treat herself to a new dress or handbag. Now she had to count every penny and think twice before buying anything new.

But then she had never thought about her father's absolute power over her either, or questioned anything he demanded of her. Well, not until that Friday night, when everything had suddenly fallen apart. And from there it had been one short step to getting up at five-thirty every morning, serving tables and living on the Mansfield estate.

The strange thing was that she wasn't unhappy. She no longer had that dread of hearing the front door open and close of an evening and wondering what mood her father would be in. She no longer had to bend to his will, to tiptoe round him, to be the perfect daughter he demanded. And as regards Clive, she didn't miss him half as much as she thought she would. Her life, although bound by different restrictions, had a new liberty about it.

The Mansfield, even though she was gradually growing accustomed to it, still held an air of menace for her. When she left in the mornings the estate was always quiet, almost deserted, and although it was busier when she came home in the afternoon, she remained constantly wary, always vigilant for any trouble that could be heading her way. It was the young men she feared most, the ones who hung around in groups or loitered near the passageways. Like a gazelle being watched by hungry lions, she would feel their eyes on her as she walked down the path.

As regards her flatmates, Carmen was still getting to know them. Beth was small and intense, her life revolving around strident causes – women's rights, CND, anti-apartheid – her driving force being to effect change and make a difference. Deana was the very opposite, tall and languid, living for the day and not giving a damn about what tomorrow might bring. She liked them both in different ways. And how could *she*, Carmen, be described? A work in progress, she decided, just starting out on the journey.

The bus terminated at Victoria bus station, and Carmen got off and followed the directions Annie had given her to a nearby café called Deano's. As she walked, it occurred to her that she had spent a disproportionate amount of time in cafeterias recently. She shuddered as she thought of her meeting with Joe Quinn, remembering his cruel, malicious face and the violent way he'd met his end. He had been her distant blood, but she had felt nothing towards him but fear and disgust.

On approaching the café door, Carmen had a sudden dread: what if this was some kind of ambush and her father was waiting for her? There were net curtains across the window, and she couldn't see inside. It was an irrational thought – Annie would never play such a trick on her – but one that temporarily stopped her in her tracks. She hesitated for a moment, her heart skipping a beat, but then forced herself forward.

54

Carmen's gaze quickly scoured the room as she stepped inside, and she exhaled as she saw Annie sitting alone in the far corner of the café. As their eyes met, Annie raised a hand, waved and stood up to greet her. She gave Carmen a hug, and then, holding on to her arms, pushed her slightly back and looked her up and down.

'You've lost weight. I'm sure of it. Are you eating properly?'

'Three square meals a day. I promise. I work in a caff, remember? Food's the one thing I'm never short of.'

They sat down opposite each other, smiling and yet slightly awkward, as if it was years since they'd last met rather than weeks. 'I got tea,' Annie said. 'Is that all right? I can order something else if you like.'

'Tea's fine,' Carmen said.

Annie was a motherly-looking woman, her waist thickening, her brown hair streaked with grey. She lifted the lid on the pot, gave the contents a stir and poured out two cups. 'Are you sure you're all right? I've been so worried about you. It's a terrible business this. I don't know what's wrong with your father.'

'I should have called you before. I'm sorry about that. But, yes, I'm doing okay. I've got a job and somewhere to live – a flatshare with a couple of other girls.'

'You should have come to us. There's plenty of room.'

'Dad wouldn't have liked that. You know he wouldn't. It would only have caused trouble for you and Pat.'

'Nothing we couldn't have dealt with, love. I'd never see you without a roof over your head, not while I've got breath in my body. So if you change your mind, or it doesn't work out where you are, the door's always open, any time day or night.'

'Thanks, Annie. I appreciate it.'

'And don't you go worrying about how your dad might feel. That's neither here nor there. Me and Pat, we'd both be happy to have you stay.'

Carmen doubted if Pat *would* be happy – he had to work with her father, after all – but she nodded and smiled and said thank you again. She suspected that Annie was lonely in that big old house of hers now that Eddie had moved out. Her marriage to Pat was a mystery to Carmen, a relationship that appeared to be based on familiarity rather than anything more loving. But then what did she know? Her knowledge of marriage was limited to what she saw on the television or read in magazines.

'And how is everyone?' Carmen asked. 'How are you? How're Eddie and Pat?'

'Oh, the same as always. Nothing changes much in the Foster household. Eddie's still at the bookshop. I don't know where he got this thing about books. It certainly wasn't from me or his father, but it seems to make him happy, so . . .'

'And Pat?'

'Still working all the hours God sends. I barely see him, to be honest. He reckons your father's going through a bad time.' Here Annie paused and raised her eyes to the heavens as if to dissociate herself from her husband's opinion. 'Apparently this whole Michael Quinn business has got him in a tizz.'

'*Michael* Quinn?' Carmen said, confused. 'I thought it was Joe he was upset about.'

'Oh, him too, but there's not much point in wasting your energy on a dead man. Did you know that he was . . .?'

Carmen nodded. 'Yes, I heard. And I didn't go looking for him, whatever Dad thinks. One of his henchmen recognised me and I was summoned to a meeting. It's hard to say no to a man like that. I'm sure he only wanted to see me to wind Dad up.'

'He was a bad lot, that Joe. I don't suppose there are many who are sorry he's gone.' Annie took a sip of tea and looked at Carmen over the rim of her cup. 'Well, now your father has got this idea in his head that he saw Michael outside the office. It was a few weeks back, maybe even a month when I come to think about it. Anyway, ever since then he's been convinced that Michael's still alive, that he's come back. Pat reckons it's all in his imagination.'

'And what do you think?'

Annie hesitated, and then sighed. 'I don't know. I used to think Michael would never have left without telling Rosa, but there's no telling with some people. But if he has come back, why would he be skulking round Rex's office? Why not just go in? There's no rhyme or reason to it. It doesn't make any sense.'

'What was he like? No one ever talked about Michael when I was growing up.'

'You'd have got on, I think. He was a nice enough bloke, tough but quiet. Don't get me wrong, he and Rex got up to all sorts in their younger days, but he was decent at heart. Or at least I always thought he was. Maybe he had another side to him. Men can be selfish creatures at times, only ever looking out for themselves.'

Carmen nodded, thinking of Clive.

'I probably shouldn't say this, but he never wanted your mum and dad to get married. He didn't think Rex would treat her well.'

Carmen, who was already aware of this, courtesy of Terry Street, gave another nod. 'And he was right, wasn't he? He didn't.'

'Your dad always wanted what he thought he couldn't have, and then when he got it . . . well, it wasn't so desirable any more.'

'I suppose she must have loved him once.'

'She did, of course she did, in those early days. But your mother was no pushover; she could give as good as she got. I've never met another woman who could keep Rex Darby in line the way she did. It was only after she had Marian, after she got sick, that it all began to go wrong.'

Carmen wanted to ask if what Marian had told her was true, if her mother had really wanted to get rid of her, but she knew that Annie, hoping to spare her feelings, would only deny it. And what was the point in dwelling on the past? She could not change her mother's feelings or transform her into the kind of happy healthy woman who would have welcomed having a third child. As these distressing thoughts ran through her mind, she absent-mindedly twisted the engagement ring on her finger.

Annie, mistaking the gesture as a sign of Carmen's feelings for her ex, asked gently, 'Have you heard from Clive?'

'No, nothing. Apparently, I'm not so appealing now my father has disowned me.'

'He's a fool, then.'

'I thought he loved me. You know, *for me*.' Carmen, afraid of sounding pathetic, smiled wryly. 'I suppose that makes me the fool.'

Annie reached across and laid her hand over Carmen's. 'No

more than any of us. You had a lucky escape if you ask me. Better you find out now than later.'

'Do you think I should give the ring back?'

'Heavens, why would you do that? It would be different if *you'd* been the one to walk away, but ... no, that ring is yours to keep, love. Don't even think about giving it back. It's the least he owes you.'

'I suppose,' Carmen said. And then, because she didn't want to ponder too much on Clive's treachery, she rapidly moved the conversation on. 'Annie, could I ask you something? Going back to Michael, why would Joe Quinn think that Dad had something to do with his disappearance?'

'That was just Joe talking. He and your dad never got on. As soon as Michael went missing, he couldn't wait to point the finger.'

'So you don't think there's any truth in it?'

Annie shook her head. 'He and Michael might not have seen eye to eye on his marrying your mum, and they weren't as close as they once were, but I can't see any reason for your dad to ... well, I don't think even *he* would go that far. I mean, where's the motive? Why would he? No, I'm never first in the queue to defend Rex Darby, but I don't believe he had anything to do with it.'

Carmen hoped she was right. Having a murderer for a father, in addition to a mother who hadn't wanted her, might be too much to take. But despite all Annie's reassurances, something still niggled in the back of her mind. Her father's capacity for anger, for holding a grudge, knew no bounds. What if Joe Quinn had been right?

55

Rex Darby lifted the glass to his lips and took a long steady pull on his pint. While he drank, he scanned the other customers, plenty of regulars, some strangers, but none of them with the face he was searching for.

'Easy does it,' said Pat, who'd just had to queue for ten minutes at the busy bar and didn't fancy a return trip anytime soon. 'What's the hurry?'

Rex gave a grunt and put his glass down on the table. 'Too many people in here this evening.' He was sitting where he could observe the door, a habit he'd acquired long ago when it had been essential to be able to see any threat that might be heading in his direction. Now those threats felt closer to home. The girls, he was sure, were plotting against him, and Jonny was circling like one of those laughing hyenas you saw on the wildlife programmes. These days even Elizabeth looked at him strangely, her eyes cold and unforgiving. And then, of course, there was Michael . . .

'Have you made a decision yet?' Pat said.

Rex knew he was talking about the inheritance – it was all anyone ever talked about at present – but he just shrugged and shook his head. 'Let them sweat for a while. It won't do them any harm. All they want to do is flog everything and go on a spending spree. What they don't understand is when it's gone it's gone. How many times have I told them? You can enjoy the profits, but you don't touch the capital.'

'You're preaching to the converted.'

'You should have talked me out of it. They're not ready for any kind of responsibility.'

'Come off it, Rex. When have I ever been able to talk you out of anything?' Pat followed his gaze towards the door. 'You expecting someone?'

What Rex was expecting was for the pub door to open and Michael Quinn to walk in. He couldn't help it. The expectation was there, sitting heavily in his gut, like a hard black stone. But he didn't share this dread with Pat. Instead, he looked around and said, 'Why's it so bloody busy? I can't hear myself think.'

'Too many people wanting a pint before they go home.'

'Or needing one,' Rex said, remembering all the times he'd come here after work to avoid Rosa.

'What's eating Elizabeth? She's had a right face on her all afternoon. You two had a falling out?'

'Not to my knowledge.' In truth, Rex didn't think much about Elizabeth these days, didn't talk to her much either unless he needed a cup of tea or a letter typing. 'Why didn't you ask her?'

'Yeah, right, that would have gone down like a lead balloon. She always expects you to know what's bugging her even when you haven't got a clue.'

'Women,' Rex said. 'They're more bloody trouble than they're worth. She's probably got the hump over Marian being in this morning. She doesn't like her sharing the reception space.'

'She doesn't need to take it out on me.'

Rex glanced towards the door again. 'Have you thought any more about that other matter?' He lowered his voice. 'Michael, I mean.'

Pat's face went pale. 'Don't start that again, Rex. It's a shit idea. You know it is.'

'I know what I saw.'

'What you thought you saw.'

How many times had they had this conversation, going round in the same circles? It was infuriating that Pat wouldn't believe him, like he was fucking senile or something. 'We can check. Why not? Then we'll know for certain.'

Pat's reply was fast and testy and barely audible. 'You know why not. What are you thinking here, the bloody resurrection? He's dead, Rex, nothing but bones, and he's never coming back. Haven't you ever heard that saying, the one about not returning to the scene of the crime? Let it rest, for God's sake. Let *him* rest.'

Rex knew where the body was, where the grave had been dug in among the trees. Or did he? It had been twenty-five years since he'd last been there. Things changed. Nature changed them, and men did too. Perhaps he wouldn't be able to find the spot again. Could Michael have clawed his way out of that hole in the ground even if he had still been alive? It didn't seem possible, and yet ...

'I won't go back there,' Pat said. There was a thin sheen of sweat on his forehead and his hands had closed into fists. 'Don't ask me to.'

Rex nodded. There was only so much you could expect from a man, even one as loyal as Pat. Everyone had their limits, the point beyond which they wouldn't go. No, he would just have to wait and see what happened. Except he knew what was going to happen. Michael would come for him eventually. It was inevitable. It was only a matter of time. He would need to be prepared, to be ready for that moment, to not be taken by surprise.

'You'll leave it then, Rex. Promise me?'

Rex didn't answer. He had barely heard the plea. Instead, he was thinking about the gun. It was still hidden in the attic. He should have thrown it away, chucked it in the Thames, but he hadn't. He was glad of that now.

56

Even as Milo was stepping over the threshold, Marian was saying in that cool, dismissive way of hers, 'I can't be long. I have to meet Hazel for dinner at eight.'

Once upon a time he wouldn't have minded a quick fuck, ten minutes in the sack before they went their separate ways, but this evening the prospect filled him with resentment. He deserved better. She treated him like an unpaid gigolo, only there to satisfy her demands and then to be dismissed. As she headed for the bedroom, already peeling off her clothes, he hung back, deciding to play the game by his rules for once.

'What's the matter?' she said, stopping at the door and looking back at him.

'I had a very odd conversation with Jonny last night.'

Marian wrinkled her nose, impatient to be getting on with business. 'Ugh, spare me the details.'

'No, I mean *really* odd. It was almost as if he was asking me to …' Here Milo paused, making it seem like he was in two minds as to whether to carry on. 'Maybe I shouldn't say.'

'Oh, for God's sake, Milo. You know you're dying to tell me so just spit it out.'

Milo ran his tongue across dry lips. He was on edge but excited too. How Marian reacted could determine his whole future. 'I could be wrong, but I'm sure he was asking me to kill your father.'

Whatever Marian had been expecting, it wasn't this. She gave a light laugh, saw that *he* wasn't laughing, and became instantly serious. 'You're kidding, right?'

'I swear,' Milo said. 'I mean he didn't come right out and ask, but he did everything but. Going round the houses, you know, trying to sound me out, see if I'd be up for it.'

There was a long silence while Marian stared at him. There had always been the possibility of outrage or horror, but neither of these emotions graced her face. Instead, after she'd thought about it for a while, she simply asked, 'And what did you say?'

Milo's own face grew sly. 'What would you have liked me to say?'

Marian slowly walked back over to him, her hips swaying. She pressed her body against his, ran her fingers through his hair, placed her mouth close to his ear, and murmured, 'When? That's what you should have said. *When* do you want me to do it?'

Milo wasn't shocked by her reaction. He had always known she had a visceral hatred of her father, a loathing she usually kept under wraps unless she'd had a few drinks. But she wasn't drunk tonight. However, he kept his tone light-hearted in case she was playing with him, just indulging in an entertaining fantasy. 'And why would I agree to that?'

'Because I'd make it worth your while.' Marian undid the buttons of his shirt and slid her palm across his chest. 'Name your price.'

'Things like this don't come cheap.'

'I don't do cheap. But it's got to be soon.'

'What's the hurry?' Milo slid his fingers down the length of her spine and roughly pulled her closer. His hand moved under her skirt to skim her thighs and hips. He felt the blood coursing through his veins and was aware of the harsh uneven rhythm of his breathing.

'I don't like waiting for what I want. You should know that by now.'

Milo's hand slid between her legs, and he heard a soft moan escape from her lips. His mouth covered hers, pressing hungrily, but then suddenly, deliberately, as his avarice caught up with his arousal, he stopped and stood back. 'I'd need money up front.'

Marian smiled and moved forward, closing the distance between them, pressing her body against his. She took his hand, kissed it and laid it over her left breast. 'You can have whatever you want.'

'Don't promise what you can't deliver.'

'Anything,' she repeated as she led him into the bedroom, her eyes bright with lust and excitement.

57

Jonny let himself into the basement of the Royal, poured himself a large drink from the collection of bottles on the small bar, sat down in one of the mock leather armchairs and gazed around. He had done what he could with the money at his disposal, but there was still a long way to go. And he was starting to think the new carpet could have been a mistake: already there were a couple of cigarette burns in it and a bad stain where some stupid bastard had spilled a pint of lager.

He'd held four games now – Fridays and Saturdays for the past couple of weeks – and made a few quid, but it had been barely enough to cover expenses once Milo had taken his share. And some of the punters had been less than desirable, bad losers who'd kicked up a fuss and had to be thrown out when the cards hadn't gone their way. What he needed was a better class of clientele, men who had money to spend and were happy to spend it here.

Oddly enough, he'd walked out of the house earlier and almost bumped straight into Lucan. Jonny had said a breezy

'Good morning' and had received a brusque nod in return. Well, that was progress. Give it a few weeks and they'd be chatting about the weather. A few more and the talk might turn to Jonny's exclusive club in the heart of Soho and an invitation to drop in any time the lucky lord felt like it. By then, hopefully, he'd be opening longer hours, have the place up to scratch and be attracting a better class of punter.

But improving the club would mean spending more money, money that Jonny didn't currently have. He'd already exhausted most of the saleable items in the attic – the rest of the pictures, some silver candlesticks, an antique coffee service, a few vases and another fur coat – but was still a long way from acquiring the funds he needed. And now Rex was withholding the money he usually gave Hazel every month and threatening to pull out of the early inheritance he had so generously bestowed on his seventieth birthday.

It was all going downhill fast. What if Rex discovered the thefts from the attic? What if he changed his will? It would be end of story. Hazel would probably get the same treatment as Carmen. Rex wouldn't believe that she'd known nothing about it. There was only one solution. The time to strike was now, before his father-in-law did something truly drastic.

Jonny thought about Milo. He liked to think of himself as having the charm, and Milo as having the muscle, which made for a useful partnership when it came to business. But could he be persuaded to go the extra mile and eliminate Rex? This brought him neatly round to the conversation he'd had last night when he'd been sounding out Milo about the perfect murder. Had Milo caught his drift? He reckoned he had. Milo wasn't the sharpest knife in the drawer, but he wasn't completely stupid either.

*

'What are you looking so pleased about?' Hazel said as Marian sat down opposite her. 'And you're late. Eight o'clock, we said. I've been sitting here on my own like Billy no-mates for twenty minutes.'

'The traffic was bad. I got here as fast as I could.'

Hazel shoved a menu towards her. 'An apology would be nice.'

Marian sighed, took the menu, and quickly skimmed the options. 'I'm sorry I'm late. I'm sorry the traffic was bad and the cab couldn't go any faster. I'm sorry you had to wait on your own. There, happy now? I think I'll have the fish.'

'Something's happened, hasn't it?' Hazel said.

Marian poured herself a large glass of Chablis from the bottle on the table. 'Nothing's happened. Where's Jonny this evening?'

'Why are you changing the subject?'

'I'm not. I was just thinking we should all get together some time, have a chat about everything that's going on. You know, Dad rapidly backtracking on the whole inheritance thing.'

'That's only for me,' Hazel said sulkily. 'You don't need to worry.'

'I wouldn't be so sure.'

'What do you mean?'

The waiter, a good-looking young man with an American accent, came over to take their order. Marian flirted with him, her gaze blatantly roaming over his body, while she enquired where he came from and asked about the specials. She could see Hazel impatiently playing with her knife and fork but took no notice. Some time soon there would be a space in her comfortable Camden bed, and she intended to fill it with the best male specimen she could find.

When the waiter had left, Hazel rolled her eyes and said, 'Well, that wasn't obvious or anything.'

'Good. That was the point. I wouldn't want to leave him in any doubt as to my intentions.'

'Job done, then,' Hazel said, a touch sneeringly.

'And since when did you become so holier-than-thou? I'm only having a bit of fun.'

'I thought you came here to tell me something, not to try and pick up some dumb Yank.'

'Do you think he's dumb?' Marian gazed across the room at him, wondering how you could assess someone's intelligence from what had been a fairly limited exchange of words. 'To be honest, I don't mind that. Better dumb than a smart alec. I can't stand clever men.'

'Stop looking at that bloke and listen to me. What did you mean about not being sure?'

Marian reluctantly dragged her eyes from the waiter. 'Oh, that. Yes, well, brace yourself, but I overheard Dad talking to Pat today and . . . you mustn't tell him about this or he'll know I was eavesdropping.'

'Just get on with it. Of course I won't tell.'

'You're not going to like it, but Dad's thinking of changing the terms of our inheritance and putting it all in a trust fund until we're forty.'

'Forty!' Hazel squealed. 'That's eleven bloody years.'

'All right, keep your voice down. I know how long it is.' Marian had concocted this story in the cab on the way over and thought it sounded feasible enough. In fact, she wouldn't put it past her father to come up with something along similar lines. She had needed to put forward a prospect that would both anger and terrify her sister. How else was she going to get her to agree? She had toyed with the idea of not telling her about the murder plan at all – surely the fewer people who knew the better? – but then had realised that she'd get landed with the whole bill for paying Milo and couldn't see how that was fair.

'So what are we going to do?'

'I've no idea. But whatever it is, we'd better do it soon. The minute he changes his will we're buggered.'

Hazel's eyes grew wide. 'What if we're too late? What if he's already changed it?'

'He hasn't. I told you: he was just throwing the idea around with Pat.'

'So it might not even happen?'

'You want to take that chance? He seemed pretty keen, from what I heard. I mean, Jesus, we're going to be old women by the time we get our hands on that money.'

'I don't see what we can do about it,' Hazel said, staring down at the table and running grooves through the crisp white table-cloth with a fingernail. She glanced up at Marian, a panicky expression on her face. 'You can't tell Jonny about this.'

'Why not? Do you think he'll leave you?'

'Christ, what kind of thing is that to say?'

Marian shrugged. 'I'm sure he loves you, sweetheart, in his own way, but this isn't exactly what he signed up for. Jonny likes being a kept man, doing what he wants when he wants, and not having to think about how much that costs. He's hardly a scrimper, is he? I get the feeling that—'

'Feeling that *what*?' Hazel snapped.

'Nothing,' Marian said, knowing that she'd already hit the mark and didn't need to rub it in. Hazel was stupid over Jonny and would do anything to hold on to him. 'I shouldn't have said that. Sorry.'

'I wish he was dead,' Hazel hissed.

'Who? Jonny?'

'Not Jonny. *Dad*. I wish he was bloody dead.'

Marian sighed into the bright chatter of the restaurant. 'Well, yes, that would solve a lot of problems.'

283

58

Carmen didn't know how she'd let Deana talk her into it. Well, that wasn't exactly true. What she really meant was that she didn't know why she hadn't had the sense to say no. And yet – she might as well be honest with herself – she knew the answer to that too. The wages she got from the café were only enough to cover the bare essentials and she yearned for some of life's little luxuries: something stylish to wear, a bottle of perfume, a different lipstick.

'They're always short of girls,' Deana had said. 'I can get you an interview. I'm sure they'll take you on. You can just work Friday and Saturday night. They're the busiest times and it's when you'll make the most money.'

'But what do hostesses *do*?'

Beth had looked up from the copy of *Spare Rib* she was reading and given a snort. 'What do you *think* they do?'

'Don't listen to her. She doesn't know what she's talking about.'

'I know that women shouldn't be treated like pieces of meat. You should have more respect for yourself.'

Deana ignored her. 'All you have to do is keep the customers company, smile and chat and pretend to be interested. Laugh at their dreadful jokes and don't be too serious. You get a percentage of the drinks they order: the more bottles of champagne they buy, the more commission you get. You can only drink the non-alcoholic cocktails, but you get a share of those too. It's easy. It's like getting paid for a night out.'

So here Carmen was, sitting at a table in Scandal, wearing the obligatory little black dress and white high-heeled shoes and feeling as vulnerable as a timid mouse at a party for tomcats. She was trying to look confident as she looked around, but probably failing. Perhaps Beth had been right. Perhaps this wasn't the place for her.

The club was crowded, and music filled the air, mingling with voices and laughter and the tinkling clink of glasses. The walls had been decorated in various shades of blue and the lighting was discreet, lamps judiciously placed to cast flattering shadows wherever they were needed. In front of her was a stage where a troupe of girls danced, wearing just enough to not be breaking any laws but not enough to pass for decent. Their long legs kicked into the air while their mouths were permanently fixed in wide, white-toothed smiles. They all had small waists and neat bums, and breasts exaggerated by what looked like lacy corsets.

Most of the customers were men, although there were a few women in the parties too. The atmosphere was simultaneously sophisticated and louche, as if high rank and money was able to transform what could have been tacky into something more civilised. Scandal was an exclusive club, and its members, according to Deana, were society's elite: MPs, judges, wealthy businessmen, actors and the like. But that, of course, didn't make them any different to other men: it just made them richer.

Carmen was wishing that she smoked, for something to do with her hands while she waited. What if nobody chose her? She could be sitting here all night like an unwanted bonbon in a sweetshop window. Her gaze quickly skimmed across the tables, viewing the customers, and she hoped there wasn't anyone in the room who recognised her. What if Clive heard that she was working here? She screwed up her face, annoyed that the thought had even entered her head. It was none of his business any more: he could go to hell.

'I wouldn't like to be in his shoes.'

Carmen looked up to see a tall, slim, debonair man in his late forties. He had short, slicked-back, greying hair and a charming if rather predatory smile. 'I'm sorry?'

'Whoever it was you were thinking about. I'm presuming it was a man.'

'Not much of one,' she said.

He laughed, put out his hand and said, 'Richard Torn. Pleased to meet you.'

'Carly,' she replied, wondering if she'd heard his name correctly. Torn was an odd surname – she had an idea there had been an American actor called that – but maybe he'd said Tawn. Although that was unusual too. While these irrelevant thoughts were flashing through her brain, her fingers were being squeezed in his cool, firm grip.

'Would you join me for a drink, Carly? My table's just over there.'

'Thank you. I'd like that.'

Relief battled with nerves as she rose to her feet. At last, her first customer. *Don't blow it, Carmen. Don't say anything annoying or stupid. Just be natural. Just relax.* They went to one of the quieter tables, away from the main throng, where he pulled out her chair, sat down opposite, ordered drinks, and proceeded to gaze at her for a few seconds.

'How lovely you are,' he said, pausing before he added, 'when you're not being angry with some dreadful man.'

'I'm not angry.' And then, because this sounded too abrupt, too defensive, she smiled and tried to soften the reply with humour. 'You'd know if I was angry.'

For a moment she wondered if she'd said the wrong thing – why didn't she think before she opened her mouth? – but then Torn laughed again, throwing back his head as if she'd uttered something enormously amusing. 'You're new here, aren't you? I'm sure I haven't seen you before.'

'It's my first night,' she said.

'I knew it. And you're not like the other girls. I can tell.'

This, Carmen suspected, was a line he used on all the girls. Richard Torn was a born flatterer. But she smiled and pretended she was pleased to be singled out this way. After all, what did it matter? This wasn't a date. She wasn't planning on spending the rest of her life with him. All she had to do was talk and listen and give the impression she was having a good time.

Fortunately, Richard Torn was exceedingly keen on the sound of his own voice. For the next couple of hours, he regaled her with amusing anecdotes and fed her titbits of gossip about the other customers. For all his frivolity, he was clearly a clever and well-read man, the sort who had been to public school and Oxbridge and who moved through life with the ease of the entitled. When the cabaret was over, they danced together twice, his hands, on both occasions, roaming a little too close to her backside for comfort.

Torn appeared to know almost everyone and numerous people dropped by the table, sitting down for a while, quaffing some champagne, and then moving on. Introductions were made, name after name, most of which Carmen instantly forgot. The time flew by and before she knew it Torn was looking at his watch, sighing, apologising and saying that unfortunately he had to go.

Carmen wondered if there was a wife waiting for him at home. She wouldn't have been surprised. There was a code, she imagined, in clubs like these, that whatever men did never went beyond these four walls. What happened in Scandal stayed in Scandal. That way members were free to chat and dance with the hostesses, to flirt outrageously and to boost their egos with no fear of repercussions.

'We should have dinner,' he said. 'When are you free?'

Carmen had not expected the invitation, had no intention of accepting it and thankfully had a handy get-out clause. 'Thank you, but I'm afraid we're not allowed to meet members outside the club. It's a rule.'

'Oh, rules,' he said dismissively, waving a hand. 'No one takes any notice of those.'

'I think *I* should,' she said, 'especially on my first night.'

Richard Torn smiled and said, 'That's a shame. Still, I'm sure I'll see you again. Do take care of yourself. And be careful. This place is full of wolves, you know.'

Carmen wasn't sure if he was joking or not. When it came to wolves, he was hardly out of the category himself. Still, she'd known worse company and wasn't displeased that he'd singled her out to spend part of the evening with him. With her confidence boosted, she sat up straight and prepared to face whatever other wildlife might come her way.

It was another few minutes before it suddenly occurred to her that there was something about Richard Torn that reminded her of her father – something suave and cold and utterly ruthless . . .

59

The last four weeks had been challenging ones for Terry Street, but he'd battled through them – quite literally on some occasions – and had now reached a point where his position as head of the firm – if not exactly undisputed – was gradually being accepted. Gordie was still hanging around like a bad smell, undecided as to which way to jump, but a few other men, Quinn's old cronies, had fallen by the wayside or gone off to attach themselves to other firms. He wouldn't lose any sleep over them. Those who weren't for him were against him.

Now that the milk run had been re-established, money was coming in on a regular basis. He'd installed a new madam, a woman he could trust, at the Albert Road brothel, and trade was brisk. A new supplier also meant that a steady supply of weed was being distributed throughout Kellston and beyond. He was keeping an eye on his dealers, double checking that none of them were ripping him off. He would stamp on anyone who thought they could take him for a fool.

Once he was sure that everything was holding, everything

running smoothly, then he would start to expand his interests into the West End. A couple of clubs to begin with, he thought, and maybe a casino too. Everybody wanted to gamble these days, to have a flutter on the roulette wheel or chance their arm on the turn of a card. A mug's game – as Jonny Cornish had found out to his cost – but it never stopped them trying.

Terry was still considering Jonny's debt and whether he should pursue it or not. Just because Joe was dead didn't mean the slate had been wiped clean: a grand was a lot of money to write off, and strictly speaking it was still owed to the firm. He'd heard that Jonny had started a small gambling club in the basement of the Royal and wondered if it was worth paying him a visit.

Although he never usually let personal feelings get in the way of business, he was aware that Jonny was Carly's brother-in-law. He had no idea how good or bad that relationship was and didn't want to screw up his chances with her by making trouble where he didn't need to. Maybe, for the sake of equanimity, he'd let it go.

Terry was never short of female company, but Carly's apparent lack of interest had only increased his own. He hadn't seen much of her recently, only a couple of times at the caff. She was still wearing that ring, but that didn't mean anything. He suspected that Clive Grainger was out of the picture. He wondered what she had argued about with her father, but she didn't seem prepared to tell him. Of course Joe hadn't helped matters, stirring up strife like he always had.

He didn't dwell on the Friday night he had killed Joe Quinn. It all had a faintly dreamlike quality, as if someone else had lifted that baseball bat and brought it down on the old gangster's skull. He had only done what he had to. Joe had killed men and now he had been killed. That was the way of this world: dog eat dog. If Joe had been smarter, he would have seen it coming, but he'd never been big in the brains department.

Terry knew that he would always have to watch his back, that taking the crown was one thing, keeping it quite another. He slept with a bat under the bed and a gun in the drawer of the bedside table. It was his intention to not just get rich, but to get old too. And to stay out of nick. He wasn't going to be one of those men who spent half their lives behind bars. With this in mind, he was taking care to keep the law on side and to make sure that the local cops who mattered had their meagre salaries amply supplemented.

Onwards and upwards: that was his mantra. He was going places, and nobody was going to stop him. Terry Street was on the road to success. He thought about Carly again and grinned. Maybe it would be nice to have a little company on that road.

60

Milo felt no guilt at the prospect of ending Rex Darby's life. The man had done all right – three score years and ten – so really, he had sod all to complain about. It was better he went now, nice and clean, before he slid down that slippery slope and completely lost his marbles. Already the old man was starting to imagine things, seeing ghosts from the past and acting paranoid. All things considered, he'd be doing him a favour.

No, it wasn't the act itself that bothered Milo but whether he could get away with it. It was all very well Marian saying that he wouldn't be suspected of the murder, that he had no motive, but the law would still put the screws on him. He'd be on the list because he worked for Rex, maybe held a grudge, maybe envied him because he was rich and powerful and lived in a smart house in Belgravia. None of which he could deny. He knew they'd keep him down the nick for hours, trying to fashion a reasonable motive just to put him in the frame.

'It'll be the same for all of us,' Jonny said after Milo voiced his concerns. 'Worse, in fact. If anyone's going to be top of their list, it's me. They'll soon find out about the money I owed Joe Quinn: if Pat doesn't tell them, Elizabeth will. They'll know Rex had a go at me about it, that the two of us weren't exactly on good terms.'

'So perhaps we should wait for all that shit to calm down,' Milo said. 'Give it a month or two and then—'

Marian shook her head. 'We haven't got time. It needs to be done in the next few days, before Dad has a chance to change his will. If he goes with this idea about the trust funds, we'll be looking at another ten years before we even get a whiff of the money.'

Milo didn't like being rushed, but he didn't want to lose face either. He'd told Marian he'd do it and backing out now wasn't an option. But he was going to make damn sure that they paid him well for the job. 'Okay, but I want a flat, one of those Mayfair ones. And a hundred grand, cash.'

Marian laughed. 'Mayfair? Don't be ridiculous! How suspicious is that going to look to the police? One minute you're sharing with your mum in a tatty block off Tottenham Court Road, and the next you're living in the lap of luxury. For God's sake, Milo, have some sense.'

'So where? I need a place to live. There's already been an offer on the flat and—'

'You can have the one in Camden,' Jonny said. 'You don't mind do you, Marian?'

'Do I have a choice?'

'It's the perfect solution. You can stay at the Gryphon when you're in London like you used to.' Jonny addressed Milo again. 'We can draw up a rental agreement so it all looks above board and then once things have settled down we'll pass the property over to you.'

'And the money?'

'You'll get your money, but you'll have to be patient. None of us have got that kind of cash right now. You'll get it when we get it.'

'We've got a couple of hundred,' Marian said, taking a brown envelope from her bag and holding it out. 'It's the best we can do.'

Milo took the envelope and slipped it into his inside jacket pocket. 'And what if you don't pay me the rest?' He had already had this conversation with Jonny, albeit in a more oblique form, but the questions remained the same. 'What the fuck am I supposed to do then?'

'That's the chance you take. Don't do it if you don't trust us. But we've got no reason to screw you over, have we? It's not as though we won't be able to afford it.'

In Milo's experience it was always the people *with* money who didn't like spending it. But he knew he was going to go for it anyway. This was his one big chance of making some serious dosh and he wasn't about to chuck it away.

Jonny had been surprised when his wife had raised the subject of getting shot of her father. Not shocked, though. He'd lived with her long enough to know how much she hated the old man. And there was no arguing with the fact that he was a nasty, manipulative bastard who'd tried to control his daughters from the day they'd been born. No, the surprise had come from the fact that he'd only recently raised the subject of murder with Milo. It seemed like too much of a coincidence. Had Milo been talking to Hazel?

Jonny was still mulling this over as he sat in the basement of the Royal with Milo and his sister-in-law, thrashing out the details of Rex's imminent demise. It was bothering him, niggling away like a bad itch that couldn't be scratched. But

Hazel was hardly ever in the Ebury Street office so he couldn't see how or when Milo could have passed the information on, unless . . .

Although he was never faithful himself, Jonny expected his wife to be. It was different for him – he was hot-wired to chase – but the thought of Hazel spreading her legs for another man sent a ripple of anger through him. He drank some whisky, his fingers tightening around the glass. He glared at Milo. Was it possible? Would she really sleep with *that*. But instantly another explanation occurred to him, that Milo had told Marian, and Marian had passed it on to Hazel. Which meant that something was going on between Milo and his sister-in-law.

For the next few minutes Jonny studied them both closely, searching for signs, stolen glances, anything to indicate that his co-conspirators were sharing more than murder plans. But it was hard to tell, especially with Marian. She flirted with most men just for the hell of it, honing her skills for the ones who mattered, the ones she'd eventually go on and sleep with. Marian was as faithful to Hugh as he was to Hazel, and from what he'd heard she didn't mind a bit of rough. In his eyes that made her a slapper, albeit a good-looking one. That, however, was neither here nor there: what mattered was if their fling (if that's what it was) would affect the plans as regards Rex.

Jonny drank more whisky and wondered if he was overthinking it all. Perhaps it wouldn't be that surprising if Hazel and Marian had, completely independently, come to the same conclusion as him. Perhaps Milo hadn't talked to anyone. They'd all been pushed to the limit over these past weeks, offered a pot of gold and then had it snatched away.

The big question, of course, the only question, was whether Milo could be trusted not to screw it up.

*

Marian was aware of Jonny studying her, his eyes lingering a little too long on places that they shouldn't. Someone should teach the man some boundaries. He thought he was God's gift, but he was nothing special. She noticed how he talked to Milo as though it was *his* money rather than Hazel's, as though *he* was the one being done out of his rightful inheritance. If Hazel had any sense, she'd get rid of him, trade him in for a husband who wasn't going to drain her dry.

The three of them – she, Jonny and Milo – had decided to leave Hazel out of this meeting today: Hazel wasn't a planner and would be more useful keeping a check on things at the office. It wasn't safe to leave their father unobserved, not when his head was full of ghosts and wild ideas. Someone had to be there to make sure he didn't do anything stupid.

Marian gazed around the basement room, wondering what Jonny was trying to do with it. Private parties he claimed, but she couldn't see the appeal. It was more like a downmarket gentleman's club, plain and charmless and lacking in taste. From what she could remember, upstairs wasn't much better: a shabby club for shabby people. She was glad the place hadn't been left to her.

For the past hour plans had been discussed, argued over, dismissed and re-instated. Finally, a decision had been made. She looked at Milo, sure that he could do it – the man had no scruples – and sure too that once he had they would need to get rid of him. Milo could only ever be a liability. There would have to be some suitable accident in the not-too-distant future, otherwise he'd be extorting money from them for the rest of their lives.

In the meantime, it would be her job to keep her father busy and away from the office for most of tomorrow. She would ask his advice about some of her properties and drag him round

London for the day. While he was doing that, he couldn't be having discussions with Pat or talking to solicitors. After that she would head over to Suffolk for the weekend, putting plenty of distance between herself and the murder.

Marian had a few ideas about how she could deflect suspicion from them all. There was the mysterious reappearance of Michael Quinn for starters. And then there was Carmen: no one had more reason to hate their father than her. She smiled. The first thing she would do on leaving the basement was call her.

61

Rex sat in his office with his eyes fixed on the window. He watched the men and women who passed by, dismissing them one by one – wrong sex, wrong height, wrong face. It had become a constant, this people watching, almost second nature, as instinctive as taking a piss. He couldn't help himself. Everywhere he went his eyes darted around, searching for the man he knew was out there somewhere. And just as he was watching, he felt watched too, permanently under surveillance, his every move scrutinised and logged.

Last night the doorbell had rung at quarter past ten, but when he'd opened the door no one had been there. Just empty space. He could have sworn he'd heard footsteps running down the street, although when he'd looked, he couldn't see anyone. The night air had been cool, the sky full of stars. For a while he had stood, ears pricked, listening. The distant sound of a car door closing? Perhaps. But no engine starting, no further sound. He had stayed there until it occurred to him that he was the perfect target, his body silhouetted against the brightness of the hall light. Then he had gone inside, slammed the door, walked into the drawing room and poured himself a stiff Scotch.

Rex knew that he needed protection. It was foolish not to be prepared, not to be ready if the worst happened. He would go up to the attic and retrieve the gun. The old Welrod was stashed where he'd left it all those years ago, high up on one of the beams where children couldn't reach. It wasn't the sleekest or most efficient of weapons, but as long as the target was close enough, it would do its job. Armed, he would be a match for anyone, even enemies from beyond the grave. There were five bullets left in the magazine. The sixth had ripped through the flesh and bone of Michael Quinn.

62

On Friday afternoon, Carmen got off the bus at Victoria, checked the station clock and decided to walk to Upper Belgrave Street. The sun was out, and she still had fifteen minutes before she was expected at the house. The call from Marian had finally come last night. If she wanted to pick up her things from home, she should be there at five o'clock.

'Hazel will let you in. I'll be out with Dad all day, so he won't know anything about it.'

'Could we make it a bit earlier?' Carmen had asked, thinking of how she would have to pack, make a rush-hour journey back to Kellston, dump her suitcase, get changed and be at Scandal for seven.

'Do you want your things or not? That's the only time Hazel can manage. It's up to you.'

Afraid that the offer might be withdrawn, Carmen had quickly agreed to the arrangement. 'Five o'clock then. That's fine. I'll be there. Thank you.'

'Right, I'll let her know,' Marian had replied, and hung up without saying goodbye.

Carmen didn't mind the walk. It was a sunny October day, mild and cloudless, and she was glad of the chance to stretch her legs and steady her nerves. There was no reason why she should bump into her father – he was bound to drop into the office after his day out with Marian, and then go on to the pub for his usual session with Pat – but routines weren't set in stone, and it would be just her luck if he came home while she was there.

All the streets were familiar and yet it felt like a long time since she'd last walked along them. She slowed a little as she approached the house, taking care to look around. She had to think about Pat and Elizabeth too; if either of them saw her, they were bound to tell her father. Ebury Street wasn't far away, and he could be here in minutes. He was still seething, she was sure, from her meeting with Joe Quinn – and even Joe's death wouldn't have softened his rage.

At five o'clock exactly she rang the doorbell. There was no response. She pressed the bell again, two long rings, hoping that she hadn't had a wasted journey. Eventually she heard movement from inside, the tapping of high heels on the marble floor, and Hazel opened the door.

'Oh, you're here at last,' she remarked, as if she'd been waiting for hours.

'I'm not late, am I? Marian said five o'clock.'

'You'd better come in.'

Carmen stepped into the hallway and closed the door behind her. 'Thanks for doing this.'

'It wasn't my idea.'

'So what's it like being back home?'

'Oh, you know, pretty much like it always was.' Hazel glanced at her watch. 'Will you be long? Only I've got to go soon.'

'I'll be as quick as I can.'

Carmen jogged up the stairs, unsurprised by the lukewarm

welcome. If her relationship with Marian was often fractious, with Hazel it was virtually non-existent. Even when they'd been living under the same roof, Hazel had usually ignored her. But she suspected, on this occasion, that her sister's coolness was down to more than indifference: she'd be in big trouble with their father if he ever found out that she'd let Carmen into the house.

On the second floor, Carmen opened the cupboard on the landing, pulled out the big blue suitcase that she'd always used for holidays and carried it to her bedroom. It felt odd to be back in her room again, everything unchanged, exactly as she'd left it. It was like seeing another version of her life, one where she had taken so much for granted.

But she didn't have time to muse on that. Quickly she went to the wardrobe and began rifling through her clothes, picking and disregarding, throwing everything she wanted on a heap on the bed. She did the same with the chest of drawers, retrieving sweaters and cardigans, all the stuff she'd need to get through the winter months. Underwear, tights and socks joined the pile.

Carmen was busy squeezing all this into the case when Hazel walked in, holding out a small white envelope.

'Here, take this. There's a key to the front door inside. I have to go, or I'll be late. You won't be too long, will you? Lock up when you leave and post this back through the letterbox.'

Carmen took the envelope. It had 'Hazel' written on the front and a folded sheet of paper inside. The key had been slipped between the folds. 'I'll only be five minutes.'

'I haven't got five minutes. Just don't forget to lock up, yeah?'

'I won't. How are you going to get back in?'

'I've got Jonny's key. I'm going to lock up when I go just in case . . . Well, Dad will know someone's here if he comes back and finds the door unlocked.'

'He won't, though, will he? I thought he was out with Marian.'

'He is, as far as I know. Just in case, that's all. I'll see you, then.'

And before Carmen could reply, Hazel strode off, clearly eager to get out of the house as fast as she could. She heard her sister go down the stairs and a few seconds later the front door closed. Carmen went back to her packing, rushing even more now, spurred on by the unpleasant thought of being caught in the act. She took her jewellery box from the dressing table, not even bothering to sort through it, and pushed it down between the clothes. As she examined the rows of shoes and boots, she was mentally balancing up what she really wanted to take against what she actually needed. The case was getting heavier by the minute, and she didn't relish the prospect of having to lug it back to Kellston.

When the decisions had been made and the case was pretty much full, Carmen had one last look round the room. She had already emptied the drawers of her bedside table, removing letters, her passport and all the other paperwork that had been gathered there. Her gaze fell on her mother's photograph, and she remembered Marian's words about how she had never been wanted. Was there any point in taking it? But somehow, she couldn't bear to leave it there. Rosa Darby had still been her mother, had still given birth to her. She wrapped the framed photo in a sweater and placed it carefully in the case.

Time to go.

Carmen had got as far as the landing when she heard the front door open. Instantly she froze. Could Hazel have come back for something? Or perhaps it was Jonny. But how could it be Jonny if Hazel had his key? She didn't dare call out for fear it was the one person she didn't want it to be. Holding her breath, she listened intently. Whoever it was had gone into the drawing room. She had to force her legs to move, to carry her quietly back into the bedroom, where she put down the case and waited.

Then what she had been dreading happened. Heavy footsteps, a man's, began ascending the staircase, not stopping on the first floor where her father's bedroom was but climbing up towards the second. She stood very still, too afraid to move a muscle. The man paused on the landing and for a moment there was silence. Carmen held her breath again. What if it *was* her father, and what if he'd noticed that her bedroom door was ajar? She could feel her heart beating rapidly, drumming in her chest.

Finally, thankfully, the footsteps resumed in an upward direction, and she was able to relax a little. She waited until she was sure he was out of sight before tentatively opening the door a fraction more and peering out. There was the creak of floorboards overhead as feet crossed the third-floor landing. Whoever it was, she couldn't figure out what they were doing. There were only guest bedrooms up there and those were rarely used these days.

Then she heard the loud scrape and rattle of a key in a lock and realised what was happening. Someone was going into the attic. A shudder ran through her. She had only been up there once, when Marian had locked her in and left her in the shadowy gloom for the longest ten minutes of her life. She had sat hunched on the floor, her arms wrapped around her six-year-old knees, consumed by terror and convinced that her mother's ghost would suddenly appear.

Carmen withdrew, certain now that the man must be her father. Jonny would have no reason to go into the attic. She was curious as to what he wanted up there, and hoped that whatever it was, it wouldn't take too long. Standing beside the door with her back pressed against the wall, she shifted impatiently, wanting to be out of the house, wanting to escape from the bad memories it held for her. 'Come on,' she muttered under her breath.

It was another couple of minutes before she heard the attic door being closed and the key turning in the lock again. Then came the footsteps on the stairs, hurrying down, not even pausing on the landing. A sigh of relief slipped from her lips. Hopefully, her father, having collected what he wanted, would return to the office or the pub. He was down on the ground floor now, walking along the hallway. Then, just as she was certain that he was leaving, the doorbell rang. She jumped, alarm running through her. Who the hell was that?

Carmen heard a murmur of voices but could not identify the visitor, could not even tell if it was a man or a woman. Whoever it was had been invited in and the two of them went, she thought, into the drawing room. The door closed behind them. Damn! She glanced at her watch – twenty past five – and began to worry that she could be stuck here for hours. That would mean being late for her job at Scandal, or even not making it at all. And that could mean being sacked.

Treading softly, she went out on to the landing and peered over the banister. She couldn't hear anything. She retreated to the bedroom and paced around, anxious and frustrated, praying that whoever had come would not stay long. But even if they left soon, her father might not. He could be here for the night, and she'd be stuck here too until he went to bed. Unless she somehow managed to sneak out. This might be possible, but she wouldn't be able to take the suitcase with her. There was no way she'd be able to move quickly enough with the heavy case weighing her down. It would have to stay here and be picked up at a later date.

The minutes ticked by, and Carmen spent them in an ever-increasing agony of impatience. How long should she wait before attempting an escape? Her father and his visitor could be there for hours. She could take the chance of going right now, but what if he looked out of the window? No, she would have to wait until it was dark, until the drawing-room curtains had been pulled across, and that would be a while yet.

Then, just as she was despairing of ever making it to Scandal on time, she heard movement from downstairs. Footsteps on the marble floor of the hall. One pair of feet or two? She couldn't tell, but no one was talking. She hurried quietly out of the bedroom and cautiously leaned over the banister again but was too late to see who was leaving. The front door closed and then there was silence.

Carmen stayed where she was, gazing down into the space of the hall. It felt like the house was empty, that no one other than herself was breathing in it, but that might just be wishful thinking. No movement came from downstairs. Her fingers curled around the smooth worn wood of the banister rail. She listened hard, straining to hear the slightest sound, the rustle of a newspaper or the chink of a glass.

She stood, undecided, too wary to venture any further. If she'd been thinking straight, she would have gone straight to the bedroom window as soon as she heard the door close and seen who was leaving. But it was too late for that now. She would have to be patient, wait it out for a while longer, be sure that she was alone before she ventured downstairs.

63

The day had not gone exactly as Marian had planned. She'd intended to take her father on a time-consuming tour of the various hotels she now theoretically owned so she could look around and he could introduce her to the management, but despite her best attempts to keep him occupied, he'd insisted on returning to the office within a couple of hours. He had seemed distracted, his mind on something else. When she'd asked what was so important that he had to hurry back, he'd brusquely waved the query away. 'Nothing for you to worry about.'

'I thought we were spending the day together.'

'A business doesn't run itself, Marian.'

'Pat can deal with anything urgent.'

But he'd been adamant that he had to return to Ebury Street. As a result, Marian had been forced to spend the early part of the afternoon in the hostile surroundings of the reception area where Elizabeth, still quietly seething, had glowered at her from behind the typewriter. When the secretary had gone to the ladies, she'd grabbed the opportunity to check her father's appointment book, but the page for the day was empty – no ominous meetings booked in with his solicitor, or with anyone else for that matter.

At three o'clock her father had come out of his office, passed some paperwork for filing to Elizabeth, stared hard out of the window, cleared his throat, and said to Marian, 'You should get on the road if you want to miss the traffic. You know what it's like on a Friday.' She had wondered if he was trying to get rid of her but could think of no reasonable excuse to stay.

So here she was, winding her way through the country lanes of Suffolk, knowing that the goodbye she'd said to him would be her very last. Her fingers gripped the steering wheel, and her jaw clenched. But she refused to feel guilty about what they had planned. How guilty had *he* felt about driving her mother to suicide? How guilty about taking out his frustrations on his daughters? The old brute had never thought about anyone but himself.

The telephone call, if everything went to plan, would come in the early hours of the morning, when Hazel and Jonny got home and found the body. Or maybe the police would send someone round from the local station. Marian glanced at the clock on the dashboard – almost half past five – and wondered if Carmen had shown up at the house. Her sister's presence there might not put her exactly in the frame, but it would certainly raise some questions.

Jonny sat with a pint at the bar of the French House in Soho, impatient for Hazel to arrive. He and Marian had decided not to tell her that tonight was the night; she could easily lose her nerve. Hazel said things, agreed to things, but she might panic and change her mind at the last minute. He was trying not to fidget, trying not to glance at his watch, trying not to look like a man who had organised a murder. A long evening stretched ahead. Already he had made a point of chatting to the barman and to a couple of girls who had been waiting to be served. The most important thing about tonight was being remembered. They would eat dinner at a restaurant where they were familiar to the staff, and then go on to a club where there would be people they knew.

Jonny's only worry, and it wasn't a small one, was that Milo would fuck up. At least he wasn't likely to snitch to the law. But suddenly something else occurred to him: what if he double-crossed them? What if he went to Rex and told him what they had planned? No sooner had the thought entered his head then he dismissed it. There was nothing in it for Milo, not even the guarantee of a financial reward.

Jonny's shoulders were tight, and he tried to relax. In a few months, he'd be a rich man. And this time tomorrow he'd be celebrating. Well, not cracking open the champagne perhaps – the law would still be sniffing around – but quietly revelling in the millions that were about to fall into his lap.

Milo's palms were sweating. He wiped his hands on his trousers and lit a fag, puffing on it greedily while he waited for his nerves to stop rattling and for his pulse to slow. He was parked up round the corner from Rex's house on Upper Belgrave Street. Don't drive away too quickly, he told himself. Stay calm. Don't draw attention to yourself.

He'd arrived at Ebury Street at quarter past five to find everyone on the point of leaving. Elizabeth, looking flustered, had her coat on, and Pat was locking up his office.

'What's going on?' Milo had asked Elizabeth. 'You usually stay open till six.'

'Mr Darby has decided to close early.'

'Why's that then?'

But Elizabeth had just pursed her lips as if questioning Rex Darby's decisions was hardly a matter for the rent collector. 'Did you want something?'

'It's Friday. I've come for my wages.'

'Oh,' she'd said, sighing softly at the inconvenience of paying him what he was owed.

She'd opened her desk drawer, pulled out a small brown envelope and passed it over. Milo had slipped the envelope into the inside pocket of his jacket. He'd been annoyed, knowing that if he'd got there five minutes later the office would have been locked up with his hard-earned money still inside it. But no one gave a toss about that, not even his father, who was already trying to hustle him out.

'What's the rush?'

Pat had shrugged and shaken his head, offering up no explanation.

That was when Rex had come out of his room looking nervy but determined, his jaw set, his movements jerky and impatient. He had stared straight through Milo as if he wasn't there. 'Right, are we all done here?'

'Could I have a word, Rex?' Pat had asked.

But Rex was already striding towards the door. 'No time, I'm afraid. We can talk tomorrow.'

And thirty seconds later the three of them, a mismatched trio, were standing on the pavement watching Rex Darby stride purposefully towards his home. They had drifted apart shortly after with vague waves and muttered goodbyes.

Milo wound down the car window and puffed some more on his fag. The change in routine had been like a red flag for him. In all the time he'd worked for Rex, he'd never known the office to close before six. Something was up. He'd decided

310

in that moment to ditch the plan that had been so carefully worked out. After collecting his wages he'd been supposed to drive home, to buy a bottle of rum from the off-licence and to wait until it got dark before making his way back to Belgravia.

He put his right hand in his pocket and pulled out the three sleeping pills Jonny had given him, enough to knock his mother out once they were crushed and mixed with the rum. She would have been his alibi when the law started asking questions, the person who could swear that he hadn't left the flat again that evening. Not that the law would necessarily have believed her, but it was better than nothing.

However, Milo, on reflection, had decided to take a completely different path. Plans were all very well, but sometimes you had to follow your instincts.

64

Carmen waited another ten minutes before creeping down, shoeless, to the first-floor landing. Here she leaned over the banister again and studied the half-open door to the drawing room. She could only see a small expanse of silver-grey carpet, offering her no guarantee that the room was empty. He could be sitting in the armchair by the fireplace or relaxing on the sofa.

Except Rex Darby was not a still sort of person, not meditative or thoughtful, not the type to remain motionless for minutes on end. He was a man who liked to move, to make noise, to constantly remind the world of his existence. She inclined her head, listening hard. There was no cough, no sigh, no rustle of papers. Asleep? She didn't think so. Even in sleep, he wasn't quiet, muttering under his breath or emitting loud rolling snores.

Tentatively she began to walk down the stairs, carefully avoiding the ones that creaked. She paused frequently to listen for the slightest sound. There was an odd smell in the air, something almost sulphurous, an odour she couldn't put a name to.

She gently sniffed. Perhaps she was imagining it. She held her breath as she descended, knowing that shortly she would reach the point of no return. If her father suddenly emerged now, she'd have nowhere to go, nowhere to hide.

But as her feet made contact with the hall floor, she was certain she was safe. He wasn't in the room. She was stressing over nothing. The silence was too strong, too deep, to contain another human being. And she needed to get a move on. Time was ticking by. She had to get back to Kellston and dump the case. A cab, she decided, knowing that the bus would take for ever. It would be worth the expense if she could make it to Scandal without being late.

Carmen took the last few steps to the drawing room and put her ear against the door. That smell again, reminding her of Bonfire Night. Gently, with her fingertips, she nudged the door further open. And now, finally, she was able to look properly inside. The armchair was unoccupied, the sofa too. Nobody was standing by the window. A whispery sigh of relief slipped from her lips.

She was about to retreat, to dash upstairs and collect her case, when her gaze dropped to the floor. At first, she didn't comprehend what she was seeing – an ankle, a foot in a well-polished shoe, sticking out from the side of the sofa – and it took a moment for her brain to absorb it. Then, with a start, she lurched forward, stifling a cry as she saw the rest of the body, supine on the carpet, eyes wide open, the white shirt front crimson with blood.

'Dad,' she said, as she dropped to the floor beside him, laying a hand on his shoulder, wanting to shake him awake even though she knew he was dead. For a moment, a few seconds, she felt paralysed, weirdly disconnected, as if she had floated outside herself and was up on the ceiling looking down. Then horror flowed over her as the reality sank in. She shrank back, leaned forward again, and found herself overcome with helplessness.

Carmen could hear her own breath coming in short, fast pants as if she couldn't get enough oxygen into her lungs. Her father's face was neither peaceful nor frightened but wore an expression of mild surprise. He would be angry, she thought, at a good shirt being ruined. What? Random thoughts were jumping into her head, thoughts she couldn't control. She touched his forehead – still warm – and stroked his hair.

'Dad.' Her voice sounded hoarse, odd, like it was someone else's. Information seemed to be reaching her in tiny parcels, the contents of which had to be ripped open and digested before she could move on to the next: her father was dead; her father had been murdered; the person who had rung the bell had killed him; she had to do something. It was this something that seemed beyond her.

She had started to shiver now, her teeth chattering. She tried to get to her feet, but her knees buckled under her. It was then that she saw it, the odd-looking gun lying on the carpet, abandoned. Dull grey with a long barrel. Why hadn't she heard the shot? Even with the door closed she should have heard it. Instinctively she reached out a hand and as quickly withdrew it. *Don't touch the gun.*

Carmen tried to stand upright again, staggered a little but finally managed it. She stumbled across the room towards the phone. She was feeling hot and cold, clammy, sick. She should have made up with her father, or at least tried. Now it was too late. She couldn't look at him again. She had to look at him. Who had done this? Why? Even as she snatched up the phone, as she dialled 999, she couldn't begin to make sense of it all.

Somehow, erratically, disjointedly, in some mad garbled fashion, she managed to convey the fact that her father had been shot, that he was dead, that help was needed. The call was ended, and the receiver replaced. Then she stood, not knowing what to do next. She could not bear to be in the same room as her father's body but could not bear to leave him alone either. Shot. Dead. Murdered. These facts punctuated her every thought, leaving her lost and devastated, incapable of properly grasping it and yet filled with a dreadful despair.

Carmen stood by the window waiting for the police to arrive. Sometimes she would look over her shoulder and murmur a few useless words. 'I'm so sorry, Dad,' or 'Why? What happened? I don't understand.' Her father had always seemed immortal, his character so strong, his determination so rigid, that even death would think twice before approaching him. And yet in a matter of seconds an unheard bullet had penetrated his chest and stopped him breathing for ever.

Carmen was gulping for breath herself, her chest heaving. She had been upstairs, someone had come to the door, and her father had let them in. She had suspected nothing. He had been lying here murdered for ten or fifteen minutes and she'd had no idea. It came to her that perhaps there were other phone calls she should make, to Marian and Pat, but she could not bring herself to utter those awful words again. The police would deal with that, wouldn't they? They could break the news to everyone else. She had no idea where Hazel and Jonny had gone, but they probably wouldn't be back till late.

Time had slowed, becoming something sluggish and drawn out. Outside, life continued as normal, people passing as they walked home from work. She had a mad urge to hammer on the glass, to cry out, to shout at them: 'What are you doing? Why are you behaving as though nothing has happened? There's a dead man in here. My dad's been murdered!' But instead, she stood silent and frozen, only her eyes moving as they searched up and down the street for any sign of the police. She was beginning to wonder if she had even rung 999 or if the call had just been a product of her overwrought imagination when she finally saw the first car draw up outside the house.

'Here they are,' she said, as if her father could hear. Then, as fast as her shaky legs could carry her, she stumbled towards the front door.

65

After talking to the man in charge, a DCI Neil Hennessy, Carmen found herself in the kitchen, sitting at the old, scarred oak table and drinking tea with a young WPC called Sandra Best. The girl, a redhead, had a fine scattering of freckles on her pale face. She was calm and collected, with an air of efficiency about her. There was sugar in the tea, which meant that Sandra must have made it, but Carmen didn't remember hearing the kettle boil or the tea being placed in the pot, or the bottle of milk being retrieved from the fridge. And yet all these things must have happened right in front of her. The house was full of uniforms, tramping through every room, the tread of their boots heavy on the ceiling.

'What are they looking for?' Carmen asked.

'It's just routine,' Sandra said. 'Nothing to worry about. Are you sure there isn't someone we can call to be with you?'

The only person Carmen could think of was Annie, but she knew Pat would need his wife when the news was broken to him. She shook her head. 'No, it's all right.'

Sandra glanced at the diamond engagement ring on Carmen's finger. 'No one?'

'No,' Carmen repeated firmly.

'This must all have been a dreadful shock for you. Were you and your dad close?'

Although Sandra was, on the surface, being nothing but kind and solicitous, her eyes and her words expressing only sympathy, Carmen suspected ulterior motives. As if she had been left with the female constable in the hope that she would talk more openly with another woman. As if the police were not entirely convinced that her story was true. 'We were, I suppose. But not so much recently. I moved out in September.'

'Oh, why was that?'

Carmen sensed entrapment in the question, but there was no point in lying. If she didn't tell her, someone else would. 'We had a falling out. I only came back today to pick up some things.'

'But you didn't talk to your dad when you heard him come home?'

'I didn't want him to know I was here. It would only have caused another row and . . . I thought it would be easier to just wait upstairs. I thought he'd only come back to pick something up. He never normally left the office before six, and on Fridays he always went for a drink after the office closed. So, I just kept my head down and waited. Then someone called round – well, I've told the DCI all this – and later, when I came downstairs . . .'

Sandra reached out and laid her hand briefly on Carmen's wrist. 'It must have been terrible finding him like that. Do you have any idea who might have been at the door? A man or a woman? Any idea at all?'

Carmen shook her head. 'I could hear voices, murmurs, but nothing loud enough to put a name to. He must have known them, I suppose, whoever it was, or he wouldn't have let them in. Anyway, they went into the drawing room and after that I didn't hear anything else until there were footsteps in the hall and then the front door closing. I wasn't sure if one person went out or two, so I stayed where I was for a while.' She lifted the mug to her lips, blew on the surface of the tea, smelled the sickly sugary small and put the mug back down again. Her voice, sounding scared, rose in pitch. 'I didn't kill him if that's what you think. We might have had our differences, but I'd never have done anything like that.'

Sandra smiled her comforting smile. 'Nobody's saying that, Carmen. Please don't worry. Could I ask you about the gun, though? Have you ever seen it before?'

'No, never.'

'Do you think it could have belonged to your dad?'

'I don't think so.' Carmen frowned. 'What would he have a gun for?'

'People keep them for protection, in case there's a break-in or . . .' Sandra gave a light shrug. 'This is one of those hackneyed questions, but I have to ask. Did your dad have any enemies that you know of, anyone who bore a grudge? Anyone he might have fallen out with recently?'

'Apart from me, you mean?'

'Apart from you,' Sandra said patiently. 'Can you think of anyone? Maybe something work related?'

Carmen mimicked Sandra's shrug. 'I haven't been around lately. You'd have to ask Pat Foster about that. He's the financial director of the company. He works . . . *worked* closely with my dad. The office is in Ebury Street. He might still be there.' She glanced at her watch. It was six forty-five. The time that had dragged so much earlier now seemed to have disappeared down a black hole. 'Or in the Plumbers Arms. That's where they usually drink.'

'We'll send someone round.'

'Or his secretary, Elizabeth. Elizabeth Holmes. She's been with him for years.'

'Do you have an address for her?'

'Somewhere in Victoria. Sorry. Pat will know.'

Sandra scribbled down the names in a notebook, stood up and disappeared for a couple of minutes. While she was gone, Carmen gazed into the middle distance. Her hands remained around the mug, gripping it tightly, as if it could anchor her to sanity. *Her father had been murdered.* No, that couldn't be real. His face leapt into his mind, eyes wide open, his lips slightly apart. And the rose on his chest, blossoming where it shouldn't. Perhaps she, his daughter, had killed him. Was that possible? Could she have picked up the gun and pointed it and fired . . . and then wiped it from her memory like a cloth dragged across a blackboard?

Carmen shivered. The initial shock was wearing off to be replaced by fear and doubt and a growing sense of panic. Did the police believe her story? Did she believe it herself? She could see how ridiculous it all looked, how wrong it all sounded. And yet it was true. She was sure it was. She couldn't have done something so terrible and then forgotten about it. Her mind was just playing tricks, making her doubt herself.

Sandra came back, smiled, sat down and drank some tea. And then, as if she hadn't been away, she said, 'So there's no one you can think of? No one your dad had a problem with?'

Carmen had started to shake her head but then, out of nowhere, she suddenly remembered. 'There was someone. Joe Quinn. You've probably heard of him. But he's dead now. He was murdered too, not that long ago.'

Sandra's eyebrows shifted up. 'Joe Quinn from Kellston?'

'Joe was my mother's cousin. Do you think there could be

a connection? No, there couldn't be. He was killed by his son, wasn't he?'

Sandra had one of those expressions on her face, like she was trying not to look too interested. 'What was the problem between your dad and Joe Quinn?'

'Old family stuff, I think. And then when Joe heard I was living in Kellston, he wanted us to meet. I wasn't keen but I didn't dare refuse. We had a cup of tea together in a café called Connolly's. He only arranged it to wind Dad up, so he could make out I was being disloyal in some way.' Carmen paused, realising that she was probably digging an even bigger hole for herself. Mixing with gangsters wouldn't put her in the best of lights. 'That was the only time I met him, just that once.'

There was movement out in the hall, a fresh flurry of feet and voices, a sense that something new was happening. Carmen glanced over her shoulder, then back at Sandra. 'What's going on?'

Before she could answer, DCI Hennessy came into the kitchen. Sandra instantly sat up straighter. His voice was low, kind, almost confiding. 'Carmen, we're moving your father now.'

Carmen stiffened, then nodded. 'Will I be able to see him again?'

'Later,' Hennessy said. 'I don't see why not.'

Carmen put her elbows on the table and briefly buried her face in her hands. For all her problems with her father, for all his rages, manipulations and bitter grievances, she had never truly hated him. Now he was gone and there would be no opportunity for resolution or reconciliation. The finality of it all hit her with renewed force. Tears sprang into her eyes.

'Do you know when your sister – Hazel, isn't it? – and her husband, will be home?'

'No, sorry, I've no idea. Late, probably.'

'And you don't know where they've gone?'

'Hazel didn't say. They'll probably be in the West End some-where. Sorry, that's not very useful, is it?'

'We've arranged for Marian to be informed,' he said, as if this might be some comfort to her. 'I'm sure she'll be here before too long.'

'Is she in London or Suffolk?' Carmen asked.

'Suffolk, I believe.'

Carmen nodded, praying she would be able to get away before her sister arrived. She could imagine Marian's reaction when she found out that Carmen had been hiding upstairs while their father was being murdered. Blame would be quickly apportioned. Not that Marian would be heartbroken by the loss; she had about as much affection for the head of the family as she had for all the other inconveniences in her life. Carmen felt guilty as this thought passed through her mind – even though it was true. Once she was over the initial shock, Marian wouldn't grieve too much for the father she had lost.

'Are you sure there isn't someone we can call to be with you now?'

'No. No, thank you.'

Hennessy sat down beside Sandra and leaned forward, pre-paring to speak again. Carmen looked at him properly for what felt like the first time. He was a tall, slim man in his mid-forties with brown hair receding from a high forehead. His eyes were light blue, soft but shrewd, and had a watchful air about them.

'I know this isn't easy for you, but if we could just go through everything again? Please think very carefully. Any small detail could be important.'

'I'll try,' she said, her heart sinking at the prospect of re-living it all for the second time.

'Right, let's start from when you got here.'

66

It was one twenty-five on Saturday morning before Hennessy had talked to every member of Rex Darby's immediate circle. Starting with Carmen, he had gone on to Pat and Annie Foster, Elizabeth Holmes, Milo Grant, Marian and Hugh Loughton, and finally Hazel and her husband Jonny, who had fallen out of a black cab, tipsy and laughing, about an hour ago. There was a further list to be explored later on today: friends, employees, managers and the like. Any one of them could have held a grudge. The picture he was slowly building up was of a man not well liked even by his nearest and dearest.

DS Gary Ward placed a fresh plastic cup of coffee on Hennessy's desk and slumped his rugby-playing bulk into the chair opposite. He heaved out a sardonic sigh. 'Jesus, what a family. Where do we start? Carmen Darby. What do you think? Do you believe her story? She could have shot him. He came home, found her there, had a fit, she retaliated and . . . well, that doesn't explain the gun, of course, unless the whole thing was premeditated.'

Hennessy wasn't discounting any possibility at present. 'Is it odd the sisters arranging for her to be at the house at five o'clock? Why then? Why not earlier when there was far less chance of Darby making an appearance?'

'She doesn't finish work till two.'

'But why not half three or four?'

Ward took a sip of coffee and pulled a face. 'Christ, I don't know why I drink this stuff. You think they were trying to set her up?'

'That would be risky. She could have seen who shot Darby or heard them. And she could have ruined everything if she'd gone downstairs earlier.'

'Unless they were counting on her staying put.'

'Except they couldn't know that Darby would leave the office early. That seemed to come as a surprise to everyone. Well, when I say everyone, I mean Pat Foster and the secretary. Darby didn't receive any phone calls that afternoon, nothing to send him rushing home. And why did he go up to the attic, a place he normally never went near?'

'To collect something for his visitor, or get the gun?' Ward suggested.

'If the gun was his.'

'Weird-looking thing.'

'A Welrod' Hennessy said. 'Second World War pistol. There's still a few of them around. Not the prettiest firearm in the world but it does have one advantage over its more glamorous counterparts: an inbuilt suppressor means that when it's fired it makes hardly any noise.'

'So Carmen could have been telling the truth about not hearing the shot. And there was no blood on her clothes. Would there have been blood with a pistol like that?'

'It probably depends on how far away she was standing. We'll have to ask ballistics. Anyway, if there was some spatter, she had time to get changed before she dialled 999.'

'But then where did she put the clothes? Nothing was found during the search. And she couldn't have risked leaving the house. We checked her suitcase but that was all clear.'

'And Hazel can't remember what Carmen was wearing. Or says she can't. It was hard to get anything coherent out of her.' Hennessy twisted the plastic cup between his fingers. 'What have we got on Darby?'

Ward flicked through a thin folder and said, 'We've managed to dig up some information. He's worth a mint, apparently. Something of a slum landlord – lots of run-down properties in Notting Hill and the surrounding area – but a whole portfolio of other businesses too: hotels, restaurants, cafés and a few flash flats in Mayfair. I wonder how he made his money.'

While Ward had been left at the house in case Marian or Hazel showed up, Hennessy had gone to Victoria where one of his interviewees had proved especially useful when it had come to background on Darby. 'According to Annie Foster he grew up dirt poor in Kellston with a deadbeat third-rate villain for a father. She claims Darby made his fortune during the war and not through anything legal.'

'Not a fan then, this Annie Foster.'

'No, not a fan. Reckons he was a tyrant, a bully, a man with-out morals. Said she wasn't surprised that someone had shot him, only that it had taken so long. She would have said a lot more too if her husband hadn't stopped her. We'll have another word when he's not around.'

'Has Darby got form?'

Hennessy shook his head. 'Pulled in a few times in the distant past – for theft, mainly – but nothing stuck. Been clean as a whistle ever since. Or if not clean then smart enough not to get caught. I guess the big question is who benefits from his death. It'll be the daughters, I presume. Chase up Darby's solicitor later this morning and see if we can get a sneak preview of the will.'

'On a Saturday? You'll be lucky. I'll try but he'll probably be on the golf course. So, what do you make of the sisters? You think one of them could be up for a spot of patricide – or all of them?'

Marian was the sister who had made the greatest impression on Hennessy, but then she probably made an impression on every red-blooded male she came into contact with. Beautiful women had a habit of doing that. She had been upset but controlled, dignified in grief, as if the journey from Suffolk had given her the opportunity to come to terms with what had happened. Her morning, she'd said, had been spent with her father, and she had described him as 'distracted', as if he'd had his mind on something else.

'At the time Darby was murdered, Marian was in her car driving back to Suffolk. Not that that puts her in the clear. She could have hired someone else to do the job.'

'And Hazel and Jonny were in the West End. Mind, I wouldn't trust that Jonny Cornish as far as I could throw him. He landed on his feet marrying one of the Darby girls.'

Hennessy nodded. Of the three sisters, Hazel was the one who had been, on the surface, the most upset. There had been a lot of tears, a lot of incoherent questions. Carmen hadn't done much crying, but he put that down to the shock. Sometimes a violent death provoked hysteria, other times a withdrawal, a refusal to face up to it, a sort of numbness. You couldn't always judge by people's reactions whether they were guilty or not. He scratched his chin, in need of a shave.

'And talking of not trusting people, what about Milo Grant? He's got form: assault, handling stolen goods. He was even at the office shortly before Darby left.'

'Yeah, collecting his wages,' Ward said. 'But where's the motive? No Rex Darby, no job. And nothing to suggest he was on bad terms with his boss. Although he hasn't got much of an alibi. Well, he hasn't got an alibi at all. His mother *thinks* he got home about quarter to six, but it could have been a bit earlier or a bit later. And either way he would have had time to go round to Upper Belgrave Street, shoot Darby and drive straight home.'

'Pat Foster's illegitimate son. Is that important?' Hennessy frowned. 'Perhaps the two of them were in it together. Pat's the finance man. We'll get someone to go through Darby's books and make sure everything's as it should be.'

'Syphoning off the profits, you mean?'

'It's not impossible. Darby finds out, or he's on the verge of finding out, and he has to be eliminated.' Hennessy, needing the caffeine, risked a gulp of coffee. 'Anything from the finger-print boys?'

Ward shook his head. 'Nothing yet other than the expected ones.'

'Neighbours?'

'Nothing. Sod all. No one even saw Darby come back to the house, never mind his visitor.' Ward gave a snort. 'Too bloody posh to look out of their windows.'

Hennessy grinned. 'Money buys you privacy, mate. It's one of the perks. See no evil, hear no evil, and keep your nose out of it.'

'Very helpful, I'm sure.'

Hennessy visualised the big house on Upper Belgrave Street, empty now of all its usual occupants, a crime scene with the door sealed. A house of secrets, he thought. His grin gradually faded away. His mind conjured up the three sisters, the three dark-haired girls who had just lost their father. Marian and Hazel, along with their husbands, had booked into the Gryphon for the night while Carmen had been driven back to her flat in Kellston. Carmen hadn't even waited for Marian to arrive before leaving.

'What's bothering you?' Ward asked, after a silence had settled on the room.

'That family, those girls: there's something off about them.'

'Off? Peculiar, you mean? Or guilty as sin?'

But Hennessy didn't elaborate. 'You should go home, get some sleep,' he said. 'It's late.'

67

Showered, shaved and in a fresh set of clothes, Hennessy was keeping his tone chatty, his manner informal, as if rather than interrogating her he was simply grateful for whatever assistance she could give. However, Annie Foster continued to sit stiff-backed in the worn plastic chair, her eyes warier than yesterday, her opinions less vociferous. This could have been the result of finding herself in the less than salubrious surroundings of a police interview room or, just as likely, the result of a firm pep talk from her husband.

Pat Foster, as it transpired, was no stranger to the law, having been convicted for fraud back in his twenties. He'd served a couple of jail terms but since teaming up with Rex Darby his fortunes had taken a turn for the better, and now he was comfortably off with a good job, a house that was worth a few bob, and money in the bank.

'Your husband worked with Rex for a long time.'

'Over thirty years,' she said.

'They must have got on.'

Annie nodded. She was a small, plump woman, with greying hair that she didn't attempt to disguise. There was something motherly, homely, about her, but there was a forcefulness too, a strength beneath the surface. He suspected that if anyone tried to hurt the people she loved, she'd show her claws and lash out like a mother cat.

'Pat's more tolerant than me. He's the easy-going sort.'

'You didn't like Rex.' Hennessy presented it as a statement rather than a question.

'He was a difficult man. No one will tell you otherwise.' There was a defensiveness in her tone, and she glared at Hennessy. 'He was a bully. I've already told you that. He rubbed people up the wrong way. And no, I didn't like him: there was nothing *to* like about him. He seemed to take pleasure in making other people miserable.'

'Like his daughters, for example?'

As if sensing a trap, Annie hesitated. 'If you're looking to lay this at their feet, you're barking up the wrong tree. I'm not saying it was all sunshine and roses, but he was still their dad. They wouldn't do anything to harm him.' She paused, frowned, and said, 'Do you know how Carmen is? I tried to call her last night, but no one answered the phone. She shouldn't be on her own at a time like this. The others have got their husbands, someone to take care of them, but she hasn't got anyone.'

'I believe she's with her flatmates.'

'Flatmates,' Annie scoffed. 'She's barely known them five minutes. She should be with people who care about her.'

'No boyfriend, then?' Hennessy asked, remembering the diamond ring on Carmen's finger.

'There was. They split up.'

'Why was that?'

'It's not down to me to say. You'll have to ask her.'

'Can you give me a name at least?'

Annie's face darkened, and her hands gripped the edge of the table. 'Clive Grainger. He's the manager of Lola's. She's had a lucky escape if you ask me. That man was only ever after her money. The minute he saw it slipping away, his interest slipped away too. He turned his back on her when she needed him most.' Annie stopped abruptly, chewing on her lower lip as if she'd said more than she meant to.

'Slipping away?'

'You know, after the birthday dinner, after Rex and Carmen fell out.'

'That seems kind of . . . extreme. Grainger thought the falling out was more than just a passing tiff, I take it. That there was no going back?'

'I've no idea what he thought.'

'But you said—'

Flustered, Annie reached for the handbag that she'd placed on the table. 'I've told you everything I know. Can I go now?'

'Just one last thing if you wouldn't mind, Mrs Foster.' Hennessy steepled his fingers, widened his lips and gave her what passed for a cordial smile. 'What exactly happened at Rex Darby's birthday dinner?'

Elizabeth Holmes had that puffy look that women get when they've been crying a lot. She sat down on the still-warm plastic chair recently vacated by Annie, gazing around at the four blank walls before eventually returning her attention to Hennessy.

'It still doesn't feel real,' she said. 'Him being gone. I can't take it in. It's like . . .'

But whatever it was like she couldn't find the words for it. Hennessy nodded in sympathy. 'It's all very shocking. Murder always is. Thank you for talking to us again. I can see how difficult it is for you.'

'We'll try not to keep you too long,' WPC Sandra Best said. 'Anything more you can remember could be useful, though. Perhaps we could go over yesterday afternoon. Why do you think Mr Darby left the office in such a hurry?'

'He didn't say. He just announced that we were closing early and that was that. There wasn't any explanation. If I'd have known ... God, it's just so terrible.' She paused for a moment and then said, 'To be honest, he hadn't been the same since that birthday party. All that retirement nonsense! As if he could leave the business in *their* hands. Years it took him to build up and those daughters of his don't have a clue. I think he was starting to realise that. It was affecting him, making him nervy. And then there was Carmen throwing his generosity back in his face. Rex was devastated. And then all this Michael Quinn business.'

'Michael Quinn? What was that about?'

'Didn't Pat tell you?'

Sandra made one of those indeterminate noises that could have meant anything. 'It would be interesting to get your take on it.'

Hennessy sat back, happy for Sandra to take the lead. She had done an excellent job with Carmen Darby, and it was always good to get the female perspective on things. It also gave him a chance to watch Elizabeth's reactions more closely.

Elizabeth's eyes darted round the room again, her gaze never settling. 'I dare say it was something and nothing, but he got this idea recently that he'd seen Michael outside the office and ... well, it seemed to upset him, put him on edge, because he didn't understand why Michael wouldn't just come in.'

'Did he give the impression of being frightened of Michael?'

'Frightened? No, I don't think so. Why should he be? They were old friends. But he'd gone away years ago – Michael, I mean – and Rex was ... he was ... I don't know, *upset* about it, bewildered, as if he didn't understand why he'd show up again after all this time. He asked me to look out for him, but I wouldn't have known Michael if he'd walked straight past me on the street. I only ever met him once or twice and that was a long time ago.'

Sandra nodded. 'Do you think Rex actually saw him or do you think he made a mistake?'

'What are you trying to say? That Rex was imagining things? He might have been seventy, but he still had all his faculties. He wasn't gaga, if that's what you're getting at. He had years left in him, *years*. And someone took that away and ...'

Elizabeth retrieved a small lacy handkerchief from the sleeve of her sweater and dabbed at her eyes. Her face twisted, becoming ugly. For a few seconds there was no sound in the room but a thin snivelling. Then suddenly she glanced up, her gaze hard and bright and directed straight at Hennessy. 'So you haven't arrested anyone yet? If I were you, I'd take a good hard look at those girls. They couldn't wait to get their hands on his money. Selfish, greedy little cows, the three of them! Who had the motive? That's what you've got to ask. *They* did!'

They were sitting in the comfort of the Gryphon's lounge, empty at the moment apart from them and Rex Darby's son-in-law. For the present, Hennessy had decided against pulling any of the family into the station, aware that without hard evidence as to their guilt it could appear heavy-handed and unsympathetic.

Jonny Cornish stretched out his long legs, linked his fingers in his lap, and sighed in reply to the question he'd been asked. 'Ah, the birthday dinner, yes. Rex's seventieth. That was the night he announced his retirement.'

'Did that come as a surprise?' DS Ward asked.

'A surprise? Yes, I suppose so. I never really imagined him

333

retiring. He was something of a workaholic, always in the office, always on the go. Not a pipe and slippers type of man, if you know what I mean.'

'And not just retiring,' Ward continued, 'not just stepping down, but sharing out his wealth between his daughters too. Quite a windfall, I should imagine. Something to celebrate.'

'There was some champagne if I remember rightly.'

Hennessy thought Jonny looked smug, but that might just have been his normal expression. 'Then things took a turn if I'm not mistaken. Between Mr Darby and his youngest daughter?'

'There was a stupid row, yes. Rex was drunk, very drunk, and decided Carmen wasn't living up to expectations. Not fawning enough, you see, not showing enough gratitude. Putting it mildly, he got the hump and asked her to leave.'

'And *was* she being ungrateful?'

'Not as far as I could see. But Carmen's the quiet one. You never know what's going on inside her head.'

'It seemed to develop into quite a rift. She moved out, didn't she?'

'She did. Although I don't think she expected it to be quite as permanent as it became. Neither of them was prepared to compromise so . . .' Jonny shrugged, crossed his legs at the ankles, and gave a small eye roll. 'Families. What can you do? I always tried to stay out of it.'

Ward glanced at his notebook. 'Didn't you move into Upper Belgrave Street shortly after Carmen moved out?'

'That was Hazel's doing. If I'd had my way . . . well, I was happy enough living where we were. But she was worried about her dad being on his own. Thought we should move in, so he'd have some company.'

'And how is your wife?' Hennessy asked.

Jonny shook his head. 'Not good, I'm afraid. This has all been devastating for her. The doctor gave her something to make her sleep. I suppose you'll want to talk to her again at some point but I'm not sure she'll be up to it today. Marian's with her, just in case she wakes up.' He glanced at his watch. 'Will this take much longer?'

'Just a few more questions,' Hennessy said. 'I'd like to ask about the falling out that *you* had with Rex Darby. Over a gambling debt, wasn't it?'

'Oh, *that*. It was nothing. Rex only had the hump because it was Joe Quinn I owed the money to. We didn't exactly fall out over it. I told him I was going to pay the debt and that was that.'

'So he didn't threaten to put a freeze on Hazel's inheritance because of your gambling habit?'

Jonny lit a cigarette and grinned. 'Ah, who have you been talking to? Elizabeth, was it, or Pat? Those two always know how to make a mountain out of a molehill. Rex would have come round. He wasn't being serious. He just liked to flex his muscles and show everybody who was boss.'

'Still, it must have been a worry. One minute your wife is in line for a tidy little fortune, the next she's having it snatched away from her.'

'Like I said, it wouldn't have come to that.' Jonny pulled on his cigarette and squinted through the smoke at Hennessy. 'I hope you're not trying to pin Rex's murder on me, chief inspector. I wasn't anywhere near the house yesterday afternoon. And I'm hardly going to kill my wife's father. What do you think I am? Some kind of monster?'

'You've got a record, though.' Ward said.

'Minor stuff. Nothing violent. And Jesus, that was years ago. I'm not a bloody murderer.'

Ward glanced down at his notebook again. 'Have you ever been in the attic at Upper Belgrave Street?'

'What? No.'

'So just out of interest, Mr Cornish, could you tell us why your fingerprints are on the door and the walls?'

Hennessy thought it was the first time Jonny had looked even faintly rattled. A frown appeared between his eyes. His mouth opened and closed, before his face suddenly cleared. 'Ah, yes, I know what that was. I wanted to check if there was any storage space up there. But that was weeks ago, just after we'd moved in. Sorry, I'd forgotten all about it. I only went up for a minute or two. When I told Hazel, she said to leave it, that no one used the attic any more on account of . . . well, you know.'

'I don't know, Mr Cornish,' Hennessy said. 'Why don't you enlighten us?'

Jonny gave a thin smile. 'On account of Rosa Darby having killed herself up there.'

Marian was next in line to face Hennessy and Ward. She was all grace and charm, courteous to the point where it felt like she was bestowing a favour even by agreeing to talk to them. They spoke about the birthday dinner, about her father's row with Carmen, about her movements the previous day, about Michael Quinn, going over everything and finding no contradictions in her answers. Then, when the subject of Carmen came up again, she casually dropped the bombshell.

'I suppose it must have been a dreadful shock when I told her that Dad was cutting her out of his will.'

Hennessy's ears pricked up. 'When was this?'

'Oh, weeks ago.' Marian waved an elegantly manicured hand. 'I don't remember exactly.'

'And how did she react to the news?'

'She made out she didn't care, but that can hardly be true, can it? I mean, nobody wants to work in a backstreet café for the rest of their lives. I can't imagine what she was thinking: all she had to do was apologise and that would have been that.'

'So why didn't she?'

'Your guess is as good as mine. Sheer stubbornness, I suppose. Neither of them was prepared to back down. And then Carmen just made everything worse by having a cosy cup of tea with that awful Joe Quinn. That was the last straw as far as Dad was concerned.' Marian paused, her face crumpling slightly. She wiped away an invisible tear. 'Poor Dad. It's all so awful. He only ever wanted the best for us.'

'Do you know if your father went through with his threat?' Hennessy asked. 'To disinherit Carmen?'

'I've no idea. You'd have to ask his solicitor. Robin Spencer.'

'We would if we could find him,' Ward said. 'He's not at his office or his home address.'

'Have you tried his club? The Athenaeum? He might be there.'

'Thank you. We'll do that.'

'Or Pat might know. About the will, I mean. There could be a copy at the office.'

Ward shook his head. 'He says not.'

Marian looked disappointed, but quickly changed her expression to something more neutral. 'Spencer's a dreadful bore,' she said. 'A stickler for the rules. You'd better have the right paperwork if you want him to cooperate.'

'We'll bear that in mind.'

'Was there anything else? Only I really should be getting back. Hazel's in a terrible state. I'd like to be there when she wakes up.'

'That's all,' Hennessy said. 'For now.'

When Marian departed from the lounge, she left in her wake a soft, subtle, and yet enduring perfume that lingered in the air long after she'd gone.

68

Since the discovery of Rex's body, Jonny hadn't had the opportunity to talk to Marian alone. By the time he and Hazel had returned to Upper Belgrave Street last night, Marian had already installed herself and Hugh at the Gryphon. Jonny had booked into the hotel too, but by then it was the early hours of the morning, Hugh was sticking close to Marian's side, and they'd all had enough on their hands with Hazel flipping out.

At first, when they'd been informed of the murder, Jonny had thought Hazel was acting, even *overacting*, but it had soon become clear that she wasn't. As if it had all come as a complete shock to her. As if she hadn't known it was going to happen. As if she had thought that all the planning was just some sort of game that they'd been playing. Still, at least it had stopped the law from grilling her. Close to hysteria, Hazel had been barely capable of understanding their questions, never mind answering them.

Whatever the doctor had given her had knocked her out cold. Jonny was worried that when she did wake up, she'd blurt something out to the law. He sat beside the bed watching her closely while he went over his conversation with Hennessy. There was no doubt that the cop had his suspicions, that the family was firmly in his sights, but he didn't have a shred of evidence.

And Jonny wanted to keep it that way. The stuff about the attic had caught him off guard. What had that been about? Hennessy had caught him out in a lie, and he wasn't sure how important it was. But this problem and Hazel's meltdown weren't the only things on his mind. Nothing had gone exactly to plan last night, and he couldn't grasp why.

There was a light knock on the door and Marian came into the room. 'Still asleep?' she asked softly.

Jonny nodded. 'Where's Hugh?'

'Gone for a walk.'

Jonny stood up and gestured towards the en suite bathroom. Once they were inside, he shut the door and leaned against it. Then all his frustrations bubbled over. 'For fuck's sake, what's Milo playing at?' he hissed. 'After ten, we agreed. When it was dark. When no one was likely to see him. When the neighbours would have their curtains closed. What the hell was he doing going there in the afternoon?'

Marian, cool as always, smoothed down her hair and gave a vague shrug of her shoulders. 'I don't know what you're asking me for. How would I know? But it's done now so I don't suppose it really matters what *time* it was done.'

'Of course it bloody matters. Carmen was still there, wasn't she? What if she saw him, or heard him?'

'If she had, they'd have arrested him by now.'

'And how do you know they haven't?'

Marian sighed. 'Because Hennessy wouldn't be wasting his time on us, would he? He'd be down the police station giving Milo the third degree.'

'Unless the little scrote's already spilled his guts. He could have said that we were behind it all, that we're paying him, that none of it was *his* idea.'

'If that was the case, we'd all be down the station too. I hope you're not losing your nerve, Jonny. We've already got Hazel to deal with without inventing more problems. We'll have to keep her away from the police until we're sure she won't say anything stupid. And stop stressing over Carmen. It could be useful that she was there. We're hardly going to arrange for her to pick up her things at the very same time we've organised a hit.'

Jonny could see she had a point, but he still didn't like the way Milo had gone off-piste. It only proved what he'd suspected all along: the man was a loose cannon and couldn't be trusted. 'Do you know what Carmen's told the law?'

'Your guess is as good as mine. But if she *did* see Milo, she'd have told them. She's got no reason not to.'

'What about this attic business?'

'What?'

'Did Hennessy ask you about the attic?'

'No, what's the attic got to do with anything?'

Jonny might not be losing his nerve, but his nerves were certainly frayed. He would have liked to pace but there wasn't enough space in the bathroom with the two of them in there. 'I don't know. Nothing, probably. Maybe you should talk to Carmen, find out what actually happened last night.'

'We know what happened.'

'Not all of it.'

Marian looked uninterested in the idea. Instead, she glanced around as if assessing the decor and deciding how to change it now that she was the owner of the place. Her gaze settled briefly on the bath, the towels and the pale green cabinet. Then her eyes focused on Jonny again. 'I could, I suppose. It might seem odd if I don't get in touch.'

'Just be careful what you say.'

'Thanks for the advice. I'd never have thought of that myself.'

'I'm just saying, that's all. Don't get antsy. They could have the phones bugged, anything. I wouldn't be surprised if they put a tail on us. We're going to be under suspicion for weeks, months even.'

Marian brushed an invisible speck from the shoulder of her jacket. 'Hennessy can't prove a thing. For all he knows, Michael Quinn could have done it. Or Carmen, come to that.' Her lips slid into a sly smile. 'Motive and opportunity: that's what Hennessy's looking for. All we have to do is keep our cool and we'll be fine. Do you think you can manage that?'

'It's not me you need to worry about.'

'I can deal with Hazel. She's up to her neck in it, like the rest of us. Maybe she needs reminding of that. If she doesn't want to spend the next twenty years behind bars, she'll get her act together and toughen up. I'm not going to prison because she's had a sudden attack of conscience.'

'*I'll* deal with Hazel,' Jonny said.

'You'd better. Just remember what's at stake here.'

But Jonny wasn't likely to forget. He was looking forward to the future he had risked so much for, when he could be master of the house in Upper Belgrave Street, when no one could ever look down on him again, when he could start living the life he'd always wanted.

69

Annie Foster closed her umbrella and shook the rain out of it. She followed her husband into the office on Ebury Street, aware of a silence in reception that was almost eerie. Pat had insisted on coming over – to clear up after the police, he said, although she suspected it was just to be doing something – and she hadn't wanted him to be on his own. Rex's death had knocked him for six. He seemed to have aged overnight, the lines deepening on his face, his eyes dulled with shock and disbelief.

The reception area was untidy but not catastrophically messy. Drawers had been left open in Elizabeth's desk and in some of the filing cabinets, as if the effort of closing them had proved too much. Assorted paperwork lay in heaps, picked up, examined and rejected. The phone was facing the wrong way, and a jar containing pens had been emptied out. It was like a careless burglar had been in, rummaging through everything in the hope of finding an item of value.

Pat sighed and walked across the room into the short corridor that led to his own office, opened the door, and looked inside.

Annie stood on her toes and peered over his shoulder. It was much the same in here.

'What were they searching for, do you think?'

'Evidence,' Pat said. 'Anything that might give them a clue as to why Rex was . . .' Here his voice broke, and he swallowed hard. 'Accounts, business contracts, letters from disgruntled tenants.'

'Accounts? What use are those?'

'In case I've been cooking the books,' Pat said. 'Syphoning off cash to fund my lavish lifestyle.'

'And what lavish lifestyle would that be?'

'Well, you know what I mean.'

'But they can't suspect you.'

'Why not? Money's as good a motive as any. Maybe Rex had caught on to what I was doing. Maybe everything was about to come crashing down. I could have easily gone round to the house, shot him and walked home.' Pat took a breath. 'But I didn't, in case you're wondering.'

'I wasn't wondering. Of course you didn't. Anyone could have done it. Even Elizabeth or . . .' She had been about to say Milo but smartly bit her tongue. Now wasn't the time to be throwing accusations at his other son. 'Or someone who held a grudge.'

Pat went into his office and started tidying up. 'I can't see Elizabeth wielding a gun somehow,' he said, as he moved papers from one spot to another. 'She's taken it hard. I told her to take some time off, but she wasn't having it. Said she'd be in on Monday as usual.'

Annie nodded. 'Best to keep busy, I suppose.' Strangely, she *could* imagine Elizabeth wielding a gun, all those pent-up frustrations of hers rising to the surface in a moment of madness. Resentment could be a powerful force, and she'd had good reason to resent Rex. All those years he'd kept her dangling, and nothing at the end of it. But Annie couldn't feel sorry for her. The woman had reaped what she'd sown.

Annie gazed around the office, trying to remember the last occasion she'd been here. Before Rosa had died, she thought. With no desire to see either Rex or Elizabeth when she didn't need to, she'd stayed well away. 'What will happen to the business?'

'That's down to the girls. Once probate has gone through, it will belong to them.'

'And in the meantime?'

'I'll keep things ticking over – if they want me to.'

'They're lucky to have you,' Annie said. 'What about Carmen?'

Pat sighed again. 'I don't know, love. That depends on whether Rex changed his will. He threatened to, but whether he did or not . . .'

Annie's lip curled. Even in death, she thought, Rex could still cause harm. Although she regretted saying what she had to the police – she had let her emotions get the better of her – this was only because it never paid to tell the truth about disliking someone. Especially when that someone was a murder victim. However, she had meant every word. She had never been a hypocrite and couldn't and wouldn't grieve for Rex Darby.

Milo was keeping his head down, staying home and waiting to see what happened next. He had kept his cool with the law despite all the provocation. Having a record for GBH, for fencing, apparently meant he was a murderer too. But he knew no one had come forward to identify him, or even give a rough description. If they had, he'd have been in a line-up by now. The neighbours hadn't been paying attention yesterday and he was glad of it.

Hennessy had taken Milo's clothes to be examined by

344

forensics. Well, good luck to him with that. And no doubt he was out there right now, trying to dig more dirt. Milo would have liked to talk to Marian or Jonny but knew that it would be a big mistake to call. No, he'd keep himself to himself and let things take their course.

His mother was circling round, giving him evils. First thing she'd said this morning, even before he'd had his breakfast, was, 'You'd better not be involved in this, Milo. I ain't coming all the way from Spain to visit you in the nick.'

'What would I want to top Darby for? He pays my bleedin' wages. Or used to. Now I probably ain't even got a job.'

'If you're lying to me ...'

Milo had just rolled his eyes. 'First the law and now you. I don't know which is worse. I liked old Rex: him and me got on fine. Have I ever said a bad word about him? I mean, Jesus, we even used to go to the pub together. I'm not saying we were best mates or nothin' but I'm hardly going to shoot the geezer.'

'Yeah, well, I know that temper of yours. Once you get into an argument—'

'There was no argument, for God's sake. Ask Pat. Ask Elizabeth. I didn't see him again after he left the office. How many times have I told you? I walked to the car and drove back here. End of story.'

But his mother had a suspicious mind. She kept asking questions, drip-feeding them to him, repeating them, as if she was hoping to eventually catch him out. He was sticking to his story, though, refusing to budge. She could badger him all she liked but it wasn't going to make a damn bit of difference. It was a rum do, he thought, when even your own flesh and blood didn't trust you.

70

Carmen pushed the remains of her scrambled egg – which was most of it – around the plate. It reminded her of the breakfast Clive had cooked for her when everything had first gone wrong. She wasn't hungry, couldn't think straight, could barely breathe properly. It was as if her body had partly shut down, unable to deal with the enormity of what had happened. Last night she had lain awake, gazing into the darkness, going over it all step by step, trying to turn the unbelievable into something her brain could comprehend. Now her eyes felt tired and scratchy, and her limbs were like lead weights. Everything she did was an effort.

Beth leaned against the sink with her arms folded across her chest. 'You should try and eat. I know it's not easy.'

But Carmen had a lump in her throat, like a giant stone. Every time she tried to swallow, she wanted to gag. *Her father was dead*. He had not been a man who was easy to love, but he'd still been her flesh and blood. She put down her fork and said, 'The police are coming again today.'

'Be careful what you say to them.'

Carmen gazed at her, wide-eyed, reminded of the fear she'd felt yesterday, the dread of being accused. Her mouth went dry. 'But I haven't done anything wrong.'

'The family are always the first they suspect. The cops can be lazy bastards, and lying bastards too, when it comes to it. Just be on your guard, yeah? Don't let them put words in your mouth.'

It had been after nine when Carmen had got home yesterday evening. Deana had already gone to work, and Beth had been the only one in. Up to this point she had not made any kind of bond with her, but last night her flatmate had been a godsend, listening calmly while she'd blurted out the story in jerky incoherent sentences. In the end, Beth had proved both compassionate and efficient, offering consolation as well as practical help, even calling Scandal to tell them there had been a bereavement in the family and that Carmen wouldn't be in until the following Friday.

'Thanks for everything you did last night.'

Beth gave a shrug. 'I didn't do much. Are you sure you don't want me to call the caff, too? You should take a few days off while you sort your head out.'

Carmen knew it would take more than a few days. 'No, I'd rather stay busy. I'll go in on Monday as usual. I mean, what am I going to be doing here? Just sitting around and dwelling on it.'

'You could be right. But let me know if you change your mind. Or come home if you can't deal with it.'

'I will,' Carmen said. She pushed her plate away, giving up on the food. The phone rang and she jumped. 'If it's for me, I'm not here. Unless it's the police. I don't want to talk to anyone.'

Beth went through to the living room and picked up the phone. Carmen tried to listen, but the radio was on. Ken Boothe was singing 'Everything I Own', the kind of plaintive song that she really didn't want to hear right now. If she'd had the strength she would have stood up, walked over to the windowsill and turned the radio off.

'Annie Foster,' Beth said, coming back into the kitchen. 'I told her you were down the police station. She said she'd try again later.'

'Thanks.' There had been a couple of calls last night too, but she had let them ring out. She felt guilty for not answering now, knowing that Annie would be worried. 'I'll ring her in a bit.'

'Didn't you say you had sisters?'

'Two,' Carmen said.

'I take it you're not close, then.'

'They're both much older than me.' As if this was an adequate reply, as if it explained everything. But she didn't want to go into the detail of their troubled relationship. It made her feel faintly ashamed. Like it was her fault. Like she was the kind of person that other people – even those who *should* have cared – found themselves incapable of loving.

'But at a time like this. Perhaps . . .'

Carmen shook her head. It had been the same with her mother, she thought. And Clive. Perhaps there *was* something about her, something that repelled rather than attracted, a trait in her nature that singled her out as being unworthy of affection.

The doorbell went, three sharp rings, and Carmen looked at Beth. 'That'll be the police.'

'I'll get it,' Beth said. 'Don't forget what I told you.'

Carmen stood up, took her plate over to the bin, scraped the food into it, and dropped the plate into the sink. She pushed back her shoulders and tried to arrange her features into a mask of innocence. Well, she *was* innocent, but she could feel a trembling inside her, an anxiety that couldn't be worse if she had pulled the trigger.

DCI Hennessy came into the kitchen accompanied by WPC

Sandra Best. It was Sandra who smiled and nodded and said, 'Hello Carmen. How are you doing today?'

'Oh, you know. Still trying to . . .'

Before the conversation could proceed, Beth cast the police officers a scathing glance and said to Carmen, 'Would you like me to stay with you? I don't mind.'

But Carmen shook her head, deciding she would be even more nervous, even more self-conscious, with Beth sitting beside her. 'It's all right, thanks.'

'Okay. I'll be in my room if you need me.'

Once Beth had gone, Carmen gestured for the officers to sit down. 'Do you have any news? Any leads. Has anyone been arrested?'

'I'm afraid not,' Hennessy said. 'Early days. We just wanted to run over a few things with you.'

'It's nothing to worry about,' Sandra said.

In Carmen's experience, *nothing to worry about* usually meant something. She asked if they'd like a hot drink – both declined – and then laid her hands on the table, linking her fingers together, hoping they wouldn't start to shake.

For a while Hennessy went over old ground, asking the same questions he'd asked the night before, talking about the sequence of events, the arrival of the visitor, the discovery of her father's body. Then they moved on to the birthday dinner and the row, her job at the café, Joe Quinn, and the phone call from Marian.

'Marian came to see you at the café, didn't she?' Sandra said. 'A few weeks ago?'

'Yes. It was a while back.'

'She says she told you that your father was going to write you out of his will. That must have been upsetting. How did you cope with that?'

Carmen could have said that the delight with which Marian had delivered this news was equally upsetting but sensed that now was not the time to be badmouthing her sister. 'It didn't come as any big surprise. My father was . . . a strong-willed man. He didn't like to be disobeyed.'

Hennessy cleared his throat and leaned forward. 'That's quite extreme, though – disinheriting you? How did you feel about that?'

The same question twice, Carmen thought, phrased a little differently but fundamentally the same. She gave a small, frustrated shift of her shoulders. 'It seemed very . . . final, I suppose, like he was cutting me out of his life completely.'

'Did that make you angry?'

Carmen gave a hollow laugh. 'Angry enough to kill him, you mean? No, I'd already come to the conclusion that I was better off taking care of myself.'

'Even if that meant sacrificing a fortune?'

'I didn't really think about it.'

Hennessy gave her a sceptical look. 'Aren't we talking millions here?' His gaze swept quickly over the kitchen as if he was mentally comparing it to the one in Upper Belgrave Street. 'Surely that must have had an impact on you.'

'I mean, I was preoccupied with other things: a new job, a new flat. I couldn't stop my father from doing whatever he wanted to do, so I didn't dwell on it.'

Hennessy didn't respond immediately, and when he did, his request startled her. 'Tell me about Milo Grant.'

'Milo? I hardly know him.'

'But he worked for your father.'

'Yes, but I didn't see him often. In the office occasionally, but that was it. We've never had much to do with each other.'

'You don't get on?'

350

Carmen, inwardly recoiling, thought of Milo's lascivious glances and crude chat-up lines. 'I just don't know him very well. Why are you asking? You don't think . . .? But why would Milo kill Dad? What would be the reason for it?'

'We're not claiming that he did,' Hennessy said. 'We're just looking into everyone who was with your father before he left work yesterday.'

Except they hadn't asked about the others, Carmen thought, not Pat or Elizabeth. Surely they must have been there too? She thought Milo was more than capable – there was something cold about him, something brutish – but she couldn't see a motive.

'You must have *some* thoughts on him,' Hennessy persisted.

'To be honest, I've always tried to avoid him.'

'And why was that?'

Carmen didn't want to explain, to have to go into it all, but once she'd come out with the stupid avoiding comment – why had she said that? – she wasn't left with a choice. Her hands did a small dance on the table while she tried to phrase the words in her head. 'Because it was awkward, with him being Pat's illegitimate son. I mean, that wasn't Milo's fault, but I felt bad for Annie, so I just stayed away from him. It was easier that way. I didn't want to take sides.'

'There was bad feeling then between Annie Foster and Milo?'

'No, I didn't mean that. She didn't blame him. Why would she?'

'But she did blame her husband? He was unfaithful to her, after all.'

'I don't know. It was a long time ago.'

'But the evidence of that affair was ever present, wasn't it? Annie can't have been happy about your father giving Milo a job, about her husband working alongside his other son every day?'

'We've never talked about it.'

'Was Pat close to your father?'

'They were best friends,' Carmen said.

'And close to his son? Was he close to Milo?'

'I suppose so.'

Carmen felt like she was getting entangled in a web, a sticky, complex snare that was tightening around her. Did they suspect Pat of killing him? Maybe with Milo? Or perhaps they even thought that Annie had pulled the trigger. But that was ridiculous. 'Why are you asking me all this? What's it got to do with my dad's death?'

'We're just trying to form a picture.'

'You're looking at the wrong people.'

Hennessy, as if to catch her off guard, abruptly returned to his earlier subject. 'Do you know if your father actually changed his will?'

'I should think so,' Carmen said. 'He wasn't one for idle threats.'

'Well, we're still trying to track down your father's solicitor. As soon as we do, we'll know for sure.'

Carmen was aware of two pairs of eyes on her, both closely watching her response. But she knew there wasn't any winning reaction. She could have murdered her father to stop him changing his will, or she could have murdered him *because* he'd changed it. Either way, it left her firmly in the frame.

71

On Monday morning, Carmen was back at the Station Café, glad to be out of the confines of the flat and to have something to think about other than the murder of her father. Even the relentless delivery of bacon and eggs, toast and countless cups of tea was preferable to being alone with her thoughts. Beth would be at work all day, and Deana didn't get out of bed before midday. Deana's eyes had grown wide as saucers when she'd been told what had happened, and Carmen had made her promise not to tell anyone at Scandal. Pity and suspicion were the last two things she needed right now.

The afternoon before she had walked down here and repeated the story to Joan. They had sat upstairs in the kitchen of the flat, drinking strong coffee while Lottie watched the TV in the living room. It had been time, she'd decided, to come clean before someone else did it for her. She'd apologised for lying about her name, about who she really was, but Joan had brushed the apology aside.

'Everyone in Kellston has something to hide, love. It's not

the end of the world. But this is an awful business with your dad. Terrible. You should take some time off. Me and Lottie can manage.'

But Carmen had shaken her head. 'I'd rather be working – if you still want me. I'll understand if you don't.'

Joan, however, wasn't fazed by a murder inquiry, or the fact that Carmen was still a possible suspect. 'It's up to you, but don't feel that you have to. And I won't tell anyone if you'd rather I didn't. Although it's hard to keep anything quiet round here. You can't go for a pee without everyone knowing about it.'

Carmen remembered this as she hurried along the aisles, fetching and carrying, exchanging small talk with the customers. There were newspapers on almost every table – mainly the *Sun* and the *Daily Mirror* – with news of Harold Wilson's victory in the second general election of the year. She kept her eyes averted from them, knowing that inside there would be reports on her father's killing, perhaps even photographs of him. And of her, too? She prayed not. Most of the coverage would have been over the weekend but the papers would still be writing about it.

Gordie came in and sat down at one of the few empty tables. Carmen approached him with trepidation. *He* knew who she really was. No doubt he would have heard about the murder of her father too. If she still retained any hope that he hadn't, it was quickly extinguished.

'At work then?' he said, lifting his eyebrows.

'It looks that way.'

'Bad business with your old man.'

'What can I get you?'

But Gordie wasn't going to be deflected so easily. 'Yeah, a bad business. First Joe and now your old man. It's one tragedy after another, ain't it? I'm surprised you're here, to be honest.

I wouldn't have thought you'd want to be working at a time like this.'

'A brew, is it? Or would you like some breakfast?'

'Just a brew, ta.' Gordie smirked. 'I suppose you've had the law crawling all over you.' He looked her up and down as if he meant it literally. 'It always helps to have a pretty face.'

Carmen was wishing he'd lower his voice in case anyone else heard. The place was busy, but he had the kind of voice that carried. She didn't want to be the talk of the café. 'I'll get you that brew.'

Joan, seeing the expression on her face, asked if she was all right when she went back over to the counter. Then she glared over towards Gordie and said, 'What's his game? What's he been saying?'

'He knows. And I don't suppose he'll be slow in making sure everyone else does too.'

'Well, you take no notice of him. He's a stirrer, that one, a nasty bit of work. Anyway, even if people do talk it won't be for long. They'll soon find something else to gossip about. You hold your head up, love. You've got nothing to be ashamed of.'

Carmen nodded. Given the choice, she would have preferred to put a bag over said head and go and hide in the back with Lottie. Given that this option wasn't open to her, she took the mug of tea, placed it on the table in front of Gordie and tried to make a fast getaway. But he wasn't having any of it.

'Hey, hold on,' he said, even though he could see she was busy.

'Did you want to order something else?'

'What's the deal between you and Terry?'

Startled, Carmen stared at him. 'What deal? I don't know what you're talking about.'

'Sure you don't,' he said snidely.

'I haven't seen Terry in ages.' Which was true. Since Joe

355

Quinn's death, she'd barely set eyes on him. He'd come into the caff once, weeks ago, but since then their paths hadn't crossed at all. 'What deal? What do you mean?'

'Never mind,' he said, turning his face away and picking up his mug.

Carmen was too busy to pursue it and didn't want to prolong the exchange anyway. For the rest of the time Gordie was in the café he watched her through crafty eyes, following every movement as she hurried up and down the aisles. She tried to take no notice, to ignore him, but his gaze was like a predatory wolf's surveying its prey.

She was still thinking about Gordie, and what he was up to, when she took her break late morning. While she ate a sandwich, she pointedly ignored the paper lying on the table. She couldn't bear the thought of opening it, of turning over the pages and finding her father's face looking out at her. Had Hennessy made any progress? When the murderer was found, some sense might be made of all the awfulness, but until then the horror would continue. It was like being stuck in a nightmare, so many questions and no answers, and with a cloud of suspicion hanging over her.

Marian had rung yesterday, a brief call to say that she and Hugh were returning to Suffolk. 'How are you?' she'd asked, but she hadn't waited for Carmen to reply before continuing. 'I suppose the police are giving you a hard time with you being at the house and everything. They do tend to leap to the most obvious conclusions. It really is a terrible business, isn't it? Hazel's taken it very hard. It was the shock, I suppose. It's been a shock for everyone.'

Carmen still had those 'most obvious conclusions' in her mind when Lottie came out from the back and sat down beside her.

'Why aren't you wearing your engagement ring?'

'Because I'm not engaged any more.'

'Have you and Don split up?'

'Yes, we've split.'

Lottie twisted her long brown hair between her fingers. 'Are you sad? You look sad.'

'No,' Carmen said. 'Not about that.' She thought about Clive and how he'd run a mile when the fortune he thought was coming his way began to slip from his grasp. 'We were never really suited. It's like that sometimes. You think you care for someone but you're not seeing them clearly. He wasn't a nice person, not deep down.'

'You'll find someone nicer,' Lottie said. 'Is that why you came round yesterday? To tell Gran about you and Don?'

'Something like that.'

Lottie reached across the table and took her hand. 'I'm glad you're not getting married, Carly. Do you mind me saying that? Only you would have left and had babies or moved away, and then you wouldn't work here. And if you didn't work here, I wouldn't have anyone to sit with at break times.'

'It's all for the best, then,' Carmen said, oddly touched that Lottie would miss her, even if it was only as a companion at break. She had decided it was finally time to remove the ring, to cut the fragile ties to Clive, to face the world as a single woman ... and, in all probability, a poor one. No more lies or pretence. Well, there was still her name, but everyone had got used to calling her Carly now. And perhaps a new life needed a new identity too.

Carmen left work as usual at two o'clock. She was halfway down the high street when she felt a peculiar prickling on the back of her neck. Someone's eyes on her. She glanced over her shoulder, but the street was busy, and she couldn't single out her tail. Or was she just imagining it? No, she knew that someone was there, someone dogging her footsteps. She upped her pace, striding on towards the Mansfield. It was the police, she presumed, checking out her movements, watching to see who she met up with, still unconvinced of her innocence.

Carmen could not remember a time before when she'd actually been pleased to enter the estate. But now the high grey towers with their hundreds of windows and graffiti-covered walls felt more like a place of safety, of sanctuary, than the concrete jungle she had always presumed it to be. Like a fugitive, she hunched her shoulders and hurried forwards.

72

DCI Hennessy was hitting one brick wall after another. It was Monday afternoon, three days after the murder, and the only lead he had was a family with motive, and his innate suspicion. He had, by now, interviewed and interviewed again all those closest to Rex Darby, but he was no nearer to finding the perpetrator. The house in Upper Belgrave Street had yielded nothing, and neither had forensics. There were no random fingerprints, nothing was missing, and all the clothes they had examined from possible suspects were clean. A scrutiny of the company accounts had showed up nothing untoward – no missing monies, no fortune syphoned off by a greedy employee – other than a skilful use of tax avoidance. Permission had been given to delve into bank accounts, but there had been no substantial amounts of cash withdrawn or deposited over the last six months.

Their only success to date had been tracking down the solicitor Robin Spencer on Saturday who had, eventually, and with much persuasion, agreed to leave the comfort of his club and reveal the contents of the will.

'So, what do you think?' Hennessy said, waving a copy of the document at his colleague.

DS Ward had his jaws around a ham salad roll, devouring it like he hadn't eaten for a week. A lank piece of lettuce leaf fell on to the desk and lay there abandoned. Still with his mouth full he said, 'Well, if we're looking for motive it's all there in black and white. Money – and lots of it. The daughters stand to inherit a fortune. And it puts Pat Foster and Elizabeth Holmes back in the picture – if they were ever out of it – with a windfall of twenty grand each. People have killed for a lot less.'

'But did they even know it was coming their way? Did Darby tell them? If they say not, we can't prove otherwise.'

'Bad news for Carmen,' Ward said, lifting the lettuce from the desk with his fingertips and dropping it into the bin. 'Jesus, that must have been some bloody row to make him cut her out of the will.'

Hennessy thought of the swish house in Belgravia, with its deep-pile carpets and elegant furniture. 'But does it eliminate her from the list of suspects? She could have been angry enough to shoot him. Or hopeful enough that he hadn't changed his will to shoot him before he did.'

'True. But if Pat Foster was going to inherit, it gives Milo a motive. Maybe the two of them were in it together. Father and son, a sweet little partnership.'

'Foster's not short of money, though. I mean, if we were talking millions I could understand, but is he going to risk going to jail for twenty k? Ten k if you're talking fifty-fifty.'

'It's not peanuts.'

'Granted, but it's not life changing either. I can't see Foster risking everything for that amount of money.'

'Milo Grant's got form for violence.'

Hennessy shrugged. 'He's got a weak alibi too. But why

wouldn't he have got himself a better one? If this was premeditated, he'd have known he was going to be in the frame.'

'Because he's an amateur? Or stupid? Or both?'

'We should talk to the other son. Eddie, is it? His mother reckons he never had much to do with Darby, but he was still at his birthday dinner.'

'And we can't rule out Elizabeth Holmes, the loyal secretary. Maybe she'd had enough of nine-to-five and decided to cash in her inheritance early.'

Hennessy nodded. 'All three of them – Foster, Milo, and Elizabeth – had opportunity. And Carmen, of course. And possibly Hazel too, if she didn't leave when she said she did.' He had finally got to talk to Hazel again this morning, but she had seemed woozy and not entirely with it. Her story, however, had remained the same. In between bouts of weeping, she had stumblingly related the same set of details as the first time.

'What do you make of Hugh Loughton?'

'Upper class, polite, benign. Not a huge fan of Rex Darby's, but then there aren't too many who were.'

'And loaded,' Ward said. 'He's got a big estate in the country.'

'Yeah, well, it's all relative. Our idea of loaded and that of the landed gentry are two completely different things. Those houses aren't cheap to run.'

Ward grinned. 'I shouldn't think his wife is either.'

Hennessy thought of the fragrant Marian and grinned back. She would certainly be a woman who didn't come cheap, but was she callous enough, greedy enough, to arrange the murder of her own father? 'If we want to get the inside line on the family, we should have another word with Mrs Cooper. The cleaner always knows what's what. And she's worked for Darby for years. She wasn't saying much on Saturday, but now she's had a few days to think about it, she might be more forthcoming.'

'There's Clive Grainger too, Carmen's ex-fiancé. He runs one of Darby's clubs, Lola's. Not a bad joint as it happens. Bit pricey, but the entertainment's decent.'

'We're clearly paying you too much. Do you know Grainger?'

'No, but I've seen him there. Suave bloke, very slick. Likes to charm the VIP customers. Do we have the lowdown on why the happy couple split up?'

'Not exactly. But if I was being cynical, I might suggest some connection to Carmen Darby losing her fortune. And that would give her another motive for wanting her father dead.'

Ward sat back in his chair and pulled a face. 'Wouldn't she be more likely to just shoot Grainger? A woman scorned and all that.'

But Hennessy wasn't so sure. Women, in his experience, didn't always blame the people you'd expect them to. 'We'll have a chat, see what he says.' Then, because he didn't want to get completely caught up in focusing on the Darby girls – single vision could lead you down all sorts of blind alleys – he glanced down at the file he'd had transferred from Cowan Road and said, 'What about this Michael Quinn business?'

'Anything in it, do you think?'

'Michael disappeared about twenty-five years ago. He was reported as a missing person by his mother, now deceased. There was bad blood between Joe Quinn and Darby about it. Quinn was of the opinion that Michael was dead, and that Darby had killed him.'

'Any good reason for that?'

Hennessy opened the file and flicked through the pages until he found the place he wanted. 'Michael and Darby were close pals, apparently. They worked together during the war – and by work I don't mean anything legal – but then there was a falling out over Darby marrying Rosa. Not good enough for his sister, perhaps. She was a lot younger than him. Anyway, after that the friendship cooled, but it was another four or five years before Michael went missing.'

Ward gazed up at the ceiling while he pondered on this. 'Well, Joe Quinn's out of the picture – he died before Darby. And his two sons are currently banged up for his murder, so neither of them could have topped him either.' He looked back down to Hennessy. 'Families,' he added scornfully. 'Michael could have just got in a spot of bother and left the area. There's nothing to say he was actually murdered.'

'No, and no body was ever found. But then no one ever saw him again, either.'

'Until Rex Darby claimed to have spotted him walking past his office.'

'Yeah, and that's the big question: *did* he see him, or did he just think he'd seen him?'

Ward shrugged his heavy shoulders. 'And why would Michael want to kill him after all these years?'

'I don't know, but if the Welrod *was* Darby's, and he went up to the attic to retrieve it, he must have been convinced he'd need it. So whoever he was expecting, Michael Quinn or someone else, he felt worried enough to try and protect himself. Darby's wife committed suicide, which could have been reason enough for Michael to bear a grudge. Perhaps he blamed Darby for her death.'

'Nothing suspicious about it, was there?'

'Not according to the records. Vodka and a bottle of pills. No foul play suspected. She had a history of depression, but just because she took her own life doesn't mean that Michael wouldn't hold Darby responsible in some way.'

'So we're chasing after a ghost.'

Hennessy placed his hands, palms down, on the table,

examined them for a moment and then glanced up at Ward. 'Not chasing after him exactly, just not dismissing the possibility of his existence.'

There was a knock on the door and WPC Sandra Best came in. 'Sorry to disturb you, guv, but there's been a call, an anonymous call, about Carmen Darby. Some bloke from Kellston claiming that she's in a relationship with Terry Street.'

'And who's Terry Street when he's at home?'

'Well, that's what I wondered too, so I rang Cowan Road to see if they had any information on him. Seems like he was part of Joe Quinn's firm and he's looking to take over now his boss has met a sticky end. There might be nothing in it, just someone stirring, but I thought I ought to let you know.'

Hennessy's eyes brightened. 'Interesting. Thank you.' His fingers lifted and dropped, drumming out a fast beat on the tabletop. 'Maybe our Carmen isn't quite as innocent as she makes out.'

73

It was Annie Foster who called Carmen to tell her about the contents of the will. Her voice sounded uncharacteristically tentative as she explained how she'd been told by Pat who in turn had been told by an indignant Robin Spencer, who'd been forced to leave his gentleman's club on Saturday to share Rex Darby's final wishes with the police.

'I thought it was better you heard it from me than from one of those coppers,' Annie said after she'd broken the news. 'It's not fair, love, not fair at all. I hope those sisters of yours will do the decent thing and share the money with you.'

Carmen smiled wryly into the receiver, thinking that the prospect was unlikely. Her sisters had never shared anything in their lives. 'It's no big surprise, Annie. Marian told me that was what he was planning to do.'

'But he'd have changed his mind. I'm sure he would. He wasn't thinking straight. It was all done in a fit of pique. He'd have come around, given time.'

But time was what her father didn't have. There could be no second thoughts now, no change of heart, no going back.

Carmen thought of him lying dead in the drawing room and a shudder ran through her. 'I'll be okay. Money isn't everything.'

Annie sighed down the line as if to say, *Oh, that old cliché.* 'But Rosa would have wanted you to have something. She'd be horrified by what he's done. You're always welcome at ours, love. You know that, don't you? There's plenty of room in the house.'

'Thanks. I appreciate it. But the flat's handy for work so I'll probably stay here for now.'

'The offer's always open. Are you sure you're all right, Carmen?'

Carmen assured her that she was, thanked her again, said her goodbyes and put the phone down. No sooner had she replaced the receiver than the doorbell went. Her first thought was the police, come to break the bad news about the will and to watch how she took it. She took a deep breath, glanced at the clock – almost three – and prepared herself for yet another ordeal.

It was a surprise, therefore, when she opened the door to find Terry Street standing on the other side of it. At the sight of her his mouth started to slide into its familiar trademark grin before he realised that this was not the time to be practising his flirtatious charm.

'Hey,' he said. 'I heard about your old man. You okay?'

Carmen stood aside to let him come in. 'I thought you were the police.'

Terry, who had taken a step forward, stopped abruptly and frowned. 'Are you expecting them?'

She shook her head. 'Well, there's nothing arranged but they're bound to show up again at some point.'

Terry seemed to relax a little. He turned, had a quick look along the corridor, and then closed the door behind him. 'Did they give you a hard time?'

'No, not really. I don't know. They were here again on Saturday. They just kept asking the same questions.'

In the living room Terry went over to the window, keeping to one side while he stared down at the estate. 'Did you know the law are watching the gates? They've got a car parked on Mansfield Road. It might not be for us, but I wouldn't be surprised if it was.'

'Us?' Carmen repeated, not understanding. 'What do you mean?'

Terry left the window and sat down on the sofa. 'Is everyone out? We need to talk.'

'Yes, I'm on my own.'

'I got pulled into Cowan Road this morning where I found DCI Hennessy waiting for me. He'd made a little trip across town just for the pleasure of my company.'

Carmen, confused, slumped down into the armchair. 'Hennessy? What did *he* want?'

'Apparently someone tipped him off that we were having a ... relationship.'

'What?' Carmen's jaw had dropped. 'That's ridiculous!'

'All right,' Terry said. 'No need to sound so outraged. You could give a bloke a complex.'

'No, I just meant ...'

Terry grinned. 'Yeah, I know what you meant. Anyway, he's quickly put two and two together and decided that I could have had something to do with your old man's death. Like I've suddenly taken up doing hits in my spare time. Lucky I've got an alibi, or I'd be well in the frame.'

'But who'd do something like that? Who'd say we were together?'

'I've got an idea.'

And suddenly Carmen had an idea too. 'Gordie,' she said. 'He was in the café this morning being weird.'

'What sort of weird?'

'Asking what the deal was between you and me. Looking all smug like he knew something I didn't. And he mentioned my dad, so he knows what's happened. But why would he go to the police?'

'To try and stitch me up,' Terry said. 'The bloke's a toerag.'

'What are you going to do?'

'Nothing ... for now.' Terry relaxed and stretched his arm out across the back of the sofa. 'Keep your enemies close, right? He doesn't like me muscling in on Joe's manor. Thinks someone else could do a better job. He's old school, the sort who reckons the place should be run by bleedin' geriatrics. New ideas don't appeal to him.'

Carmen thought about this, decided she had nothing to add on the subject of Joe's succession, and said instead, 'I'm sure someone followed me home from work today. Do you think it was the police?'

'Oh, yeah, I reckon so. They'll be watching all of you, all the family, until they've got a better suspect.'

'But what for?'

'In case you're associating with undesirables like me.'

Carmen frowned. 'So doesn't that make it a bad idea for you to be here?'

'It would,' Terry agreed, 'if they knew about it. But I didn't come through the main gates. I came over the wall.'

Carmen gazed blankly back at him.

'There's a wall,' he explained, 'round the back of Haslow, where the bins are. From there you can use the tunnel to Carlton and get into the foyer without being seen from the street.'

'Unless the police are hanging round the foyer.'

'Nah, the law don't come on to the estate unless they have to. It's not a welcoming place for them. And if they do, everyone knows about it in two minutes flat. We're okay.'

'What did you tell the police about "us"?' Carmen asked.

'The truth, more or less. That I know you from the caff, that I put you in touch with a mate about this flat, that I took you to see Joe, that there's nothing going on between us.'

'And did they believe you?'

'I shouldn't think so.' Terry shrugged, indifferent apparently to what the police believed. 'Not about the last thing anyway. Typical, ain't it? They're accusing me of the one thing I'm *not* guilty of.'

'Good thing we never had that drink.'

'I wouldn't go that far,' Terry said. 'The offer's still open if you ever change your mind. I mean, not right now, obviously, but when this is all over.'

All over. Carmen could barely imagine what that would be like. Everything still felt so fresh and raw and painful. She glanced down at her left hand, oddly bare now she had taken the engagement ring off. That image of her father, dead on the floor, jumped into her head again. She flinched and smiled vaguely but didn't reply.

'They asked me about Michael Quinn,' Terry said, moving swiftly on. 'If I'd heard anything, if anyone had seen him recently. I told them that all I knew was what I'd heard on the grapevine about Joe blaming your old man for his disappearance.'

'Is Michael a suspect then?'

'He's not being ruled out by the sound of it, but I don't reckon Hennessy's got much to go on. He wouldn't be sniffing round me if he did. Do you have a brief?'

Carmen shook her head. 'Do I need one, do you think?'

'Best to be prepared.' Terry reached into the inside pocket of his jacket, took out his wallet and removed a business card. 'Here,' he said, placing the card on the coffee table. 'This bloke knows his stuff. He won't let the law walk all over you.'

'Is he expensive?'

'What price freedom?' Terry said.

Carmen gave a sigh. 'I can't afford expensive lawyers.'

'He won't need the money up front. He'll know you're good for it.'

'How am I good for it? I'm a waitress, for heaven's sake.'

'You're also Rex Darby's daughter.'

Carmen gave a mirthless laugh. 'That's not going to help much. He wrote me out of his will, so I won't be rolling in it any time soon.'

'Christ, did he really?' A thin whistle escaped from Terry's lips. 'I guess that puts a different slant on things.'

'The sort of slant that doesn't allow for pricey solicitors.'

'No, I meant that could be good for you when it comes to the law. Kind of takes away your motive, don't it? Unless you didn't know. Did you know?'

'Yes, my sister told me that's what he was going to do.'

'Good,' Terry said. 'That should give Hennessy something to think about it. And don't worry about the brief. If you need him, I can cover it.'

'I couldn't let you do that.'

'Why not? We're mates ain't we? Least I like to think so. And don't stress, there's no strings attached if that's what you're wondering. I ain't that sort of bloke. I'd do the same for Deana or anyone else I like.'

'Thank you, but—'

'The number's there if you need it,' Terry insisted, nodding towards the card. 'Don't make any decisions now. And if it makes you feel better, you can pay me back. An interest-free loan. How about that? You can just pay whatever you can afford, weekly or monthly. I'll leave it up to you.'

Carmen was grateful for the offer, although she didn't intend to take him up on it. She knew where his money came from – drugs and brothels and people like Joan – and didn't want to be a part of any of that. But she didn't want to come across as churlish or ungracious either. 'Thanks. I'll think about it.' Then she quickly changed the subject. 'Terry, could I ask you something? Are there any rumours out there on that grapevine of yours? About my dad's murder, I mean. Have you heard anything?'

'You don't want to go listening to gossip. People talk but it doesn't mean it's anything worth listening to.'

'So people *are* talking?'

Terry briefly looked away before meeting her eyes again. 'I just meant . . . people always think the worst. It's human nature ain't it?'

'They think it was one of the family.'

'Some of them, maybe. Like I said, I wouldn't take any notice of it.'

'But you'll tell me, won't you? If you hear anything that you think *is* worth listening to.'

'Sure,' he said. 'I promise.'

74

It was Thursday before Jonny was informed that the house in Upper Belgrave Street had been cleared as a crime scene and they were free to return. When he broke the good news to Hazel, she widened her eyes and stared at him.

'I'm never stepping foot in that place again. Not *ever*. I'm staying right here until we find somewhere else to live.'

It was getting on Jonny's nerves, the whole shocked, grief-stricken daughter thing. As if she hadn't played any part in the murder. The truth was that she was just as guilty as the rest of them. She had wanted Rex Darby dead and now he was dead, so what the hell was she whining about? 'Suit yourself, but I'm not living in one room for months when there's a whole house going begging. I'll call Mrs Cooper and get her to go over and clean up. I dare say plod have left a bleedin' mess behind.'

'I don't know how you can even think about going back there. Not after what happened.'

But Jonny didn't share Hazel's scruples. And he was sure that she would change her mind once she realised that he wasn't going to change his. Anyway, he had come on his own to Belgravia and now he was roaming from room to room, aware of the dusting powder on every surface and of drawers and cupboards that had been ransacked. The lazy buggers, as expected, hadn't even tidied up after themselves. Although it hadn't been empty for long, the house had a weird abandoned smell, and a peculiar silence as if it was still absorbing the events of last Friday.

He was relieved to see that there was no blood on the carpet in the drawing room. Even Mrs Cooper would have baulked at that. She'd already insisted on double time, claiming it was the least she deserved, that there were plenty who wouldn't go near a place where someone had been murdered. He'd been tempted to tell her to do one – she wasn't the only cleaner in London – but then decided that it wasn't worth the hassle. He had better things to do than trawl through the Yellow Pages for a replacement.

Jonny went to the cabinet, opened it, and removed the ten-pound note he'd found during his earlier explorations. With a grin of satisfaction, he slipped it into his new wallet, surprised that the law hadn't snaffled it. There wouldn't be a shortage once the estate was sorted out, but until then he'd have to make do with whatever he could scavenge. There were plenty of valuable items in the house – Rex had liked expensive things – but he had to be careful what he took. Anything obvious and he'd have Marian on his back.

Unfortunately, the law had opened the safe, emptied out its contents and removed them. The combination must have been provided by Rex's solicitor. He had no idea exactly what had been inside but could hazard a guess at ready cash and jewellery. It irked him that he couldn't get his hands on it, that he'd have to wait until the property was returned.

Jonny fancied himself as master of the house. No one could look down on him if he owned a place like this. Could he persuade Hazel to buy Marian out? He had a sudden image of Lucan sitting in one of the pale-yellow chairs, sipping a whisky, while they talked man to man. Having an associate like Lord Lucan would open doors for him, move him into the kind of society he craved. And they were virtually neighbours. There was no reason why they shouldn't become friends. Unless something went wrong, unless Hennessy dug out the truth, unless it all came tumbling down.

He walked upstairs, frowning. His main anxiety, other than Milo caving under pressure, was what Pat Foster would tell the law. If he started prattling on about how Rex was beginning to have second thoughts about the inheritance, it could look bad for them. But would he? Pat was no friend of the Old Bill and maybe he wouldn't want to cause additional stress for the family. Elizabeth, however, was a different matter. No doubt she'd be happy to spread a little poison wherever she could.

In Rex's bedroom, Jonny rifled through the drawers in the dressing table. He found a selection of watches and tried to remember if he had ever seen Rex wearing them. There were a couple of Rolexes, an Omega and a Patek Philippe. He checked the latter for an engraving on its back, found none, and put it in his pocket. One wouldn't be missed, he decided. And even if it was, there would be no way of knowing whether Rex had sold it on or traded it in for something he preferred.

Jonny moved on to a selection of cufflinks, quickly opening and closing the boxes, searching for the ones that were made of the heaviest gold. He chose two pairs and placed these in his pocket too. Best not to sell them in London, he thought, already savouring a drive out of the city to Kent or Surrey. Not today, though. He didn't want to leave Hazel on her own for too long in case the law turned up. In her current state, she couldn't be trusted to keep her mouth shut.

Milo had turned up at the office on Monday morning and every morning since. On Monday the phones had been ringing off the hook, with half the company's managers and employees calling to find out what the situation was, if they still had a job, and if they were going to be paid. Elizabeth had been saying 'Business as usual' in a small tight voice, informing them that Mr Foster would be running things for the time being. There was a box of tissues on her desk, and her eyes were damp.

Milo was doing what any lowly member of staff would do in the circumstances – acting shocked, keeping his head down and getting on with things. It would be a few months before the estate was sorted and he got his flat and his money. Until then he had no choice but to carry on as usual, collecting the rents, dealing with tardy tenants and running any errands that Pat deemed essential. His father looked old and weary, almost haggard, and the two of them had barely exchanged more than half a dozen words since the beginning of the week.

When Jonny strolled into the office, Milo was pleased. He'd been desperate to talk but hadn't dared communicate by phone. Now was his chance to make sure that the arrangement was fully understood, and that Jonny knew exactly who he was dealing with. If he had killed one man, he could kill two. He deserved respect and wanted to see it.

'How are you, Elizabeth?' Jonny asked, all solicitous, after barely nodding at Milo. 'Hazel asked me to thank you for working through this dreadful time.'

Elizabeth sniffed and reached for the tissues again. 'It's what Mr Darby would have wanted.'

'I'm sure he would. But we all appreciate what you're doing. We're extremely grateful.'

Before Jonny could lay on any more smarmy charm, the internal phone rang. Elizabeth snatched it up, exchanged a few words with Pat, and put the receiver down. She picked up her notebook and a pen, got to her feet and said, 'If one of you could just keep an eye on reception, I'll be back in five minutes.'

'Of course,' Jonny said.

Elizabeth nodded. 'Did you want to see Pat?'

'Whenever he has time. I know he must be busy.'

'I'll tell him you're here.'

As soon as Elizabeth had gone through to Pat's office, Jonny turned on Milo and hissed, 'What the fuck do you think you were playing at? After dark, we agreed. After ten. You could have blown everything.'

Milo glared back at him. 'What's your problem?'

'My fuckin' problem is that we had a plan and you decided to ignore it. What if the neighbours had seen you? What if Carmen had? I mean, Jesus, she was upstairs when you did it. What if you'd screwed up our alibis by going in early?'

'And did any of those things happen? No. All I did was grab an opportunity that came my way. You got what you wanted and everyone's happy.'

'You took a bloody stupid risk.'

'I took a calculated risk, and it paid off.'

Jonny glanced towards the interior door, checking that Elizabeth wasn't on her way back. 'And what about the gun? How did you get hold of it? We agreed you were going to use a knife. Why—'

'What you don't know, you don't need to know.' Milo took a step forward and thrust his face close to Jonny's. 'Just drop it, yeah? Concentrate on your own story, not mine. I can deal with the law. They can't prove nothin'.'

'You'd better hope one of those neighbours doesn't suddenly remember something. Or Carmen, come to that. Broad bloody daylight. What the hell were you thinking?'

Milo didn't appreciate the attitude. 'If you were so fuckin' fussy, you should have done it yourself. What's the matter, Jonny? What's with all the grief? You losing your nerve? You'd better not be. I'm not going down because you're falling apart.'

'No one's falling apart.'

'Good, because I'm the one who's in the firing line here. And I'm going to need some readies to get by on until things are sorted.'

'You've already had money. You've had two hundred quid.'

'I've had peanuts. It's not enough. Get Pat to release some cash from the business. Or Hazel can flog some of that fancy jewellery of hers. Sort it out, Jonny. It's the bloody least I deserve.'

'Or what? You going to tell the law what you did?' Jonny barked out a laugh. 'Don't start calling the shots with me. We can't give you what we haven't got. You'll just have to be patient like the rest of us.'

Milo didn't like that smug look on Jonny's face and had a sudden urge to deck him. His hands curled into two tight fists. But this wasn't the time or the place. Instead, he grinned and said softly, 'No, not the law, mate, but I could tell Hazel about that little tart Mimi you've been seeing. Be a shame if the missus kicked you out just when you're so close to getting what you want.'

Jonny's face was a picture. First it went white, then red, like he'd been hit by a blast of heat. 'You say a word to Hazel and I'll—'

But Jonny's threat, whatever it was going to be, remained

unuttered. The door to Pat's office opened and closed and seconds later Elizabeth came back into reception. The two men stepped apart, but the antagonism remained, a brute force hanging in the air. Had Elizabeth been less preoccupied she might have noticed the hostility. Instead, she made her way to her desk, sat down, glanced up at Jonny and said, 'He'll see you now.'

As Jonny headed for the door, Milo couldn't resist a parting shot. 'Give Hazel my best when you see her.'

75

It was Friday evening, a full week since the murder, and Carmen was on the top deck of a bus, on her way to Scandal with Deana. Hopefully the club would distract her from the mess in her head and stop her thinking about the things she didn't want to think about, and she could make some much-needed money at the same time. Beth had stared disapprovingly at them both as they left the flat but hadn't said anything. The expression on her face, however, had said it all: she'd rather starve to death than pander to the egos of rich entitled men who thought of women as nothing more than playthings. And maybe she had a point. But then Deana's point of view was valid too, that it was all just a bit of fun and that if anyone had the upper hand it was the women.

Carmen was balancing these two opposing opinions as the bus swept along the darkening streets. She had spent the whole day, and the preceding ones, in a state of nervous tension, waiting for the police to turn up, and for the endless questions to start again. Terry, with his talk of solicitors, had rattled her already unsteady nerves, and she feared that Hennessy might decide that she was the guilty party and come to arrest her. Would Terry visit her in prison? It was a random thought, and she had no idea why it had entered her head.

Deana was talking about some girl who had once worked at Scandal, who'd met a rich man there and married him. 'He was an earl,' she said. 'Imagine that! And Janey was just an out-of-work actress. Now she lives in the country in this *huge* mansion and spends all her summers in Monaco.'

'Is she happy?' Carmen asked, just to show she was listening, although she hadn't been for most of it.

Deana laughed. 'Of course she's happy. Why wouldn't she be? As much money as she can spend, new clothes every season and a diamond engagement ring the size of a house. Honestly, you should have seen it. It must have cost a fortune.'

Carmen pressed the side of her face against the coolness of the window and sighed. Her feet had been aching after the shift at the café, and now, after forcing them into a pair of high heels, they were hurting even more. She'd have blisters by the end of the night, she was sure of it.

Deana, perhaps mistaking her sigh for regret over her broken engagement, touched her arm and said, 'Oh, sorry. You don't want to hear about Janey.'

'No, I was just—'

Deana took a silver-coloured flask out of her bag, unscrewed the lid, took a swig, wiped the top and passed it to her.

'What is it?'

'Vodka, babe. Have some. You look like you need it.'

Carmen took a gulp, wincing as the neat spirit hit the back of her throat. But almost instantly, probably because she hadn't eaten much that day, she could feel its effect, a warmth that spread through her, a softening around the edges of her sharp painful thoughts. They passed the flask back and forth a few times before Deana said, 'You hang on to it. Don't let the boss catch you drinking, though. He'll fire you on the spot.'

By nine o'clock Scandal was filling up, and by ten it was crowded with customers letting off steam after a hard week's work. There were City boys flashing the cash, a few MPs, some aristocrats, actors and musicians, and probably a smattering of villains too. The champagne flowed and the music played, and the dance floor was always busy. Carmen soon discovered how much easier it was to flirt with men when she wasn't completely sober. She drank her fruit cocktails, smiled, laughed, danced and occasionally visited the ladies where she topped up her alcohol level with a few furtive swigs of vodka.

There was not enough in the flask to render her visibly drunk, but it kept sobriety at bay. She was able to blend into the fashionable excitable crowd as if she belonged to it, as if having fun was her very reason for living. The horror of her father's death, of Clive's abandonment, retreated into the shadows until all that was left was a girl called Carly Baxter who had no dreadful secrets and was open as a book.

It was after eleven when Richard Torn turned up – tall and elegant and determined to monopolise her. He chased away the younger men like an alpha lion staking a claim to his prey, chose a table and ordered drinks.

'Where were you last week?' he said, mock accusingly. 'I came specially to see you but there was no Carly.'

'Oh, just family stuff,' she said, carefully watching his face in case he betrayed any sign of knowing who she really was. He didn't. She relaxed.

'You condemned me to an evening of unutterable boredom.'

'I'm sure you found a way to keep yourself entertained.'

Carmen glanced around, her gaze alighting on a couple of shapely hostesses sitting a couple of tables away. 'There are lots of lovely girls here.'

'Lovely girls are two a penny. I can find them anywhere. They're not special like you.' His eyes grazed over her, narrowing slightly. 'Once I set my heart on something, nothing else will do.'

Richard was a blatant flatterer, but Carmen didn't mind. In fact, it was just what she needed. Being the chosen one, the object of his doubtless temporary affections, made her feel significant for once. She could bask in his attention and become, for a while, the girl she wanted to be, the one who was light and unburdened and not forever waiting for the knock on the door.

He wanted to dance, and so they did, moving slowly around the floor while he held her close and whispered into her ear: compliments and snippets of gossip and clever asides that made her laugh. The rhythm of the music flowed through her. She had not been in such intimate proximity to a man since Clive, and it felt odd – although not unpleasant – to have a different pair of arms around her.

Later, back at the table, Richard continued to charm, regaling her with funny stories and showing an interest in what she liked, what she did and who she was. He listened attentively to everything she told him, even though what she told him was only from her imagination. Here, tonight, she could be anyone she wanted and what she wanted most was to not be Carmen Darby.

The hours passed quickly, and at quarter to one, fifteen minutes before Scandal closed, Richard leaned across the table and said, 'Come for a drink with me. A proper drink. There's a nice little bar I know down the road. We can have a cocktail together and then I'll put you in a cab. What do you say? Say yes. It's too early to end the evening.'

A sensible, sober Carmen would have refused the offer, not just because it was against the rules, but because she sensed Richard wasn't entirely trustworthy. But the vodka had dissolved her better judgement. Her earlier tiredness had disappeared and been replaced by a restive feeling. She felt an impulse to do something out of character, and what harm was there in one last drink away from the prying eyes of the management?

'I'm not supposed to,' Carmen said. Although she'd already made up her mind, she was unwilling to appear too keen. 'I could get fired for it.'

Richard smiled at her across the table, a wolfish sort of smile. 'Not supposed to isn't the same as won't.'

76

Carmen picked up her pay for the evening, boosted by the commission on the multiple bottles of champagne Richard had bought. He had not drunk that much himself, but like the last time, had shared the bottles with endless visitors to the table. Deana was going on to a house party with some of the other girls, but Carmen excused herself, saying she was tired and would get a cab home.

Once she was outside, Carmen turned left as she'd been instructed, walking towards the corner where Richard had arranged to meet her. As she made her way along the busy Soho street, still bustling at this early hour of the morning, she felt if not exactly happy, then certainly less *un*happy than she'd been for the past week. Even her feet had stopped complaining. She sashayed slightly as she walked, her confidence boosted by Richard's attentions.

Richard was waiting for her, a broad smile in place. He took her arm and linked it through his. 'Just along here,' he said, and led her to a lounge bar that was all welcoming squishy sofas, with soft jazz playing in the background. The lighting was dim, the walls covered in modern paintings, and there were enough potted palms to start a small jungle. The atmosphere was relaxed, laid back: a completely different vibe from Scandal.

They found an empty sofa near the rear of the bar and settled into it. 'Now, what would you like to drink?' Richard asked. 'A cocktail of course.'

'What do they have here?'

'How about a Martini? You look like a Martini sort of girl.'

'And what does a Martini sort of girl look like?'

'Classy,' Richard said smoothly. He caught the eye of a passing waitress, put in the order and immediately returned his attention to Carmen. 'Have I told you that you're looking radiant tonight?'

'Once or twice, but it's not anything you get tired of hearing.'

Their drinks arrived and they talked, and talked, although later she would not remember exactly what they had talked about, or what had made her laugh so much, or why she had flirted so outrageously. They were sitting side by side and occasionally she would feel the soft pressure of his thigh against hers. She could have moved her leg, but she didn't. The rhythm of the jazz swirled over and around her.

By the time she had finished her second Martini, Carmen was starting to feel light-headed. The cocktails had been strong, and she had drunk them on top of the vodka she'd been swigging all night. Now, suddenly, she felt her focus going, a kind of slipping away. Declining a third drink, she decided to do the smart thing and go home.

'We'll find you a cab,' Richard said as they rose to their feet, and he helped her into her coat.

The night air had a cold sting to it. The street was quieter now and their footsteps made an echoey sound. Orange light from the streetlamps cast an eerie glow. Carmen stumbled in her high heels and would have fallen over if Richard hadn't grabbed her elbow.

'What you need is a coffee,' he said.

'No, really, I'm . . .'

'Coffee,' he repeated firmly. 'I could do with one too. You'll feel much better after.'

Carmen didn't have the energy to argue. Her earlier spark had fizzled out and left only a weariness in its wake. She had to concentrate on walking in case she turned over in her heels again. 'Is there a late-night café round here?'

Perhaps Richard hadn't heard, her voice whispery, maybe drowned out by a car going by, because he didn't reply. A few yards further along he stopped by a door with blue flaky paint and took a key out of his pocket.

'Where are we?' she asked. 'What is this place?'

'Just a little flat I use when I'm in town.'

'Oh, I'm not sure if . . .'

But Richard already had the key in the lock and was stepping inside, switching on a light. She hesitated for a moment on the doorstep, looking up a narrow flight of stairs.

'Come on,' he said. 'Don't let the cold in.'

Carmen knew that she wasn't thinking straight, that the booze had impaired her judgement, but she didn't seem able to find the words to refuse. It would look like she didn't trust him, and then he would probably take offence. And it was only a cup of coffee. She could be in and out in ten minutes. As soon as she'd drunk it, she would go.

She closed the door behind her and followed him up. The flat was on the first floor, a poky apartment with a worn brown carpet and a dubious smell. She looked around at the place. It was barely furnished and what was there – a beige sofa, a coffee

386

table, a couple of lamps – was purely utilitarian. There was nothing personal about the place, nothing cosy or welcoming. There were no pictures on the walls, no photographs on display. A tiny kitchenette was in the corner, and off to the right, its door open, was a bedroom.

Richard turned on the gas fire and bluey-gold flames leapt into life. 'There, that's better.'

Carmen smiled weakly.

'Here, let me take your coat,' he said.

As he slid it from her shoulders his fingertips brushed along her bare arms. Accidentally or on purpose? The room wasn't cold, but she felt a shiver run through her. Instinctively she moved away from him. The air felt charged, and her earlier confidence had started to ebb.

Richard laid the coat over the back of the sofa.

Carmen said, 'Shall I put the kettle on?'

But Richard had something else on his mind. As she went to walk towards the kitchenette, he grabbed her forcefully by the arms and pulled her towards him. Almost immediately his lips were pressing against hers, his hands roaming over her body. She twisted her head, freeing herself from his hungry mouth. 'What are you doing?'

Richard's face grew hard, his voice sarcastic. 'Don't be a tease, Carly. We both know you didn't come up here for coffee.'

Carmen tried to push him off, but this only seemed to increase his ardour. As if this was a game where she protested and he ignored it, where she tried to fight and he overcame her. He held her tighter. She could feel his breath on her neck, fast and excited. This was a different Richard from the one in Scandal, from the one in the cocktail bar, a man possessed, a man who wasn't going to take no for an answer. And then she was being hauled towards the bedroom, and he was too strong, too determined, for her to resist. Words came out of her mouth, but he wasn't listening. He didn't want to hear what she had to say, didn't care.

Richard threw her down on the bed and climbed on top of her. He wound his fingers through her hair and held it so tight that she could barely move her head. His mouth closed over hers again and she could taste the Martini on him, taste the cigar he had smoked an hour ago. His fingers clawed between her legs, groping, ripping at the lacy edges of her pants. She heard the thin metallic sound of his zip being released. It was all happening so quickly, almost as if it was happening to someone else, as if a part of her had removed itself and was watching like a frightened child from the dark corner of the room.

Carmen's struggles had ceased. There was nothing she could do. She could try to fight, but that would only make it worse. Fear and shock and a dreadful resignation had paralysed her. One way or another, Richard was going to take what he wanted. Tears slid from the corners of her eyes, but he was oblivious. He had her firmly pinned down and was on the verge of victory. She was limp and unresponsive, no more than an empty receptacle for his pleasure.

Then, as his legs roughly forced hers apart, something in her snapped. She wasn't going to be the victim here. She'd had a lifetime of being bullied, of being controlled, of being manipulated by men who thought it was their right to oppress and dominate. Instinctively, her right arm flailed wildly out to her side and her hand grasped for something, anything, to make it all stop. She felt the edge of the bedside table and then the cool metal of a lamp. Her fingers curled around the slender stem and with one fast movement she sent it crashing into the side of Richard's head.

A gasp escaped from his mouth, a half cry. Then he suddenly

collapsed, the full weight of his body on her for a few seconds – so heavy she couldn't breathe, a dead weight on her chest – before eventually rolling off. His hands clutched at his head, a low moaning filling the room. Was there blood? She thought there was, a darkening in his grey hair.

Carmen didn't hang about. The moment she was free she flung the lamp on the floor and leapt off the bed. Without a backward glance, she ran into the living room, grabbed her coat and bag, and fled.

77

Even when she was back on the street, Carmen didn't slow down. She ran and stumbled, ran again, continuously looking over her shoulder in case he suddenly appeared behind her. She could hear her breath coming in short, fast bursts and felt the frantic beating of her heart. Sobs caught in her throat, but she swallowed them down. Until she was somewhere safe, she couldn't afford to fall apart.

Carmen was moving forward only by instinct, one foot in front of the other, hardly aware of where she was. But a voice in the back of her mind was telling her to find a main road, to get away from Soho's maze of winding streets and alleyways. Somehow, eventually, she found herself on Charing Cross Road, saw a black cab approaching with its light on, staggered into the road and flung out her arm. The cabbie slowed, gave her a brief assessing glance, and drove straight past.

She came to a halt, staring after the disappearing cab, distraught that he hadn't stopped. How could he leave her standing there? It was like the final straw in a night of horrors. Perhaps he had thought she was drunk and would throw up in the back of his taxi. Perhaps both of those things were true. Except she didn't feel drunk any more, only hollow and abused and incredibly stupid.

It had started to rain, a thin slanting drizzle that gathered at the nape of her neck. How was she going to get home? There were buses to Kellston from Tottenham Court Road, but she had no idea if they ran at night. And now was the very middle of the night. They say that London never sleeps, but it was certainly dozing at this hour – her watch told her it was half past three – and the street was only thinly populated.

Suddenly the few people who were still around, all of them men, felt more like a threat than a reassuring presence. She searched for another cab but there wasn't one in sight. She would just have to keep on walking. With her shoulders hunched against the rain, she set off again, trying to maintain a brisk pace even though her shoes were killing her. And not just the shoes. Her mind kept flashing back to the dingy apartment, to Richard, to the pain and humiliation he'd inflicted on her.

As she went past a bookshop – the road was full of them – she was reminded that Eddie lived round here somewhere. What was the shop called? As she walked her gaze skimmed over the many shopfronts, hoping one of the signs would jog her memory. It was another couple of minutes before she saw it. *Egan's*. Yes, that was it. She stopped again and gazed across the road.

There were no lights, unsurprisingly, in the flat above the shop. Carmen felt guilty at the thought of waking him up, but the guilt was outweighed by her desire to get off the street and to be in a safe place. She waited for a car to pass and then dashed across the road. She pressed the bell to the flat. For a while, nothing happened, and she was just at the point of ringing again when she heard the sound of a window scraping open.

391

'Hello?' Eddie called out from the first floor.

Carmen took a step back and looked up. 'It's me,' she said. 'Sorry it's so late. Can I come in?'

Eddie peered down into the semi-darkness, sleepily trying to put a face to the voice. 'Oh, hey, yeah. Hang on.'

The window shut again, and shortly after she heard the clatter of Eddie's footsteps on the stairs. He opened the door and stood back to let her in. His eyes were half closed, his hair mussed, and he had slung on a dressing gown over a pair of striped pyjamas. 'You okay?'

'Sorry,' Carmen said again. 'I'm really sorry. I've got a bit stranded. I won't stay long. If I could just call a cab. Do you have a phone?' She was saying all this to him as she walked up the stairs, the words tumbling out of her mouth, utterly relieved to be inside but trying to hide it, trying to act as if nothing terrible had happened to her tonight, as if she was just a girl who had landed herself in an awkward situation and needed some practical assistance.

Eddie's flat was very different from the one she had just been in: cosy and cluttered and littered with books. It was clean but untidy, the walls a soft shade of green, some of the furniture familiar. There was an old corduroy sofa that had once graced his mother's living room, and a table that she remembered being in Annie's kitchen many years ago. Like relics from the past, there was something comforting about them.

'Do you have the number for a cab company?' she asked. 'Then I can leave you in peace. I feel awful just turning up like this in the middle of the night.'

Eddie looked at her properly for the first time, examining her face in the light. Whatever he saw must have alarmed him. His brow furrowed, and two deep lines appeared between his eyes. 'Are you all right, Carmen?'

She nodded, feeling suddenly overcome, and not trusting herself to speak. It was as if everything was catching up with her, as if she'd been holding her breath and was gradually releasing it.

'Would you like a coffee?'

It was that question, those five simple words, that finally broke her. And before she knew it, she had slumped down on the sofa and started to cry. Then she was telling him everything, the whole wretched story from start to finish. He sat and listened without interrupting, his face full of concern, his hands planted on his thighs. She only glanced at him once and didn't look again. Instead, she stared hard at the carpet, focusing on the flecks of colour, the green and the grey, while the horrors spilled from her lips in a fast tremulous monologue.

After she was done, Eddie leapt to his feet. 'Christ, what a bastard! You have to report him to the police. Would you like me to call them?'

'No,' she said, vehemently shaking her head. 'No police. I don't want them involved.'

'But ...'

'No, I can't talk to them. I mean, what's the point? I can't *prove* anything. It'll be my word against his. He'll say I consented, I'll say I didn't, and who are they going to believe? I went to that flat, Eddie. Nobody made me. I'd had too much to drink and I did something stupid.'

'Don't start blaming yourself. Don't ever go down that road. It wasn't your fault. *He* did this to you.'

'I know, but it's a battle that I'm never going to win.' Carmen had heard too many stories from Beth – stories from the refuge, of what women endured when they reported an assault, especially one like this where the lines could easily be blurred – to want to go through the same experience. 'It'll just make everything worse, having to go over it again and again.

393

The minute they hear I work at Scandal, they'll put a label on me. I'll be the girl who chats up men for money. I'll be the girl who went back to his flat. I'll be the girl who was asking for it.'

'He shouldn't be allowed to get away with it.'

'No, but he will. His type always do. And anyway, I've had enough of the police to last me a lifetime.'

Eddie paced over to the window, looked out briefly, and came to sit down again. 'God, yes, I haven't seen you since . . . Your dad, Jesus, that was a shock. Mum told me you were there when it happened. That must have been dreadful.'

Carmen stiffened at the mention of her father. She had started this evening trying to escape the horror of his death and had instead found herself in a different kind of nightmare. 'You won't tell anyone, will you, Eddie? About tonight? Not even your mum. I don't want anyone to know.'

'Of course not. If that's what you want.'

'It is. Thank you. Look, I should be getting home. Do you have the number of a cab firm?'

'I can't just put you in a cab. I've got the car parked round the corner. I'll drive you there. Is anyone at the flat? I don't think you should be on your own.'

'Yes, Beth's there, and Deana probably. My flatmates. But you don't have to do that. I'll be all right.'

'Humour me,' he said. 'Give me two minutes to get dressed and I'll be with you.'

While he was gone, Carmen went back to studying the carpet. She tried to focus her mind on anyone, anything, but Richard Torn. But blanking out what had happened was impossible. She could still smell him, taste him, could still feel his vile determined arms holding her down.

78

True to his word, Eddie was back in two minutes, dressed now in jeans and trainers and a navy-blue sweater. They left the flat and walked together to a side road where his car was parked. The sky was gunmetal grey and starless with no sign yet of dawn. It was still raining, heavier than it had been, and the London air smelled of damp and diesel.

'I'll put the heating on. It'll soon warm up,' Eddie said as they got into the Datsun. 'Kellston, isn't it? It shouldn't take long to get there, not at this time of the morning.'

'The Mansfield. Do you know where it is?'

'I've got an idea.'

Eddie switched on the engine, indicated to pull out and then paused. 'You can still change your mind about the police,' he said. 'I'm not saying that you should – it's your decision – only that you can.'

'I'm not going to change my mind.'

'Okay.'

As they set off, Carmen was aware of how tense Eddie was,

his hands gripping the steering wheel, his frustration almost palpable. He wanted to help her but didn't know how. In truth, there was nothing he could do, other than what he was already doing, to make things easier for her. She didn't want to talk any more about what had happened, but she feared silence too, as if it was a black hole she might fall into and never clamber out.

'Did the police speak to you about Dad?' she asked, just for something to say.

Eddie nodded. 'They wanted to know about the birthday dinner. And Michael Quinn. Not that I could tell them much. I can't even remember what he looked like.'

'Do you think they're serious about that? About him being involved?'

'Hard to tell. Covering all the bases, I suppose, just in case. Dad doesn't give it any credence. He thinks they're wasting their time.'

'What else did they ask?'

'Just what your father was like, if he had any enemies that I knew of, the usual stuff. Oh, yeah, and they asked about Milo. They seemed pretty interested in *him*.' Eddie, as if determined to be fair even if it went against his better judgement, quickly added, 'Although I can't see why he'd do something like that.'

'No,' Carmen said, although it had crossed her mind that Milo was more than capable. 'I reckon Hennessy still thinks it was one of us. One of the family, I mean.'

'Don't take it personally. It's always the first place they look. Have you heard from Marian or Hazel?'

Carmen gazed out through the windscreen, looking at the street, the shops, the houses, but not really seeing any of it. 'Marian called me. She's gone back to Suffolk, I think.'

'She should have stood up for you at the dinner. Both of them should.'

'It wasn't their argument.'

'Marian can be a selfish cow.'

Carmen glanced at him, surprised by the vehemence in his voice. She thought she saw a flash of anger cross his face. 'I thought you two were close.'

'Whatever gave you that idea?'

'Well, not so much now, but when you were younger. The two of you seemed to be inseparable.'

'I don't know about that. She used to make my life a misery. One day she was my best friend, the next she'd ignore me. It was like a weird game she used to play. How far she could push me before I finally snapped. But I always went back for more, so I guess I'm partly to blame. I had a massive crush on her, and the older we got the worse it became.' Eddie gave a long sigh. 'God, I don't know why I'm telling you all this. The confessions of a bookshop worker.'

Carmen guessed that he was trying to distract her, to give her something else to think about, and was grateful for the attempt. It was odd how she had known him all her life, and yet she didn't really know him at all. He was from her sisters' generation, already a grown-up before she was even a teenager. 'Marian can be difficult.'

'That's one way of putting it. She always knows exactly where to plunge the knife.'

'That's true. She told me that Mum ... no, it doesn't matter.'

'Told you what?'

Carmen shook her head. 'Another time. You've had enough of my angst for one evening.'

'I liked your mother. She was always kind to me.'

There was an edge to the way he said it that made Carmen give him another quick sideways glance. His face was sad,

397

regretful, but she sensed something more, some deeper under-lying meaning to the comment. 'Was she? I never knew her.'

'Yes, that was a shame. She was a lovely woman. She had her problems, but she had a good heart. And your father didn't treat her well. He pushed and pushed until she ...' Almost imme-diately Eddie shut his mouth, pressing his lips together as if to prevent himself from saying things that he shouldn't.

'Don't stop on my account. He didn't treat anyone well.'

Eddie was quiet for a moment. 'It was terrible what she did, awful for her, awful for all of you. It should never have hap-pened. I can still remember that afternoon. It was one of those days that was so hot, so close, your clothes stuck to your back. Everything was *so* still. I often think if only ...' Abruptly he came to a halt again, as if he couldn't find the right words, as if just talking about her mother brought him pain.

Carmen had never considered before how the suicide had affected him. 'If only?'

Eddie frowned at the road ahead. Like he'd predicted, they were making good progress, the West End already behind them, the East End approaching. With very little traffic they were driving across London in record time. 'All I mean is that if she'd got the help she'd needed, she might still be around today. Rex handed her over to his pet quacks, men who'd dose her up to the eyeballs and leave her like a zombie. Who wants to live like that? She certainly didn't.' He paused, sighed again, and said, 'Sorry, you don't want to hear this.'

'At least you talk about her. No one ever did when I was growing up. If her name was even mentioned, Dad would fly into a rage. It was like he wanted to pretend she'd never existed.'

'He saw it as a slur on his judgement that he'd married some-one who suffered with mental problems. He was ashamed of her. I mean, Jesus, she deserved better, she really did.'

They fell into silence. Carmen tried to concentrate on the road ahead, the way the rain danced in the beams from the streetlights, and the puddles in the gutters. Richard Torn kept nudging at the edges of her thoughts, as if even now, when she was miles from him, he still had the power to crawl under her skin. Fear and loathing gathered inside her. She had only escaped by the skin of her teeth. Another few seconds and ... She briefly squeezed shut her eyes, refusing to be dominated by him again.

It was a relief when she finally saw the three tall towers of the Mansfield looming ahead. 'Straight on,' she said. From a distance she could see that a number of windows were still lit – early risers or insomniacs or people who'd just forgotten to turn the lights off – and she wondered what they were all doing at this time of the morning.

'I've been thinking,' Eddie said as he drove through the gates and, following her instructions, pulled up outside Carlton House. 'I know you don't want to go to the police – I get that – but maybe you should warn the other girls at Scandal. Just in case he tries the same thing again.'

Carmen considered this, pulled a face, but then nodded. Eddie had a point. Much as she wanted to keep quiet about the whole harrowing experience, pretend it had never happened, she wouldn't forgive herself if Richard Torn assaulted someone else. The other girls were probably too smart to fall for his smarmy charm, but it wasn't worth taking the risk. 'Okay,' she said as she got out of the car. 'I'm not going back there but I'll tell Deana.'

Eddie got out too.

'I'll be all right from here,' she said. 'You don't need to come in with me. Thanks for everything.'

'I'll just walk you into the foyer. That way I can be sure you're safely home. What floor are you on?'

'The ninth,' she said. 'I'll take the lift up.'

They walked together across the forecourt. The whole place was deserted, even the dealers having given up and retired to their beds. The estate, usually so busy, had an eerie, abandoned feel. There was only the sound of the rain and their footsteps on the concrete. Eddie didn't comment on the graffiti or the litter or the general air of gloom. The light still flickered in the foyer.

'Well, thanks again,' she said, pressing the button to open the lift doors. 'I don't know what I'd have done without you.'

Eddie shrugged as if it was no big deal having a distraught girl show up on his doorstep in the middle of the night. 'It's not a problem. You should drop by the shop some time. Anytime.' He glanced down at the floor and up at her again. 'Are you sure you'll be all right?'

'I will. Thanks again. Have a safe journey home.'

The doors closed, blocking out Eddie's face. It was only as the lift began to ascend that her teeth started to chatter. Now that she was alone, the fear was coming back. She had a sudden appalling thought: what if Richard Torn had reported *her* to the police? Could he? Would he dare? What if he had gone down West End Central with his bloodied skull and made a statement accusing her of assault? He might say *she* attacked him. It would be his word against hers.

The lift came to a juddering halt and the doors slid open. As Carmen stepped out of the foul-smelling box, she almost expected to see the police waiting outside the flat. But there was no one there. She strode along the corridor, unlocked the door and closed it behind her with a sigh of relief.

Quietly she went to her bedroom, stripped off her clothes – none of which she ever intended to wear again – put on her dressing gown and hurried to the bathroom, hoping the sound of running water wouldn't wake up Deana or Beth. She brushed her teeth vigorously, trying to get the taste of Richard out of her mouth. She stared at her reflection in the mirror. The girl who looked back was pale faced and empty eyed, a girl she barely recognised.

79

DCI Hennessy was a patient man. Even at five o'clock in the morning, as he lay wide awake, there was no panic in his thoughts. Instead, he was methodically going through the evidence, reviewing everything he'd seen and heard. While his wife slept peacefully beside him, oblivious to such horrors as corpses with bullets in their chests, he was carefully sifting through the conversations he'd had in the last seven days.

After the family had been interviewed, along with Darby's closest associates, he had widened the net to include other people of interest. Clive Grainger had been one of these, an interviewee Hennessy hadn't taken to, one who had a patronising charm and clearly saw the police as an inconvenience to his busy schedule. Grainger had glossed over his broken engagement to Carmen, describing it as 'a clash of personalities', and insisted that his relationship with Darby had been 'business-like'. Hennessy had got the impression of ruthless, cold ambition and a total lack of empathy.

He had liked Eddie Foster more but couldn't rule him out

as a possible suspect. Like his mother, he had made no attempt to disguise his dislike of Rex Darby. There was history there, a history of simmering resentment and blatant hostility. His alibi wasn't exactly watertight – he claimed he'd been working in the shop until five but could easily have closed earlier – and Hennessy wasn't about to discount both past and present grudges as possible motives for murder.

'Well, I don't like to speak ill of the dead,' Mrs Cooper had said, before proceeding to do just that. The cleaner had had plenty to say about her late employer and none of it had been good: bad-tempered, inconsiderate, controlling and greedy. 'But then the rich don't get rich by being nice, do they? He was what he was and there's no point in sugar-coating it.' She had worked for Darby for over ten years and borne witness to his many moods and tantrums. 'I don't know how poor Carmen put up with it. Nothing was ever good enough. And her without a mother and all. You'd think he'd show a bit more kindness.'

Hennessy carefully shifted on to his back and placed his hands behind his head. If there was one conclusion that could be drawn from his many interviews, it was that few people had held much affection for the victim. What he sensed was a kind of toxicity, a poison that sat at the very heart of everything. What had occurred to trigger the murder? Something in the past or something more recent? Something to do with Rosa and her suicide? With Michael Quinn? Or was it all tied in with the inheritance?

These questions, and plenty more, rolled through his mind, coming to rest in a tidy pile in a corner of his brain. There was only one thing he knew for sure and that was that sooner or later the killer would make a mistake. In the meantime, he'd continue to put the pressure on, continue digging, stirring

403

things up, pushing, probing, hassling, until the cracks finally started to appear.

Milo had spent his Saturday morning collecting the outstanding rents, before taking the money back to the office, exchanging a few words with his father, signing off for the day, and then setting about the business of losing his tail. He was not surprised that the filth were following him. Hennessy still had him firmly in the frame. A couple of plain-clothes officers had been shadowing his every move, accompanying him as he went from house to house, from flat to flat, as glaringly obvious as two pigs in a bathroom.

Milo, however, knew his way around London, knew all the alleys and the shortcuts and the places his small car could squeeze through and their larger one couldn't. Within fifteen minutes of leaving Belgravia, he'd shaken them off and was on his way to Bethnal Green to see a man about a shooter. It wasn't money that Milo wanted to spend, but he'd seen the expression on Jonny's face and wasn't prepared to remain unprotected.

Alfie Monk was a small skinny bloke with bad skin and eyes that never stopped moving. He slid into Milo's car, bringing with him the smell of dope and cheap aftershave. Even as he was settling into the passenger seat, his gaze was already darting left and right like one of those nervous meercats out in the desert, forever on the lookout for hungry predators.

The gun was a snub-nosed revolver, black with a brown grip, and sized to fit easily into a jacket pocket. It came with five rounds of ammunition. Milo handed over the cash, took the gun, nodded at Alfie and their business was complete. The whole exchange had taken less than a minute.

Milo didn't drive off straight away. He had things to think about. He knew that if the filth caught him with the gun he'd be in big trouble, but if Jonny caught him *without* it, he could be dead. He'd always suspected that once the hit was done, Jonny would try and find a way to get rid of him. The irony, of course, was that ... but he was getting ahead of himself. He needed to go back a week – well, a week and a day – and go over what had happened on that fateful Friday.

It was Rex leaving early that had started it all off: an uncharacteristic change to the usual routine, a red flag. Something smelled bad. Standing outside the office, Milo had said goodbye to his father and Elizabeth and walked to his car, which, although parked just round the corner from Upper Belgrave Street, still had a view of the house. And there he had done exactly what he was doing now: staring through the windscreen while he mulled things over.

It had been while he was trying to decide whether Rex's odd behaviour would or should affect his plans when he had realised, suddenly, that he would not be coming back later, that he was not going to murder Rex Darby, that it was not worth the bloody risk. Jonny couldn't be trusted and nor could Marian. There'd be hell to pay but he didn't care. He wasn't going to spend the next twenty years banged up.

He'd had no reason to feign shock, therefore, when Pat had called him the following morning to break the news that Rex had been shot dead, that he should expect a visit from the law, that they were talking to everyone. What? Shot? When? What time? And when Pat had told him, Milo had known exactly who'd pulled the trigger. From where he'd been sitting in his car the previous evening, he had observed the murderer calling at the house and seen Rex Darby let them in.

But never one to look a gift horse in the mouth, Milo had decided after due consideration that he may as well take advantage of the situation. Counting on the fact that the filth couldn't convict him of something he hadn't done – there wouldn't be a shred of evidence – he saw no good reason to disabuse Jonny and Marian of the notion that he'd gone ahead with the killing himself. The deal was therefore still on. Money was owing, and Milo intended to have it.

80

Terry Street walked into the White Swan in Hackney, ordered a Scotch and drank it at the bar. Casually, he let his gaze roam over the room until it came to rest on the customer he was looking for. Sam Dell, one of his pet squealers, was hunched over what remained of a pint of mild, his eyes apparently fixed on a copy of the *Sun*, his nicotine-stained fingers slowly turning the pages while his ears remained alert to any useful conversations that might be going on around him. Terry waited until he was sure Dell had noted his presence before finishing his drink and leaving the pub.

The car was parked a few streets away. He got in and lit a fag, knowing that the man would be another five or ten minutes, that he wouldn't leave the pub unless he was sure that his departure wouldn't be linked to Terry's. Caution was the number one word in Dell's vocabulary: he couldn't afford to make his connections public.

Terry was on his second cigarette before he saw the shambling figure in his rear-view mirror. It was hard to tell how old Dell was, anything from seventy to ninety, small and hunched with a face etched with wrinkles and most of his teeth missing. He was one of those lowlifes who subsidised his meagre pension from scrounging off others and selling information to the law.

'Afternoon, Mr Street,' Dell said as he clambered into the passenger seat. 'You got somethin' on your mind?'

'Yeah, I want you to have a word with that pal of yours down Cowan Road. If he's interested in a stash of shooters, tell him you heard a whisper, tell him to check out Gordie's place on Beeston Road. Number fourteen.'

Dell nodded. 'Number fourteen. Understood.'

'And tell him to do it fast before they're shifted on again.'

'I'll do it today, Mr Street.'

'Make sure you do.'

Terry peeled off a couple of notes from the wad in his wallet. He'd heard on the grapevine that Gordie was hanging out with some third-rate mob from Whitechapel, a firm who fancied their chances when it came to taking over Joe Quinn's manor. *His* manor now, and he wasn't going to let anyone else muscle in. He'd heard too that this mob had passed some guns over to Gordie and knew that he would have them hidden under the bed or somewhere equally stupid. Gordie, he was sure, had been the one to drop him in it with the law, to tell the lie that he was seeing Carmen Darby. It was time to teach the fucker a lesson: no one messed with Terry Street and got away with it.

'One more thing. You heard any whispers about who did Rex Darby? Any rumours doing the rounds?'

'Nothin' much. Just gossip.'

'What kind of gossip?'

'There's some say Joe Quinn ordered it before he went to meet his maker, others that it's an inside job.'

'The family?'

408

'Yeah. One of them daughters of his – or all of 'em.' Dell scratched at the white bristles on his chin. 'I remember Darby from way back. From the war and after. He were doin' lorries mainly, and petrol coupons, making a pretty penny out of it too. Anythin' you wanted – furs, booze, stockings for the ladies – you name it, Darby could get it for you. Course everything was different in them days. I reckon—'

Before Dell could embark on one of his infamously long trips down memory lane, Terry interrupted him. 'Sorry, mate, but I've got to get off. And don't spend all bleedin' day in the pub. Make sure you pass that message on.'

Ten minutes later, Terry was driving down Kellston high street feeling pleased with himself. Gordie was going to get an unpleasant surprise, and a well-deserved one. You reap what you sow and all that. Hopefully the law would put him away and Terry wouldn't have to see his ugly mug for a while.

He noticed Deana coming out of the Spar with a pint of milk in her hand and, much to the annoyance of the traffic behind him, quickly pulled in to the kerb, stretched across the passenger seat, wound down the window and yelled, 'Hey, Deana!'

She came over to the car and leaned down to talk to him. 'Hi, babe. What are you up to?'

'Hop in and I'll give you a lift home.'

Terry smelled a sweetening of the air – soap or shampoo – as she opened the door and climbed into the passenger seat. 'If it stinks in here, it's not me. I just had some whiffy company a short while ago.'

Deana wrinkled her nose, sniffed and glanced down at the seat as if the whiff might be emanating from something left on it. 'You should choose your company more carefully. Keep the windows open and let some fresh air in.'

Terry grinned and did a U-turn in the road to a loud chorus

of honking horns. As he headed for the Mansfield he asked, 'So how's Carly doing? Did you hear the law gave me a tug? They were trying to put me in the frame for her old man's murder.'

'Yeah, she told me. I'm presuming you put them straight.'

'As straight as you ever can be with those fuckers.'

It only took a minute to reach the estate. Terry stopped the car outside Carlton House and switched off the engine. 'You going to invite me in for a coffee, then?'

'Do you mind if I don't? We're having a bit of a girls' day to be honest, just chilling out. No men allowed. Thanks for the lift, though.'

'Ah, come on. I just want a quick word with Carly. Five minutes. You'll barely notice I'm there.'

But Deana shook her head. 'Honestly, Terry, she's not in a great place right now. Give her some space. Give it a few days, huh? What with her dad and then . . .' Deana half raised her hand to her mouth as if she'd almost said something she shouldn't. 'It's not a good time.'

'What aren't you telling me? Has Carly said something? Has she said she doesn't want to see me?'

'No, of course not. Nothing like that.'

'What then?'

'She's just . . . you know, upset about things. It's nothing to do with you. I'll tell her you were asking after her.'

Terry could tell Deana was being evasive, that there was something she wasn't saying. Her gaze kept sliding away like she didn't want to meet his eyes. 'Is it about the law, about her and me? Only that's all been sorted. She doesn't have to worry about—'

'God, Terry, how many times? It's *nothing* to do with you.'

'So what is it to do with?'

Deana frowned at him. 'Just drop it, yeah?'

410

'Something else has happened, hasn't it? Come on, Deana. If you don't tell me, I'll go up and ask her myself.'

'You can't do that.'

Terry made as if to get out of the car but, as he'd expected, Deana put a hand on his arm to restrain him.

'I can't tell you. She made me promise.'

'Promise not to tell *me*?'

'No, not anyone, apart from ... apart from the people who need to know. It's private. She doesn't want everyone ... she wants to keep it quiet.'

'You can trust me,' Terry said. 'I ain't going to go shooting my mouth off.'

'I know you won't but ...'

'But what?'

Deana shifted in the passenger seat, looked at him and looked away. 'I can't. I said I wouldn't. I would if I could.'

'It'll only be between you and me. I won't tell another soul.'

Deana glanced up at the tower as if they might be being watched. She passed the carton of milk from one hand to the other. 'I don't know. Why does it matter? She'll tell you herself if she wants to.'

Terry could see that her resolve was weakening. 'It'll be easier if you tell me. And if you don't, I'll just keep on asking until you spill. You'll get sick of it before I will.'

Deana pondered on this for a few seconds and then suddenly blurted out, 'God, it was all my fault. I should never have given her that vodka. But she just looked so tense, I thought it might help her to relax. I didn't realise she'd drink it all. I shouldn't have left her to go home on her own. I should have ... Christ, I can't believe that scumbag did that to her.'

'Hey, slow down. How about starting at the beginning?'

It took a while to get the full story, with Deana making him promise every ten seconds not to tell Carly that she'd told him. And by the time she'd reached the end, Terry was just about ready to tear the bloke's head off. 'What's his name, this geezer?'

'No, I know you, Terry. You'll go and do something stupid, and she'll end up in even more trouble with the law.'

'So you think he should just get away with it? He ain't going to stop, Deana. Shitheads like that never do. Not until someone teaches them a lesson. You think it's right what he did?'

'Of course I don't think it's bloody right.' Deana started passing the carton of milk between her hands again, as if she was weighing up the rights and wrongs and trying to decide what to do next.

'So tell me his name and then go up to the flat and forget about it.'

Deana hesitated, but not for long. 'Richard Torn,' she said, and proceeded to give him a brief description. 'He's in Scandal most Fridays. But whatever you do, you've got to make sure it doesn't come back on Carly.'

'It won't.'

Deana got out of the car, leaned down to say goodbye, gave him a long look and then closed the door. Terry watched her walk towards the block, her long fair hair swinging round her shoulders. *Richard Torn*, he repeated to himself. He slapped his palms against the steering wheel, anger surging through him. The number one sin anyone could commit was to hurt the people he cared about. But he'd sort it. Torn would live to regret the day he'd ever tried to take what wasn't his.

81

'You have to stop it,' Beth said firmly, frowning across the kitchen table. The kettle had boiled, but they were still waiting for Deana to get back with the milk. 'It isn't going to help.'

Carmen, lost in thought, looked up at her, startled. 'Stop doing what?'

'Blaming yourself. I know you are.'

'I had too much to drink.'

'So what? Being drunk doesn't give a man the licence to take advantage. He knew you'd had one too many. In fact, he probably made sure of it. There was only one thing on his mind all night.'

Carmen knew that Beth was talking sense, but she still couldn't shake the idea that she'd somehow contributed to her own fate, that if she hadn't gone for that drink, if she hadn't flirted with him, if she hadn't climbed those stairs to that nasty little flat, none of it would ever have happened. 'I wasn't being smart. I knew what he was like. Well, I had a pretty good idea. I messed up, *really* messed up. I could have got a cab and come home but I didn't.'

'Could have, would have – none of it matters. Forget all that. He still didn't have the right to assault you. You didn't consent and he didn't care. He'd have gone ahead if you hadn't clobbered him.'

Carmen drew in a breath. 'And that's another thing. What if I really hurt him? He could be in hospital or . . . or worse. His head was bleeding. What if he never made it out of the flat? He could still be there. What if . . .'

'Stop stressing about *him*, for God's sake. It's you you need to take care of. I'm sure all he's got is a bad headache and that's the least he deserves. Maybe it'll make him think twice about doing the same thing again.'

The exchange was interrupted by the opening and closing of the front door, closely followed by the appearance of Deana holding aloft a carton of milk. 'Sorry I've been so long. I bumped into Terry on the high street.' She looked at Carmen. 'He said to say hi. He wanted to come up, but I told him we were having a girls' day.'

'You didn't . . .?'

'No, of course not. He just wanted to check that you were okay.'

'And what did you tell him?'

'That you were as okay as you could be in the circumstances. You know, with your dad and everything.'

Carmen nodded. 'Thanks.' There were two reasons she didn't want Terry to hear about last night's ordeal. One was that he was the sort of man who probably felt an obligation to defend the honour of his female friends, the other was that she didn't want him to think of her as some sort of victim. But what did it matter what he thought of her? She quickly shrugged this disconcerting question aside. She wasn't interested in Terry Street. That was her story, and she was sticking to it.

82

Although he was usually back by one on a Saturday, it was twenty past two before Pat came home from work. Annie knew he'd been down the pub – she could smell the booze on him – and that the time he'd spent there had made him maudlin. Too many memories of Rex. She took his lunch out of the oven and put it on the table. He went to the fridge, not entirely steady on his feet, and got himself another beer.

'Everything all right?' she asked.

Pat sat down and shrugged. 'We're just keeping things ticking over until the estate's sorted out. People keep ringing up wanting to know what's going to happen now that Rex ... but all I can do is fob them off, say it's business as usual.'

'Well, you can only do what you can do. Have you heard anything more from the police? They must have some idea by now. It's been over a week.'

'No, nothing. If they've got any leads, they're keeping it to themselves. Milo reckons they've been following him.'

'What would they want to do that for?' Annie said, although

she had a pretty good idea. If she was the police, she'd have him in her sights too. From what she had gathered through rumour and gossip, Milo was a thug who enjoyed intimidating people. He'd found the perfect job with Rex: the opportunity to dole out threats and violence to any tenants who were unfortunate enough to be behind with their rent.

'Perhaps it's not just him. Perhaps they're following all of us.'

'They'd have a pretty thin time of it with me,' Annie said. 'Unless they view shopping as suspicious activity.'

Pat pushed the food around his plate, eating occasional mouthfuls in a distracted fashion. There was silence for a while and then, out of the blue, he said, 'You know what Rex told me once? He told me that he'd killed a man.'

Annie almost dropped the tea towel she was holding. She stiffened, staring at him. 'What? Who? God, was it Michael?'

'Of course it wasn't Michael. Why would it be Michael? No, it was some feller during the war. Rex was in a pub and this bloke he didn't know from Adam accused him of chatting up his bird. He probably was – you know what he was like, never could resist a bit of skirt. There were words exchanged, a scuffle, nothing serious, but later, when he left, the bloke was waiting outside for him with a knife.' Pat took a swig of beer. 'It wasn't Rex's fault. He had to defend himself, didn't he?'

'So what happened?'

'Nothing happened. It was the Blitz and bodies were turning up all over the place. By the time they found him, Rex was long gone. He never heard anything about it again. No one came forward to accuse him and he was never interviewed by the law.'

Annie put down the tea towel, frowning. 'Do you think this could be connected to his murder?'

'I can't see it. It was years ago.'

'Some people have long memories. Perhaps you should tell the police.'

Pat shook his head. 'And have the girls know that their dad killed a man? No, it wouldn't feel right. They've got enough to deal with right now.'

Personally, Annie didn't think it would come as any great surprise – the three of them knew what their father had been capable of – but didn't argue the point. All things considered it did seem unlikely that Rex's death was connected to the life he had taken. 'I suppose so.'

Pat shifted his food around some more, decided he'd had enough, and pushed the plate away. 'Sorry, love, I'm not very hungry. I can't stop thinking about it, all of it. Where's the sense? Rex gone. It doesn't seem possible. I can't get my head around it.'

But Annie was of a different opinion. What goes around comes around, she thought as she picked up his plate, scraped the remains of the food into the bin, and dropped it into the sink. Suddenly she had one of those odd déjà vu feelings, as if she'd done all this before. The past tumbled in on her – Rosa's death, Michael's disappearance – and her hands trembled as she turned on the tap and tried to wash the memories away.

83

For the next couple of weeks Carmen was on tenterhooks, constantly expecting the café door to open and for the police to walk in. Deana had warned the other girls at Scandal, but to date Richard Torn hadn't shown his face again. She scoured the newspapers daily, dreading a report on him found murdered in Soho, or a story about his disappearance. If Joan noticed her distracted state, she didn't say anything, probably putting it down to the loss of her father. And that, of course, was preying on her mind too, his death still unsolved and no one arrested.

Carmen felt like she was lurching from day to day, going through the motions, her head frazzled, her body on automatic pilot. She got up, went to work, went home and then did it all again. She was glad of the café though, glad to be occupied and to have something to do, even if she didn't remember much about it by the time she clocked off.

Gordie stopped coming in – there was a rumour he'd been arrested for the possession of firearms – and Carmen couldn't say she was sorry. The bloke had always put her on edge, and she was pleased to see the back of him. It was the big guy Vinnie who showed up to collect the money on a Friday now. Terry came in occasionally, looking at her with those dark eyes of his, asking how she was, less full of banter than usual. 'Anything you need, just let me know,' he'd say. But she didn't know what she needed other than an end to the nightmares that haunted her sleep.

One evening Marian rang to tell her that their father's body had been released by the police and they could now go ahead with the funeral. He had, apparently, left full instructions with his solicitor – the church, the hymns, the prayers, the full order of service. 'We've arranged it for next Thursday,' Marian said. 'November the seventh at three o'clock, and then back to the house for the wake.'

'But it can't be at the house,' Carmen objected. 'How can it? Not after . . . not after what happened there.'

'It's what Dad wanted. We can't go against his wishes.'

'Yes, but that was before—'

'It's all written down in black and white, Carmen. Don't start kicking up a fuss. If that's what he wanted, that's what he's going to have. It's all organised now. And we can close off the drawing room; there's no reason for anyone to go in there.'

Carmen thought it was a macabre decision – she had no desire to ever set foot in that house again – but it was clear she had no choice in the matter. Well, she did have a choice, she could choose not to go, but somehow that felt wrong too.

84

The church was packed, crowded to the extent that some of the late-coming mourners had been unable to get a seat and were gathered in the foyer like disgruntled spectators sidelined from the main event. Carmen suspected that most of them had come more out of curiosity or a desire to curry favour with the family than any tender or sentimental feelings for her late father. But what were *her* feelings? On the whole, she was trying to avoid them, pushing them down like she always did, keeping them out of reach. Her eyes, averted from the mahogany coffin on its plinth, were fixed on the stained-glass window behind the altar.

It had been a relief when Annie had called to ask if she would like to come with the Fosters to the funeral. Now she was positioned in the front right-hand pew, with Annie on one side of her and Eddie on the other. She could have sat with her sisters but she'd not been able to face it. Her place in the family felt ambiguous and, at a time like this, she preferred to be with those who she knew would support her.

Carmen lowered her gaze from the window and looked left

across the aisle to the adjacent pew, where Marian and Hugh were seated alongside Hazel and Jonny. Jonny had a sour expression, and Hazel kept throwing him tight, angry glances. A row. A falling out of some sort. Even on a day like this the two of them were at loggerheads. She wondered what it was about and then realised that she didn't care.

As the service began, Carmen tried to conjure up some happy memories of her father, but all that came to mind was the bad stuff, the tempers, the violence, the rejection of her as his daughter. She took slow, deep breaths. Prayers were said, hymns were sung, and the priest – who had clearly never known Rex Darby – piously extolled his virtues. She thought she heard faint rumblings from among the congregation, but she might just have been imagining it.

Most of her father's employees were present, although Clive, thankfully, hadn't shown up. Elizabeth was seated behind her, Milo half a dozen rows back. It occurred to her, with a shiver, that the murderer could be right here. DCI Hennessy must have had the same idea because he and DS Ward had positioned themselves at the back of the church, their eyes keeping close watch, hoping perhaps for some dramatic sign of remorse from the killer.

Jonny was deliberately avoiding Hazel's gaze. Despite this he could still feel the anger rising off her like steam. If looks could kill, he'd be the one in the coffin rather than Rex. He'd been careless, that was the problem. He'd intended to drive out of town to dispose of the watch and cufflinks, but necessity had overcome caution and, needing some ready cash, he'd flogged the lot to a pawnbroker in Lambeth. Leaving the receipt in his suit pocket – what the hell had she been doing going through his pockets anyway? – had been his downfall.

A blazing row had ensued, the aftermath of which was still burning brightly. He had no right to steal her father's things and sell them behind her back, she'd said. To which he'd responded by claiming that it was hardly stealing, that it all belonged to her anyway now, and what belonged to her belonged to him. Which hadn't gone down well. And then he'd compounded that by adding, 'So it's all right to plot the murder of your father, but beyond the pale when I flog a few bits and pieces?'

Hazel, like her father, knew how to hold a grudge. She would feed it, nurture it, and use it against him at every opportunity. And that wasn't all he had to worry about. The law were seated at the back of the church, watching everything and everyone. He'd warned Hazel, told her that now was not the time, but it was like talking to a brick wall.

Milo, instead of following the service, was busy stoking old resentments. While his father sat up front, he had once again been pushed aside and left to find himself a seat. That he'd got one at all was down to sheer force of will, shoving his way through the crowd and using his elbows to secure a place in a pew. How was that right? He was pissed at Marian too; she had blanked him outside the church, her gaze sweeping over him as though he wasn't there. Yeah, playing the part of the grieving daughter, he knew, but that was no excuse for not even acknowledging his presence.

Milo, feeling aggrieved, decided that he was going to confront Rex's killer at the wake. It was time to let them know that they hadn't got away with it. Double bubble was what he was thinking: money from Marian and Jonny, and from the actual murderer too. Being paid for something he hadn't done was going to be gratifying, but being paid by the killer would be the icing on the cake.

*

To Eddie the church service had seemed interminable, an endless litany of prayers and readings. For a man who had never had time for God while he was alive, Rex had certainly tried to hedge his bets in death. Whether the Almighty would be impressed was another matter altogether. The burial was an equally dreary affair. Not that interment was ever a joyful occasion, but this one was made even more gloomy by the failing light and the pouring rain.

As the priest intoned the words – perhaps a little faster than he normally would – the ground began to turn to mud and the gathered mourners, eager to be out of the rain, shuffled on their wet feet with a less-than-decorous impatience. *Earth to earth, ashes to ashes, dust to dust . . .*

DCI Hennessy, alongside his sergeant, was standing well back in the graveyard, sheltering under the branches of a dripping tree. A canopy of umbrellas disguised the faces of most of the mourners and he had to be content with reading their body language. Unsurprisingly, Rex Darby's killer hadn't broken down pleading for forgiveness as the coffin was lowered into the ground, but he suspected something interesting might happen when all the main suspects gathered for the wake in Upper Belgrave Street. He would gladly pay to be a fly on the wall in the house, but there were some places even the police couldn't go uninvited. They could, however, wait and watch from outside, and that was exactly what they intended to do.

85

Like Carmen, none of the Fosters had any enthusiasm for going on to the wake. That they would not go, however, seemed out of the question. One way or another it would have to be endured. Pat looked upset but resigned, Annie exasperated – 'I don't know what Marian was thinking' – while Eddie just shrugged as if to say that the workings of Marian's mind were one of the many mysteries of the universe.

Carmen girded herself as they approached the house. This was the first time she'd been back since she'd found her father's body. The door was open and the lights were blazing. Already the mourners were streaming in, eager to get their hands on a strong drink and whatever food might be on offer.

'You don't have to go if you don't want to,' Eddie said to her. 'I can run you home and come back for Mum and Dad.'

Carmen shook her head. No matter how much she dreaded it, she couldn't run away. It wasn't just to do with looking guilty, as if she had a bad conscience and couldn't face this final part of the farewell to her father; she needed to prove to herself that she

had the strength to see it through. And why shouldn't she? But even as she asked herself the question, she knew that Richard Torn had ripped apart what little had remained of her resilience. To hold her head up high was going to take the greatest effort of her life.

She was aware of a frisson of excitement as they stepped through the door into the busy hall. Rumour and speculation would, of course, have been doing the rounds. The Darby girls, all three of them, would remain under a black cloud until the real killer was brought to justice. An almost gleeful suspicion lay in the eyes of the mourners, whispers rippling through the crowd.

'Just stick with us, love, and you'll be fine,' Annie said, while simultaneously staring down anyone who had the audacity to look too hard at Carmen.

The drawing room had been roped off, as had the staircase to the upper floors. Jonny was doing his best to encourage people out of the hall and into one of the large rooms at the rear of the house. Carmen averted her gaze from the drawing-room door, trying to blank out what had happened on the other side of it. There was something surreal, disturbing, about the wake being held here. She could imagine her father, invisible but present, watching everything and everyone, judging even from beyond the grave.

They walked through to the back where Pat stopped a passing waitress and secured drinks for them all – white wine for her and Annie, a whisky for himself and an orange juice for Eddie. Carmen had vowed to stay off the alcohol, but now that she was here, now that so many eyes were on her, she felt the need for some Dutch courage.

There was a crush in the room with people trying to balance glasses and cigarettes and plates of food. Despite a window being open, it was hot and stuffy and smelled of wet coats.

Marian was centre stage, holding court with Hugh beside her. She noticed Eddie stare at her for a moment before quickly looking away. Carmen caught sight of Hazel too, with her nose in a gin and tonic, and her expression as tight and angry as it had been in the church.

For the next half hour, as various mourners descended on her, Carmen had to endure all the hollow words of sympathy, the insincere declarations of sorrow and the endless pronouncements of what a fine man her father had been. She nodded and said thank you, drank, and drank some more. The wine made everything a little more bearable. It was, of course, what was unspoken that was hardest to take. It hung in the air like the cigarette smoke, a fug of distrust and suspicion.

At some point she got separated from the others, decided she needed to eat and headed for the long trestle table underneath the window. Here there were rows of sandwiches, carved meats, bread and cheese. By chance she ended up standing beside Elizabeth. The secretary, dressed in a severe black suit, was clutching a white lacy handkerchief which she continuously pulled through her fingers or used to dab at her eyes, her lips quivering like a grieving widow's.

'Quite a turnout,' Carmen said, feeling obliged to say something even if wasn't anything very original.

Elizabeth scowled. 'Look at them,' she said, glancing round the room. 'Nothing but vultures. As if any of them cared about your father. They're only here to eat and drink and pick over the bones.' Then she turned her gaze on Carmen, her eyes cold and angry. 'And I'm surprised *you've* shown your face after everything you put him through.'

Carmen, taken aback, almost choked on the sandwich she was eating. She felt a flush rise into her cheeks. 'You don't know what you're talking about. I realise you're upset but—'

'I know all right. Take, take, take, is all you girls ever did. And what thanks did he get for the sacrifices he made? None! It broke his heart the way you treated him.'

'Sacrifices?' Carmen repeated, lifting her eyebrows as she wondered just what exactly he had relinquished over the years. It seemed to her that he had always done exactly what he liked when he liked. But then it dawned on her what Elizabeth was actually getting at. 'Oh, you mean *your* relationship with him. Well, there was nothing stopping him from marrying you after Mum died. If he'd wanted to.'

Elizabeth glared at her. 'He always put you three girls first. Family was everything to him.'

Suddenly Hazel was by Carmen's side, knocking against her shoulder as she leaned unsteadily forward towards Elizabeth. 'Family! Don't be so bloody sanctimonious! Was he thinking about family when he was shagging you behind my mother's back? You should be ashamed of yourself.'

Elizabeth blanched, her lips tightening into a thin straight line.

'Don't give me that look,' Hazel continued. 'And don't think you were the only one either. He didn't know the meaning of monogamy. You and all the other slappers made my mother's life a misery. No wonder she killed herself! You've got a lot to answer for.'

Elizabeth, finding herself not just outnumbered but also without the moral high ground, decided to beat a hasty retreat. She gave an angry toss of her head, muttered something under her breath, pushed past them both and merged into the crowd.

'Good riddance,' Hazel said.

'I thought that was me,' Carmen said.

Hazel looked at her, frowning. 'Thought what was you?'

'The person who killed Mum.' The wine had loosened

427

Carmen's tongue, but she was still cautious enough to keep her voice down. 'Marian said it was all my fault, that she didn't want another child and that's why she . . . you know.'

'Oh, bloody Marian! She says whatever suits her.' Hazel replenished her glass from the bottles on the table and took a large swig. 'I mean, Jesus, if you're playing that game, you could as easily claim that it was having *her* that made Mum ill in the first place. It was all downhill from there. But anyway, it wasn't just one thing. It never is. And our beloved father didn't help matters, did he? Or tarts like Elizabeth.' Hazel gave her glass to Carmen to hold, scrabbled in her bag for a cigarette, lit it, sighed, and took back her glass. 'Marian is just so . . . so . . . and Jonny's no better. They go their own sweet way, not even considering anyone else. I mean, you say things, don't you, in the heat of the moment, but it doesn't follow that you've actually *agreed* to anything.'

Carmen wasn't really following Hazel's train of thought – if she even had one – but she nodded anyway. 'No, I don't suppose so.'

'It's my life too. Did either of them consider that? No, they bloody didn't. Whatever Marian and Jonny want, they get. End of story.'

'What do they want?'

Hazel seemed momentarily fazed by the question. 'What?'

'What do Marian and Jonny want?'

'What are you getting at?' Hazel's eyes narrowed with anger. 'Jesus, you're as bad as the rest of them. Why does everyone think that *we* had something to do with it? I mean, he was my dad for God's sake! How could anyone—'

Carmen swiftly interrupted to put her straight. 'Hey, I wasn't saying that. Did I say that? If anyone's getting the finger pointed at them, it's me. I was there, remember? You weren't.'

428

Hazel thought about this – as much as she was able to think about anything in her drunken state – gulped the gin, took another drag on her cigarette, squinted through the smoke, looked around and said, 'I hate this damn house. You know Jonny wants to move back in? As if I'd ever want to live in this place again. Have you seen Jonny? Do you know where he is? Chatting up some bloody tart probably.'

'Have you two fallen out?'

'He's a bloody liar.'

Milo chose that moment to gatecrash the conversation. 'Hello, girls. I hope that's not me you're talking about.'

'Jonny,' Hazel said. 'Have you seen him? Do you know where he is?'

'In the doghouse, is he?'

'Yes, he's in the bloody doghouse. He's a lying, cheating good-for-nothing.'

Milo pulled a mock-serious face. 'Oh, you found out then. I told him he was a fool. Why eat hamburger when you've got steak at home?' He gave Hazel a lascivious grin. 'That Mimi's not a patch on you.'

Hazel's face turned white, then red. 'What?'

86

Annie, who'd had enough of listening to small talk, sly digs and innuendo, was now on the search for her husband. Duty had been done and there was nothing wrong with making an escape after a respectable period of time. And that time, she'd decided, had come. She scoured the room, pushing through the crowd, but couldn't see him anywhere. Exasperation dogged her footsteps. Earlier she'd had an awkward conversation with Marian, her suggestion that Rex's inheritance should, perhaps, be shared with Carmen being met with stone-faced disdain.

'I don't think this is the occasion to be discussing such things.'

'You'll think about it, though? I'm sure your father didn't want her to be left with nothing.'

'I believe my father made his intentions quite clear in his will.'

Annie, remembering the exchange, was dismayed by Marian's coldness. All those millions and she wasn't prepared to share any of it with her youngest sister. Rosa would be turning in her grave. But then Marian always had been hard as nails, single-minded, greedy and selfish. She might be beautiful on the outside, but inside she was pure ruthlessness.

The presence of Milo hadn't improved her mood either. Although they'd never been formally introduced, she knew him by sight. And even if she hadn't, his relationship to Pat would have been obvious – the same build, the same facial features, even some of the same expressions. It was as if all his DNA had come straight down the paternal line with barely a nod to his mother.

Annie went through to the hall, only sparsely populated now, but Pat wasn't there either. She hung around outside the locked downstairs bathroom, wondering if he was taking a pee, but the occupant, when she finally came out, turned out to be a young woman wearing red lipstick and a black hat that was slightly askew. The disharmonious smell of perfume and alcohol wafted off her.

Disappointed, Annie continued her search, opening and closing doors until she eventually found Pat in Rex's study. He was sitting in an armchair next to the fireplace nursing a large glass of Scotch.

'Ah, so this is where you're hiding.'

Pat looked up, smiling wanly.

Annie went inside, unsurprised that he was seeking sanctuary from the rest of the guests. She'd had enough of them herself. 'Shall we go home? I don't know about you, but I've had enough for one day.'

'Have you heard them out there?' Pat said, his voice a little slurred. 'People are suggesting that the girls had something to do with Rex's death. I mean, they're not coming straight out and saying it, but it's what they think.'

'Who cares what they think? Just idle gossips the lot of them. They'll soon find something else to talk about.'

'It's not fair on them, though. Why should they have to put up with that?'

'Come on, let's go home.'

But Pat showed no inclination to move.

Annie glanced around the study. It was lined with books, none of which Rex had ever taken off the shelves. When he'd bought the house, he'd bought the library too, the previous owner having gone to a place where they no longer required the distraction of reading. Everything had been for show with Rex, a façade to disguise who and what he really was.

Seeing as Pat seemed unwilling or incapable of standing up, she sat down too. This was, perhaps, the last time he would be in the house – it was bound to be sold – and if he didn't want to hurry home, she wasn't going to make him. People said goodbye in their own way. Pat was doing it by getting blind drunk. But she wasn't worried. She had Eddie to help her get him into the car when he was ready.

'It's not fair on the girls,' Pat said, repeating himself.

'Stop worrying about the girls. The truth will come out soon enough. It always does in the end.'

Pat shook his head. 'You don't understand. I can't do this any more.'

Annie felt a chill run through her. 'Can't do what? What are you talking about?'

There was a long silence, broken only by the ticking of the old mantel clock. From beyond the door, at the other end of the house, came the rise and fall of distant voices. 'It was an accident,' he said eventually. 'I swear it was.' He gazed at her pleadingly. 'You believe me, don't you?'

And now that chill in her body had turned into a block of ice. 'Oh God, Pat. Don't say it. Please don't say it.'

'I only came here that Friday to try and talk him out of it. But he wouldn't listen. He'd lost his mind. He started ranting and raving and waving the gun around and I tried to take it from him, and it went off and . . .'

While Annie was still trying to absorb the horror of this, to let it slowly sink into her uncomprehending mind, Pat continued talking.

'I don't even know why he still had the gun. He swore he'd got rid of it, years ago. But he was convinced that Michael was still alive, said he was going to prove it once and for all, that he was going to drive over to Epping, find the place where he was . . .' Pat stopped as if the words had got caught in his throat and he couldn't get them out. He swallowed hard. A sheen of sweat glistened on his forehead.

Annie's hands flew to her face. 'Where he was buried. Is that what you mean? Rex killed him, didn't he? Rex killed Michael.'

'We buried him in the forest.'

'You helped him.' A groan escaped from Annie's lips. She stared hard at her husband, trying to push down the nausea. 'How could you? All those years Rosa didn't know where Michael was, what had happened to him, and all the time he was dead and buried in some godforsaken forest. How could you be so cruel?'

Pat's expression abruptly changed, his face becoming tight and red. A pulse throbbed in the corner of his left eye. 'It isn't Rosa you're bothered about. Tell the truth for Christ's sake! Rosa wasn't the one who was going to run away with him. That was you, Annie. You and Michael bloody Quinn. You think I didn't know what the two of you were up to behind my back? You always were a bad liar.'

Annie felt her chest constrict, felt the sudden acceleration of her heartbeat. Michael Quinn, the man she had loved once, the man she'd been planning to leave with. Until he'd suddenly

433

disappeared. Cold feet, she'd thought, and had hated him for it. So many years of hating him, her heart broken, her future in tatters. With a jolt, the truth came to her, a truth so dreadful it could barely be spoken. '*You* killed him, didn't you? It was you. It wasn't Rex.'

'You were going to take Eddie away. How could you even think about doing that?'

A volcanic anger rose in Annie. She leapt to her feet, but her legs were unsteady, and she almost fell back into the chair again. 'How could *you* ever think about fathering another son and not telling me about it? And you call me a liar. All those years sneaking around behind my back, making a fool out of me. Michael understood how that made me feel. And I understood how *he* felt about the way Rex treated Rosa.'

'How lovely for you both.'

Annie had to fight against the urge to strike him. The fingers of her right hand clenched into a fist. 'Tell me what you did. Where you killed him. How.'

'What does that matter now?'

'It matters to me.'

Pat reached for his Scotch and drained half the glass. He looked at her briefly and then focused his eyes on the wall. 'I went to the Royal. He was down in the basement sorting out some stock for Rex. I went to talk, man to man, to ask him to stop, to beg him to leave my family alone. But he wouldn't listen. I got desperate. I didn't want to lose you, Annie. I didn't want to lose you and Eddie. When he wouldn't . . . that's when I took out the gun.'

'You took a gun with you?'

'I never meant to use it.'

'But you did.'

'He said I didn't deserve you, that you'd be better off without me. He laughed when I said I'd kill him before I let him take my family away. It was that, the way he laughed, that made me do it. I just saw red. I lost it. I pulled the trigger and . . .'

Annie, who could no longer bear to look at him, turned her back and stared at the long rows of books: volumes of Shakespeare and Dickens, Hardy and Austen. All of them containing their own sorry stories of love and loss, of power and revenge. 'And Rex helped you to cover it up. Well, of course he did. That's what friends are for, right?'

'He said he'd got rid of the gun, that he'd thrown it in the Thames.'

Annie whirled round to face him again. 'I don't care about the bloody gun! Where did you bury Michael? Where is he?'

'I've told you. In Epping Forest.'

'*Where* in Epping Forest?'

Pat hesitated, but eventually came out with it. 'Near Jack's Hill. There's a walk there, pathways.'

Annie was trying not to imagine Michael's bones mouldering in the ground, but she could think of little else. Shivers coursed through her, a trembling that once it had started wouldn't stop. And she had doubted him, hated him, despised him for running off and leaving her when all the time . . . Shame consumed her, shame and guilt. She should have known better. She should have trusted in the love they'd had for each other. Her voice when she spoke again was low and cold. 'What will you do now?'

'Go to the police. Tell them everything.'

Perhaps he was hoping that she would try and talk him out of it, but Annie had no such intention. She had no pity for him, only loathing. He had murdered Michael, taken his life, deprived him of a decent burial and robbed her of the happiness she might have had. That he had killed Rex too was of no consequence except insofar as it felt almost fitting: one dreadful man turning on another, the two of them eventually destroyed by their own terrible acts.

Annie could no longer stand being in the same room as him. She took one last look at her husband and fled into the hall.

87

Carmen was standing near the door to the rear reception room, sipping on another glass of wine, when Annie, looking pink and agitated, appeared by her side.

'Do you know where Eddie is?'

Carmen glanced around but couldn't spot him in the crowd. 'I haven't seen him for a while. Are you all right?'

Annie nodded, although her whole demeanour said otherwise. 'Yes, yes, I'm just ... just tired, that's all. Will you try and find him for me? I need some fresh air. I'll wait by the car.'

And then, before Carmen could say anything else, she hurried off towards the front door. Clearly something had happened, and it must have been bad to shake the normally unflappable Annie. Or had the day simply been too much for her? Funerals were guaranteed to dredge up old emotions, to put a strain on the strongest of people. She was only coping with it herself by taking refuge in alcohol.

While she searched for Eddie, pressing through the crowd and peering into every corner, Carmen thought about her earlier conversation with Hazel. Why was it niggling away at her? For a while, Milo's big revelation about Jonny and Mimi had pushed it out of her mind, but now it was back, looming large and demanding her attention. What were the words Hazel had used? Something along the lines of saying things in the heat of the moment but it not following that you'd actually agreed to it.

Carmen frowned, not liking the suspicion that was lurking in her head. Don't be ridiculous, she told herself. It was just the drink addling her brain, twisting innocent comments into something more sinister. Hazel could never have meant *that*. Even Marian and Jonny weren't capable of murder.

Once Carmen was certain that Eddie wasn't in the vicinity, she extended her search to the rest of the ground floor. He wasn't in the other reception room or the kitchen or the downstairs bathroom. She opened the door to the study, saw Pat sitting in the armchair hunched over with his head in his hands, sensed that she was intruding and quickly withdrew.

The drawing room was still roped off, so Eddie couldn't be in there either. Her gaze fixed on the door, a sudden bombshell of memory crashing down on her. Her breath quickened, her pulse accelerating. She could feel the steady thump of her heart in her chest. All day she had been trying to keep her emotions at bay, to hold them back in case they broke like a dam and overwhelmed her. But now . . .

No, she couldn't give in. If she did, she'd be lost. Her mouth had gone dry. She imagined for one crazy moment that her father was still lying on the floor, still waiting to be found, his judging eyes staring up towards the ceiling. A tumult of emotions crowded in on her. She swallowed hard and wrapped her arms around her chest. *Think about something else.* She had to find Eddie. For Annie's sake. Annie who was outside right now, standing in the cold, waiting for her son to let her into the car.

By a sheer effort of will, Carmen turned away from the drawing room and all its dreadful memories. She was almost out of ideas, but then realised that Eddie could have gone upstairs to use one of the other bathrooms. She ducked under the rope of gold braid that had been slung between the rails of the banisters and hurried up to the first floor.

'Eddie?' she called out on the landing.

Nothing.

She tried the big bathroom but that was empty, poked her head into the bedrooms but they were empty too. It was only when she reached the third floor that she saw that the door to the attic was open, and the light was on. She stopped short. Someone was up there. It might be Eddie, but it might not. It could be any of the mourners. Or someone could have just walked in off the street. A thief, perhaps? Someone who wanted to take what wasn't theirs.

Carmen very quietly climbed the wooden stairs. Had she drunk a little less she might have been more cautious, taken more precautions, but her own safety didn't even enter her head. Well, not until she was approaching the top steps, when the reality of confronting a possible burglar began to dawn on her. But it was too late to retreat now. She launched herself up into the attic and quickly looked around.

At first, she thought there was no one there. It was just an empty room full of storage boxes and discarded furniture. But then she saw him, hunkered down by one of the crates, leaning against the wall with his arms wrapped around his knees. Eddie. She smiled, relieved that it was him and not an intruder.

'What are you doing up here?'

It was only then, as he raised his face, that Carmen saw he'd been crying. The shock of it wiped her smile away. She frowned, rapidly crossed the room, and crouched down beside him.

'What's wrong? What's happened?'

439

Eddie shook his head.

'Tell me.'

'I can't.'

'Of course you can. You can tell me anything.' She thought of Annie's agitated state and said, 'Is it to do with your mum?'

'No. No, it's nothing to do with her.'

'What then?'

Eddie's eyes wouldn't meet hers. He seemed lost, disconnected, struggling to hold on to whatever little remained of his self-possession.

Carmen laid a hand on his knee. 'Eddie?'

'She was sitting right here,' he said eventually. 'In this exact spot.' His hands dropped to the floor, his fingers splayed out, as if he could still feel the imprint of her. 'I was trying to get away from Marian and I thought she'd never find me in the attic. I thought I'd be safe up here, but I wasn't the only one trying to escape.'

Carmen's eyes widened as she realised who he was talking about.

'She was wearing a green dress with white buttons down the front, and her feet were bare. There was a bottle of vodka. Smirnoff. I remember the label. And there was this little pile of white pills by her right foot. She saw me and she smiled, and she put her finger to her lips and said, "Don't tell anyone I'm here, Eddie. It's our secret. Do you promise?" And I went back downstairs. And I didn't tell anyone.' His voice was shaky, hardly more than a whisper. 'I let your mother kill herself. I should have told someone, told Mum, told Rex. If it hadn't been for me, she'd still be alive today.'

Carmen, who'd been holding her breath, released it in a sigh. A tiny flame of resentment towards him flickered in her but was quickly extinguished. 'Jesus, Eddie, you can't think like that. You were only a kid. What were you – ten, eleven? You can't blame yourself.'

440

'Who is to blame, then?'

'Can you really put your hand on your heart and swear that you *knew* what she was doing?'

'I knew that something was wrong. I knew that adults didn't usually skulk in the attic with bottles of vodka. I knew that Rosa – your mum – was doing something that she shouldn't.'

Carmen shook her head. 'That's not the same. *She* was the one who made the decision, not you. If it hadn't been that day, it would have been another.' She wasn't sure if this was true but decided that it probably was. 'Once she'd made up her mind, nothing was going to stop her.'

'You're just trying to make me feel better.'

'I'm being honest. I never knew her but from what I've heard she was desperately unhappy. And you told me she was a kind person. Do you think she'd want you to feel like this?'

Eddie shrugged.

'Well, she wouldn't. Not in a million years.' Carmen got to her feet and held out her hand. 'Come on, let's get out of here.'

Eddie hesitated, wiped his face with his sleeve, and finally took her hand to let her haul him up.

'You have to leave it all behind,' she said. 'The guilt, the secrets, everything. *You* didn't kill her. She killed herself.' Carmen understood now how it must have been an agony for him every time he was forced to visit this house. 'Neither of us ever have to come back here again.'

Eddie stopped at the base of the stairs and looked back over his shoulder. She wondered what he was seeing. The ghost of a woman in a green dress, perhaps, a woman who had haunted him all his life.

When they were down in the hall, she shoved him gently towards the front door. 'Your mum's waiting outside. I'll go and fetch your dad.'

88

Jonny, escaping Hazel's wrath, had fled the house and taken refuge in the Plumbers Arms. Here he quietly seethed over his pint, deciding once and for all that Milo Grant's days were numbered and he needed to be eliminated before he caused even more damage. At best he was a loose cannon, at worst a bloody liability. The sooner he was off the scene the better.

That the wake was still in progress only added to his aggravation. How long did it take to mourn a bloke who hardly anyone had liked? It was just an excuse to get bladdered at the Darbys' expense. Already it was after nine and nobody showed any sign of leaving. By the time they did push off, the back room would be a mess. He resented this incursion on to his property – he did think of it as *his* property now – and swore that none of those free-riding leeches would ever set foot in it again.

This resolution brought him some solace. And once Hazel had been placated, once he'd managed to wheedle his way back into her good books, everything could get back on track. He was still pondering how exactly he'd achieve this when the door to the pub flew open and a woman with blood pouring down her face ran in.

'Help me, help me, somebody's just murdered my nanny!' she screamed.

While the other customers gathered round, Jonny realised with a start that it was Lord Lucan's wife. What was her name? Veronica, he thought. He jumped up and stared at her, shocked. But there was nothing he could do. The barman was already calling the police, others were trying to help and comfort her. Then suddenly, out of nowhere, he saw an opportunity: if he could apprehend the murderer, catch him before he got away, then he might finally make some meaningful contact with Lucan. Wouldn't he be grateful? Grateful enough, perhaps, to join him in the Royal basement one night.

Jonny, drunk but determined, left the pub and all its commotion, and began running along Lower Belgrave Street. The cold night air slapped against his face. He felt excited, pumped up. Nothing about what he was doing felt odd or wrong. He was just being a good citizen, his less than sober brain told him. He was doing the right thing, the heroic thing, even if he did have his own selfish reasons for it.

Somewhere, on the periphery of his senses, he heard the roar of a sports car being driven too fast, but by this time he was already lunging across the road towards the Lucan house. The driver, young, male and probably over the limit, slammed on the brakes, but it was too late.

Jonny was still conscious after he bounced off the bonnet and hit the ground. Pain travelled through him. He was aware of noise, voices, of an engine turning over. Then a car door slamming somewhere down the road. Then running footsteps. The last thing he saw before his sight flickered and he blacked out was DCI Hennessy leaning over him.

443

89

Milo was finally enjoying himself. The free booze – his favourite kind – was flowing freely and he was taking advantage of it. His earlier bad mood had evaporated to be replaced by a strange euphoria. He was in control, in command. Things were going his way. He hadn't intended to drop Jonny in it with Hazel like that but didn't much care that he had. He'd made a point of chatting to Hugh Loughton too, just to unnerve Marian. It was time they all understood who was pulling the strings.

But he still had something important to do. His hand reached into his pocket to feel the reassuring solidity of the gun. He shouldn't need it, but you never knew how people would react when their future was in the balance. He'd seen his father go into a room off the hall over half an hour ago, and that's where he headed now.

Milo didn't bother to knock but turned the handle and walked straight in. The room, full of books, was lit by a single lamp. Shadows filled the corners. Pat was sitting alone by the fireplace with his nose in a glass. He glanced up but didn't speak.

'Getting away from it all?' Milo said cheerfully. 'Mind if I join you?'

If Pat did mind, he didn't say. Milo sat down in the armchair opposite, leaned forward, and placed his hands on his thighs. 'We need to talk.'

Pat just stared at him.

'I know,' Milo said, launching straight in. 'I know what you did. I was parked down the road when you came here that Friday. I saw you come into the house.' Pat still didn't speak. He didn't even look surprised, which Milo found unnerving. 'I've kept my mouth shut, though. I mean, you're my dad, aren't you, flesh and blood? I'm not going to grass you up to the filth.'

'What do you want, Milo?'

Pat's voice sounded weary, almost indifferent. Milo wondered how drunk he was. But he persevered. 'Of course, I'm the one getting all the heat, but I can deal with that. They've got nothing on me. Still, it don't seem fair, me getting all the attention when you're the one who wasted him. I was thinking you could help me out. A few quid for my troubles? Let's say twenty k.' Marian had informed him of the contents of the will. 'A little bird told me that's what Rex left you, so I reckon that would just about equal things out.'

'You're too late.'

'And what the hell is that supposed to mean?'

'I've already told Annie. When I leave here, I'm going to the police.'

Milo felt a heat rising in him, a rage that all his plans were about to be thwarted. If Pat confessed, then Marian and Jonny wouldn't pay him another penny. He could see his whole future laid to waste. He could feel the blood pounding behind his eyes. 'So tell her to keep her bloody mouth shut! Does she want everyone to know she's got a murderer for a husband? And what about Eddie? No, you're not going nowhere near the filth. It's out of the question.'

'It's not your decision, Milo.'

'No, I'm not having it.'

'You can't stop me.'

Milo leapt up from the chair and stood over his father. 'You're not fuckin' thinking straight. What's wrong with you? Do you want to spend the rest of your life banged up?'

'That's up to me, not you.' Pat rose slowly to his feet. 'In fact, I may as well get it over and done with.'

Milo, panicking, pulled the gun out of his pocket and aimed it straight at Pat. 'You're going nowhere.'

But Pat only gave a small infuriating smile. 'What are you going to do? Shoot me?'

'If I have to. Now sit back down. We need to talk about this. You've had one too many, that's all. You go to the filth now and you'll regret it for the rest of your life. We can sort this.' He waved the gun at him. 'I said sit down.'

As if the effort of arguing was too much, Pat slumped back down in the chair. 'You're wasting your time. If I don't tell the police, Annie will.'

'We'll see about that.'

'It's over, Milo. There's nothing you can do.'

Milo was breathing quickly, his thoughts racing, his rage and frustration increasing by the second. Nothing he could do? He wasn't going to accept that. If Pat couldn't shut his wife up, then he'd have to do it for him. There was too much at stake to let it all slip away. 'No, no way, I'm not going to let her—'

But before he could complete the threat, the door suddenly opened, and Carmen Darby walked in. There was a split-second delay before her eyes took in what was happening right in front of her. Her body stiffened and he heard the harsh intake of her breath. Milo took a step forward and put the gun to Pat's head. 'Close the door and come over here,' he hissed. 'And don't even think about screaming or I'll blow his bloody brains out.'

90

Carmen did as she was told, walking slowly across the room. Shock had overtaken her, jolting her into an odd state of disbelief. As if this was a dream, a nightmare, something that wasn't completely real. And yet Milo was real, and the gun was real and the floor beneath her feet was solidly real too.

'Stand behind him,' Milo demanded, moving away from Pat. 'Stand behind the chair.'

'What's going on?' she asked stupidly. It was perfectly clear what was happening, but what she meant was *why*?

Milo glared at her. 'My old man here has some strange ideas. I'm trying to persuade him of the error of his ways.'

Carmen, behind the chair now, found herself in the direct line of fire. The gun was small and black and pointed straight at her. Even an incompetent shot, one made with an unsteady hand, couldn't miss from that distance. This was not the time for provocation, but the words slipped from her mouth before she had time to properly consider them.

'So it was you,' she said. 'You killed my father.'

Milo laughed unpleasantly. 'You're barking up the wrong tree there, love. I never laid a finger on him.'

Carmen knew he was lying. He had to be. Why else would he be standing there with a gun? Pat had found out and now Milo was threatening to kill him too.

'Let the girl go,' Pat said. 'She's got nothing to do with this.'

'Shut up! Haven't you caused enough trouble?' Milo was shifting from foot to foot, getting more agitated by the second. 'Oh yeah, let her go, let her go. And what then?'

'She won't say anything, will you, Carmen? Me and Milo just had a falling out, a difference of opinion let's call it. Things got a bit out of hand. Why don't you put the gun away, son? There's no need for it.'

But Milo wasn't going to be so easily persuaded. His hand tightened around the grip, his forefinger on the trigger. 'What do you take me for, a bloody fool? The minute she's out of here, she'll go blabbing to the filth.'

'I won't,' Carmen said. 'I swear. If Pat doesn't want me to say anything, I won't.'

'You're a liar, just like your sisters.'

'And what have they lied about?'

Milo bared his teeth like an animal. 'Evil bitches, both of them. Standing out there pretending they're so bloody sad that Rex is dead. They don't give a damn! You know what they think? They think *I* killed him. And they don't care so long as they can get their hands on his money.'

'That's not true,' Carmen said.

'Why don't you go and ask them?' Milo gave her an evil grin. 'Oh yeah, you can't, can you? Well, they're not getting away with it. I want my share and I'm going to have it.'

Pat intervened again. 'Stop it, Milo. Just put the gun away and go home. I'll talk to Carmen, explain things to her.'

'You're not explaining nothin',' Milo said. 'Keep quiet, both of you, or I'll close your fuckin' mouths for ever. I need to think about this.'

Carmen found herself thinking too, of all the men who'd decided they could say or do what they liked to her through the years – her father, Clive, Richard Torn, and now Milo – and felt the resentment rise in her. Despite his order to stay silent, she couldn't. 'If you didn't kill my father, why are you pointing a gun at us? It doesn't make any sense.'

'What did I tell you? Shut the fuck up.'

'If you're going to shoot me, I'd like to know why.'

'Being a Darby is enough,' Milo said nastily. 'I don't need no other reason.'

Pat sighed into the tense, fraught atmosphere of the study. 'Come on, Milo. It's all too late. You know it is. This isn't getting you anywhere. Just walk away.'

Carmen could tell that Milo didn't know what to do next, but she wasn't sure if this made him more or less dangerous. She was still convinced that he was the murderer, regardless of his claims to the contrary.

Milo glared at his father, but before he could even begin to compose an answer there was a commotion from out in the hall – heavy footsteps, boots echoing on marble – followed by a bellowing voice coming from the entrance to the reception room. 'This is the police. Please could I have your attention?'

Carmen saw the panic enter Milo's eyes. He flinched, recoiled and looked towards the window as if it might provide some form of escape. It was at that very moment that Pat leapt up off the chair and lunged at him. The gunshot was explosive, piercing, a noise that filled the whole room.

Pat crumpled to the ground and Carmen screamed.

91

Three hours later, DCI Hennessy was still trying to unravel it all. He had two more dead bodies on his hands: Jonny Cornish, who had sprinted past the police car, across the road, and straight into the path of an oncoming motorist; and Pat Foster, who had died at the hands of his own son. Hennessy and Ward had only gone into the house to inform Hazel of the fatal accident but had been met instead by the sound of a gunshot.

Milo Grant had already been interviewed and charged. He was not denying that he'd shot his father but was claiming it was an accident, that Pat Foster had lunged at him and the gun had gone off by mistake. Carmen Darby, the sole witness, backed up this version of events although with the proviso that she was sure Milo must have killed her dad, that Pat had found out and his son was trying to silence him. When asked why he'd been carrying a gun in the first place, Milo had refused to answer.

Annie Foster had put a whole different slant on things. Pat had, she claimed, admitted to killing Rex Darby and Michael Quinn too. She'd been white-faced and trembling, although whether that was from the shock of her husband's death, or his earlier confession, was hard to tell. So, maybe three more bodies rather than two.

Now Hennessy was wondering if Milo had been trying to blackmail Pat over the murder of Rex and/or the murder of Michael Quinn. He'd already denied it and would probably go on doing so. The stand-off in the study continued to revolve in Hennessy's thoughts, a dramatic scene with a brutal ending.

The beautiful Marian had looked shocked and confused when he'd told her about Pat Foster's confession. '*He* killed Dad?' There had been something in her face, just for a moment, that betrayed more than surprise. It had been there, and then as quickly vanished, leaving a question mark in his mind.

And there were other questions that he hadn't yet got satisfactory answers to. What Milo had really been up to and where the two hundred quid they'd found in his flat had come from. Why Carmen and Eddie had been in the attic. Why Jonny Cornish was in such a hurry to get back to the house. Why everyone connected to the Darby family seemed to be hiding something.

Hennessy put his feet up on the desk and eyed his plastic cup of coffee with misgivings. There had been another murder this evening not so far away. In Lower Belgrave Street, Lord Lucan had allegedly bludgeoned to death the family nanny, attacked his wife, and then disappeared into thin air. He shook his head. It was like the world had suddenly gone mad.

Still, three murders solved in one evening. What more could he ask for? Well, the whole truth, perhaps, and nothing but the truth, but he had the feeling that was always going to evade him.

EPILOGUE

One year later

For Carmen, the past twelve months had been a period of change. She had moved out of Kellston, found herself a bedsit in Finsbury Park and got a new job in a small West End gallery where she was bottom of the pile and spent most of her time making cups of tea. So, no big change from the café, but at least she'd got a foot on the career ladder. Occasionally she still missed the caff with its noise and bustle, its chatter and gossip, although she didn't miss getting up at five thirty every morning.

Annie had sold the house in Victoria and moved to a bungalow near Clacton. She seemed happier out of London and away from all the bad memories. On Sundays Carmen and Eddie would drive over for a roast dinner, a catch-up and a walk by the sea. And sometimes they took Joan and Lottie with them, further additions to what had become a close if somewhat unconventional family unit. Even Beth came along occasionally. Carmen had no contact with her sisters now, but Annie had become like a mother to her, and Eddie like the brother she'd never had.

In June an announcement in the paper that Clive Grainger was engaged to an American heiress, Tara McKinley, had momentarily shaken her. But then, realising that she'd had a lucky escape, she'd turned over the page and consigned him to that distant part of her mind that was labelled 'mistakes made and done with'.

Another report, this one in the *Evening News*, had held her attention for longer. It had been about a seemingly random attack on a businessman late at night in Soho. Nothing had been stolen from Richard Torn, not even his wallet, but he'd been left with a broken nose and multiple bruises. She had read this several times, unable to resist a growing feeling of satisfaction – his vile actions had finally caught up with him – but also wishing there had been a better way to bring him to justice. Should she have gone to the police? But she knew, now as then, what the outcome would have been, knew that he'd have got away with it. Although Deana denied having told Terry Street about the assault – her gaze sliding away, her expression turning shifty – Carmen instinctively suspected his hand in this act of retribution.

It was over eight months since she'd last seen Terry. She still thought about him sometimes, about what might have been, but to fall for him would have been to accept his way of life and that was something she could never have done. Anyway, Terry, like her father, was single-minded and probably not inclined towards monogamy. Yes, she had made the right decision. She wanted a different future, one she made for herself, one she could be proud of.

Annie Foster had slipped into her new life with ease. From the bungalow she could see a long stretch of sand and a line of blue-grey sea, a view that never failed to bring her pleasure. Although she was still coming to terms with what her husband had done, it seemed to her now that she had never properly known him and had spent years living with a stranger. The police had searched for Michael's body, but it had not been found: the forest was vast and there was no way of locating exactly where he'd been buried. Jack's Hill, Pat had said, but it had not been enough. She would sometimes drive there, walk along the path that led from the car park, and leave flowers in the undergrowth. It brought a sense of peace to her, as if Michael knew that she was not so far away.

Sunday was the day she looked forward to most, when she could fuss over her visitors and have the full house she had always dreamed of. But it was her son, of course, whom she loved seeing most. Eddie was changing, coming out of himself, starting to uncoil and stretch like a small wary creature emerging from hibernation. Was he happy? Not quite there, perhaps, but he had a lightness she hadn't seen in him before. Despite all evidence to the contrary, she harboured secret hopes of Eddie and Carmen getting together. At the moment their relationship seemed easy, familiar, more like brother and sister than anything more romantic, but a mother could still dream . . .

Marian was happy. She told herself this every morning when she woke up in her opulent Mayfair flat. She was rich and free and able to live how she wanted, picking up men and dropping them at will, drinking too much champagne and falling out of nightclubs in the early hours. She shopped and lunched and screwed around, thinking of nothing but her own pleasure. If an element of doubt ever crept into her head, if she sensed a hollowness at the centre of it all, she chose to ignore it, reaching for the bottle and blanking out the voices that she didn't want to hear.

Milo had scuppered her marriage by writing to Hugh from

jail and providing the details of their fling – dates, times, places, everything the little double-dealing bastard could remember. She had denied it all, naturally, but even Hugh had his limits. He'd filed for divorce with custody of the children, and she wasn't going to contest it. She would still see the boys, probably as much as she ever had, and they would have a far better time visiting her in London than in the desolate surroundings of the countryside.

The one thing Milo hadn't been able to do was implicate her in the plot to kill her father, not without implicating himself too. It had come as a shock that he hadn't been the one to end Rex Darby's life. Still, at least she had the pleasure of knowing he'd be locked up for years. Not for as long as she'd have liked – he'd managed to successfully plead manslaughter – but long enough for her to take pleasure in every day he was behind bars.

Marian didn't often think about her father, or her long-dead mother either. Hazel, after a short period of mourning for Jonny, had got involved with another charming con man, one who would, undoubtedly, take her for every penny she had. And Carmen? Hazel had no idea what she was doing, maybe still waiting on tables in Kellston.

Terry Street had everything he wanted – money, power, respect, women – and no regrets. Well, maybe one. Carmen Darby still slid into his mind from time to time. There had been something there, a spark, an attraction that he couldn't quite forget. Had she heard about Richard Torn? He had got what was coming to him, and Terry had taken pleasure in meting out some much-deserved justice.

Deana said she had no idea where Carmen had gone, and even Lottie, if she knew, wasn't letting on. A few months ago, he'd been driving along Charing Cross Road when he thought he'd seen her go into a bookshop, but by the time he'd found somewhere to park and walked back she'd disappeared. Perhaps it hadn't been her at all. It was the ones who got away that haunted you, the might-have-beens, the lost ones.

Carmen was slowly putting her life back together. Although her father's death, her mother's, Pat's, even Michael's, continued to cast shadows, she was building something new. She still got flashbacks to the day she'd found her father's body, to the dreadful moment that Milo's gun had gone off, but she was learning to deal with them. The future lay ahead – unknown, exciting, even scary – and she was facing it with a new-found courage and a sense of optimism.

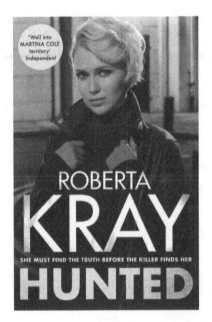

'Well into MARTINA COLE territory' Independent

ROBERTA KRAY

SHE MUST FIND THE TRUTH BEFORE THE KILLER FINDS HER

HUNTED

Full of the same danger and grit as its London setting, this is bestselling author Roberta Kray at the top of her game. Get ready for a KILLER read . . .